MARKED

BY THE

DRAGON

THOPHAT
KLODIAN KEEP
SLIA

OMINION
THE LONG SANDS

OTHER BOOKS

Dragon Riders of Osnen

The Price of Honor
Trial by Sorcery
A Bond of Flame
The Warrior's Call
The Coin of Souls
Wing of Terror
Eyes of Stone
Tooth and Claw
The Servant of Souls
Smoke and Shadow
The Dark Rider
The Song of Bones
Sword and Crown
Tides of Darkness
Wrath and Ruin

The Fallen King Chronicles

Dragonsphere
The Fallen King
The Valiant King
The Restored King

Dragons of Isentol

Throne of Deceit
Rune Marked
Empire of Serpents

Galactic Mercenaries

Steel for Hire
Steel for Free
Steel for All

MARKED
BY THE
DRAGON

RICHARD FIERCE

Dragonfire Press

Print ISBN: 978-1-958354-56-8

First Edition: 2023

CURSE

OF THE

DRAGON

THE MORNING SUN FILTERED THROUGH the canopy above as Mina made her way along the winding forest path. Her worn shoes crunched on the undergrowth, the familiar sounds of the woods calming her restless mind.

Mina breathed in deeply, savoring the scent of pine and moss. This was her favorite place, where mysteries lingered behind every tree and adventure waited around each bend.

As a twelve-year-old girl living in a small farming village, life was often dull. But out here, deep in the forest, she was free. Here, she could pretend she was the High Princess, or follow the tracks of a legendary beast. Her imagination knew no bounds amidst these trees.

Most days she spent her free time exploring, climbing rocks, crossing streams, and mentally mapping new routes. Her parents worried about her, but she was resourceful. Mina knew which berries and plants were edible, and how to navigate her way home as darkness fell. The villagers had long since given up trying to keep her out of the woods. Mina belonged there as much as the wild animals.

Today she wandered further than ever before, lured by the promise of discovery. She'd found strange markings on the trees and an unfamiliar animal print in the mud. What sort of creature could it be? Mina quickened her pace, her senses heightened. The forest was calling her deeper, into a world of mystery.

She shook her head, smiling to herself at her overactive imagination. Yet still she walked onward, unable to resist the pull of the unknown. The sun sank low on the horizon, shadows lengthening between the trees. Nightfall was approaching, but Mina did not turn back. The forest had gripped her in its embrace, and she willingly followed where it led.

It was just getting dark by the time she trudged into the village. Leaves and twigs were tangled in her unruly hair, and some of the nearby villagers glanced up at the familiar sound of her approach, concern marking their expressions.

"You shouldn't be traipsing about this late," Dela, the baker's wife, scolded. "Your parents have been looking for you. Off on one of your adventures again, were you?"

Mina grinned sheepishly. "I was following some strange markings I found. I didn't mean to be gone so long, but I lost track of time."

The baker shooed his wife inside their shop and stared at her with amusement. "One of these days you'll wander too far and we'll have to come searching for you."

"I'm always careful," Mina protested.

The villagers knew she could fend for herself, but for some reason, they still worried about her. She appreciated their concern, but there was nothing to fear out there.

"Did you finish laying the traps for Tarrow?"

"Yes, I did that before going into the woods."

She often aided the people in her village with such tasks despite her age.

"Very good. I knew he could count on you. Have a good night."

Mina's cheeks flushed. It was not easy to get a compliment from the old baker. She waved and continued to her parents' farm. Darkness had settled over the village by the time she reached the dirt path that led to the house.

Her parents would be finished with their chores, tired and worn from a long day of labor in the fields. They worked from dawn until dusk, struggling to grow enough crops to feed themselves and pay the high taxes imposed by their Dominion lord.

Despite their hardships, her parents always had a smile for her when she returned home. They were proud of the things she did for their fellow villagers, but she often wished she could help them in a bigger way. Perhaps one day she would be able to.

Mina sighed, eyeing the broken fence and crumbling stone cottage that was their home. She loved her family, but part of her yearned for something more. A life of adventure, where every day brought something new.

Her gaze drifted to the forest, dark and forbidding in the fading light. Somewhere in that sea of trees and shadows lay the answer to her restless dreams. She just had to be persistent enough to keep searching for it.

Pushing the thoughts aside, Mina went inside to help prepare their meager dinner. Her parents would need her help, and helping them cook was the least she could do. No matter how strong the call of adventure sang in her blood, her duty was here. To her family and her village, who had given her so much and asked for nothing in return.

The next morning, Mina rose with the sun and set about her daily chores. She fed the chickens, milked the cow, and collected eggs from the henhouse. Though mundane, she found comfort in the routine. Her parents were still asleep, worn out from the previous long day of plowing the fields.

After a quick breakfast, Mina ventured into the village. Many of the townsfolk greeted her warmly, waving from their shops and cottages. She stopped by the baker's and traded a dozen eggs for a loaf of bread and sweet bun, knowing it would be a welcome surprise for her parents.

The village blacksmith hailed Mina as she walked past his forge. "My wife's taken ill today. Do you think you could deliver this to the miller for me?" He held out a large iron horseshoe, still warm from the fire.

"Of course," Mina said, taking the horseshoe carefully. She balanced it on one hand, careful not to burn herself, and set off down the road toward the mill.

The miller thanked her profusely when she arrived, pressing a copper coin into her palm. Though she tried to refuse it, he insisted. "You're a lifesaver, Mina. We're lucky to have you."

Mina flushed at the praise, though inwardly she swelled with pride. No matter how difficult life became, she would always do her best to help others. It was her duty, and the right thing to do. Her parents had raised her to be kind and selfless, values she intended to live by.

With the errand complete, Mina returned home to find her parents awake. She gave them the treats she had brought, and her father ruffled her hair affectionately. "What would we do without you?"

Mina smiled, warmth flooding her chest. She might dream of adventure, but this? This was all she needed. Home and family, a place where she belonged. It might not be an extravagant life, but it was a good one. And that was enough.

The following day dawned bright and clear. Mina rose early as she always did, eager to check the snares on the edge of fields to see if they had caught anything. Her stomach rumbled at the thought of fresh meat; they hadn't had much of it lately.

She made her way across the field, following a winding path only she seemed to know. The snares were empty, but she spotted some mushrooms peeking out from under a log near the edge of the forest and gathered them. Every little bit helped.

When she returned to the village, she found old widow Cora struggling to repair the hole in her roof. Mina didn't hesitate, climbing the ladder and tackling the job with enthusiasm. By the time the sun was directly overhead, the roof was mended.

Cora clasped her hands, eyes shining with gratitude. "Thank you, dear one. I don't know how I can ever repay you."

Mina shook her head. "No need. I'm happy to help."

"You have a gift, child," Cora said softly. "Far too wise and kind for your years. Never lose that, you hear?"

Mina bowed her head. She never thought of herself as special. She simply did what anyone would do in her place. Helping others came as naturally as breathing. But she appreciated Cora's words nonetheless.

With the roof repaired, Mina set off to check the remaining snares, hoping today's efforts would yield better results. She thought of Cora's praise and smiled. As long as there were people in need of aid, she would do her best to provide it. And she would never stop trying to make the world a little bit better, one good deed at a time.

Unfortunately, those snares were also empty, so she headed into the woods. The sunlight slanted through the leafy canopy above in dappled patterns, causing shadows to dance across the winding trail.

The air was lush and verdant, scents of moss and fern mingling with the sharper tang of pine.

A red fox peered at her from behind a tree, unafraid. Mina smiled, waving a hand as she walked past. The fox watched her, sniffing the air, before slipping back into the underbrush.

The deeper Mina traveled, the more alive the forest grew. Squirrels chattered in the branches, and a woodpecker rapped against a tree somewhere in the distance. Something rustled in the bushes, and Mina caught a glimpse of tawny fur and bright eyes. She kept walking, hands swinging at her sides, drinking in the vibrant palette of greens and browns.

Here, she could lose herself for hours. Exploring the twisting trails and hidden glens, discovering secrets tucked away in quiet hollows. The forest was endlessly fascinating, filled with mystery and wonder.

By the time Mina made her way home, dusk was falling. Shadows lengthened between the trees as the woods grew hushed with twilight. An owl hooted softly in the distance.

She emerged from the forest and paused, looking back. The trees stood like silent sentinels as night descended, cloaked in darkness thick as velvet. She might live on a farm, but the woods were her real home.

*

Mina chased a yellow butterfly, heading deep into the woods. She had wandered far from home in her pursuit of adventure, as she often did, her curiosity driving her onward.

She paused, realizing she didn't recognize where she was. Strange rock formations jutted up around her, unlike anything she'd seen before. Her heart raced with excitement. She was discovering new lands!

Approaching one of the rocky outcroppings, Mina ran her hands along the ancient stones. "How did you get here?" she whispered in wonder.

A glint of reflected light caught her eye through a crack in the rocks. Mina peered inside, her heart pounding. There was a whole hidden chamber inside! She had to see more. Gripping the edge of the rock, she started to pull herself up to get a better look.

Without warning, the ground caved in around her. She fell, landing hard on the floor of an enormous cave. A sharp pain pierced her leg, and she cried out, grabbing at her calf. Something hard was embedded in her flesh, and blood slicked her fingers.

Panic rose in Mina's chest as she stared at the strange object stuck in her leg. She had to get help. Struggling to her feet, she made her way out of the giant hole and limped as quickly as she could, leaving the mysterious rock formation behind.

Mina winced with every step, sweat beading on her forehead. She didn't know what was in her leg, but she knew it was bad. Her heart pounded as she ran toward the village, desperate to find someone who could help her. She had discovered more adventure than she'd bargained for this day.

"Help!" she cried, collapsing to the ground. Her leg burned, and she was growing lightheaded from blood loss.

A few villagers rushed to her side, gasping at the sight of the strange object embedded in her leg.

"What is that?" Deka asked, leaning down to examine Mina's injury. She grasped the object and tried to pull it out, but Mina screamed in agony.

"Stop!" Mina cried. "It hurts too much!"

The old widow Cora joined the crowd that surrounded her and inspected the wound. In her younger days, she'd worked as a healer in the Dracan Dominion.

"I've never seen anything like this. It's … fused to her flesh. I can't remove it without causing greater injury."

Mina began to sob, clutching her leg. She didn't understand what was happening. All she wanted was for the pain to go away.

"There, there," Cora said gently. "I'll do all I can to keep the wound clean and prevent infection, but I'm afraid you'll have to learn to live with this … thing. It looks like a dragon scale."

Live with it? Mina stared at the scale in horror. She didn't want this thing to be part of her body, but it seemed that was not an option.

If Cora couldn't work her healing abilities on it, then it was bad indeed. Her life had changed in that hidden chamber, all because of her curiosity and thirst for adventure.

*

Mina hobbled back home, leaning on her mother for support. Each step sent waves of pain radiating from the scale in her leg. She bit her lip, trying not to cry any more tears.

Back home, she collapsed onto her bed. Her mother brought her a warm cup of tea, the herbs soothing her frayed nerves.

"The pain will lessen in time," her mother said gently. "You'll grow accustomed to it."

Mina shook her head. "I don't want to grow accustomed to it. I just want it out of my leg."

Her mother sighed and sat beside her on the bed. She took Mina's right hand in her own, calloused yet comforting. "I know this is difficult to understand, but maybe this is a gift. Maybe this scale has a purpose we can't see yet. Only time will tell."

Mina scowled. It didn't feel like a gift. It felt like a curse. She leaned into her mother's embrace, letting the warmth and familiar scent soothe her. She knew her mother meant well. Maybe her mother was right. Maybe one day this scale would prove to be a gift. She closed her eyes, drifting off to the sound of her mother's lullaby.

The next morning, Mina awoke to birds chirping outside. For a brief moment, she felt at peace. Then a sharp pain in her leg jerked her back to the present.

The scale.

She peeled back her blanket to examine the injury. The bleeding had stopped. The scale was embedded in her flesh as before, but now she noticed something new. A tingling sensation emanated from the scale, as if it had developed a life of its own. She rubbed her fingers over the scale, and the tingling intensified into a surge of awareness. Somewhere, in the distance, was a dragon. She could feel its presence like a heartbeat.

Mina gasped and yanked her hand away. How did she know there was a dragon nearby? What dark magic was this? She had always been sensitive to the natural world, but this was something different. Something unnatural.

The tingling faded, but it left her unsettled. She had a sinking feeling that this was only the beginning. The scale had changed her in some fundamental way, and given her an ability she never asked for.

Her mother entered the room, smiling. "How are you feeling today?" Then she noticed Mina's expression. "What's wrong?"

Mina hesitated. How could she possibly explain this? Her mother wouldn't understand. No one would. She was alone in this.

Mina shook her head and forced a smile. "I'm fine. Just tired."

Her mother frowned, seeing through the lie. But she didn't press the issue. "Get some rest, then. I'll bring you some broth."

As her mother bustled out of the room, Mina curled into a ball. She pressed her hands over her ears, trying to block out the rhythmic pulsing that seemed to permeate her mind.

A dragon was out there. She could feel its presence, like flames licking at the edges of her consciousness. No matter how hard she strained to ignore the sensation, it persisted.

A tear rolled down her cheek. She squeezed her eyes shut, cursing the wretched scale and the fate that had befallen her. If only she had never ventured so far into the forest. If only she hadn't been so curious.

Now she was cursed, marked by something dark and strange.

*

The whispers started as hushed murmurs in the village square, but soon spread like wildfire through the cobblestone streets.

Mina could feel the stares of villagers as she walked by, their eyes following her every move. She pulled her cloak tighter, as if she could hide from their prying gazes.

Did they know she could sense a dragon was out there? Her heart hammered in her chest at the thought. Dark magic was outlawed, and only nobles could use the magic sanctioned by the High Prince. What if they thought she was a witch?

Within days, tales of her mysterious ability had spread throughout the village. She had only told her mother, but someone must have overheard their conversation. She prayed word of her affliction didn't leave the village, but a few days later, that fear was confirmed.

Mina's parents called her into their small kitchen. Her mother wrung her hands anxiously, while her father stared out the window at their farm, brow furrowed.

Mina's stomach twisted into knots. "What's wrong?"

Her father turned to her, his eyes grave. "Lord Klodian has requested an audience with us. He wants to discuss your ... ability."

Mina paled. She knew this meant trouble. Lord Klodian did not request audiences out of idle curiosity. There was always an ulterior motive behind the actions of Dominion Lords.

"You can refuse," she said hurriedly. "We don't have to meet with him."

Her father gave her mother a knowing look.

"If we refuse, it will only anger him," her mother said.

"There must be another way. What if he wants to take me away?"

Her parents refused to meet her gaze, staring instead at the floor. The silence in the room was suffocating. Finally, her father spoke, his voice heavy with resignation. "We have agreed to meet with Lord Klodian. He has offered to give you a better life than we can provide."

"No!" Mina cried.

"It is the only way to keep our family safe."

"We're protecting you. And ourselves," her mother added. "It would not be good for any of us to defy Lord Klodian."

"I won't go with him!" Mina insisted, panic rising in her chest. "I'll run away first!"

"And then he will hunt you down," her father said. "His soldiers will scour every inch of the kingdom until you are found. It is better to go willingly than be dragged there against your will."

"I hate you!" The words burst from Mina unbidden, hot and angry. "How can you do this to me? I'm your daughter!"

Her parents flinched, but held firm in their resolve. They had made their choice, and now Mina would have to live with the consequences. Or die trying to escape them. She turned and fled from the house, tears blurring her vision as she ran into the trees. But no matter how fast or how far she ran, she could not escape the truth: she now belonged to Lord Klodian. Her life was no longer her own.

*

Mina huddled in the branches of an old oak tree, watching the winding dirt road that led to her village. Any moment now, Lord Klodian would come riding through, flanked by guards in gleaming armor. Coming to claim her.

Her heart thudded in her chest like a wild bird trying to escape. She didn't want to go with him. She didn't want to be owned and controlled, treated like some kind of prize horse. But she had no choice. Her parents had seen to that.

When the procession finally came into view, Mina squeezed her eyes shut. She couldn't watch, couldn't bear to see the look on Lord Klodian's face as he took possession of her.

"Mina!" Her father's voice rang out below. "Lord Klodian is here for you. Come down at once!"

She opened her eyes and slowly climbed down from the tree, limbs heavy with dread. This was it. The end of her freedom. The beginning of her imprisonment.

Mina blinked back the tears, steeling herself for the long journey ahead. She may be bound to Lord Klodian now, but she would never truly belong to him. Not as long as she had breath left in her body. She only hoped she could survive long enough to find a way out of his cage.

*

Lord Klodian surveyed her with a possessive gaze as the carriage rumbled along the road to his keep. Her parents' stricken faces haunted her, even now. They didn't want to sell her any more than she wanted to go. But what choice did they have? Defy Lord Klodian and face his wrath, or give up their only daughter to save all their skins?

Mina couldn't blame them for choosing the latter. She knew the stories, knew the fate of those foolish enough to cross a Dominion Lord. They did what they had to in order to survive, as always.

She sighed, gazing out the window at the rolling hills of sand that stretched endlessly into the distance. If only she had the freedom to roam the forest as before, but wishes were for children, and she was no longer a child. She was a prisoner in a gilded cage, a pawn in Lord Klodian's game of power and control. And there was no escape—not for her, and not for her parents.

They were all dancing to the tune of the Dominion Lord now.

SCALE

OF THE

DRAGON

1

THE SUN GLARED OVERHEAD, REMINDING Mina why she dreaded Lord Klodian's summer hunting trips. He was almost obsessive in his desire to hunt dragons for sport, and he used Mina like a hound to sniff them out.

Her life hadn't always been so exciting. Once, she'd been a normal girl that worked the farm with her family … until they sold her to Lord Klodian. Those days seemed so long ago now. At least the memories no longer brought her to tears. She'd cried enough to last her the rest of her life, as far as she was concerned.

"Which way, girl?"

Mina's pace had slowed, prompting Lord Klodian's demand. She looked over her shoulder at him. He sat astride his black warhorse, his polished plate armor glinting in the sunlight. The visor of his helm was up, and he glared at her impatiently.

To his right rode a group of his retainers, and on his left was Vhan, Klodian's squire. The retainers stared at her with a bored expression plastered on their faces, but Vhan looked excited. The squire was always thrilled when it came to dragon hunts.

"This way," Mina replied.

She continued trudging along the dunes, following the subtle pull she felt from the scale embedded in her leg. It infuriated her that Klodian forced her to walk while he and his entourage got to ride horses. Certainly, he knew it would be quicker if she were mounted, but then again, he probably did it just to spite her.

Mina was Klodian's slave, and she knew it. Whether or not it was legal was another issue, but from what Mina had gathered so far in her young life, Dominion Lords did whatever pleased them so long as it didn't get them into trouble with the High Prince.

She supposed it was a small blessing to belong to Klodian. There were rumors that other Dominion Lords could be very abusive, violent even. While Klodian had never raised a hand toward her, he was manipulative and impetuous. Growing up amidst the wealthy and elite seemed to breed those qualities into people, though.

Ahead, Mina spotted a tall mesa that rose several hundred feet above the surrounding landscape. The top was flat, and the sides were steep and straight as if some underground creature had pushed it directly up out of the ground. The rock formation was various shades of red all intermingled, but that wasn't what caught Mina's attention.

It was the shadowed cave entrance.

She angled her steps toward the mountain and the scale in her leg began to burn. It was only slightly uncomfortable, but once they got within a few hundred feet of the dragon, the pain would be excruciating. It happened every time, but that never stopped her. It wasn't the fear that Klodian would punish her that kept her from turning away. It was her hatred for dragons.

They were the source of her misery. Or rather, one of them was. That didn't matter to Mina. The only good dragon was a dead one, and so she would continue to lead Lord Klodian on his hunts with the hope that—one day—he would kill the beast whose scale made her life a nightmare.

"It's there," Mina said. "Inside the cave."

"You're certain?" Klodian asked. "It's not on top, preparing to swoop down on us?"

She turned to regard him. Klodian hadn't kept his title as Dominion Lord for no reason. He'd been born to the position, certainly, but that didn't guarantee someone the title for life. There was always some young upstart who wanted the power and fame for themselves, and Klodian's quick wits and suspicion had saved him from many assassination attempts.

"I'm certain, my Lord. The scale may be a curse, but it never lies."

"One man's curse is another man's godsend. You may not like your ability, girl, but your gift has increased my wealth fourfold."

That was another thing that bothered Mina. Lord Klodian always referred to her as 'girl' and never by her actual name. She supposed he did that out of spite, as well.

"You are entitled to your opinion, as am I. And I say it is a curse."

Klodian laughed and slid off his mount, landing with a clatter as his plate mail jounced about. He unsheathed his sword from his waistbelt and quickly looked it over, then returned it. He motioned to Vhan, and the squire also dismounted. Vhan carried a spear, but the weapon wasn't his. He hadn't earned the privilege of learning to fight yet.

"Wait for me out here," Klodian ordered, taking the spear from Vhan. "I'll be back shortly."

Mina watched him disappear inside the cave. The retainers began talking amongst themselves, sharing gossip and discussing things that made Mina wish a dragon would swoop down on them. Whether it ate them or her didn't matter, so long as it put her out of her misery.

Vhan slowly sidled around to where Mina stood, a grin on his face.

"Don't even ask," Mina said.

"I've never seen it," Vhan replied. "And I *really* want to see it."

"Why? So you can make fun of me, too? No, thank you."

"I wouldn't make fun of you. I think having a dragon scale in your leg is neat. I'd have one if I could. How did you get that, anyway?"

"I'm sure you've heard the stories," Mina said.

"I've heard rumors, which is usually far from the truth. And I've never heard the story from you, so …"

Vhan stared at her expectantly.

"I fell on it."

"Care to elaborate?"

Mina heaved a sigh, knowing Vhan would irritate her until she gave in.

"I was playing in the hills when I was young, and a hole opened up beneath me. I fell into a dragon's nest and landed on a pile of scales. This one," Mina slapped her thigh, "happened to penetrate my skin."

Vhan's eyes were wide. "Seriously? That must have been amazing. Being in a dragon's nest, I mean."

"The nest was abandoned. And it wasn't amazing at all. It ruined my life."

"You're alive, aren't you?" Vhan asked.

"I exist, but I wouldn't exactly call being a slave to Klodian living."

"Some people don't like him, but I do. He's always nice to me. I have a warm bed and food to eat, so I can't complain. There wasn't much to go around at my home, so being the squire to Lord Klodian has been the best thing that's happened to me."

Mina offered him a fake smile in the hopes that he'd get the hint and stop talking, but he kept yammering on about how great it was to be part of Klodian's Dominion. Mina tuned his voice out and watched the cave entrance, wondering how long it would take Klodian to kill the dragon. Her leg was still burning, which meant it wasn't dead yet. At least he hadn't forced them to go into the cave with him.

After a while, Vhan left her alone and wandered over to listen to the retainers. Mina rubbed her leg, massaging the skin around the edges of the scale. She didn't fear for Klodian's safety. If he died, then she'd have an opportunity to escape. It wasn't likely he'd be killed, though. Not when he had the power of his runes. That was another perk the wealthy nobles enjoyed: magic.

Rune magic was sanctioned by the High Prince, and it was only lawful for nobles to employ it. Everything else was outlawed, but that didn't stop people from practicing it in secret. Although Mina had never met any illegal sorcerers, she knew they were out there. It was whispered that on the fringes of the Dominions, there were people who openly sold their services to others.

The burning in Mina's leg ceased abruptly, and she smiled. Another dragon was dead. *Good riddance,* she thought. A moment later, Lord Klodian stepped out from the cave. He was covered in dust and blood, and he carried a severed horn in one hand. Vhan rushed over and fawned over him, ever the loyal squire. Mina found the display annoying and turned her gaze away, looking up at the mesa's jagged walls.

"That's the first dragon of the season," Vhan said.

"The first of many," Klodian replied. "Girl."

Mina looked at him, and he tossed the horn to her. She caught it and turned it over, examining it. It was small, and she guessed the dragon must have been an adolescent.

"For your collection," Klodian said.

"Thank you, my Lord."

"Ride back to the castle and summon the workers," Klodian instructed Vhan. "Tell them to bring plenty of wagons. The beast was hoarding enough trinkets to fund an army."

"Right away, sir."

Vhan got on his horse and rode off. The retainers gathered around Klodian and listened to him relay how he killed the dragon. Mina ran her fingers along the horn, feeling the coarse lines that grooved its surface. Every horn was different, but they all had similarities. She glanced at the cave and thought she saw glowing eyes staring back at her from the shadows. She blinked a few times and squinted, but there was nothing there.

It was probably her imagination. She waited for Klodian to finish bragging about his kill, and then they began the trek back to the castle. Mina clutched the horn in her hands, hoping that the next dragon to be killed would be the one to set her free.

How she hated dragons.

2

IT HAD BEEN A GRUELING day for Caden.

He'd faced a series of challenges that tested both his mind and his body, and he'd pushed his limits further than he ever believed possible. Feats of strength, tactical challenges, and many other trials meant to determine whether he was worthy of being a Runesman had been his sole focus.

And he'd made the cut.

Caden stood in line, waiting for his turn to be marked. A few of his fellows had suffered minor injuries, and the man in front of him was bleeding from a cut on the back of his head. It didn't seem to bother him, so Caden didn't point it out.

Both exhausted and dirty, Caden was ready to rest. The challenges had been physically taxing, true, but his mind had been tested even harder. He'd tried to only think about his tasks, but that hadn't helped. The entire time he'd been questioning himself, worried that he'd fail somehow. When given the news that he'd been accepted as a Runesman, it was as if a heavy weight had been lifted from his shoulders.

If there was one thing that Caden wanted in life, it was fame. And riches. So, two things. They usually came hand in hand, anyway. He didn't want to be a Dominion Lord—and couldn't be one—but he *did* want everything they had. And the easiest way to gain both was to become a Runesman.

Since he lived in the Thophate Dominion, that meant that he'd been forced to enlist in Lord Ardit Klodian's army. That wasn't necessarily a problem in itself, but Lord Klodian didn't wage war against the other Dominions enough for Caden to earn the renown he wanted. So, he'd devised a plan. A plan of simplicity that had little chance of failing in his mind.

He would enlist with Lord Klodian, then request a citizen's transfer to another Dominion. Transferring to another Dominion wasn't unheard of, and with the right coaxing, there would be no reason Lord Klodian should refuse him.

The only flaw Caden could find with his plan was that he didn't know which Dominion was in good standing with Lord Klodian. They fell in and out of favor with one another as often as the wind changed direction, which meant that Caden would have to keep his ears open. If he requested a transfer to one of Klodain's enemies, well … that would be bad.

"Step forward."

A portly middle-aged man sat behind a wooden table, scrawling names onto a parchment with a feather-pen. He dipped the quill into an inkwell and gazed up at Caden. The man wore thin spectacles, and they hovered at the edge of his nose, threatening to slip free at any moment.

"Name?"

"Caden Davtyan," Caden said.

The man repeated the name under his breath as he wrote Caden's name down, misspelling his surname. Caden didn't bother correcting him. No one had ever managed to spell his surname properly, and Caden's father had taught him long ago that a man must pick his battles carefully.

"Do you own a blade?"

"Not yet," Caden replied, giving the man a grin.

"Right then. Go to the red tent where those men are and wait for Captain Eduard. He'll determine the best rune for you."

"Thank you."

Caden strolled over to the tent the steward had motioned to, joining the group of men waiting there, and glanced around the field. They were outside the castle, and various obstacles had been set up for the day's festivities. Enlistment day only came around once every few months, and Caden had waited a long time for this moment. Now that the Runesmen had been chosen, servants were working on clearing the field.

Turning his attention to the other members of his group, Caden spotted a man with long braided hair. He thought it was odd until the man turned around and he realized it wasn't a man at all, but a woman.

"What are you looking at?" she snapped.

"Nothing," Caden answered calmly. He didn't avert his eyes, though. He matched her stare.

"You don't think I should be here, do you? Well, I've got just as much right to be here as you. And I guarantee I could kick your butt across this field without breaking a sweat."

"Calm down, Thais," one of the others said. "Save your energy."

"Shut your mouth," Thais growled back at him. "Or I'll pummel you, too."

She shot Caden another glare before turning away. Caden shook his head, finding it funny that a woman would want to join the Runesmen. He supposed she had her reasons, just as he did, and that he shouldn't look down on her.

Captain Eduard, an imposing man decked out in chainmail and leather armor, strode over to the tent and began assigning people their runes. Some of them left to other tents, but Caden and a handful of others were instructed to stay where they were.

"Each of you showed proficiency in many areas, but those of you standing here excelled at one thing in particular. Strength."

Captain Eduard looked at each of them, meeting their gaze for a moment before looking to the next person.

"Being a Runesman is something most envy, but not everyone is cut from the same cloth. Some of your fellows will be marked for sight, and others for speed. Though you may have different runes, you are all a brotherhood dedicated to the same cause. Defend the Thophate and protect Lord Klodian. Do you all swear allegiance to your new lord until the day you die?"

"I swear it," Caden said, his voice joining the chorus of his fellows.

"Good. The Marking will hurt, but only for a short while. It burns more than anything, at least it did for me. Remove your shirts and take a seat. The scribes will perform their work, and then you will be escorted to the barracks."

Caden removed his shirt and stuffed it into his belt. Everyone else removed theirs as well, except for Thais. She stood rooted in place, her face a mask of stoicism.

"Is there a problem?" Captain Eduard asked.

Thais cleared her throat. "Must I remove my shirt?"

"If you want to be a Runesman. Are you having second thoughts?"

"No, sir."

Caden eyed her from his peripheral, wondering if she was actually going to go through with it. After a brief moment of hesitation, she removed her shirt. Thais's jaw tightened and Caden knew if anyone said anything inappropriate, she wouldn't hesitate to lay them out on their back.

No one said a word.

Everyone took a seat upon a wooden chair. The chairs were designed differently than anything Caden had seen before, with the back of the chair actually being in the front. The design allowed the person sitting to lean forward, and as Caden did so, he understood the idea behind the design.

A group of elderly men joined them under the tent, and each one carried a bucket filled with supplies. Caden's scribe set his bucket down and removed clean strips of cloth, inkwells, and some sort of metal instrument. He laid them out on the table and used one of the cloth strips to cleanse a spot on Caden's back, just below his neckline.

None of the scribes spoke as they worked. Caden gritted his teeth against the pain as sharp pinpricks stabbed the flesh along his spine. And it burned, just as Captain Eduard had said it would. From his side view, Caden watched another scribe work on Thais. Her eyes were closed, but she flinched here and there as the old man stabbed her with his metal instrument.

He dipped the tip of it into an inkwell, then jabbed it into Thais's flesh. As far as Caden could tell, each scribe followed the same process. While he knew that being a Runesman granted his lord the ability to borrow an attribute, he knew nothing about how the magic of the runes actually operated.

As he watched the scribe work, he assumed the magic imbued within the rune had something to do with the ink being used. The scribes were tattooing a rune into their flesh, and since that rune connected them to their lord, it seemed logical to Caden that the ink was magical in some way.

Thais opened her eyes and glanced at him, scowling. Caden turned his gaze straight ahead and tried not to think about Thais beating him to a pulp. He also tried not to think about her naked upper half, as that would cause other problems. She reminded him of a feral animal, wild and dangerous. And yet, he was attracted to her. She was pretty, there was no denying that, but her personality clashed with her looks enough that Caden knew he'd never pursue anything with her.

His conflicting thoughts were interrupted as a sharp pain lanced down his back, and he felt his feet go numb. The scribe tattooing him slathered something thick and greasy onto his flesh, rubbing it in thoroughly. The numbness faded, but his back still burned like fire.

"The rune is complete," the old man said.

Caden sat up, stretching the stiffness from his muscles. He watched the old man place everything back into his bucket, and then he left. Captain Eduard came over to inspect the rune and nodded his approval.

"Well done, Runesman."

Caden couldn't help but grin like a fool.

3

WHEN THE RED STONE WALLS of Klodian Keep came into view, Mina breathed a sigh of relief. She'd had the feeling that someone was watching them. The idea was ludicrous, she knew, but the feeling was intense. Lord Klodian and his retinue were oblivious, still talking about his prowess in killing the dragon from the mesa.

Even Vhan wasn't paying attention to their surroundings. Granted, they were within the boundaries of the Thophate Dominion, but that didn't mean that enemies weren't lurking, waiting for a chance to eliminate Lord Klodian. Mina rubbed at the scale on her leg absently and wondered whether the glowing eyes she had seen had truly just been her imagination.

It was hot and she was thirsty, so maybe she had seen a mirage. The more she considered it, the more she became convinced that's what it had been. As they got closer to the castle, Mina could see that Enlistment Day was nearing an end. Klodian customarily watched over the proceedings, but today had been different.

Klodian and the others rode at a slow pace, allowing Mina to keep up with them. He usually left her behind, knowing that she would eventually make her way back to the castle. Vhan occasionally looked back at her, and she assumed he was checking on her. Vhan seemed like a nice person, but Mina had learned long ago not to trust anyone.

When they reached the field where the newest Runesmen were, Klodian stopped and dismounted. Vhan hurriedly followed suit, trailing after the lord like a puppy. Mina kept her distance from them, but she did glance over the faces of Klodian's newest soldiers. She didn't recognize any of them, but she did spot a woman among the mix. That was a first.

"Lord Klodian," Captain Eduard greeted, bowing.

"Captain."

"How was the hunt?"

"It was good," Klodian replied, removing his helmet. "I'll tell you about it later. How many new Runesmen do we have?"

"Sixty."

Mina could tell by the way the Eduard said it that he knew Klodian wouldn't be pleased. The Dominion Lord scanned the sea of new faces and finally nodded.

"Why so few?"

"You have high standards, my Lord. It is my duty to enforce those standards and only enlist the best."

"What of the Marking? Any problems?"

"Three," Captain Eduard answered. "Three died during the process."

Mina was surprised to hear that. It was rare for anyone to die during the Marking, but it wasn't impossible. Those too weak to accept the magical rune were typically released from their oath and they went on to find another pursuit in life, but with a few new scars. For three to have died … well, the scribes responsible would be put to death as punishment.

Klodian frowned. "I see. How about the assignments?"

"Ten were marked for strength. Five for haste, and five for vision. The rest were given the common rune."

"I needed more footmen, so I'm happy to hear that. Hopefully, we'll see more talent at the next enlistment. Carry on, Captain. I'll see you at the feast tonight."

Klodian and Vhan climbed back onto their horses and returned to the castle, leaving Mina behind. She offered a bow to the captain, but he ignored her and walked off, shouting orders at the servants clearing the field.

Mina regarded the female Runesman curiously. She'd never seen a woman as a soldier, nor had she ever heard of such a tale. The woman returned her stare, fire in her eyes.

"Do you have a problem?"

"No," Mina replied.

"Then why are you looking at me?"

"I'm curious is all. Why would you want to be a soldier?"

"That's my business," the woman spat. "Keep your nose out of it."

"For Hadon's sake, Thais. Not everyone is your enemy."

The woman named Thais turned to the man who'd spoken and punched him in the face, knocking him to the ground.

"Everyone is your enemy until they prove otherwise," she growled. "And you!" Thais turned back to Mina, her right hand balled into a fist. She took a few steps forward, but another man stepped into her path.

"Just stop," he said.

"Move out of my way unless you want to get thumped next!"

The man crossed his arms and refused to move. The two stared at one another, neither one backing down. Mina's face flushed with embarrassment. No one had ever defended her, and it felt odd to have a stranger do it.

"Please," Mina begged. "I meant no disrespect. Don't fight because of me. I'm leaving now."

"You aren't going anywhere until I bash your face in!" Thais shouted.

"Go cool off somewhere," the man said.

"No one tells me what to do!"

Thais leaped forward, and the two clashed. They tumbled to the ground and fought, punching and rolling around. Mina watched, horrified. Thais gained the upper hand, pinning the man's arms with her knees. Just as she was about to punch the man in the face, Captain Eduard came rushing over, driving his right knee into the side of Thais's head. Her face scrunched in confusion and she toppled over with a groan.

"Did you so quickly forget your oath?" Captain Eduard demanded. "We are a brotherhood with the same cause. No one here is your enemy. You would do well to remember that."

The captain paused, looking from Thais to the man.

"I think five lashings for the both of you will be a fit reminder. Report to me after dinner. I'll deal with you then."

Captain Eduard stalked off, shooting a glare in Mina's direction. He could have punished her too, with Klodian's approval, but Mina guessed he didn't think it was worth the effort. Mina might be a slave, but she was a valuable one.

Thais slowly rose to her feet and staggered off. The man waited until she was gone, then he sat up and smiled at Mina.

"Sorry about her," he said. "I've only met her today. She's got a bit of a temper."

Mina had been taken aback before, but now doubly so. Not only had a stranger helped her, but he'd fought a fellow Runesman to do it. If the day got anymore strange, she'd have to assume she was dreaming.

"No, it's me that should apologize," Mina replied. "I shouldn't be standing around out here."

"Nonsense." The man got up and brushed a trail of blood from his lips with the back of his hand. "I'm Caden. What's your name?"

"Mina."

Caden's brows rose slightly. "Lord Klodian's fortune finder?" He glanced down at her legs briefly, and Mina knew what he was looking for.

"The same," she answered curtly.

"I apologize, that sounded less rude in my head."

"Don't worry about it. I'm used to it."

Caden was taller than her by roughly a full foot. He was well-muscled and clean shaven, with short brown hair and green eyes. Despite the dirt and grime, Mina found him rather alluring. The silence stretched until it became awkward, and Caden cleared his throat.

"I don't want to start on the wrong foot," he said. "I'm sorry if I offended you. That wasn't my intent."

His tone was sincere, but Mina didn't trust him. He was a stranger, and despite his actions to defend her, she wouldn't let her guard down, no matter how handsome he was.

"All is forgiven," she said. "As I said, I'm used to it."

She was clutching her dragon horn tightly, feeling uncomfortable. Part of it was her attraction to Caden, but she also still felt as if someone was watching her. She was confident that once she got inside the castle, the feeling would subside.

"I should be going."

"Would you like me to escort you?" Caden asked. "In case Thais hasn't learned her lesson?"

"No," Mina said quickly. "I'll be fine."

She speed-walked across the field, heading to the castle. She could tell her cheeks were flushed by the way they burned. Aside from her discomfort around Caden, she also needed to get the dragon horn to her room so she could take the necessary steps to preserve it. If she waited too long, the horn would dry out from the desert heat and slowly rot from the inside, becoming brittle.

Mina reached her room and barely remembered her trek through the confusing network of hallways. Klodian hadn't built the castle, but he had made several changes to the interior when he'd taken up his father's mantle, transforming it into a literal maze.

He'd claimed it was to make the castle a more formidable fortress, but no one had ever attacked the Thophate Dominion before. It was on the border of The Long Sands, much too far for an enemy army to march to, let alone conquer. The heat itself stopped most people from coming to Thophate, and only merchants and traders with deep pockets braved the trip.

After she'd treated the horn, Mina cleaned herself and changed clothes, then ate the small meal that was delivered to her bed. As she went about her evening tasks, she couldn't help but think of the Runesman from earlier.

"Caden," she whispered, a smile pulling at her lips.

4

AFTER THE DARK OF NIGHT had fallen, and he'd received his five lashings, Caden laid on his cot in the barracks, trying not to move much. Even breathing sent pain flaring through his wounds, but he didn't regret his actions.

Thais had been wrong to threaten Mina or anyone else for that matter. She had some serious anger issues, or perhaps someone had deeply hurt her in the past. Either way, Caden wasn't sure how to handle her. He never expected to fight a woman, but she had attacked him. And she would have knocked him unconscious if it weren't for Captain Eduard intervening.

Something creaked, and Caden lifted his head. The barracks were dark, but he saw a shadow moving slowly in his direction.

"Who's there?" he whispered.

"Shut your mouth," Thais's voice whispered back.

Caden laid his head back down and sighed. If she was here to fight him again, he knew he would lose to her. She'd been lashed too, but he thought she handled the pain with much more grace than he had. He chalked it up to her having a higher pain threshold. Thais reached his bed and stood over him. Her face was hidden by the shadows, but her posture didn't seem menacing.

"What do you want?" Caden asked lowly.

"I wanted to apologize for beating you up," Thais replied. "I expected more of a challenge."

"Go away."

There was a brief moment of silence.

"No one has ever stood up to me the way you did."

"That's surprising. You're a bully, Thais. Eventually, someone always puts the bully down."

"I …" She sighed. "Where I come from, soft people die. I had to learn to be tough and trust no one because I didn't want to die. You may not understand that, but it's the truth."

Caden stared up at her shadowy figure, mulling over her words. Perhaps she wasn't as terrible a person as he first assumed.

"You don't have to apologize to me," he finally said. "But you might want to apologize to Mina."

"The girl from earlier?"

"Yes. That's Lord Klodian's girl. The one who leads him to his dragons."

Thais stiffened. "I didn't know. Do you think she'll rat me out to Lord Klodian?"

Caden smiled. He didn't believe Mina would do that, but it wouldn't hurt to keep a little fear in the air. "Possibly. If you apologize quickly, she may let it pass."

"I'll talk to her first thing tomorrow."

"Good idea. Now, can I try to get some sleep?"

Thais climbed onto the cot with him and laid her head on his chest. Caden froze, unsure of what she was doing. She didn't move or try to seduce him, and he eventually relaxed when he realized she had fallen asleep. He decided that Thais was more like a wild animal than he first realized, and it seemed like she needed a friend. And that was something he could be for her if she needed it. Until he transferred Dominions, anyway.

When he awoke the next morning, Thais was gone. Judging by the lack of light coming through the windows, dawn hadn't quite arrived. Caden sat up slowly and was surprised to find that he didn't feel any pain at all from the previous day's punishment. He left the cot and headed for the washroom, where he splashed cold water onto his face. A small mirror hung on the wall, and he removed his shirt and twisted awkwardly to get a look at his back.

The rune was there, an onyx symbol that looked like a pillar. A set of eyes sat between the crossbars of the upper portion, and two swords crossed over the center. The details were intricate, and Caden understood now why the Marking had taken so long. What surprised him, however, was the absence of his wounds.

There was no sign that he'd been lashed at all, not even reddened or upraised flesh. He stared at his back in disbelief. How was that possible?

"Pretty neat trick, huh?"

Caden whirled around to see Thais in the doorway. "What trick?"

"The rune healed our wounds."

"How?"

"Magic, probably. What good would we be as Runesmen if we couldn't heal quickly? The Dominion Lords would have a tough time keeping their ranks full, especially in the Dominions that are always warring with one another."

Caden took a final look at his back and slipped his shirt back on.

"You seem to be in a better mood today," he said, turning to face Thais.

"I got some sleep," she replied, shrugging. "I'm not always a raging b—"

A horn blared outside the barracks, cutting off her words. The main quarters erupted in chaos as people scrambled out of bed, swiftly dressing and rushing out into the courtyard. Caden and Thais hurriedly followed their fellows.

Captain Eduard was standing with his arms clasped behind his back. Instead of his chainmail and leather armor, he was wearing black pants and a brown shirt. An olive-colored cloak draped his shoulders, tied at the neck. Strapped at his waist was a sword with a black hilt, and the pommel was a large clear stone. Once everyone had lined up, Captain Eduard cleared his throat.

"What is the purpose of a Runesman?" he asked.

"To protect the Dominion and its lord," someone shouted.

"Correct, at least on the surface. If you dig a little deeper, what do you find?"

Silence met his question, and he flicked his gaze across the line.

"I wouldn't expect any of you to know yet, but I'm always hoping for a surprise. We are a brotherhood unlike any other. Are we soldiers? Yes, but we are more than that. We have been given a gift that many will never receive. Having this rune on your body isn't just a sign of who you serve. It's an honor that you uphold.

"Do you know why Lord Klodian made me the captain of his Runesmen? Not simply because I've proven myself to him countless times. It is because I know what it means to be a warrior. And I am going to teach you to be warriors."

Thais raised her hand.

"Yes?" Captain Eduard asked.

"We're already warriors, aren't we? We're here to kill, and I'm sure any of us can do that."

"There's more to being a warrior than killing someone. War without purpose is brutality. We are not tyrants. If that is what you are here for, you can leave now. Listen carefully, all of you. Your first lesson is this: Courage, above all things, is the first quality of a warrior. It takes courage to do the right thing, especially in the face of adversity.

"Beginning tomorrow, you will wake before dawn and run ten laps around the castle. The horn that woke you this morning will blare every morning at the same time. I suggest you do not ignore it unless you enjoy being punished. After you finish your morning run, you can enter the castle for breakfast. You will eat, and you will return here for your training. Are there any questions?"

Caden glanced down the line, but nobody spoke.

"Good. Start running. Ten laps, all the way around. If you don't finish, you don't eat."

Caden wasted no time. He broke from the line and took off, jogging at a swift pace. He made sure not to push himself too hard, fearing that if he was forced to walk at all, he'd be lashed again. A couple of people sprinted past him, but he ignored them and focused on keeping a steady stride. Thais eventually joined him, matching his steps and jogging beside him.

He wasn't sure, but he suspected that she liked him.

5

AS A CHILD, MINA'S PARENTS never taught her to read. In retrospect, she assumed it was because they didn't know how themselves. They were farmers, after all, and had no use for such privileges.

She stared at the spines of the books as she dusted the shelves they rested upon, wondering what the letters spelled out. The colors of the books varied from black to navy to green, and they were all in pristine condition. This was Lord Klodian's private study, and he demanded only the best.

Mina paused in her work when she spotted a book that had gold lettering. She glanced around, making certain she was alone and pulled the book out. It had some heft to it, and she cracked it open and idly flipped through the pages. Flowing script filled every inch of parchment space. Mina was disappointed to find that there were no pictures.

The sound of approaching footsteps startled her and she quickly replaced the book and continued dusting.

"Where is that blasted girl?" It was Lord Klodian. "Girl!"

Mina rushed toward the open door, reaching it just as Klodian stepped into view.

"I'm here, my Lord."

"Where have you been? I've been searching the entire castle for you."

"I was completing my chores, as you commanded."

"Never mind that. You're coming with me."

"Now, my Lord?" Mina asked.

"Yes, now. Don't fall behind, girl. We haven't got much time."

Klodian spun around and hurried down the hall. Mina followed after him, her eyes wide with terror. She'd never seen him in such a rush. As she tried to keep up with him, she looked around for a place to leave her duster. A servant stepped out of one of the rooms and paused, bowing her head as Klodian passed her.

"Here," Mina handed her the duster, smiling at the girl's confusion.

Klodian hurried through the hallways with sure steps, never once pausing as Mina usually did. He'd designed the maze of hallways, so she wasn't surprised that he knew exactly where he was going. They exited the castle and were immediately greeted by Captain Eduard in the courtyard.

"Are the Runesmen ready?" Klodian asked.

"Yes," Eduard hesitated. "You didn't give me much time to prepare, so I'll have to use some of the recruits. Most of the seasoned men are out on patrol along the border. We're ready to follow your lead."

"Very good. I won't let this stand, no matter what must be done."

Mina didn't understand what he was talking about, but she knew it must be important if he was taking Runesmen with him. Captain Eduard bowed and departed, heading for the barracks. Klodian continued onward and Mina spotted a carriage ahead. The horses pawed at the ground anxiously as if they were aware of Klodian's urgency.

"Get inside," Klodian ordered.

Mina looked at him in surprise, but he wasn't paying her any heed. He walked to the front of the carriage and spoke with the driver. Not wanting to lose the opportunity, Mina climbed into the carriage and sat down, marveling at the interior.

The benches were covered with plush cushions, and the walls and ceiling were elaborately decorated with velvet. Mina ran her fingertips along the soft material. Aside from everything being an ugly gold color, she found the entire experience quite amazing.

Lord Klodian stepped into the carriage and shut the door, then took a seat opposite Mina. She clasped her hands in her lap and lowered her gaze, keeping her eyes on Klodian's shoes. When the carriage didn't move, Mina cast a furtive glance at Klodian. He was staring out of the window and seemed to be waiting on something.

A few moments later, Captain Eduard's face appeared in the glass and he knocked on the carriage door twice. The carriage jerked as it began moving, and Mina sat back, trying to figure out where they might be going.

"I suppose you are curious?" Klodian asked.

"Very, my Lord."

"We're going on a hunt, but it is not like the usual trips. I'm not looking for gold and sport this time, but for blood. A dragon attacked Slia."

Mina's face scrunched in disbelief. A dragon had attacked a human settlement?

"Is that normal?" she asked.

Klodian snorted. "No, girl. I suspect it might be a young one that strayed too far from home."

"Dragons are wild animals. They aren't capable of things like retaliation, are they?" Mina didn't think so, but she envisioned the glowing eyes staring at her from the cave entrance, and she wasn't so sure.

"Of course not," Klodian replied. "But they are territorial, like any other animal. It probably left its nest and ventured far enough that it lost the scent of its fellows. It's unfortunate that it won't live long enough to learn from its mistake."

That made sense to Mina. She wondered how much damage the creature had done to Slia. She'd never been there before, but she knew the name. It was a smaller city within the Thophate Dominion, and it was the closest community to Klodian Keep.

As the time slipped away, Mina began dozing off, occasionally jolting and startling herself. Afraid that Klodian would yell at her, she tried rubbing her eyes and digging her nails into her palms, but it did little to help keep her awake. When the carriage finally stopped, she had no idea how much time had passed.

Klodian stood and stepped out of the carriage. Mina blinked repeatedly and followed after him. Now that she was moving around, she didn't feel as tired. The crunch of dirt signaled the approach of the Runesmen. Mina shielded her eyes with her right hand and saw Captain Eduard leading the small contingent of soldiers on horseback. She spotted two other familiar faces as well. Caden and Thais.

Thais.

Mina glared at her briefly before turning away. Thais was rude. And violent. Mina wanted nothing to do with the woman. She walked over to stand beside Klodian, so enwrapped in her thoughts that she didn't notice the smell of smoke in the air. She kept her eyes on the ground until a few flakes of gray ash landed at her feet. Mina realized something was wrong and lifted her head. She gasped.

Slia had been destroyed.

At least, it appeared that way to Mina. As Klodian strode forth, he motioned for her to follow him. She obeyed, gazing wide-eyed at the destruction around her. Buildings were nothing more than piles of rubble, smoke drifted into the sky in lazy plumes, and there was a terrible scent faintly masked by the smoke. Mina would later learn that it was the smell of burnt flesh.

"This is another reason why I hunt the creatures," Klodian said. "Dragons are dangerous. When they grow in numbers, their food sources become scarce. They start looking for alternatives, and that usually leads them to our cities."

"I thought you said it was a young one? If a small dragon can do this …" Mina trailed off.

"That was my assumption before we got here, but this isn't the work of one dragon. Do you sense anything?"

"No, nothing."

"I doubt the dragons have gone far. Let me know the moment you feel even the slightest hint of something."

"Yes, my Lord."

Mina winced and averted her gaze as they passed a corpse. It had been badly burned, and the lower half of it was missing entirely. She could feel bile rising in her throat, but she swallowed her saliva, forcing it back down. Klodian didn't stop moving. He continued walking through the ruined city, and it slowly became apparent to Mina that he was looking for something.

They turned left onto another street and Klodian paused. He seemed uncertain, which was out of character for him. Mina suddenly grew wary. What if the dragons were still here and she couldn't sense them? They would all be killed, and it would be her fault.

On the bright side, if she did die, at least she would finally be free, from both Klodian's leash and her curse. Such dark thoughts used to bother her, but now … now they didn't. She didn't know if that was a good thing.

"Your ability to sense the closeness of dragons is invaluable, and not just to me. If the other Dominion Lords knew of your sixth sense, they would try to steal you from me."

Mina frowned. Why was he telling her this? Klodian grunted to himself and continued walking. Mina rubbed her leg, pressing against the scale under her pants. She didn't feel the presence of any dragons.

Klodian stopped again after a few feet. He pushed some debris around with his foot and turned to look past Mina. She glanced over her shoulder and saw Captain Eduard and the Runesmen approaching.

"This was the Dominate's house," Klodian said. "I can see his body."

"Should we search for survivors?" Eduard asked.

"Yes, but be quick. And keep your eyes open. I have a feeling the dragons that did this are still in the area."

Eduard paired the Runesmen in groups of two and sent them in various directions. Mina watched them scatter, wringing her hands anxiously. She wanted to help Klodian find the dragons responsible, but the scale wasn't giving her anything. He was probably going to be angry with her if she couldn't track them, yet what could she do?

Mina.

She whirled around at the sound of her name, but no one was there. Her eyes widened. Lord Klodian was gone.

6

So, Klodian *had* brought Mina. Caden assumed he might have, especially if the whispers of a dragon attack were true. Judging by the destruction, there was more truth to those whispers than Caden liked. After all, he hadn't signed up as a soldier to fight dragons.

"Thais and Caden, you two take the northeast side of the city. Shout if you find anything."

Caden barely heard Captain Eduard's command. He was staring at Mina. Her blonde hair seemed to shimmer in the sunlight, and she was rubbing her leg. Did she sense the dragons nearby? Fighting a man was one thing, but a dragon … he swallowed hard and tried to summon his courage.

"Come on," Thais said, pulling his arm.

They backtracked to the main street and turned left, following it east. Caden surveyed the damage as they walked. Almost all of the buildings had been decimated. The dead littered the streets, and the smell of smoke was suffocating. The heat was always rough, but with the fires still burning, it was much worse. Every so often, a slight breeze would stir, giving him the opportunity to take a fresh breath.

"I know dragons are powerful, but is this really the work of a dragon?" Thais asked. "I mean, there's nothing left."

"Lord Klodian thinks it was more than one, and I have to agree. How else would an entire city be destroyed in such a short time frame? It had to be multiple dragons."

"I suppose you're right. I just hope those beasts aren't still around."

Caden hoped so too, but he didn't say it. They reached a fork in the road. The main thoroughfare continued ahead, and a side street angled north.

"We should split up," Thais said. "We'll cover more ground that way. Besides, I don't like the feeling I get from this place."

"I don't know if that's a good idea. Captain Eduard assigned us in groups for a reason. What if something happens to you?"

Thais smirked at him. "Your concern is touching, really, but I'm a big girl. I can take care of myself."

"That's not what I meant," Caden scoffed.

"Sure you didn't. I'll take the side street. You continue ahead. If the roads don't converge at some point, we meet back here."

Caden looked back the way they'd came, unsure. "Fine," he muttered.

"See you shortly."

Thais left, and Caden watched her go. He tried not to stare, but he found it difficult. She was beautiful, he couldn't deny that, but there was something about Mina that captured more than his eyes. He barely knew the girl, true, but his attraction was more than physical. He just couldn't put his finger on it.

"Focus," he berated himself.

He continued along the main street, listening for anything other than the occasional whistle of wind through the rubble. There had to be survivors, even if there were only a few. Caden paused here and there to dig through the rubble, but all he found was death. Bodies, both burned and mutilated, were buried everywhere. The stench stung his nostrils and he vomited. He'd been in fights before and had even killed, but this was something different entirely.

Caden spat several times to clean his mouth out, then wiped his lips with the back of his hand. His throat burned, but he'd left his canteen on the saddle of his horse. It wasn't the first time he'd needed water and gone without, and it wouldn't be the last. He continued walking and tried not to breathe through his nose.

The street ended, branching off to the left and right. Stone and wood from a collapsed building blocked the way to the right, so he went left. Judging by the direction, Caden assumed he'd meet up with Thais again on this route. A scrabbling noise caught his attention, and he climbed over some rubble on the left side of the street.

He lifted a large wooden beam and shifted it aside, clearing the way into a building. He stuck his head in and looked around, but there didn't appear to be anyone inside. The sound continued, and he eventually spotted a rat. It was pinned by debris, its claws scratching as it tried to get free. Caden was about to go through the effort of saving the little thing, but then he saw the injuries it had sustained.

"Poor guy," Caden murmured.

The rat would succumb to its wounds soon, so he did the only thing he knew to do. He put the rat out of its misery by pushing down on the debris. It squealed once and was dead. Caden wiped the sweat from his brow and climbed to the top of the rubble, looking for Thais. He could see some of the other Runesmen in the distance, but there was no sign of his volatile partner.

A tingling sensation began in his neck, quickly spreading along his shoulders and down his spine. Caden looked to the sky, fearing it had something to do with a dragon. He didn't see anything other than the blinding sun. He suddenly felt weak, and his knees gave out. He slumped down face-first among the wreckage.

"Gods, what's happening to me?"

His muscles felt like jelly and refused to budge. After a few moments of panic, the realization that Lord Klodian had enacted the rune magic struck him. Was this what it would feel like all the time? He hoped not. It rendered him useless. How could he do his duty and protect the Dominion and his lord if the moment his strength was borrowed, he fell like a sack of potatoes?

As he lay there unable to move, his gaze roamed among the hill of debris under him. Through the stones and wood, he spotted something glowing. It was small, but it blazed red as if it had been superheated. Caden kept his eyes on it, afraid that if it cooled, he'd lose sight of it. His weakness only lasted a few minutes, and then his strength came flooding back.

He hurriedly began moving the debris out of the way in an attempt to reach the glowing item. It was buried under two feet of rubble, but he managed to clear enough of it away so that he could stick his arm down through the rest to reach it. His fingers hovered around it, and despite its glow, he didn't feel any heat coming off of it.

Gritting his teeth, Caden grabbed onto it. He expected to get burned, but it was cool to the touch. He pulled his arm free and inspected the curious trinket. It had some weight to it, and he guessed it was metal. The glow faded, revealing a unique pattern of thin lines engraved on its surface.

Caden had no idea what it was, but it looked interesting. He palmed it and headed back down the mountain of ruined buildings to the street. There was still no sign of Thais, and he wondered if she'd turned back. He decided to give her a few more minutes, then he'd go searching.

While he waited, he continued to check for survivors. He didn't find any, but he did find a charred corpse and had accidentally put his hand through it when lifting a large stone. He felt his throat constrict and he gagged, but there was nothing to vomit up. He was sweaty and hot, and his patience was long gone.

"Thais!" he yelled. "Where are you?"

There was no reply. Caden growled in frustration and stormed along the street, cursing under his breath. If she had turned around…

A scream stopped him in his tracks. His best guess told him it had come from the west, and it was the scream of a woman. He sprinted toward the sound.

7

Mina screamed.

She hadn't meant to, but when Thais unexpectedly walked around the bend, it had taken her by surprise. What was she doing here? She was supposed to be looking for survivors. Mina eyed her distrustfully.

"Don't come any closer," she warned.

Thais stopped where she was, a disarming smile on her face. "Your name is Mina, right?"

Mina took a step back, her heart racing in her chest. Thais had threatened to beat her yesterday, and no one was around to stop her from acting on her words.

"Please don't run," Thais said. "I'm not going to hurt you."

"Why should I believe you?"

"It's clear that you don't. I don't blame you. Where I come from, trusting another person can get you killed. So, I won't convince you to trust me. You shouldn't. But at least hear me out."

Mina glanced over her shoulder, making note of the path she would take if she needed to flee. She looked back at Thais and tried to calm her nerves.

"What do you want to say?"

"I want to apologize. I know I can be a bit…" Thais waved her hand as if searching for the word.

"Rude?" Mina offered.

"I was going to say brash, but that works, too."

Mina stared at Thais intently. The woman was beautiful. Her hair was long and black, woven in multiple braids that stretched past her shoulders. She wasn't much taller than Mina, but she was slightly thicker because of her sinewy form. Her eyes were a piercing blue, and they held a fire in them that seemed unquenchable. The tan hue of her skin revealed her seafaring lineage, one that was riddled with warmongering and ruthlessness before the High Prince had bent them to his will.

"Why would you apologize to me? I'm nobody."

"You are Lord Klodian's dragon finder. I hardly think that's the position of a nobody."

Thais knew nothing about her, nor about how Klodian treated her. No one did, not really. Perhaps other people didn't see her as a slave, but Mina was no fool. She knew what her role in life was, whether she liked it or not.

"While you are bound by a willing oath, I am bound against my will," Mina replied. "I am nothing more than a purchased item."

Thais shook her head. "You are more than that. Don't believe that your worth is tied to your place in life. We all have value in the eyes of Hermóðr."

Mina was surprised that Thais had apologized, but more so that she was being nice to her. She was tempted to let her guard down, but she knew better than that. Thais was playing her for a fool. That was fine. Mina would play along. For now.

"If I forgive you, will you stop talking to me?"

"If that is what you want, then yes."

"I forgive you," Mina said.

"Good. Then we are on even ground now."

Before Mina could tell Thais to leave, Caden bounded into view. He slid to a stop, looking from Thais to Mina with a confused expression.

"What's going on?" he demanded. "I heard a scream."

"That was her," Thais said, motioning to Mina. "I startled her."

"It's true," Mina replied. "I was looking for Lord Klodian and didn't see her."

"Lord Klodian is missing?" Caden asked.

"I can't find him, but that doesn't mean he's lost. I assume he's looking for the dragons."

"They're still here?" Caden's face paled slightly.

"I don't think so," Mina answered. "I don't feel any nearby, but Lord Klodian can be … stubborn sometimes. As I said, I'm only assuming that's what he's doing."

"He used the strength rune a few moments ago," Thais said, glancing to Caden. He nodded.

"Perhaps he was lifting something heavy," Mina offered.

"Or perhaps your little ability isn't working," Thais returned. "How does it work, anyway?"

Mina felt her face flush. She didn't like attention. Thankfully, Caden diverted it elsewhere.

"We don't have time to discuss that. We need to make sure he's all right. It's our duty. Where's the last place you saw him?"

"Over there," Mina answered, pointing to where he'd been. "He was there one moment, and gone the next."

"You didn't see or hear anything?"

Mina shook her head. She didn't believe the voice she'd heard had been real, and she certainly didn't want to tell anyone about it even if it was.

Caden frowned and walked over to where Mina had pointed. He knelt and sifted the dirt around with his fingers, hobbling along the ground like some sort of crab. Mina peeked over at Thais to see if she was just as curious about his actions. The woman watched Caden with an amused smile, but there was something else in her look that told Mina that she liked him.

A pang of jealousy flashed through Mina. She wasn't sure why she felt that way. She didn't like him, not in *that* way. At least, she didn't think she did. He'd been nice to her by defending her, but that didn't mean anything … did it?

"I found his tracks," Caden said. "He went this way."

Caden stood and walked off the street, climbing over rubble and disappearing behind a crumbling building. Thais hurried after him, leaving Mina wondering if she should follow them. She decided she didn't want to be alone and ran to catch up, almost twisting her ankle attempting to balance her steps over the wreckage.

As she came around the corner of the ruined building, a strange feeling washed over her. She paused, touching the scale on her leg. The sensation was different from what she normally felt when a dragon was near, but it was definitely coming from the scale.

Caden was searching ahead, but Thais had gone a different route. Mina watched them as she tried to get her bearings, but a wave of nausea caused her to double over. She clutched her stomach and gritted her teeth, curling into a ball on the ground. Her mouth opened, but nothing came out except a gasp of air.

"Help," she managed to say, but it was barely above a whisper.

The air in front of her seemed to ripple like the surface of a pond disturbed by something. She fought against the ill feeling and stretched her hand toward it. Her nausea intensified and she recoiled, screaming within her mind as tears escaped her eyes.

Gods, make it go away!

Mina lay there tremoring, holding herself. Eventually, the sensation faded, leaving her feeling weak and tired. Once her strength returned, she sat up and brushed her hair out of her eyes. The air was no longer rippling. She touched her leg. Nothing was coming from the scale. Had that been the presence of a dragon? If so, it must have been powerful indeed to have such an effect on her.

Fear coursed through her. If that had been a dragon, then Klodian might be dead. Mina scrambled to her feet, leaning against the rubble momentarily. She needed to find him. If he had been killed, then her curse would never be lifted.

"Over here!" Caden shouted. "I found him!"

8

Caden knelt beside Lord Klodian's prone form.

His chest moved up and down with his breathing, and Caden heaved a sigh of relief. At first, he'd feared his lord was dead. A glance at their surroundings didn't reveal much. Everything was a mass of rubble like the rest of the city, and there were no signs that anything foul had caused Klodian to fall unconscious.

Still, the man wasn't lying on the ground for no reason. Caden kept his hand on the hilt of his sword just in case, though he didn't know what he would be able to do against a dragon. Thais joined him first. Her eyes widened in surprise.

"He's alive, but I'm not sure what happened. I found him here like this."

"If a dragon attacked him, there'd be nothing left," Thais said.

"My thoughts exactly. That doesn't mean we're clear of danger, though. Go find Captain Eduard. We need to get Lord Klodian to safety."

"I don't like being told what to do, but I'll make an exception this time. Next time I better hear the word 'please.'"

Thais flashed him a grin and rushed off. A moment later, Mina cautiously approached. Her face was pale and she looked like she might faint.

"Is he…"

"No, he's fine. For now, at least. Thais went to get help. Are you all right? You look sick."

"It's nothing," Mina replied.

It was obvious she was lying, but Caden decided not to press her. He nodded instead and lifted the visor of Klodian's helm. His eyelids were open, but only the whites of his eyes were showing. Caden gently pulled the helm off completely and set it aside.

"Has he ever gone unconscious before? Maybe when he uses the rune magic?"

"No, never."

Mina seemed nervous, which confused him. He wondered why she was so concerned about Klodian. If he died, she would no longer be a slave. She would also no longer have a home, but to Caden, freedom seemed more important than things like food and shelter. Mina swayed on her feet, and she blinked lazily.

"You should probably sit down," Caden said. "You don't look so good."

"I'm fine. Just focus on Lord Klodian."

They both went silent. The time ticked along, seeming to last indefinitely until the sound of several people approaching broke the stillness. Thais had returned, leading Captain Eduard and a few other Runesmen.

"What happened?" Eduard demanded.

"I'm not sure. He was already down when I found him."

Eduard motioned to the other Runesmen. "Find something stable to put him on. We'll carry him out of here and have the physicians look at him back at the castle."

In short order, a thin flat piece of wood was brought over and they lifted Lord Klodian and placed him onto it, using the board as a makeshift stretcher. Eduard ordered everyone to grab a side, and together, they raised it off the ground and started navigating slowly over the rubble. Caden glanced over his shoulder at Mina.

She followed them, but she seemed to be struggling. Caden was forced to keep his main focus on Klodian, namely keeping his end of the board up high enough without tripping, but he continually checked on Mina when there was a pause.

As they made it onto the street, Caden heard a groan and looked back just in time to see Mina stumble and fall. She hit the ground hard and didn't move.

"Captain! The girl!"

Eduard called a halt and walked over to her, but he made no move to help her. He stood over her in silence for a moment, then turned to look at Caden.

"We can come back for her."

Caden scrunched his face. "Sir?"

"Lord Klodian's well-being is more important than hers. After we've tended to him, we can worry about her."

"I'm sorry sir, but I don't think Lord Klodian would approve." Eduard gave him a hard stare. "She's the key to his wealth. If we left her out here, I'd hate to see the punishment he'd inflict on the one responsible."

Caden caught a slight change in Eduard's demeanor. It was subtle, but it was there.

"Good point, Runesman. You can carry her."

Eduard strode past Caden and ordered the others to continue. Caden hoped he hadn't overstepped a line with the captain, but he couldn't in good conscience leave someone to die. And he knew he wasn't wrong. If Klodian found out they'd intentionally left Mina, he would probably lash the entire lot of them.

Caden lifted Mina in his arms and slung her over his shoulder, then hurried to catch up with the others. They trudged through the ruined city back to where the carriage and their mounts waited. The desert was always a quiet place, but Caden found the stillness of Slia to be eerie.

He reached the carriage just as Lord Klodian had been placed inside. Captain Eduard offered him a nod as he stepped out, which led Caden to believe he hadn't completely messed up.

"Put the girl in there and ride along with them. I can't be in two places at once, so keep your eyes on Lord Klodian. If anything happens, knock twice on the front wall. The driver will stop and I'll know there's a problem."

Caden wasn't sure if his assignment was a punishment or a reward. He didn't mind riding in the cool shade, but he also didn't want the other Runesmen to think he'd been elevated above them without merit. Perhaps he was overthinking things, but he knew how petty people could be.

"Yes, sir."

Eduard waited until Caden had entered the carriage, then he closed the door and began shouting orders. Lord Klodian was lying on one side of the carriage, stretched out across the pillowed bench.

Caden placed Mina on the other side, in the same position, and stood in the center. The carriage started moving and he held onto the wall for support.

His gaze flicked back and forth between Lord Klodian and Mina, making sure they were breathing normally. Aside from being unconscious, Lord Klodian didn't seem to have sustained any wounds. It was a mystery, but one that would hopefully be solved by the physicians. After a long while, Mina's eyes fluttered open.

"How are you feeling?" he asked.

She watched him with a thoughtful expression on her face and slowly sat up, hugging her knees to her chest.

"I feel better," she replied.

"You scared me back there. I'm glad you're all right."

Mina's cheeks blushed, but she didn't say anything. They rode in silence, both of them watching over Lord Klodian. Eventually, Mina released her legs and let them hang down off the bench. That's when Caden spotted a glint of copper. She must have torn her pants when she'd fallen. Mina followed his gaze and her eyes widened. She tried to cover the scale with her hands, cursing lowly.

"I'm not bothered by it," Caden said.

"Maybe not, but I am. I hate this cursed thing."

"Some would see it as a blessing rather than a curse."

"And such people would be wrong," Mina retorted. "No one knows what it's like to feel the presence of those creatures in their mind. I wouldn't wish it on my worst enemies."

As he listened to her, Caden wondered if he would have the fortitude to deal with something like that. It was unheard of. A human who could sense dragons. He'd heard the things whispered about her. Some called her a witch, others a demon spawn. They were all wrong, he knew. She was just different, and people had trouble understanding that.

"Were you born in Klodan's court?" Caden asked.

"No. My parents sold me to him when I was young."

"They *sold* you? Isn't that illegal?"

Mina snorted. "Many things are illegal, but that doesn't stop anyone."

"I know that, it's just… your own family sold you. I can't believe anyone would do that."

"I blame this stupid scale. And the dragon that it belongs to. That's why I help him, you know."

"Why?"

"To rid the world of the beasts. Dragons are mindless animals, good for nothing other than their treasure troves. Lord Klodian grows richer, and I get a little bit of revenge with each one that is killed."

Caden was surprised at how much hatred she harbored. She seemed like such a meek woman, and yet as she spoke, he could hear the unbridled rage burning within her voice. She didn't just dislike dragons, she despised them.

"How did it happen?" Caden asked.

Mina stared at him, and he assumed he'd offended her. He was about to apologize when she answered.

"I fell into the nest of a dragon. While I was playing in the hills, I stepped on a weak spot and it collapsed. The nest was abandoned, thank the gods, but they had left a great pile of discarded scales. I landed on it and this was my reward."

She removed her hands from her leg and Caden got a better look at it. It was a deep copper color and pentagonal in shape. The two sides were longer, while the top and bottom edges were shorter in diameter. It was curved flush with her thigh, which Caden found intriguing. He'd assumed the scale would be protruding out of her, but given that she wore normal clothes, he realized that was a foolish assumption.

"Did your parents try to remove it?"

"They did. And so too did the local physicians. The scale fused into my flesh somehow and … became a part of me. My parents were told that the only option was to remove my leg. They probably would have gone through with that option had it not been for the other thing."

"What do you mean?"

"The ability to sense dragons. I didn't know that's what it was until I followed the pull. I led my parents to a den of dragons and almost got us all killed. I think that's when they realized that I wasn't just deformed. I was cursed. Lord Klodian heard the rumors about me and my parents sold me to him. There's not much else to tell."

Caden sat down on the bench beside her and tried to fathom how parents could sell their own flesh and blood. By the time they returned to the castle, he still didn't have an answer.

9

Mina's strength didn't fully return until evening fell.

The chaos that had engulfed the castle had finally died down, though the servants talked about the steady stream of physicians still coming and going from Lord Klodian's chambers. Mina had spent the remainder of the day in her bed, but she hadn't been able to sleep. She didn't have the energy to finish her chores, and she doubted anyone would notice they weren't done.

Lord Klodian would, but since he was still unconscious, she wasn't afraid of earning his wrath. Left to her own devices for the first time in a while, her mind replayed the events at Slia over and over again. The odd sensation she'd felt still troubled her. It had definitely originated from the scale, but it didn't feel like any dragon she'd sensed before.

"How are you feeling?" Vhan's voice broke her reverie and she rolled over to look at him.

"Better," she replied.

"That's good."

"What of Lord Klodian?"

"Nothing to report yet. The physicians all seem stumped. He hasn't suffered any visible wounds, but they can't explain why he hasn't awakened yet. Despite that, they seem to agree that he should be all right. They're saying it might take some time for him to come out of whatever state he's in."

Mina wasn't sure those old men knew what they were talking about. If there were no wounds and he hadn't awakened yet, something was wrong. There was nothing she could do about it, though, so she tried not to think about what would happen if Klodian died.

"Are you hungry?" Vhan changed the subject. "Dinner is almost ready. If you don't think you can make it to the dining hall, I can bring you something."

"I appreciate the offer, but I think I can manage," Mina said.

She was hungry, and she felt like herself again, so she sat up and slipped her ragged shoes on. She was waiting until she had enough money to buy a new pair of sturdy boots, but since Klodian didn't pay her, it was taking a long time to scrape the coins together.

"I wouldn't mind some company if you don't have anything else to do."

Vhan smiled. "I've got the night off, believe it or not."

"So do I. It's kind of odd, isn't it?"

"It really is," Vhan agreed. "I almost don't know what to do with myself."

Mina laughed, which wasn't something she did often. It felt good to feel unburdened, even if it wouldn't last long.

"Come on, I'm famished."

Vhan walked beside her as they navigated the maze of halls, and they reached the dining hall to find that the Runesmen were being served. Mina usually didn't eat until later in the evening, so she was surprised to see so many people in the hall at one time. Caden and Thais were there too, talking amongst themselves at the end of one of the long tables.

Mina and Vhan joined the line of people waiting to be served, eventually getting a plate full of steaming chicken smothered in a cheese sauce and a bowl of broth. The food at Klodian Keep was the only thing that Mina had never complained about. Lord Klodian didn't scrimp when it came to nourishing his soldiers and staff, and although Mina was a slave, he didn't exclude her.

She followed Vhan to an empty section of one of the tables and they ate in silence. The room, however, wasn't quiet. The Runesmen were a rowdy bunch. Bits and pieces of loud conversations reached Mina's ears, and she heard everything from stories about where people were from to the destruction of Slia. The loudness was a little overwhelming, and after she finished her meal, she rose to her feet.

"Thank you for eating with me," she said to Vhan. "I should probably get some rest."

"You're welcome," he grinned at her like a fool. "Does this mean you'll let me see the scale?"

Mina rolled her eyes at him. "No."

"It was worth a try," he said with a chuckle, then shrugged. "Just leave your plate and bowl here. The kitchen staff will collect them."

"Are you sure?"

"Yes. It's their job, you know."

"Oh, right. Well, good night, Vhan. I'll see you tomorrow."

"See you tomorrow."

Mina left the noisy dining hall and returned to her bed. With her stomach full, it didn't take her long to fall asleep. Her dreams didn't let her rest, and she tossed and turned from continuous nightmares. She felt as if she had just fallen back to sleep when someone touched her shoulder.

She opened her eyes to see Captain Eduard. He pressed his finger to his lips and motioned to the hall. Mina got up and followed him, wondering why he was summoning her. Her heart began racing in her chest. Once they were out of the room, Eduard spoke lowly.

"Lord Klodian wants to see you."

"He's awake?"

"Yes, but he's very weak. I told him it could wait until morning, but he demanded I come and get you."

"Is he going to be all right?"

"He'll be fine. Let's go. I'd like to get *some* sleep tonight."

Captain Eduard escorted her to Lord Klodian's bedchamber. At the door, he stopped and nodded for her to enter. She pushed the door open and stepped inside. Eduard shut it behind her, and she heard his receding footsteps echo down the hall as he left.

The room was mostly dark, but a few candles were lit, their flames burning steady. She walked further into the room and paused when she saw Lord Klodian. He was sitting up in his bed, his back against the headboard. A mound of pillows surrounded him. Mina paused. He appeared to be sleeping. She was about to turn around when he spoke.

"Sit, girl."

His voice was little more than a rasp. In the dimly lit room, it was almost creepy. Mina stepped toward a chair against the wall, and Klodian hissed in disapproval.

"Over here. On the floor."

She obeyed, sitting on the plush rug that covered the cold stones, gritting her teeth while doing it. Mina hated that he treated her like a dog. She was relieved to see that he was alive, but that didn't mean she cared about him. She only wanted her freedom, and unfortunately, he was the only key to that door.

"Did you sense a dragon at Slia today?"

"No, my Lord." She hesitated. "I … don't think I did."

"Interesting. Explain yourself."

"It's difficult to describe, but when I sense a dragon, it's very distinct. I just know that's what it is. Today I felt something, but it wasn't the same. It was … different, odd. I don't know what it was, but it made me sick."

Lord Klodian was silent for a long while, and Mina wondered if he'd fallen asleep. He stirred, reaching up to lazily scratch his cheek. She had never seen him so vulnerable before. The thought of killing him flitted through her mind, but she discounted it almost immediately. She wasn't a murderer, no matter how much she thought he might deserve it. And as much as she hated to admit it, she needed Klodian.

"I think you might have felt the touch of magic," he said.

"My Lord?"

"I didn't stutter, girl. Something, or someone, attacked me out there. I didn't see anyone, but it's the only explanation I have."

"Why do you think I felt magic? Only Runesmen can feel it when their lord uses it unless I am mistaken?"

Lord Klodian turned his head toward her.

"There are other forms of magic in the world. Even you have surely heard the rumors."

"I have, my Lord, but they are only that: rumors. The High Prince outlawed everything except rune magic."

Klodian laughed weakly, but there was no joy in it.

"The High Prince has outlawed many things, but people always find ways around the rule of law. There are rogues out there who practice banned magic. They are called mages. Their powers are far different from rune magic, and much more dangerous. I think one of them attacked me, though I have yet to figure out why. Perhaps it was another assassination attempt or a survivor from the dragon attack. Either way, I believe that scale can alert you to the presence of magic."

Mina didn't want to believe it, but it made sense. The sensation was too different to have been a dragon. There was no explanation to her aversion to it, though. It had made her physically ill, enough that she'd been useless.

"That might be true, though I desperately hope it is not."

"Of course you don't," Klodian said. "You already see your dragon sense as a curse. If you can also sense magic, I'm sure you'll hate that scale even more."

"You know me too well, my Lord."

"Not well enough, it would seem. How this evaded my notice is beyond me. Unless you knew and hid it from me?"

Although his words were weak and hoarse, the veiled threat behind his question sent a shiver along Mina's spine.

"It is as new to me as it is to you. I would not hide something like that, my Lord."

Klodian nodded slowly. "I believe you. As soon as my strength returns, we are going to put your new power to the test." He breathed heavily for a moment. "Leave me. I need to rest."

As Mina made her way back to the servant's chamber, a bad feeling was worming its way into her stomach.

10

After dinner, Caden and the other Runesmen retired to the barracks. Darkness had fallen, and there was still no word from anyone on Lord Klodian's status. Caden shuffled along behind his fellow soldiers, Thais beside him.

His thoughts kept returning to the odd thing he'd found in Slia. He'd stashed it in the upper portion of his right boot to keep from losing it, and it had eventually worked its way down until he was walking on it. It pressed painfully against the sole of his foot, but he ignored the ache and listened to Thais as she talked.

"What happens if Lord Klodian never wakes up?" she asked.

"Don't say things like that," Caden replied, glaring at her.

"Why not? Everyone's thinking it. I'm just saying it. And it's a valid question. Who takes his position if he dies?"

"How would I know? I'm a lowly peon like you. But if I had to guess, I'd say the High Prince would appoint someone else. Lord Klodian isn't married and he has no children, so there's no heir to his title."

"That's a fair assumption. I figured the next in command would be promoted, but I suppose being a Dominion Lord doesn't fall into the same line of power."

"There's something I want to show you," Caden said, lowering his voice.

"What is it?"

"Meet me at my bed once the lights go out."

Thais side-eyed him, and a flirtatious grin was pulling at her lips. Realizing that his words sounded like he was talking about something else, he laughed and shook his head.

"It's nothing like that."

"Right. I've fallen for that a time or two, but not anymore."

"I'm serious. I found something in Slia, but I don't know what it is."

"If you say so. If I find you with your clothes off …" Thais didn't finish her sentence. Caden wondered if she'd actually be mad if he did that, then quickly pushed the thought aside. He would never do something so crass. Well, maybe if he were drunk, but certainly not if he was in his right mind.

The Runesmen filed into the barracks and dispersed to their designated spots. Caden sat on his cot and pulled his boots off with a grunt, thankful to be off his feet. Despite no one seeing an enemy, dragon or otherwise, Captain Eduard had placed the castle on high alert. Lord Klodian's mysterious circumstances had everyone speculating, and all of the soldiers at the castle had been forced into taking shifts at watch.

As the day went on and nothing happened, Eduard had relaxed the shifts to allow for dinner and rest. Caden was as bothered about things as much as everyone else, but there was no use in fretting about it. Some things were outside of his control. The key was learning to accept that.

He tilted his right boot upside down and caught the metal piece as it fell out, then laid down and turned the item over in his hands. Now that it wasn't glowing at all, he could see that it was a silvery gray hue. The unique pattern of lines was still visible, too. Caden ran a finger over the ridges. They were smooth. The entire piece was smooth, aside from one jagged edge that appeared to be a break line. Whatever the thing was, it had broken off of something.

Once the lanterns were extinguished and snoring filled the air, Thais approached his cot. The room was slightly illuminated from the moonlight that filtered through the windows, and he could see that she was regarding him with a thoughtful look.

"What?" Caden asked.

"You surprised me."

"How so?"

"I expected to find you naked. I thought you were joking about finding something."

"Are you disappointed that I'm not?" Caden had his suspicions that she was attracted to him, but he wanted to be certain before he tried to pursue anything with her. It was funny how quickly he'd changed his mind about her.

"Don't worry about that. What do you want to show me?"

"This."

He held the item up so that a shaft of light caught it. Thais reached for it, and Caden pulled his hand away.

"I'm not going to steal it from you," she huffed. "I just want to see it closer."

He handed it to her, and she peered closely at it. Her left brow rose, and she turned her eyes on him.

"You found this in Slia?"

"Yes. It was buried under some debris, and it was glowing red when I first saw it, but it wasn't hot."

"Don't you know what this is?" she asked.

"Should I?"

"It's a piece of irite."

Caden stared at her blankly, shaking his head slightly. "What's that?"

"It's a type of metal, but it is only found in one place that I know of, and it isn't anywhere near here."

"Maybe someone in Slia imported it. What's the big deal?"

"Nothing really, other than it grows on a creature that lives on a volcanic mountain. It's basically a giant snail that makes its home in the vents of the volcano. The irite acts as a shield from the heat. It's an interesting creature, but they're harmless. I think it's odd you found this in Slia, given that it was attacked by a dragon."

"Why is that odd? You said it's basically a piece of a snail."

"Yes, but it's heat resistant. What do you think burns hotter, dragon fire or a volcano?"

"Probably a volcano, but what do I know?"

"Not much, apparently," Thais quipped with a grin. "You guessed right, though. People have been trying to use irite for years, but no one has figured out how. It's sort of like iron, but it has different properties. It's almost impossible to shape it."

"You seem to know a lot about it," Caden said.

Thais shrugged. "My father spent some time around merchants that had a plan to sell the stuff, but no one wanted it. I had the misfortune of having to listen to their entire conversation on the matter."

"Was your father a merchant?"

"No. He was a soldier."

"A Runesman?"

"No, he was a leader. A commander. He died in battle a few years ago."

"Did he serve Lord Klodian?" Caden was surprised that Thais was openly sharing so much with him.

"I wish he had. He served in another Dominion under Lord Culver. The man is a tyrant. When my father died, Lord Culver called him a failure and banished me and my mother from his Dominion. We came to the Thophate because no one wanted to risk Lord Culver's anger."

"Lord Klodian didn't care, huh?"

"Lord Klodian doesn't know," Thais clarified. "I shouldn't have told you that."

"Don't worry, I won't say anything," Caden replied. "What is there to gain by bringing you trouble?"

"Nothing besides a pummeling."

"What about your mother? Did you join the Runesmen to help her with money?"

"She's dead, too." Thais's expression darkened. "I'm tired of talking about this stuff."

"I didn't intend to pry into your history. I'm sorry."

"It's fine. I'm going to bed. It's been a long day."

Caden half-expected Thais to climb onto his cot again, but instead, she handed him the irite piece and went to her own bed. He put the irite under his pillow and considered her words. Was it possible someone had figured out how to use the metal? And if so, what were they doing with it?

IIT WAS STILL DARK WHEN one of the servants woke Mina.

She rolled over, bleary-eyed, and tried to focus on the girl's face. It was Kera. Or Fera. She wasn't sure, as it was hard to tell the twins apart.

"Lord Klodian has asked for you," the girl whispered.

"It's still dark," Mina groaned. "What could he possibly want at this hour?"

"Dawn is on the horizon. And you know how he can be, so please don't fall back asleep."

The girl crept back to her own bed and climbed in, pulling the blanket over her head. Mina yawned and laid there for a moment, trying to force herself into wakefulness. She felt as if she'd only just fallen asleep, and it didn't help that he'd also woken her in the middle of the night. She forced herself out of bed and sluggishly put her worn shoes on, then made her way into the hall.

Lord Klodian was waiting for her, along with two other men. They were all dressed in plain clothes, which made Mina pause. She'd never seen Klodian dressed down before. It was a peculiar sight.

"My Lord?"

Klodian looked her over. "You'll fit in as you are," he said. "Come, the carriage is waiting for us."

"Carriage? What's going on?"

"I told you, we're going to test your new skill. And I know just the place."

Mina stared at Klodian, trying to wrap her tired mind around his words. Just hours ago, he'd looked frail and tired. And now he appeared to be back to his usual self. There was no rasp to his voice or anything. It occurred to her that he was probably using his rune magic.

"We're leaving now, my Lord?"

"Yes. We're going to be traveling a fair distance, and I want to be back by nightfall."

"Where are we going?" Mina asked.

"To the borderlands, near the Phalan Dominion. Your questions are wasting time. Let's go."

Klodian turned on his heel and started walking. One of the guards followed beside him, and the other waited for Mina. She rubbed the sleep from her eyes and sighed. If the cursed scale offered her another ability, she was going to rip it out of her flesh, no matter the pain.

The four of them entered the carriage and they were off, heading north toward the border. Mina was curious as to why Klodian was dressed as a commoner, but she was more curious as to why he'd only brought two guards with him. She'd heard that the cities located along the borders of the Dominions were dangerous places, filled with people who didn't respect the laws of either Dominion. If that were true, Mina suspected that Lord Klodian was sorely understaffed.

The journey took several hours, and the trip was uneventful. Mina was surprised she stayed awake the entire time, especially considering she hadn't gotten much sleep. She kept her gaze out the window or on the floor, trying her best to avoid looking at Klodian or his men. Eventually, she spotted a sprawling metropolitan that resembled an oversized camp more than it did a city. There was no wall surrounding it, and the place was teeming with people of all cultures swarming in and out of large multicolored tents.

Once the carriage stopped, the two guards exited and surveyed the area, then motioned for Lord Klodian. He stepped out into the open and looked over his shoulder at Mina.

"This should be the ideal place for you to sense magic. Karapen is the busiest city on the border, and there are people from many other Dominions. If someone is using outlawed magic, this is where they will be."

Mina stood and subconsciously rubbed the scale on her leg. She didn't feel anything yet, but if sensing magic was the same as sensing dragons, she'd have to be within a few hundred feet of the person.

Her stomach rumbled, though she wasn't entirely sure if it was from hunger. She was anxious, and sweat was collecting on her palms.

I just want to get this over with, she thought as she slowly stepped down the carriage steps. She noticed that the heat wasn't as bad. It was still hot, but there was a heaviness to the air that she wasn't accustomed to. She glanced at Lord Klodian, wondering again why he was dressed down.

"Don't speak to anyone," Klodian said. "And don't wander off. We'll travel together at all times. If you see something suspicious, say something. I may be perceptive, but I can't be aware of every danger. My runes aren't as strong at this distance, and I'd rather avoid trouble if we can."

"Yes, my Lord."

Klodian looked at her. "Call me Ardit," he said. "I don't need anyone realizing I'm a Dominion Lord, or they'll all be petitioning their needs and wants at my feet."

"As you say, my L—" Mina paused. "Ardit."

Ardit was his first name, but Mina had never heard anyone call him by it. He was always addressed properly with his title, so it would take her some time to get accustomed to using anything else. Klodian motioned to the city.

"Karapen has a district where magical items are sold, charms and such. We'll start there and work our way through the city. With any luck, we'll determine your skill quickly and be on our way. I'm not fond of these clothes, and I don't like being this far from home without an army."

"I will do my best," Mina said.

Klodian took the lead, his two guards flanking him on either side. Mina walked behind them, gazing wide-eyed at all the foreign sights. They passed tents of all sizes and colors, and the goods being sold within them ranged from weapons and armor to bright rugs and ornate tapestries.

A few of the vendors called out to her in the common tongue, but many of them spoke in languages she'd never heard before. They continued along the main road, which was comprised of well-trampled dirt that had been packed down from use. Side streets veered off in various directions, but Klodian kept them going straight until they reached a large intersection. He led them to the left, and Mina noticed there was considerably less foot traffic.

She immediately realized why.

The tents and stalls on this street were for people looking for magical items. Potions, charms, and spellbooks were everywhere, and the people selling them were just as fascinating. Some of the vendors had strange markings inked into their flesh, while others had a variety of piercings on their faces. Despite their appearances, Mina didn't feel afraid. She was more intrigued than anything, with a host of questions forming in her mind.

"Do you sense anything?" Klodian asked lowly, looking back at her.

Mina shook her head. The scale wasn't doing anything, and she didn't feel ill or nauseous. As they traveled further down the street, the items being sold became abundantly stranger. Dead animals, talismans made of bones and teeth, and many other things that Mina didn't recognize. A feeling of darkness settled over her, and she glanced around fearfully.

"My Lo—er, Ardit?"

"Yes, girl?"

"I don't like this place. It feels … bad."

"I imagine so. These people practice shadow magic. It's banned like the other types, but shadow magic is especially dangerous. To use it, the caster must take life from something to work their spells."

"They kill people?"

"Yes, and animals. They are a wicked lot."

Mina could feel the darkness closing in around her, a heavy weight that tried to suffocate her. She swallowed hard and kept close to Klodian and his guards, but that didn't make her feel any safer. Her heart began to race, and …

Her eyes shot to the right. She could sense something, but it wasn't the odd sensation she'd felt in Slia. No, this was a familiar feeling, one she knew all too well. She focused on the pull. It was on the other side of the tents, close, but not too powerful. It had to be a young one, younger than any she'd felt before.

Mina pushed past the guards and took the lead. Klodian didn't question her. He just followed; his steps quickening to keep pace with her. The pull was guiding her to the right, but she couldn't see anything with all of the tents in the way. She hurried to the end of the street and turned the corner. A massive green and yellow tent caught her attention.

That was it.

She checked to make sure Klodian and the guards were still with her, and Klodian nodded at her. He placed his hand on the hilt of his sword, and the guards did the same. Mina turned back to the tent. While it was enormous, it didn't seem big enough to house a dragon. It had to be young indeed if it could fit inside that space. Mina paused at the entrance, her heart pounding in her ears.

"What is it, girl? Dragon or magic?"

Mina grabbed onto the tent flap and pulled it open.

12

WHEN THE MORNING HORN BLARED, Caden was already awake and prepared.

He was one of the first to rush out of the barracks and begin the morning run around the castle. Captain Eduard had told them ten laps. That had seemed easy enough, but as yesterday had proved, it was much more difficult than he first thought. Midway through his second lap, he could feel the soreness in his muscles flaring to life.

He kept a smooth pace and tried to focus on something other than the pain. His thoughts turned to Lord Klodian, and he wondered how the man was faring. Klodian seemed tough, and Caden had heard the stories about how he had evaded multiple assassination attempts. Whatever had happened to him yesterday in Slia, it hardly seemed possible to keep him down for long.

The morning air was crisp and cool. Within a few hours, the sun would start baking the land with its unforgivable heat. For now, Caden enjoyed the slight chill. He was well ahead of his fellow Runesmen, by at least two laps, but it wasn't a competition. It was about endurance and training his body. By the time he finished his final lap, the sun had driven the chill away.

Caden entered the castle for breakfast. The line was nonexistent, and he got fresh servings of scrambled eggs, two biscuits smothered in gravy, and a thick slice of ham. The steaming food made his mouth water and he devoured the meal hungrily. The other Runesmen began to file into the dining hall, and Thais carried her tray to where he was, sitting down beside him.

"You trying to show off or something?" she asked.

"No, why?"

"Just asking. You didn't wait for anyone before you bolted off like a dog on the scent of its prey."

Caden smiled. "I just love to start my days with a relaxing run, so I was eager to get going."

Thais eyed him like he was insane before his sarcasm dawned on her. She rolled her eyes and shook her head.

"Oh, we've got a jester here. Great."

"I'll be here all week," Caden said.

"You'll be here longer than that, I hope. You don't plan on dying anytime soon, do you?"

"No, of course not."

Caden considered telling her his plan, but he decided to keep his mouth shut. He'd initially assumed his days of training would be torture and that he would end up keeping to himself, a lone wolf among the pack. It was only his second full day as a Runesman and he felt more at home than he had in a long time.

It was a great feeling, but if he wanted to make a name for himself, he would still need to transfer Dominions. He was feeling conflicted, which made things confusing. Should he stay where he was and be content with the way things were, or should he forge ahead with his plan?

He didn't know the answer. Not yet.

Thais dug into her food, but she turned to him and spoke with her mouth full.

"You should show Captain Eduard what you found in Slia."

Caden's face scrunched in confusion. "Why?"

"The more I think about it, the more I'm convinced there's something strange going on. Supposedly, multiple dragons attacked and there was no sign of them when we got there."

"What does that have to do with the irite? And besides that, the attack was a couple of hours before we arrived. That's plenty of time for the creatures to flee."

"Weren't you listening to me last night? Irite is heat resistant."

"And?"

Thais was about to shovel more food into her mouth, but paused and stared incredulously at Caden.

"You're really not putting these things together? If someone could craft a shield or some kind of armor that was resistant to dragon fire, what do you think they would do with that? Slay dragons easier? Sure, maybe someone like Lord Klodian would do that. But someone like Lord Culver would think bigger, with greed as their driving force. Someone like Lord Culver would find a way to utilize irite to their advantage and force dragons to do their bidding."

Caden was silent for a long moment. Thais continued eating as if she hadn't just made a wild leap in logic, which worried him. She wasn't serious, was she?

"You think that someone orchestrated that attack on Slia? Someone who has a way of controlling dragons?"

"Yes."

"You can't be serious," Caden said, laughing nervously. "That's outlandish thinking. And it's impossible."

"How do you know it's impossible?" Thais asked.

"It's never happened before. If it was possible, I'm sure someone would have figured it out by now and we'd be waging battle from dragon back. Think about it, Thais. Really imagine that in your mind. Someone controlling a dragon?" He snorted. "I think you've been hit in the head one too many times."

"You don't have to believe what I do, but don't mock me for it. We might be friends now, but I'll still slap the fire out of your backside."

"I'm sorry, I didn't mean to offend you. It's just ... you don't really believe that, do you?"

Thais shrugged. "So what if I do? Are you going to call me crazy next? Hurl insults all you want. I can take it. I've got thicker skin than you know. But mark my words: if I'm right and something bad happens, it's all on you. I'm just saying that you should tell Captain Eduard what you found. I'll tell him what I think is happening, and if he laughs us off, then the blame is on him. If he doesn't and I turn out to be right, then we'll be heroes."

Caden couldn't believe what she was saying. There was absolutely no way he was going to tell anyone her conspiracy theory, especially not Captain Eduard. They'd both be kicked out of the Runesmen for mental instability.

"If that's what you believe, more power to you, but I'm not having any part of it. And there's no blame to be cast at me even if you are right. I found a piece of metal, nothing more. I'll see you on the field."

Caden left the dining hall and departed the castle, turning toward the practice field. The idea that someone was controlling dragons for some nefarious purpose was absurd. If he didn't know any better, and he might not, he'd say Thais *was* crazy. Maybe she was stressed. She had brought up has past last night, and those were some deep emotional wounds. The death of a parent could have that effect on anyone.

He waited for the other Runesmen so they could begin their training. Captain Eduard was the first one to join him on the field, and he offered an impressed nod to Caden.

"You did well yesterday," Eduard said. "Finding Lord Klodian like that must have been frightening."

"A little," Caden admitted. "I thought he was dead at first. Is he all right? We haven't heard anything about him."

"He's fine. He left this morning for personal business, but he'll be back tonight."

Caden felt a wave of relief wash over him. "Thank the gods. What happened to him?"

Eduard shook his head. "No one knows. He awoke in the middle of the night, weak and confused. The physicians didn't find any wounds. No poison was in his system, nothing. It's a conundrum."

"I imagine so. I'm glad he's all right."

Loud voices filled the air as the other Runesmen began to approach the field. Eduard stepped close to Caden and lowered his voice.

"You might think you've gotten away with it, but I've got my eyes on you."

"Sir?" Caden asked, confused.

"It's quite a coincidence that he was alone when you found him. He doesn't remember much, and the slave girl said he disappeared before she knew he was gone. It all sounds suspicious to me. An inside job done by a traitor. Possibly two. What would you know about that?"

"Nothing, sir. I told you everything I know."

"We'll see about that. If you're lying to me, I'll find out." Eduard turned toward the other Runesmen. "Line up!" he shouted. "Today you'll be sparring!"

Caden stared at the captain. Did he think that Caden had done something to Lord Klodian? That was more absurd than Thais's theory. As if summoned by his thoughts, Thais marched over to stand beside him in the line, a scowl on her face. He closed his eyes and sighed.

Not only was Thais upset with him, but Eduard also suspected him of a crime he didn't commit. Maybe transferring to another Dominion wasn't a bad idea after all.

13

"Welcome! Come in, come in!"

The jovial voice came from a tall dark-skinned man standing near the center of the tent. He grinned broadly and motioned for Mina to enter. She glanced around the tent and spotted the source of the pull. It *was* a dragon, but it was the smallest one she'd ever seen. It was curled up on a rug, but it snapped its brass-colored head up and gazed at her as she stepped inside.

Lord Klodian and one of the guards followed her, and she guessed the other one was standing watch outside. Klodian looked at the dragon first, then to the merchant. Mina was confused. The dark-skinned man didn't appear to be afraid of the beast. It was roughly the size of a horse, but still … it was a dragon.

"You come looking for spices, yes? I have many to choose from."

The man motioned to the racks around the tent. The shelves were filled with glass jars containing a variety of colored spices.

"Yes, we're here for spice," Lord Klodian answered. "Gareth, find me some cinnamon, would you?"

"There should be some cinnamon on the rack there," the merchant said, pointing to the rack along the far-right wall.

Klodian nodded toward the dragon. "I've never seen one like it before."

"Ah, yes. Draak isn't from this Dominion. I brought him from across the border."

"You gave it a name?" Klodian seemed appalled.

"Yes. He is my pet. Do you not name your pets, good sir?"

"Yes, but dragons are not pets. In my Dominion, we kill dragons. They are mindless creatures that cause nothing but destruction."

Mina was listening to their exchange, but she was also watching the dragon curiously. It returned her stare, sniffing at the air.

"Dragons are smarter than people realize," the merchant said. "This one can even do tricks. Draak, come here."

The dragon ignored him and continued to gaze at Mina. The merchant snapped his fingers a few times, but it didn't do any good.

"Bah! They can be stubborn things when they want."

Mina tore her eyes away from the dragon and looked at Klodian.

"How much for the cinnamon?" he asked as the guard came back holding a jar.

"Two silver, no minted images on them. I need to be able to spend them in my own Dominion."

Klodian reached into a pouch on his belt and produced the coins. He handed them to Mina, and she walked over and gave them to the merchant. The dragon sniffed the air again, and it growled at her, a low rumbling sound deep within its chest.

"Oh, come now Draak. She's harmless."

The dragon hissed and scrambled onto its legs; wings tucked against its body. It ran behind one of the racks and remained there.

"Strange," the merchant said. "I've never seen him do that before."

"It probably doesn't like her stench," Klodian said, shooting a look at Mina. "Thank you for the cinnamon."

"Come back any time!"

They left the tent, joining the other guard on the street.

"Is that the only thing you sense around here?" Klodian asked.

"Yes, my Lord."

Klodian shot her a glare, and she flinched.

"Yes, Ardit."

"Let's walk around to be certain."

Klodian led Mina down more streets than she could count, and eventually, she quit trying to keep track of them. Karapen was a strange and mystifying city. There were more wondrous things and people in this one place than she ever imagined possible, but she didn't sense anything other than the dragon, and that was only when she was close enough to feel the pull from the scale in her leg.

After several hours, Klodian grew irritated and called an end to his test. They stopped at a food stall and he bought them all a slice of dried meat, then they returned to the carriage outside the city. Mina chewed on the treat, which was slightly tough. It was seasoned and tasted good, but it took a decent amount of effort to tear through it with her teeth.

Lord Klodian took the jar of cinnamon from the guard and tossed it to the ground. The glass shattered and the cinnamon scattered across the sand. Mina risked a glance at him, wondering why he did that.

"That man is a fool if he thinks that dragon won't eat him the moment it has the opportunity. Can you believe he said they were intelligent?"

The two guards chuckled. Mina smiled, silently agreeing that the man's words were hard to believe.

"Back to the castle," Klodian said. "This was a wasted trip."

They climbed into the carriage and began the trek back to Klodian Keep. The further away from Karapen they traveled, the more Mina grew uneasy. She looked out the carriage window, but there was nothing to see.

But she *felt* it.

There was a dragon nearby, and it wasn't the same one from the city. Each one had a unique feel to it, and she'd never felt the same one twice. In all the years she'd been leading Klodian on his hunts, he had never failed to slay a dragon. She knew that it was because of his rune magic. Since he was able to draw on the strength of his soldiers, among other traits, he was stronger and faster than his prey.

And yet, despite the many dragons that had fallen to his blade, they still hadn't encountered the one that had cursed her. At least, that's what she hoped. If the dragon had been killed already, that meant its curse had outlasted its existence. And Mina couldn't bear the thought of being a slave her entire life.

"My Lord," she said, keeping her gaze out the window. "There's a dragon nearby."

Klodian tilted his head to look out the window.

"Which direction?"

"I'm not sure. It feels like it's right on top of us. Maybe if we stop, I can get a better sense of where it's at."

Klodian was silent for a moment. "No. We're still too far from the castle for the magic to be effective. I didn't bring my plate armor, either. This one can count itself lucky."

Mina frowned in disappointment. If only Lord Klodian wasn't one of the few who hunted dragons. Aside from the danger, there was only a handful of Dominion Lords. And since rune magic was only for the ruling class, the risk far outweighed the benefit for most people. That's what Mina believed, anyway.

The pull of the scale started to fade, and Mina searched the sky again. This time, she saw something. A massive dark shape shot through the sky heading west. Mina watched until it was no longer visible, her brows furrowed.

She'd never seen a black dragon before.

14

"I WANT TO SEE WHAT you've got," Captain Eduard said, his arms folded across his chest. He looked at the line of Runesmen.

"It's one thing to swing a sword around in practice, and another to battle a real enemy. Today you will pair up and you will fight. I want you to hold nothing back, but don't kill your partner. A few cuts and scrapes can be dealt with, and they'll heal. If you mortally wound your partner, you will be punished and sent to the gallows. I don't want that, and neither should any of you."

Caden had some skill with a blade, but he wasn't the best by any means. He was eager to learn from someone with more expertise. Not only would it make him a better warrior, but it would also help if he transferred to a Dominion where he would see plenty of battles.

"Thais, you're with Caden."

Eduard flicked his eyes at Caden momentarily before continuing down the line. Caden got the hint, but he wasn't going to let Thais beat him. He drew his sword and took a few steps back, swinging the blade around a few times to loosen his muscles.

Thais drew her sword, a scowl plastered across her face. She looked just like she had the other day when he'd met her. He'd already apologized. What more did she want?

"I hope you don't mind having a few scars across your face," she said smugly.

Caden groaned inwardly. He wasn't vain by any means, but that didn't mean he wanted to look like a veteran of war at such a young age. Without any warning, Thais rushed him, bringing her sword down in an overhead chopping motion. Caden sidestepped and turned to strike her, but she'd already corrected herself and blocked his blade. Metal clanged loudly as their swords clashed, and the two stepped away from each other.

"I said I was sorry," Caden said. "I didn't mean to hurt your feelings."

Thais laughed. "Oh, you thought you hurt my feelings? Please. I don't have any!"

She rushed him again, but this time Caden was prepared. He brought his sword up horizontally, blocking her attack. He allowed her momentum to force his blade downward, but he twisted his wrist at the last moment, causing her to lean far forward. The tip of her sword struck the ground, and Caden lunged forward, jabbing his blade at her ribcage. She was protected by her armor, but he scored a hit.

Thais growled and jerked her sword up, swiping at him. There was a rage in her eyes, and Caden feared that her anger might override her better judgment. She crashed into him, and the next thing he knew, he was lying flat on his back. He stared up at her in confusion, wondering how he had gotten on the ground.

"Very good, Thais," Captain Eduard congratulated. He stood over Caden and offered his hand. Caden took it and was pulled to his feet.

"Do you know why Thais knocked you down?"

"Because she ran into me?"

"Yes, and no," Eduard said. "That is *how* she knocked you down, but not why. She is brash. She saw an opening and took it, but there is a difference between calculated risk and being reckless. You could have maneuvered out of her path, but you stayed put. Why?"

"I didn't think she could hit that hard," Caden replied.

"You underestimated your opponent. If this were a real battle, you'd be dead because of that error. We are taught when we are young that mistakes are bad, and we are punished for them. Remember this: mistakes are only bad if you don't learn anything from them. Making mistakes is often the best way to learn."

Eduard leaned close to Caden and lowered his voice.

"Thais is skilled and uses her fury to her advantage, but she does have weaknesses. Find them and take a risk."

"Yes, sir."

Eduard stepped back several paces.

"Go again."

Caden and Thais circled one another again, but this time, Caden felt less prepared. Moments ago, Eduard has accused him of treachery, and now he was offering helpful advice. The man was as confusing as Thais. Caden quickly cleared his mind and silently counted to three, then rushed at Thais. She smiled at him, and before he could bring his sword up to strike her, she dodged to the side, slapping the flat of her blade against the back of his thigh. Stinging pain shot through his leg. He gritted his teeth and whirled around to face her.

"You're so predictable," she taunted.

Caden ignored her words. He could feel Eduard watching him, judging him. Was he regretting his decision to let Caden be a Runesman? Gods, he hoped not. This was his only gateway to the money and fame he wanted, but Lord Klodian's army was ultimately a stepping stone to his end goal. He couldn't afford to stumble on this stone.

"You talk too much," Caden said, slowly closing the distance between them.

Thais didn't wait for him to get close enough. She charged him, swinging her sword in an upward motion. Caden deflected the strike out wide with his blade, then dropped low and slammed the hilt into the side of her knee. She cried out in surprise and fell to the ground.

"How was that for predictable?" he asked as Thais rolled onto her back.

She shot him a glare and rubbed her knee. Caden knew she was angry. She hadn't anticipated his move, and she didn't like losing. He offered her his hand as Eduard had done for him, but she slapped it away and stood on her own.

"Best two out of three," she snapped.

"Fine by me," Caden replied.

He tilted his head from side to side, stretching his neck. There was nothing to gain from this victory. If anything, it would show Captain Eduard that he had learned something. Thais wouldn't be happy about losing, but there was no helping that. She was staring at him, and he stared back, their eyes locked.

At the same time, they ran toward each other. Their blades clanged together, and they began a dance of footwork and flurried jabs and swings. Caden threw everything he had into his maneuvers, pouring every ounce of strength, speed, and mental focus into the fight.

He wasn't her equal. No, she was more skilled than he was, but he managed to hold his own against her until the very end when he saw the weakness that Eduard had told him existed. If she had the slightest hint of what he was thinking, she could easily block him and win. And if she didn't, then he would be the victor. He kept her busy with his thrusts, but his muscles burned and his stamina was failing. Eduard had told him to take a risk. It was now or never. Caden waited until he saw Thais overextend herself as she jabbed her blade at him, then he smacked her sword up high and quickly stepped forward. He came in low and drove his shoulder into her stomach.

She grunted in surprise and pain, and his momentum pushed her off balance. She staggered backward and fell, crashing to the ground with a loud thud. He put his foot on her chest, pinning her down, and placed the tip of his sword against her neck.

"Do you yield?" he asked.

Her eyes welled with tears, but he doubted they were from embarrassment. She'd fallen hard and he was certain she was in pain. She gasped her answer, making him the winner of their bout. He removed his sword and turned to look at Captain Eduard. The other Runesmen had gathered to watch their battle, and they started cheering.

"You took a risk," Eduard said. "She left an opening and you went for it. She could have had you."

"I know. I was afraid that my eyes would give me away, but she was too consumed with emotion. It worked to my advantage."

"Congratulations. You learned something new today."

Eduard spun on the others. "The show's over. Get back to it!"

The Runesmen went back to sparring, and Caden looked at Thais. She was on her feet now, and she sheathed her blade. She limped over to him and clapped him on the shoulder.

"I'm impressed," she said. "You beat me fairly, but it won't happen again."

"We'll see," Caden replied.

"Yes, we will." Thais lowered her voice. "I still think you should tell him what you found."

"I'm not going to."

"Suit yourself." Thais shrugged. "It's your funeral if I'm right."

She headed for the barracks, and as she hobbled away, Caden felt guilty for hitting her so hard in the knee, but when he considered the rage he'd seen in her eyes, he knew she would have done the same thing.

If not worse.

15

IT HAD BEEN A WEEK since the attack on Slia.

Lord Klodian was just as fixated on revenge as he had been the day it happened, and Mina felt as if she were on the brink of exhaustion. Every day since then, Klodian had taken her on his hunts. They searched the desert plateaus, scoured the hidden caves, and trekked across the dry landscape for hours.

Granted, Klodian had killed more dragons in the last few days than he had the entire previous summer, but Mina was tired. Her skin was sunburned so much that it had blistered, and when she was sweating, the water collected beneath her flesh and made her feel like some sort of monster.

They returned every night in time for dinner, and this night was no different. Since they spent the entire day hunting, Klodian didn't make her complete her usual chores. The evenings were hers to do as she wished, and she'd been spending them in the field outside the castle, staring up at the stars.

Mina was lying in the dry grass, her stomach full. She wanted to rest, but for some reason, sleep eluded her. She had much on her mind, and it all haunted her as she lay there in the quiet of the night. Distant memories, hopes, and nightmares all barraged her. The chirping of some sort of animal in the distance crept into her ears, bringing with it madness and the desperation to make it disappear.

Above her, the night sky was clear and the stars glimmered brightly. She traced the constellation Avera with her eyes, wondering who had been the first to spot the human shape the stars formed. Avera was the goddess of fortune, and Mina had prayed to her many times when she was younger. That was before she knew the truth, that there were no gods. Or, if there were, the plight of the people mattered little to them. The sound of someone approaching broke her reverie, and she lifted her head to see Caden.

"Another quiet night," he said softly. "And another quiet shift."

He took a seat beside her and leaned back, propping himself up with his arms. He looked into the sky, and she stared at his face. He was a handsome man, but she knew that Thais desired him. It was obvious in the way she acted around him. Mina didn't mind. She wanted her freedom from the cursed scale, and the desire for romance would only detract her attention from what mattered.

She considered him a friend, though. She'd never really had many, at least not since she was a child. Before her accident, she'd had a few friends. Once word spread of the scale in her leg, she became shunned by everyone. Mina found navigating a friendship more difficult than she remembered, but she knew that Caden didn't plan on staying in the Thophate Dominion.

"Do you ever question yourself?" Mina asked.

"All the time," Caden replied. "Why?"

"I don't know. I guess I'm just curious if I'm the only one that does it."

Caden laughed and turned to look at her. "Everyone wonders whether they are on the right path at some point. Nobody is perfect."

"Some people make it seem as if they have everything planned out and their life is perfect. Like you."

"Me? My life is hardly perfect."

"Isn't it, though? Your dream was to become a Runesman, and you are one."

"Yes, but it took a lot of effort to get here. And being a Runesman is only part of what I want. I want to be wealthy. I want people to know my name, but not because of anything I've done wrong, but for the fact that a lowly peasant lifted himself out of poverty and into grandeur. To do that, I'll have to keep from dying."

"I've seen you fight," Mina said. "You're very good."

"To the untrained eye, perhaps." Caden smiled. "I'm not one of the best with a sword in my group, let alone the entire army."

"And yet you were put on guard duty so quickly."

"Only because of the circumstances. Lord Klodian has lost four patrols. They've vanished without a trace, and The Long Sands is a big place. We can't go searching for them without risking the loss of more men."

"What do you think happened to them?"

"No idea," Caden replied. "Maybe they defected, but I doubt it. There have been a lot of sand storms recently, so Captain Eduard believes they got lost. If they don't return within a few days, Lord Klodian is going to assume they are dead. Without water, it's impossible to survive out there."

Mina did find the disappearance of the patrols curious, but since it didn't affect her, she hadn't dwelled on it. It must not have bothered Lord Klodian much either, for his focus had been on hunting down dragons.

"Have you ever seen a dragon?" she asked.

"No. And I don't think I want to."

She didn't blame him. They were ferocious, and any creature that could breathe fire didn't seem like a natural creation.

"When do you think you'll go to another Dominion?"

Caden shrugged. "Captain Eduard thinks I had something to do with Lord Klodian being unconscious after the attack in Slia. Until I can prove I didn't and get in his good graces, it's probably wise not to mention it."

"I didn't know that. Why does he think it was you?"

"I was the first one to find him, so he thinks it's suspicious. If Thais and I wouldn't have split up, I doubt it would be an issue. Regardless, I'm going to work as hard as I can to show my devotion. Lord Klodian seems like a good man, but there's no way I'll find what I'm looking for out here in the desert."

"There is a way," Mina said. "But it requires slaying dragons."

"No thank you. I prefer the odds against other people, not oversized living cauldrons. Maybe if you come up with something less dangerous, I'll consider it."

It was Mina's turn to laugh. She did that often in Caden's presence, which was another thing she wasn't accustomed to.

"You may not want to see a dragon, but what about a dragon's horn?"

"Why would I want to see a dragon's horn?"

"I have a collection. Lord Klodian cuts one off of each dragon he kills and gives it to me. He knows I hate them, and I think in some small way, it's a sign of kindness from him." She didn't mention that it was the *only* kindness he showed her.

"Where do you keep them?"

"Under my bed," Mina answered.

"You know Runesmen aren't allowed in the castle except for meals, right?"

"I'm sorry, it was stupid of me to ask."

"Don't apologize," Caden said. "It's not stupid. I'd love to see them, but I don't want to break the rules. Could you bring them out here?"

"No, the chest I keep them in is too heavy. Just forget it. I don't want to get you into trouble."

The silence stretched between them until Caden finally spoke.

"I'll go if you really want me to."

It wasn't what he said, but the *way* he said it that caused Mina's heart to race. She only wanted to show him her collection, but the tone in his voice set a fire under her skin that she couldn't explain. She knew it was a bad idea, but maybe if she showed him quickly, he wouldn't be caught. The servants would still be working, so there wouldn't be anyone in the room yet. Mina stood and motioned for him.

"Let's go."

16

CADEN FOLLOWED MINA INTO THE castle, ducking into doorways and side passages as they passed by servants who were still working. He wasn't wearing his armor, and it was dark, but he didn't want to take any chances. If someone recognized him and informed Captain Eduard, or worse—Lord Klodian—he'd surely be lashed again. While the wounds would heal, the pain wasn't something he relished. After traversing numerous maze-like halls, he was growing worried.

"How much further?" he whispered.

"Not much. It's just around the corner now. Stay here and let me make sure it's clear."

Mina disappeared from sight and he glanced back the way they'd come. The longer he spent inside the castle, the more he feared he would be caught. Footsteps echoed off the walls, but he didn't know which direction they were coming from. Caden moved into a darkened doorway and stood still.

A servant came around the corner, where Mina had gone. The woman carried a candle on a small plate and passed by without seeing him, continuing down the hall, her steps fading. A moment later, Mina returned.

"Sorry," she said softly. "Kera was in there, so I told her that she was needed in the kitchens. Hopefully, they'll put her to work, but she might be back soon. We probably don't have much time. Come on."

Mina led him around the corner and into a large chamber filled with beds. At the end of each one was a large chest, which he presumed was for personal effects. The setup was very similar to the barracks, including the windows. Moonlight filtered into the room, providing plenty of light.

"I don't know why, but I just assumed the servants all had their own rooms," Caden said.

"I wish," Mina replied. "It's hard to sleep when there are so many people snoring at the same time."

Mina walked over to a cot that was against the far wall and knelt beside it. She leaned down and reached under the bed, sliding a plain wooden box out. It was smaller than the chest, but it was still a decent size. She stood and hefted the box onto the bed, opening the lid. Caden moved to stand beside her and glanced inside. Horns of all sizes rested inside, all stacked in neat rows, and they were all the same color.

"That's a lot of dead dragons," Caden said.

"It is, but it's not enough."

"Will it ever be?"

Mina went quiet for a moment. She turned her head to him. "It will be enough when this curse is gone."

Caden was tempted to ask her what she would do if the curse was never lifted, but he didn't want to upset her. She seemed proud of the horns. In a way, he understood why. She hated dragons with a passion, but she was also responsible for their deaths. Lord Klodian might be the one who killed them, but she played a large part by tracking them down.

"Aren't dragons different colors?"

"Yes," Mina answered.

"Then why are the horns all the same color?"

Mina shrugged. "I'm not sure why, but color of the horn fades once it's removed. There is a way to tell what color the dragon was, though." She grabbed one of the horns and angled the pointed end down, revealing the end that had been cut. It was smooth, but Caden noticed something else. The color on the inside was gold.

"The inside of their horns mirrors the color of their scales. This one was a gold dragon."

"How many colors are there?"

"Five that I know of. Gold, silver, bronze, brass, and copper." Mina paused, and Caden had the feeling she wanted to say more.

"Do you have horns from all the colors?"

"No. I have a horn from each one except copper. Copper dragons seem to be rarer than the others."

"You seem to know a lot about them."

"There isn't much to know, really. They're wild and untamed like any other animal, just bigger and meaner."

"Well, I'm glad I've never seen one," Caden said. "I imagine it's frightening."

"Very," Mina replied. "I've only seen a few of them. They're usually hiding in caves, and Lord Klodian kills them before I ever see them. The last one I saw made my entire body shake, and it wasn't even looking at me."

Caden knew the term for it: dragon fear. It was an overwhelming sense of irrational dread. At least, that's how he'd heard it explained. There weren't many who encountered a dragon and lived to tell of it.

"What will you do when the curse is lifted?" Caden changed the subject.

"Lord Klodian will have no use for me, so he'll either sell me or grant me my freedom. I've more than returned the investment he paid my parents. If he sells me, I'll run away, probably go to a new Dominion. Who knows, maybe I'll end up at the same one you transfer to." She smiled.

Caden doubted that Lord Klodian would grant Mina her freedom. He probably *would* sell her—to the highest bidder and then forget about her. He hoped that whatever happened, she wouldn't be hurt. There were a lot of unscrupulous people in the world, and many of them lacked the decency that Lord Klodian had. Caden didn't know Mina very well, but she deserved more from life than being a slave.

Mina met his gaze and they stared at each other in silence. He was drawn to her, like a moth to the flame. He was also drawn to Thais, and he could feel his heart warring within him. Both women were beautiful, and his feelings toward each were different, but his emotions were a confusing muddle.

Without much thought, he leaned toward Mina and kissed her. Her lips were soft, and she smelled of dust and something pleasant, but he couldn't place the scent. She didn't return the kiss, and he feared he had crossed a line with her. He broke away and smiled despite the fact that his heart raced with nervousness.

"Good night," he said, then turned and left.

He hurried down the hall and quickly realized he had no idea how to get out of the castle. Mina herself had seemed unsure of which halls to take, and it wasn't long before he was lost. It didn't help that he couldn't focus on finding the right path. His thoughts were on Mina. Had he offended her with his kiss, or had he merely surprised her? He prayed it was the latter.

Caden turned a corner and bumped into the servant he'd seen earlier. Mina had said her name was Kera. She curtsied and cast her eyes to the floor.

"Excuse me, my Lord. I wasn't watching where I was going."

It felt odd to have someone called him that. He offered his best smile and tried to keep from stammering.

"It's not a problem. I'm trying to get some fresh air in the courtyard, but I seem to have gotten turned around. Can you direct me?"

"Of course, my Lord. I'll show you the way."

Kera navigated the maze easily and once they passed the dining hall, he recognized his surroundings.

"Ah, I know my way from here. Thank you."

"Of course, my Lord. It was my honor."

He waited until she was gone, then he hurriedly escaped the castle and breathed a sigh of relief once he was outside. The air was cool and he relaxed his pace. As the excitement of the kiss faded, he felt guilty. It wasn't just that he'd kissed Mina without her permission, but he felt as if he'd somehow betrayed Thais. It was foolish of him to feel that way since he and Thais hadn't even discussed their feelings, but the guilt assailed him nonetheless.

The barracks was dark when he entered, but he could tell that most of his fellows were still awake. Caden reached his cot and laid down without taking his shoes off. He was floating somewhere between the clouds of tranquility and remorse. He should tell Thais what he'd done. She would probably be mad, but his conscience would be clear. Telling the truth was never easy, but it was the right thing to do.

Before he could sit up, a commotion near the entrance drew his attention. Captain Eduard and two others marched inside, waving torches around.

"Where's Caden?" Eduard demanded.

"I'm here, sir."

Caden rolled off the cot and stood at attention. Eduard and the other two came straight toward him.

"You're under arrest," Eduard said. "Take him to the dungeon."

"Arrest? For what?" Caden looked from Eduard to the guards as if the answer would be evident on their faces.

"I know what you did. There's no sense in feigning ignorance. That'll just make it worse. Take him."

The guards forcibly turned him around and bound his hands with rope, then hooked their arms with his and marched him through the barracks toward the door. Caden didn't understand what Eduard was talking about. He hadn't done anything wrong. Had he?

As they passed Thais's cot, she was standing beside it. Caden looked at her pleadingly, and she mouthed the words, "I'm sorry."

17

CADEN'S KISS HAUNTED HER.

Mina had never been kissed before, and the experience left her reeling and flustered. Her emotions were a confusing mess. She'd assumed that he had feelings for Thais, but clearly, she'd been mistaken. Caden was handsome and well-muscled, but she hadn't thought about him as anything more than a friend.

No, that wasn't entirely true. Mina was lying to herself, and she knew it. Perhaps it was the fear of the unknown that held her back, but she didn't want Caden to be more than a friend. There were too many things to consider.

He was a Runesman, first and foremost. His life would always be in jeopardy. She was a slave to Lord Klodian. Outside of his whims, she didn't have much control over her life. Not yet, anyway. And there was no way for her to know when she might be free … if she ever would be. Dreams were one thing, but reality was another.

Caden also wanted to leave the Thophate Dominion. If he left, Mina wouldn't be able to follow him unless she gained her freedom. Not without incurring Klodian's wrath, and she knew he would stop at nothing to find her if she ran away. His hunts and his wealth were too important to him.

Mina stared at the collection of horns in the chest for a moment before closing the lid. Some of the servants would give her odd looks when she brought them out to look at them, but they didn't understand. It wasn't for some morbid fascination that she kept them. They were trophies, the spoils of her personal war against dragons.

"No one will ever understand," she whispered.

Mina placed the chest on the floor and slid it under the bed. She hoped Caden had found his way out of the castle. It had been tempting to race after him, but she knew that Kera could return at any time. If Caden was caught breaking the rules, Mina would feel terrible. She'd convinced him to come into the castle, so any punishment he received would be her fault.

She sat on the bed and pulled her boots off. Relief flooded through her feet. Lord Klodian had been relentless the last few days, scouring the desert for dragons. Tomorrow would be no different. She sighed and laid down, staring up at the dark ceiling.

The next thing she knew, a faint light was filtering through the windows. She'd fallen asleep and she assumed she hadn't moved all night, as she was in the same position she remembered being in when she'd been thinking about Caden. With the sun rising, Lord Klodian would be readying to leave. Mina rubbed her eyes and sat up, sliding her legs off the edge of the bed. She pulled her boots on and decided to go to the barracks to see Caden before she left.

Since it was still early, the castle was silent. Most of the servants were still asleep, and Mina didn't pass anyone in the halls. She left the castle and crossed the courtyard, quietly entering the barracks. The Runesmen would be up soon to begin their next day of training, and Mina didn't want to be in the middle of the chaos.

She searched the rows of cots, but she didn't see Caden anywhere. Had he started his run around the castle early? She paused, glancing around the barracks.

"What are you doing?" Thais whispered.

Mina whirled around, her heart racing. Thais was sitting on her cot, staring at Mina.

"I was looking for Caden."

"I figured as much. He's not here."

"Is he running his laps?"

Thais shook her head. "He's in the dungeon," she replied. "Captain Eduard arrested him last night."

Mina's eyes widened. "What? Why?"

Thais shrugged. "If anyone knows, they aren't saying. Eduard hauled him off and we haven't seen or heard from either of them since."

Mina needed to find out what happened, but it would have to wait. Lord Klodian was probably waiting on her by now. "If you hear anything, please let me know. I'll do the same for you."

"Sounds fair to me."

Mina rushed out of the barracks, turning toward the stable. Just as she suspected, Lord Klodian was waiting for her when she arrived. Vhan was there as well, but none of the usual entourage was present.

"If you oversleep again, I'll drag you behind my horse," Klodian threatened.

"I'm sorry, my Lord. It won't happen again."

"See that it doesn't. You'll be riding with Vhan today. You've been walking too slow lately, and I need to get back earlier tonight. I have matters to deal with."

Mina nodded, relieved to know that they wouldn't be spending the entire day in the heat again. She walked over to Vhan's horse, and the squire offered his hand to her, pulling her into the saddle behind him. It was an uncomfortable spot to sit, but she was happy that she didn't have to go on foot.

They rode northwest, heading in the same direction they had the day before. Mina held onto Vhan to keep from falling off the horse, but he didn't seem to mind. Eventually, Lord Klodian began talking with Vhan. Mina was only half-listening, but it sounded like Klodian's advisors weren't happy with him.

"I'm the lord of this Dominion," Klodian said. "I won't be scolded like a child. If they want to keep complaining, I'll string them all up on the gallows."

"I think they're worried, my Lord." Vhan replied.

"About what?"

"You, among other things. You haven't hunted dragons this much in all the time I've been alive. And there are the rumors ..."

"Bah! Rumors are all they are. War isn't brewing in the Dominions. The High Prince would sweep down from the north with his armies and remind us all quite painfully of how he united the lands in the first place. And as for the dragon hunts, it's nobody's business but my own if I seek revenge on the blasted creatures. They destroyed Slia, and I won't let it be said that I didn't bring hell upon the dragons in response."

"I'm on your side, sir. I want to see justice as much as you."

Mina rubbed her left leg. The scale was giving her something, but it was faint.

"I'm sure you do," Klodian said. "And I appreciate your loyalty. That's why you are with me today and my advisors are not. I'm tired of hearing their constant whining."

"My ears thank you," Vhan replied, laughing.

Lord Klodian looked over at Mina. "Anything?"

"Yes, but it's not very strong yet. Maybe a little further."

Ahead, a mesa towered over the landscape. Mina suspected there was a cave there, since the closer they got, the stronger the sensation became. Once they were a few hundred feet away, Mina was certain this was it.

"It's here," she said.

The mesa was split in two by a narrow pass. It looked to Mina as though someone had cracked the mesa like an egg. The walls of the pass weren't jagged, though, but instead had a checkered pattern to them.

"The dragon is in there." Mina pointed at the narrow opening between the two massive pieces of the mesa.

They reined the horses to a stop and Lord Klodian dismounted. He grabbed his sword from the saddle and strapped it onto his waist, then looked at Vhan.

"You ready?"

"My Lord?"

"You're coming with me on this one. I want you to witness what it takes to kill one. Even with my runes, they are a challenging foe."

"I've waited a long time for this," Vhan said. He slid out of the saddle and adjusted his chainmail shirt, then looked up at Mina.

"Do you want to stay on the horse?"

"Not really."

Vhan offered her his hand, and she accepted his help with climbing down. Once she was on the ground, Lord Klodian and Vhan walked together into the pass. Mina held the reins of Vhan's horse, running her hands along its soft neck. It nickered softly and nudged her with its nose when she stopped.

"You don't have to be rude," Mina said playfully.

The scale in her leg alerted her to the presence of another dragon. And another. She turned toward the pass and scanned the sky, but there were no dragons flying overhead. There were definitely three. She could feel each one individually. Both horses seemed to grow agitated. They snorted and stamped the ground.

Something was wrong.

Mina didn't know where the other two dragons had come from, but if there were three in the pass, Lord Klodian would be outmatched. She needed to warn him before it was too late, but before she could do anything, Vhan's horse screeched and reared on its hind legs, pulling the reins from her grasp. Mina watched helplessly as both horses turned and bolted off, heading toward the castle.

The scale in her leg thrummed, and she sprinted toward the mesa.

18

THAIS HAD BETRAYED HIM.

Her apology was an admission of guilt. The image of her mouthing her contrition had replayed in his mind over and over, keeping him awake most of the night. Not only that, but it had been cold and he didn't have a blanket.

Caden sat on the frigid stone floor of his cell, his back pressed against the wall. His wrists were shackled and chained to the stones behind him. It didn't make any sense. Why would she have ratted him out about what he'd found? And why would Captain Eduard care so much? It was difficult to fathom that Eduard believed Thais's wild conspiracy theory.

Yet here he was in the dungeon.

Approaching footsteps caught his attention. Someone stopped in front of his cell, and Caden squinted, trying to see in the dimness. Keys rattled, and the cell door swung open. A figure stepped inside and paused.

"Hungry?"

It was Captain Eduard. He stepped closer and knelt, offering Caden a tray with a bowl of steaming soup and half a loaf of bread. Caden's stomach rumbled at the sight and he took the tray and began eating. Eduard rose back to his feet and stood there quietly.

"I know what you did," he finally said.

"What's that?"

Eduard half snorted and half laughed. "Are we not adults? Cease the games, Caden. You did something to Lord Klodian in Slia. Just admit it."

Caden licked the warm soup from his lips. "I didn't do anything to Lord Klodian. I told you, I found him unconscious. What would I have to gain by harming him, anyway? It's not like I'm his heir, so I couldn't take his position."

"That is true, but I'm sure you have other motivations. Your loyalty lies elsewhere anyway, does it not?"

"My loyalty lies with you and Lord Klodian," Caden replied. "I've done nothing for you to question that."

Eduard folded his arms and stared at Caden, who in turn continued to eat. He finished off the bread, dipping the last piece in the soup for added flavor.

"I was expecting moldy bread and cold food, to be honest."

"We're not tyrants," Eduard scoffed.

"And I'm thankful for that."

"Which Dominion are you from?"

"This one," Caden said. "I was born here in the Thophate."

"I don't believe you."

"Believe what you will, sir. I have no reason to lie."

"Sure you do. You're a spy from another Dominion, maybe even an assassin. Who sent you here?"

Caden slurped the last of the soup and put the bowl on the tray, then set the tray aside. He wiped his mouth with the back of his hand, the chains clanking with his movements.

"No one sent me here. I'm here of my own choice. I want to be a Runesman. I *am* a Runesman. You saw my value and selected me. Why do you question me now? Because I found Lord Klodian unconscious? Thais and Mina were there with me before we started searching for him. Did you speak to them?"

"I did," Eduard answered. "They seemed forthcoming, but Thais has an attachment to you and Mina is a slave. Her word means nothing."

"What of Thais's word? Does it mean nothing as well? You said yourself that we're a brotherhood. Even if she feels something for me, she wouldn't break her oath as a Runesman."

"Say what you will, but until you admit what you're doing here or prove your innocence, you're going to rot down here."

"How can I prove my innocence? I've told you everything and you have chosen not to believe me."

"I have evidence," Eduard said.

Caden assumed he was talking about the piece of metal he'd found in Slia. If he admitted to finding it, would Eduard release him?

"If you are referring to what I found in Slia, that's not evidence of anything. I found it in the wreckage, and I'm certain it has nothing to do with Thais's theory."

Eduard gave him a hard stare, then unfolded his arms and collected the tray. He walked to the cell door and paused, looking over his shoulder at Caden.

"You'll break eventually," he said. "And when you do, I'll be here to deal out your punishment."

Eduard closed the door behind him and locked it. His steps gradually faded and Caden was left more confused than he'd been before their conversation. Had a spy from another Dominion really infiltrated Lord Klodian's army? And if so, what was their mission? Perhaps if Caden could figure out who it was, he could offer their name to Eduard and secure his release.

Unfortunately, being locked in the dungeon hindered him from gathering information, but on the bright side, he had plenty of time to think. He began to analyze everything he knew about his fellow Runesmen. He replayed conversations, trying to find something, anything, that seemed suspicious, and he came up with … much of nothing.

As far as he could tell, everyone that had joined Lord Klodian's army at the same time as him seemed legitimate. Captain Eduard had to be wrong. That, or he'd said all those things merely to mess with his mind. Caden heaved a sigh and rested his head against the wall. He didn't want to spend the rest of his days in the dungeon, but without help from someone, he feared that would be his fate.

<h1 style="text-align:center">19</h1>

MINA STEPPED INTO THE ENTRANCE of the pass, trying to be as quiet as possible. She didn't hear the sound of fighting, and the passage that cleaved through the mesa twisted and turned, making it impossible to see what lay ahead. She hoped the silence didn't bode something bad.

The walls of the mesa stretched upward, towering high above her. Small crevices broke off to the left and right, but they were too small to enter. In the sand, two sets of footprints were clearly visible. Lord Klodian's tracks were obviously the larger of the two, and she followed the same path.

Mina could feel three distinct dragons through the scale, though one felt much stronger than the others. They were all close, too close for her comfort, but if she didn't warn Klodian before he stumbled upon them, she'd be returning to the castle alone. Of course, that would mean she was free from slavery, but she wanted to be free of the cursed scale more.

A roar filled the air, echoing off the walls. The sound was so powerful that Mina paused and almost fled. A feeling of dread washed over her, but something deep down made her continue walking. There was a metallic clang, followed by a human scream full of pain. Mina steeled herself against her fear and peered around the curved wall. The narrow passage opened up into a large space, and her eyes widened.

There were three enormous copper dragons. They were all equal in size, but the one in the center was the one that Mina could feel the strongest through the scale. A row of spines trailed from its head down its back, each one growing smaller as they reached the tail. Two long, curved horns swooped back from either side of its head, and on the tips of its wings were smaller horns.

Claws as long as daggers gouged the dirt as it stepped. Its mouth was open, saliva dripping from its teeth. And then Mina noticed Lord Klodian on the ground in front of the dragon. His sword was lying a few feet away, and he was crawling backward like a crab. She assumed he was injured by the way he was moving, and she looked for Vhan.

The squire was near one of the other dragons, but unlike Klodian, he wasn't moving. A dark puddle surrounded his body and Mina feared that the boy was dead. She didn't know what to do. Going back to the castle to get help wasn't an option. Even if the horses hadn't run off, it was too far.

Kill him.

Mina whirled around to see who was behind her, but the passage was empty. She'd heard a voice. Where had it come from?

Yes, kill him.

A second voice.

Mina looked up, but there was nothing but the blue sky overhead. Was she losing her mind? Had the curse finally taken its toll on her? What was happening?

Don't worry, brethren. The dragon slayer will die, but I want to see him squirm.

Mina froze. A hundred thoughts became a tangled mess within her mind. She slowly peered around the corner again. The dragon in the center stalked toward Klodian. Was she hearing the dragons? No, that wasn't possible. Dragons couldn't speak. They were mindless animals. They—

There's another one nearby. Hurry, brother! Before more of them show up.

The dragon that was stalking Klodian issued a throaty growl and lunged forward. Klodian dropped down flat, and the dragon's maw full of razor-sharp teeth narrowly missed him. Mina's heart leaped in her chest. This was it. Klodian was going to die. He lifted an arm as if he could block the powerful creature. When Mina stepped into their line of sight, she had no idea why she did it.

"Stop!"

All three dragons whipped their heads in her direction, and she realized she'd made a terrible mistake. Now they would all be dragon food.

It's a female. It was the dragon on the left.

A brave one. This from the one on the right.

Mina had no idea how she knew which one was speaking, she just *knew.* Perhaps it was the scale. Or perhaps she was hallucinating this entire situation. Yes, maybe the heat had gotten to her and she was actually passed out on Vhan's horse, feverishly dreaming all of this.

She will die like the dragon slayer. The leader of the group. The one she felt the strongest connection to. His presence seemed larger than life, and she thought she could feel hints of emotions and thoughts from him. He was mostly angry, but there was a hint of hunger underneath, and it was all wrapped in fear. Fear? The dragon was afraid? Of what? And why?

Time seemed to stand still. Mina stood in place, dragon fear overtaking her. She'd never been this close to one. Perhaps that's why she could hear their thoughts. She tried to move, but she was frozen with terror. The leader spread his talons and slammed his front right claw over Klodian, pinning him in place.

Mina wanted to scream, but she couldn't move her mouth. Her muscles refused to obey her will. The dragon lowered his head down, mere inches from Klodian's face. The air from the dragon's nostrils ruffled Klodian's hair, and the Dominion Lord struggled against the dragon's claw.

Justice has come for this human, killer of dragons.

May he never find rest, even in death, the other two chimed in unison.

The leader opened his jaws. Mina still couldn't move, so she did the only thing she could think of. She screamed as loud as she could within her mind, directing it at the sensations she felt from the scale in her leg.

Don't kill him!

The dragon leader stiffened, his fiery gaze landing on her. The other two dragons slowly stepped backward, and she could *smell* their fear. It was the scent of lavender. Mina didn't have time to consider how she could smell their fear. Her terror dissipated and she lifted her right hand into the air.

Don't kill him! She shouted again. The two dragons snorted and unfurled their wings. They clawed their way up the sides of the mesa and launched themselves into the air. The leader regarded her warily, and the lavender scent poured from him. Mina took a step forward and the dragon tensed.

Flee! Mina demanded.

The dragon stared at her, its eyes looking her up and down. Its gaze stopped on her leg, and Mina's cheeks flushed. It seemed even dragons judged her deformity. The dragon suddenly drew back and climbed the mesa wall, following after the other two. It leaped into the air and stretched out its wings, flapping them and gaining altitude. Despite being up as high as it was, the air from its wings stirred the sand in the clearing. Mina buried her face in the crook of her arm and waited until the dust settled, then rushed over to Klodian. She lifted the visor on his helm and met his eyes.

"You saved my life," he breathed.

She'd done it for selfish reasons, but he didn't need to know that. He was her key to freedom from the curse, which was made worse now that she knew she could hear dragons.

"We need to get you back to the castle," she said. "Can you walk? The horses are gone."

"I can manage. I'll use the runes if I need to."

Mina grabbed onto his hand and pulled with all her might. He got on his feet and Mina started to walk toward Vhan.

"Leave him," Klodian said. "He's dead."

"Are you sure, my Lord?"

"Not even I could have survived what happened to him."

Mina walked over to Vhan anyway, kneeling beside him and trying not to look at the gruesomeness. His eyes were open and staring off. Klodian was right. He *was* dead. She pressed her fingertips to his eyelids and gently closed them.

"Find rest in the spirit world," she said softly.

She rose and returned to Klodian's side, and they traversed the passage out of the mesa. Mina kept glancing skyward, but there was no sign of the dragons. She could still feel the powerful leader through the scale in her leg and she looked back at the mesa. He was probably hiding there, watching them.

"What is it?" Klodian asked.

"Nothing," Mina replied. "I'm just nervous."

"I owe you a debt, Mina. Consider what you want. No matter what it is, it shall be yours."

There were many things that Mina wanted, but at that moment, there was only one that mattered. As they trudged across the desert back to the castle, she realized that, for the first time, Klodian had called her by her name.

20

The jingling of keys roused Caden from his stupor.

He blinked several times, wondering if the sound was real or part of the daydream he'd been entertaining. When the lock clicked and the cell door swung open, he had his answer. Captain Eduard stepped inside, and he didn't look happy.

The small rectangular window high above him allowed just enough light into the cell for him to see that Eduard had a bundle of clothes tucked under his arm. The man's jaw was clenched, and he walked over to the cot and set the clothes down, then unlocked the shackles from Caden's wrists.

"What's going on?" Caden asked.

"You're being transferred to another Dominion, per Lord Klodian's orders."

Caden absently rubbed his sore wrists. He was being transferred? A multitude of questions tumbled around within his mind. Transferring to another Dominion had been his goal when he first became a Runesman over a week ago, but now he was having second thoughts. Being around Thais and Mina had made him question that goal, and he was now more conflicted than ever.

"I … don't understand," he said.

"There's no need to. It's Lord Klodian's bidding, and so it will be done. Get dressed. When you're done, you'll collect your things from the barracks and be on your way."

Eduard stepped out of the cell and hovered in the hallway. Caden didn't want to question his luck, and he quickly changed into the clean clothes Eduard had provided. They weren't his own, but they fit well enough. He tossed the dirty rags he'd been wearing onto the cot, stretched his muscles, then joined Eduard in the hall.

"Follow me."

Caden did as he was asked and trailed Eduard out of the dungeon and into the castle. They didn't talk at all, and Caden was beginning to understand that whatever had transpired between Eduard and Lord

Klodian wasn't what Eduard wanted. They exited the castle and Caden breathed in a deep breath of fresh air. He hadn't been in the dungeon long, but the stench had been overwhelming. Unbathed bodies and the desert heat were a bad combination.

The two marched across the courtyard and into the barracks. The other Runesmen were out training, and the building was empty. Caden went to his cot and gathered his meager belongings, which were nothing more than two sets of clothing, a small bag of silver coins, and the piece of metal he'd found in Slia. He stuffed them all into a leather bag and turned to Eduard.

"Can I say goodbye to a few people?"

"No."

Judging by his tone, Caden knew there was no room for debate. He nodded, not bothering to argue.

"What Dominion am I being transferred to?"

"The Dracan Dominion. It's northeast of here. You'll be given a horse, so you should get there within a few days. If you ride hard, you can make it in two."

The Dracan Dominion. Caden knew it. Everyone did. It was home to Lord Kristofel D'Lance, right hand to the High Prince himself. He boasted the largest army and had more land than any other Dominion Lord. It all confused Caden even more. The move should be for someone esteemed, not a neophyte Runesman like himself. Was his transfer a punishment, or a reward?

"One of the patrols will escort you to the border, then you are on your own from there."

"May I speak bluntly, sir?"

"You may."

"I know you still think I did something to Lord Klodian, and outside of one of the gods themselves coming to you to say otherwise, I know you won't change your mind about that. I stand by my words. I didn't do anything to him, I swear it. I don't know why I'm being transferred, but if we never meet again, I want you to know I don't hold any grudge against you. If I were in your shoes, I would believe whatever my feelings were too, but sometimes the things that seem right couldn't be further from the truth."

Captain Eduard cleared his throat.

"You're a good soldier, there's no mistaking that. Whether my suspicions are true or not doesn't matter now. You're no longer under my command. Is that everything, then?"

"Yes, sir."

"Good. Come on."

They went to the stable and Caden was surprised to find that a horse had already been readied for him. The mount was saddled and a satchel of provisions had been strapped to it. He was being transferred, given a horse and provisions, and this was somehow a punishment? Caden smiled to himself. Perhaps a fresh start was in his best interest. A clean slate in a new Dominion could be just what he needed.

Caden strapped his bag to the saddle and mounted the horse. Eduard stared up at him, and he had the feeling that the captain wanted to say something. The man remained silent, however.

"Let the winds blow in your favor to keep the dust from your eyes," Caden said.

"May the sun be at your back so that you always see your enemies," Eduard replied.

Caden took the reins in his hands and flicked them, guiding the horse toward the gates. Once he was outside the castle walls, he spotted the patrol Eduard had mentioned. The small group was waiting on him, and as he joined their ranks, they turned northeast and began the trek toward the border.

He didn't know any of the other Runesmen. They were his seniors, and they all had scars from countless battles. They must have transferred from other Dominions because it was well known that Lord Klodian rarely waged war against his fellow lords. As he considered the proverbial road ahead, he was excited. It was a chance to prove himself a capable soldier, and to find the fame and riches he'd wanted for as long as he could remember.

While the opportunity was good, he hated how it had all happened. Thais had betrayed his trust, forcing him to lose her and Mina all in one fell swoop. He hoped that Thais felt guilty. A sudden wave of anger washed over him, and he cursed her. She'd ruined things for him, and not just with Captain Eduard. He'd lost Mina as well. Caden knew the sting of her treachery would fade, but his memory of her actions would not.

As the seed of hatred began to sprout within him, he silently prayed that he would meet Thais on the battlefield one day. He couldn't right her wrong, but he could avenge himself.

And he *would* avenge himself.

21

MINA WALKED WITH HESITANT STEPS into Lord Klodian's personal chamber. He'd summoned her, and she wasn't sure if that was a good thing. She'd saved his life, true, but since he was a Dominion Lord, he owed her nothing. It was a miracle that he had granted her anything at all, but she felt confident that she'd used her favor toward a good purpose.

Lord Klodian was at his desk, flipping through parchments and muttering to himself. Mina stood to the side and waited, but he was completely enveloped in his work. She didn't want to interrupt him, but he had asked her to come to see him. Her palms were sweating with her nervousness, and she cleared her throat.

The sound caused Klodian to look up and he frowned at her. She swallowed hard, thinking he was upset with her.

"If you are busy, I can come back later, my Lord."

"What? Oh. No. No, now is fine."

He rose from his chair and came to stand in front of her. Even without his armor, he was an imposing figure. He was taller than Caden. He was more muscular, too, and his physique was more noticeable when he wore plain clothes. Tinges of gray interspersed with his brown hair, and his blue eyes were as hard as steel.

"I wanted you to know that your request for your friend to be transferred to another Dominion has been completed."

"Thank you, my Lord."

"It's the least I can do to repay my debt to you. In fact, I don't feel that it's nearly enough. You didn't even ask for something for yourself."

Mina cast her eyes to the floor. She hadn't thought of anything for herself except for a way to lift the curse of the scale, but Klodian couldn't do that unless he killed the dragon responsible. And even that was only an assumption on her part.

"Is there nothing else that you desire?"

"I don't know," Mina replied. "Perhaps there is, but I don't think you can give it to me."

Klodian smiled knowingly. "If I could remove the scale from your leg, I don't know that I would do it. It has made me very wealthy."

Mina knew he hadn't meant what he'd said about giving her anything she desired. Aside from having the scale removed, the only other thing she wanted was freedom. And she knew with certainty that he wouldn't give her that.

"That is my desire, but I know you don't have the power to remove it," she said. "I don't think anyone does."

"There must be something else," Klodian pressed. "I do not want to be indebted to anyone."

Mina shook her head and opened her mouth to speak, but he silenced her with a stern look. She felt herself shrink before him. It was a habit, ingrained into her over the years.

"I had assumed you would ask for a few different things, and you surprised me by not asking for any of them. I've thought long and hard since we left the mesa, and I know what I will give you."

Klodian lifted his arm, his hand closed. It was obvious he was holding something, and Mina slowly moved her hand underneath his. Klodian drew his fingers back and dropped something cold and circular onto her palm. She pulled her hand back and saw it was a gold bracelet. Mina looked at Klodian quizzically.

"You are no longer a slave, Mina. This bracelet is a sign of your standing within my court. From this day forth, you are now an advisor to me."

"My Lord? I-I'm no advisor," she stammered. "I'm not wise in the ways of battles or politics. How can I be an advisor?"

"I will come up with a position for you, but until then, you are simply a member of my court now. You are free to come and go as you wish, but I ask only one thing."

"What?"

"That you continue to lead me to the dragons," Klodian said.

"And if I refuse to?"

Mina saw the slight clench in Klodian's jawline, but he surprised her with his answer.

"That is your decision. As I said, you are no longer a slave."

She was speechless. He had freed her. She searched his face, waiting for the reveal of a cruel joke. Klodian returned her stare, but there was no malice in his eyes.

"You are serious, my Lord?"

"I am."

"I don't know what to say. I … thank you."

"You saved my life," he said. "There is no need to thank me. This is *me* thanking *you*."

Tears welled within Mina's eyes. She blinked several times, fighting to keep from full-on crying.

"There are some things I must see to, but if you need anything, ask the steward. I've already let him know of the changes, so you'll be well taken care of."

"Thank you again, my Lord," Mina said softly, still in disbelief.

She left the room in a daze and somehow managed to navigate the maze of halls to the servant's quarters. She walked to her bed, but something was different. A quick look around revealed that all of her belongings were missing. Panic washed over her and she looked under the bed. Her box of horns was gone.

"Your things have been moved to your new room," Kera said from behind her.

Mina looked up at the girl from the floor. "My new room?"

"Yes. The steward had us carry it all. That little box with your horns has some weight to it."

"There are a lot of horns in it," Mina said. "Can you tell me where this room is?"

"Yes, but it's probably better if I show you. Come on."

Mina followed Kera into the hall and they turned left, leaving the servant's rooms behind. A few turns later and they entered the wing reserved for the nobles and other members of the court. Mina had only been to this part of the castle a handful of times, and she knew it was going to take some adjusting to the new surroundings.

Kera stopped at one of the doors and opened it, motioning for Mina to go inside. Mina did so, and she marveled at the expensive furniture and other trinkets that decorated the room. A sword hung on one of the walls, and Mina wondered what she was supposed to do with the weapon. Kera followed her gaze.

"This was Vhan's room," she said lowly. "The sword was his. The steward left it up, but if you want me to remove it—"

"It can stay," Mina replied, cutting her off. "I like it."

"Very well. Do you need anything before I go?"

Mina shook her head.

"If you do, ring the bell on the desk there, and one of the servants will answer your call. Sound travels oddly in these halls, so it may take them a moment to figure out which room it is." Kera paused. "Anyway, I'll see you around the castle, my Lady."

Mina squirmed at the last words, but Kera was walking out of the room and didn't see her reaction. Mina's entire way of life had changed so suddenly. It wasn't a bad change, but it would take her some time to get used to being referred to as "my Lady."

Windows lined the far wall, and Mina walked over to see what kind of view she had. The courtyard was visible, and she spotted a familiar figure. Caden. He was on a horse, riding toward the gate that led to his new life. Her heart broke at the sight of him leaving, but she knew that it was what he had wanted. She wished she could have said goodbye, but she supposed that would have been more painful than just watching him ride off.

She watched until she could no longer see him, then she glanced around her new room. She still couldn't believe that Klodian had freed her. He still wanted her help to hunt dragons, and she would gladly offer it. Until the curse was broken, she wouldn't stop tracking them for him.

The scene from the mesa flashed within her mind. The deep voices of the massive dragons echoed in her thoughts, and she knew it would be a long time before she forgot the sound of them. Mina rubbed the scale on her leg and looked back at the window. The dragons were nowhere near the castle, and yet she could still feel the powerful one. Why could she hear their thoughts? Why did she still feel the leader, even now? There were too many questions, too many things that she didn't know.

But she had an idea.

It was likely to get her killed, but if she succeeded, then perhaps she could finally be free. After night had fallen, she took Vhan's sword down from the wall and carried it with her as she quietly left the castle, heading for the mesa where she knew the dragon would be. She didn't know how to use a sword, nor was she strong enough to fight a dragon, but none of that mattered. She was going to get answers.

One way or another.

EGG

OF THE

DRAGON

1

The dragon had been avoiding Mina for days.

At first, she'd thought that the beast had been able to detect her scent, but after doing numerous things to disguise her smell, she'd decided that there had to be another way that he sensed her approach. Perhaps he could see better in the dark than she knew. After all, she had been searching at night.

Today would be different. She could feel it in her bones.

Mina had slipped out of the castle after breakfast, taking Vhan's sword with her. The blasted thing was almost too heavy for her to carry, but it made her feel safe. She laid the blade over her left shoulder, using her own body as leverage. Lord Klodian had been strangely absent, and she suspected it had something to do with the rumors of war circulating around the castle.

The servants had a way of exaggerating what they heard, but with Klodian seemingly preoccupied, it did lend some credence to their words. War or not, it had nothing to do with Mina. The fact that Klodian had ceased his hunts meant that she had more time to find answers to the many questions looming in her mind.

She walked to the stable and set the sword down, placing the pointed end in the dirt and waited for Aram, one of the stable hands, to saddle a horse for her. She would have taken a horse the previous few nights, but she didn't want to arouse attention. There was enough focus on her with the momentous change in status Klodian had given her. He'd named her an advisor, of all things. Mina shook her head as she considered it.

"Where you headed to, my Lady?" Aram asked.

"Just for a ride," Mina replied. "I'll be back in a few hours."

"Tempest here should do the job. She can be a bit stubborn, but she's gentle."

"She'll do fine. Thank you."

Aram led a brown mare out and handed her the reins. The horse nuzzled Mina, and she rubbed her hand along the horse's forehead before offering a quick scratch behind the ears. The mare whinnied and pawed at the ground.

"It seems she likes you," Aram said. He handed her a small bag. "There's a few apples and some oats in there. If you're going to be out past noon, you'll need to give her something to eat. She likes to snack throughout the day."

"I'll be sure to take good care of her. Come on, Tempest."

Mina dragged the sword behind her with one hand and held onto the reins tightly with the other. She walked Tempest to the castle gate, then strapped the sword onto the saddle and did her best to mount the horse without looking too inept. She hadn't ridden a horse on her own since she'd lived on her parent's farm, but she remembered the basics well enough. Once she was firmly seated, she watched and waited.

The Runesmen were doing their morning run around the castle, and she didn't want to accidentally run anyone over. Once the stragglers had passed, Mina clenched her knees against Tempest's sides and flicked the reins. Tempest began a swift trot, and after a few moments of panic, Mina was able to guide the mare in the direction she wanted.

The sensation from the scale in her leg indicated that the dragon was northeast of the castle, the same general area she'd been searching. She rode for half an hour, slightly adjusting Tempest's course as they went. Tall mesas were scattered across the landscape, but she angled the horse toward one in particular. It was tall and wide, but she didn't immediately spot a cave entrance.

"We'll ride around the base and see if we can find one," Mina muttered to herself as much as to Tempest.

It took the better part of an hour, but once she had circled the entire mesa, Mina frowned. The dragon was here, she was certain of it, but there was no cave. She dismounted and fished an apple from the satchel Aram had given her, then fed it to Tempest. The horse took the entire thing in one bite, crunching loudly.

Mina looked up at the mesa. If there was no cave, then the dragon had to be at the top. The idea of scaling the sheer wall to get up there wasn't very appealing, but what other option did she have?

"Can I trust you not to leave me here?" she asked Tempest.

The horse nickered as if replying, and Mina patted its shoulder. She had no idea what awaited her once she finally found the dragon. The beast could easily eat her, for all she knew. She supposed that she must be a little crazy to be seeking a dragon by herself, but if she had brought Klodian on her quest, he would want to kill the dragon and claim its hoard of treasure.

At any other time, Mina would have no qualms with that. But for now, she wanted answers, which meant that she would have to speak with the dragon, not kill it. Speak with a dragon. The thought seemed foolish, but after her encounter with the enormous copper beast, she knew that there was much more about dragons that she didn't know or understand.

Mina retrieved the sword from Tempest's saddle and carried it with her to the mesa wall. It quickly became apparent that she wouldn't be able to carry it while she climbed. The surface of the mesa had enough grooves for her to find foot and handholds, but the added weight and awkwardness of the sword would only hinder her.

She heaved a sigh and set the sword down, propping it against the stone wall. Grabbing a handful of dirt from the ground, she rubbed it between her hands and then began climbing up the wall. Having small fingers ended up benefitting her, and she made quick progress until she reached what she thought was the halfway point.

Her muscles burned with exertion, and her legs began to tremor. She gritted her teeth against the pain, pausing long enough to carefully brush the sweat from each of her hands onto her pants. The sun was high overhead, and without a cloud in the sky, the heat was making her sweat in places she'd rather not think about.

"Almost there," she whispered, though she knew that was a lie.

Still, if she could make herself believe it, perhaps she wouldn't fall to her death. She breathed deeply, trying to calm herself, then continued climbing. Her pace was much slower now, and the higher she climbed, the more pain she felt in her hands. Something sticky was on her fingertips, but she didn't look to confirm if it was blood.

Finally, she reached the top of the mesa. Mina pulled herself over the edge, struggling for a moment. She almost tumbled backward, but she clawed frantically at the rocks and managed to catch herself. Her heart hammered in her chest and she laid on her back with her eyes closed, a thin shield against the sun. After a long moment of rest, she rolled onto her side and looked down at the ground far below. Tempest was nothing more than a tiny brown dot.

Mina forced herself to her feet and turned around to survey her surroundings. The top of the mesa was wide and flat. Patches of desert shrubs, all dull green, littered the surface. The scale in her leg thrummed powerfully, but she didn't see the dragon anywhere. Did they have the ability to camouflage themselves? Or could they perhaps make themselves invisible completely?

As she considered those questions, movement caught her eye. Mina squinted, but it was difficult to see what had moved. She crept forward, wiping droplets of sweat from her brow. Reaching a long line of shrubs, she realized that there was a large depression hidden behind them. Mina stepped into the thorny bushes, spurs grabbing at her clothes.

The indentation sloped down smoothly, and there at the bottom was the dragon. It lay there, basking in the sun, its wings outstretched. She swallowed hard, fighting against the fear that threatened to consume her. She'd finally found him. And now that he was within sight, her carefully crafted plan shattered into pieces.

What was she doing up here? She'd made a terrible mistake. *Blessed Avera,* Mina thought. *This beast will surely kill me.* She was frozen in place, dragon fear slowly taking over her senses. Her mind screamed at her body to turn and run, but her muscles wouldn't—or couldn't—obey. Her lips refused to part and take in air, and her lungs cried out. She fought desperately against the fear and won, gasping in a deep breath.

The dragon's eyes snapped open.

2

Velbridge was the heart of the Dracan Dominion. It was also the seat of power for the High Prince's favored ruler, Lord Kristofel D'Lance.

As Caden navigated the busy streets of the sprawling city, he marveled at the number of people that the place could accommodate. They thronged down every cobbled street, the sight reminding him of how small the Thophate in its entirety was in comparison. Vendor stalls were everywhere, even at the middle of intersections, and the scent of exotic foods filled the air, tempting Caden to see if they tasted as good as they smelled.

Behind the city loomed a castle twice the size of Lord Klodian's, and its dark gray walls stood in stark contrast to all the color that the city presented. This was his new home. It was hard for him to believe that being sent here was a punishment, but his excitement was dampened by the memory of Thais's betrayal. If she had kept her mouth shut, he'd still be in the Thophate with Mina.

There was nothing he could do about it now, though, and he tried not to dwell on it. He held the letter of his transfer in his right hand. He'd found it in the bag of provisions Captain Eduard had given him. Lord Klodian's flowing signature was at the bottom, along with his official seal. Halfway through the journey, Caden had briefly considered giving up his dreams and turning around, but it had only been an idea born of the desert heat. Once he'd reached more forgiving lands, his thoughts returned to normal.

"You there," a vendor called out to him. "You look like you could use a drink. I've got the best ale in all of Dracan. Only a hundred silver for a full barrel."

Caden smiled despite the exorbitant price and continued walking. He was heading for the castle, but navigating the crowded streets was proving to be more of a pain than he'd first thought. He pushed his way through the crowd, receiving a few elbows to the ribs that he doubted were accidental. Eventually, he found a side street that ran parallel to the main one, and he turned onto it and was able to quicken his pace. The castle seemed to grow and stretch the closer he got until he found himself at the gates.

He craned his neck back, trying to take in the view. A group of soldiers standing guard saw him gawking and laughed. Caden cleared his throat and walked confidently over to them.

"Good day," he said. "I've just transferred from the Thophate Dominion. Can one of you show me to the captain?"

"Another transfer, huh? Seems everyone is coming here lately. Stay here, gents. I'll take him."

The man who'd spoken was older than the others, with dull black hair that was beginning to turn silver. He sported a thick handlebar mustache and his face was creased with a few wrinkles. The other guards shrugged and resumed their conversation, and the older man led Caden through the gates and into the courtyard. He walked with a slight limp, but his pace was swift and Caden had trouble keeping up with him.

"What's your name?"

"Caden. Caden Davtyan."

"Well met. I'm Angus. You're from the Thophate, you said?"

"Yes, sir," Caden replied. "I just arrived today."

"I've never been there myself, but I've heard terrible things from some of the merchants. I reckon the sand and heat get old after a while. Is that what brings you to Velbridge?"

Caden chuckled. "Something like that."

He'd read over the transfer letter many times as he traveled, practically committing it to memory. There was no mention of his suspected crime or the reason he was transferred.

"You wanting to be a Runesman?"

"I am one, actually."

"Oh? Lord D'Lance has many, but he's always looking for more. Being favored by the High Prince comes at a steep cost, especially since he plays the part of a peacekeeper. All these lords who think that nobility is a pissing contest have to constantly be reminded of their proper place."

"It sounds like I'll see plenty of battle," Caden said.

"Oh, I'll wager you'll see plenty more than you'd like. Word is spreading that some upstart is talking about starting a war." Angus shook his head. "Lord D'Lance will quell it, but when the High Prince finds out, there'll be hell to pay."

Despite the severity of what Angus was saying, Caden was excited. His plan initially had been to transfer to a Dominion where he would see more battle, so his luck couldn't have been better. Now he just needed to make a name for himself on the battlefield, and the riches would follow.

"How much training have you had?"

"A week or so," Caden replied sheepishly. "I'd planned on being fully trained before transferring, but it didn't work out that way."

As they talked, Angus led him across the courtyard and around the eastern side of the castle. Roughly a hundred feet away sat a large rectangular building. It was built of the same gray stone as the castle, but the decoration was lacking. They went inside, and Caden realized it was the barracks. As with everything else he'd seen so far, it put Lord Klodian's to shame. There were two levels, and there was enough room to house a few thousand soldiers.

"Is this where I'll be staying?" Caden asked.

"Yes. This is the Runesmen barracks. The barracks for soldiers without runes is on the opposite side of the castle."

"How many Runesmen does Lord D'Lance have?"

"I believe at last count it was upwards of five thousand."

Caden's eyes widened in surprise. "When you said he had many Runesmen, you weren't exaggerating."

"If there's anything you'll learn about the Dracan Dominion, it's that Lord D'Lance has the best of everything."

Five thousand Runesmen. Caden couldn't imagine how strong Lord D'Lance could be with that many men at his disposal. Was it even possible for someone to utilize the attributes of that many people? Perhaps his excitement had been premature. How would he make a name for himself as a soldier with so much competition?

"I assume your previous lord cut the rune he gave you?"

Caden's hand instinctively went to the back of his neck, rubbing the tattoo.

"No," he replied. "Should he have?"

Angus paused and turned to look at him. "Let me see it."

Caden obliged, turning around. Angus pulled the neckline of his shirt back and muttered something he didn't catch, then said, "A strength rune. Not many of those in our ranks lately."

"Why not?"

"As I said, Lord D'Lance pays a steep price for being the favorite. Runesmen get used a lot around here. Without proper rest and time to heal, burnout becomes a problem. Some can push through, but most can't."

"They get discharged?" Caden asked.

"No. They die."

Caden was glad that Angus couldn't see his face at that moment. Angus straightened his collar and continued further into the barracks. Caden rushed to catch up, and they ascended a stairway that led to the second level. The setup was similar to the first level, but there was a walled-off area with a door at the far end. Angus took him to the door and opened it, then motioned him inside and closed the door.

"Have a seat."

Caden did so, seating himself at one of the chairs in front of a large desk. Angus walked around to the other side and sat down, clasping his fingers together and leaning forward.

"I hope you'll forgive my ruse, but we have many soldiers that transfer here, and most of them don't have what it takes to serve Lord D'Lance."

"*You're* the captain," Caden said with a nervous laugh.

"Commander, actually. Commander Angus Morin. Do you have your letter of transfer?"

"Yes, sir." Caden set the parchment on the desk and slid it forward.

Angus picked it up and read over it, then set it atop a stack of papers.

"I'm good at reading people, Caden. In my position, I have to be. I can tell you're ambitious, else you wouldn't have requested to come here of all places."

Caden smiled, but he knew that he'd had nothing to do with where he'd been sent. He didn't think it would hurt to leave that information out.

"I like you," Angus continued. "Normally, I'd send you out with the next patrol to get your feet wet with something like settling a border dispute, but I've got something different in mind. I find it curious that your rune wasn't cut. It severs the magic between you and your lord, allowing a new rune to be added."

Caden assumed he knew where the conversation was going. Angus probably thought he was a spy. Why else would his rune be intact? Had Lord Klodian believed Eduard's suspicions and sent him to the Dracan Dominion, thinking that this was his true home? Caden swallowed hard and tried not to let his emotions show.

"There was a lot going on, so it's possible that Lord Klodian forgot."

"That's possible," Angus said. "I get the feeling you think this is a bad thing. Let me put your mind at ease now. It's fine."

"I was a little worried," Caden admitted.

"Don't be. Things couldn't be better for you."

Caden relaxed, the invisible weight on his shoulders washing away.

"In fact, I think Lord D'Lance is going to take a personal interest in you."

3

You.

The dragon's voice echoed within Mina's mind. She stood still, frozen in place. For some unfathomable reason, she'd envisioned this entire situation going differently. The dragon shifted his bulk and slithered around to fully face her, his hot breath washing over her like the heat from a fire.

Why do you stalk me? Do you seek death at the claws of a dragon?

While terror kept her physically rooted in place, Mina was able to push through the fear mentally. She could feel a plethora of emotions coming from the dragon, all of them swirling together. The one that stood out the most was curiosity. It smelled sweet, reminding Mina of strawberries, with subtle notes of honey and mint.

You can *speak,* Mina said, pushing the words through the scale.

All dragons can speak.

Can they? I've always heard that dragons were ... She paused, knowing that if she completed the sentence, the dragon would likely snap her in two.

That we are dull? I can assure you that we dragons are far from lacking intelligence. Tell me, girl. Why have you come?

Abruptly, the feeling of dread she felt dissipated. Her muscles slackened, and she blinked. Her lips were chapped from the heat and the sand, and she ran her tongue across them, but it did little to help.

"Why can I hear you?"

The dragon tilted his head to the side, and his pupils became thin slits.

I believe the scale in your leg has something to do with that.

"Well, yes, but *why?*"

The dragon snorted. *How would I know?*

"The scale came from a dragon, and you are a dragon. I thought you would know."

I do not.

The two stared at one another in silence, and Mina considered how crazy it all was. She was talking to a dragon—a dragon!—and it felt normal, as though she were conversing with another person.

I hope that you did not come all this way to ask me a single question. I've eaten people for much less.

"I have many questions. Why were you afraid before? In the mesa when you tried to kill my mast—my lord?"

Dragons fear nothing, he replied heatedly. *You mistake mercy for fear.*

"Mercy? You and the other two dragons fled as if you'd seen a spirit."

I have spoken already. What else do you want to know?

"Can you remove the scale?" Mina asked.

The dragon stepped closer, snaking his head down until his eyes were level with her.

Let me see the scale.

Mina opened her mouth to protest, but the dragon glared at her. She reached down and unbuttoned her pants, then slid them down to reveal the scale. The dragon stared at it intently, then returned his gaze to her face.

It cannot be removed.

"Why not?"

It has fused into your flesh and become a part of you. To remove it would kill you.

"What of the curse? Can it be lifted?"

What curse do you speak of?

"This blasted thing allows me to feel the presence of dragons. And now I can hear you speaking through it. How do I get rid of the curse if I can't get rid of the scale?"

The dragon drew back and sat on its haunches, its tail flicking back and forth behind it. Mina pulled her pants back up.

You are the reason my brethren are being killed. A growl rumbled in the dragon's chest. *I had assumed the man killing us was using magic to find us, just as he uses it to become stronger and faster. Instead, it is* you.

Mina didn't feel guilty. She helped Klodian because she believed that ultimately it would help her be free. Her face remained impassive as she stared up at the dragon. It towered over her, but oddly, she wasn't afraid.

I can feel your hatred. Why do you despise us so much?

"Why do you think?" Mina patted her leg. "This thing ruined my life. I've been a slave most of my life because of it." She could feel the anger welling up within her.

How is that our fault? Did one of my kind force the scale into your flesh?

"No. I fell into a nest and landed on it."

And you blame us for that?

The dragon was trying to get into her head. She refused to question herself on this. Dragons *were* to blame. They had caused all of her problems, whether this one wanted to accept that or not.

"The blame lies with one of you, and I won't rest until you're all dead."

The dragon moved with lightning quickness. His massive claw snatched her from where she stood and slammed her onto the ground, pinning her in place. Mina's heart pounded wildly in her chest, and the fear she'd felt before returned full force.

You are nothing to me, girl. You pose no threat. Your words are the howling of the wind against the mountain and nothing more. I could crush you with little effort.

"Then do it."

Mina couldn't believe the words had come from her mouth. She tensed, expecting the dragon to stomp down on her. The dragon only stared at her in silence. The scent of an unfamiliar emotion poured off the dragon, but she didn't know what it was. It smelled of a mix between lemon and clove.

You are not afraid to die?

"No."

Then you are not like the others of your race. The dragon leaned down and sniffed her. *What is your name?*

"Mina."

Mina, the dragon repeated it, and her name echoed over and over within her mind.

"What is your name?"

You will know my name once you earn my trust, girl. For now, you may call me Copper.

Copper. She didn't find the nickname very original, considering his color, but it was better than nothing. She squirmed under the force of his claw, but he didn't let her up.

In exchange for sparing your life, I demand that you stop leading your lord to my brethren.

"You didn't spare my life," Mina said. "And I told you I'm not afraid to die."

The scent of your fear says otherwise. And I could have flamed you and your horse long before you reached the summit of this mesa.

"You knew I was coming here?"

Yes.

"Why didn't you evade me like you've been doing?"

Your determination made me curious.

"Could you smell me? Or how did you know I was approaching?"

The power of your scale works both ways for a dragon wise enough to know how to sense it.

Mina had suspected that, but the idea that a dragon could sense her as she was able to sense them had made her uneasy, so she chose to ignore that possibility. Now that she knew the truth, it only added to her list of questions.

Now, give me your oath.

"Let me up first."

Copper lifted his claw and Mina rolled away and got to her feet. She looked up at the dragon, weighing her options. Lord Klodian had been too busy to go on his hunts, and if there really was a war brewing, she doubted he would have the free time for one anytime soon. And if there was no war, she could just lead him around aimlessly until he gave up.

"I will not lead him to any more dragons," Mina said. "For now."

For now?

"I have more questions. As long as you answer them, I will hold up my end of this bargain."

What makes you think you have any power over this agreement?

Mina smiled. "Because Lord Klodian has one of your eggs."

4

Caden stood in the shadows of an alley behind a busy tavern called *The Dirty Serpent.*

The sound of raised voices and laughter spilled out from the place, signs that the patrons were thoroughly enjoying themselves, including his target. Angus had given him the task of removing a threat to Lord D'Lance.

"I'm a soldier, not an assassin," Caden had argued.

"I know that I am asking much from you, but this man is dangerous. He doesn't know your face, so you'll be able to get close to him before he realizes what's happening. If you are successful, I'll take it as proof of your skill. It needs to be quick, but not public."

"Why doesn't Lord D'Lance deal with him directly?"

"Politics, my boy. They are as nuanced as the weaving of a tapestry. Lord D'Lance is a public figure. He can't just go around killing his enemies without backlash. Things like this must be done delicately."

Caden understood those things, which was the only reason he agreed to do the job. He would have preferred handling a border dispute or some other task, but it seemed like Angus trusted him. Since he was eliminating a dangerous foe, he was essentially protecting Lord D'Lance's life. He would make a name for himself yet.

A soft whistling sound echoed down the alley. That was Caden's sign. He unsheathed the dagger Angus had given him and crouched beside the door that led into the kitchen. Muffled voices were speaking on the other side. Caden gripped the hilt tightly, preparing himself. He didn't feel right about killing an unarmed man, but he pushed those feelings down deep inside. The door opened and a figure stepped out into the alley.

"Joeffrey?"

"Over here, sir," Caden whispered.

"What in the blazes are you doing in the dark?"

"It's urgent, sir. I need to show you something."

The figure glanced around the alley, then walked toward Caden. As soon as he was within range, Caden leaped forward and drove the dagger into the man's stomach. There was a pained grunt, but Caden's didn't feel any blood. The man staggered back, cursing, and stepped into the moonlight. He was wearing chainmail under his shirt.

Caden tackled the man, and the two of them crashed to the ground. His target was stronger than he looked, and he almost managed to get the dagger from his grasp. Caden ended up on top of the man and leaned forward, putting all of his weight into the movement. The dagger's blade sliced through the man's hand and drove into his neck. There was a gurgled cry, and then silence.

Death was no stranger to Caden, but he'd never murdered someone before. It left a foul taste in his mouth and made him feel dirty somehow. He got to his feet and waited, watching the blood pool around the man to ensure he was dead. Satisfied, he hurried down the other end of the alley and emerged onto the main street.

The roads weren't as packed as they had been during the day, but there were still people ambling along. Most of them were probably heading to and from the many taverns in Velbridge, and Caden did his best to keep his face hidden as he passed them. No one knew what he'd done, but the guilt he felt had a funny way of making him think they did. By the time he returned to the castle, he felt horrible.

Angus met him at the gates, and they walked wordlessly to the barracks. They went up to the second level and into Angus's office, and Caden collapsed into a chair. Not only was he feeling sick from his actions, but he was tired. He'd been in Velbridge for less than a day and he had blood on his hands. Figuratively, if not literally. He looked down to see if there was any blood visible and noticed his hands were shaking.

"I assume it's done, then?" Angus asked.

Caden nodded.

"Good. You've done the Dominion a great service. Lord D'Lance will be glad to know that there is one less enemy in our midst."

"Sir, I … I don't feel right about it. That wasn't battle. It was murder."

Angus sat on the edge of his desk and stared Caden straight in the eyes. He remained silent for a moment.

"As a soldier, you need to remove your feelings from the situation. You were given a task, and you completed it. With that said, I'd be worried if you didn't feel remorse. You took a life, which is no small thing. Yet you saved Lord D'Lance from a possible assassination. The man you killed has been here for weeks, waiting for an opportunity to catch us off guard. He was an agent of the lord I told you about, the one wanting to start a war. I wasn't exaggerating when I said you've done a great service."

Angus's words eased Caden's guilt a little, but they didn't make him feel any less dirty.

"Take one of the open beds and get some rest. Work through your feelings if you must, but be ready in the morning."

"Ready for what?" Caden asked.

"To meet with Lord D'Lance. He'll be glad to have a strength Runesman, but when I tell him what you've done for the Dominion, I expect there will be great things in store for you."

"Thank you, sir."

Caden rose from the chair and left the office. He'd left his bag with his belongings in an empty chest at the end of one of the beds, and he lifted the lid to see that his stuff was still there. Between his journey and his gruesome task, he felt soiled. He grabbed a fresh pair of clothes from his bag and changed, tossing the ones Eduard had given him into the bottom of the chest. He didn't plan on wearing them again.

Most of the beds on the second level were empty, but here and there, Caden spotted sleeping soldiers. He climbed onto the cot and stared at the ceiling. He'd murdered a man. That was disturbing enough, but the more troubling thing was that it hadn't been hard for him to do. He wanted to blame it on his willingness to prove himself, but he wasn't sure that was the source.

He was still angry about Thais, and it felt good to take that anger out on someone. Did that make him a bad person? He hoped not. He pleaded silently to any god that was listening to forgive him, then his thoughts turned to Mina. He hadn't gotten to speak to her after he'd kissed her, and he still feared that he may have upset her.

Perhaps deep down, he truly was a monster.

5

Lord Klodian had found the egg a few years previous.

It had been in one of the nests that Mina had led him to, and he took the egg back to the castle. She never knew why he decided to take it, but it never hatched. Eventually, everyone around the castle had lost interest in it.

Despite that, Lord Klodian had continued to keep it secured beneath the castle. Mina didn't know exactly where it was located, but she had a general idea. The only problem she could foresee was whether he still kept the room guarded.

Since Copper had begrudgingly agreed to help her find a way to remove the scale from her leg in exchange for the egg, she had to figure out a way to abscond with it. It wasn't likely that Klodian would realize it was missing until long after it was gone, and if Mina was free of the curse, she'd be long gone as well.

"My Lady," a servant greeted as he passed her in the hall.

She smiled and continued to her room, Vhan's sword propped against her shoulder. Mina supposed she looked like a fool with the weapon. It was much too heavy for her, and she doubted she could properly swing it even if she wanted to. Still, she felt powerful when she carried it, and in a way, she considered it a remembrance of Vhan. She still couldn't believe that the squire was dead.

Lord Klodian had returned to the mesa the next day with a large force of Runesmen and retrieved the boy's body, and Mina had stood with the crowd at his pyre as he burned. Vhan had been honored, but it seemed to her as though everyone had quickly forgotten about him.

She was so deep in her thoughts that she walked right past her room without realizing it. She stopped at the edge of an open doorway and was about to turn around when she heard voices talking lowly.

"He doesn't have enough men to spare," a man said. "Lord Klodian is already hard-pressed to keep his Dominion safe from wild animals. How does Lord D'Lance expect him to send an army to aid against the brewing war?"

"Has Lord D'Lance sent a formal request?" It was a woman.

Mina didn't recognize their voices, but she knew they were nobles. Otherwise, they wouldn't be in this hall.

"Not yet, but he's bound to any day now. I have a feeling Lord Klodian will deny the appeal."

"I'm certain he will. He's been consumed with hunting dragons of late, and war in a far-off Dominion has nothing to do with him. He will deny Lord D'Lance, and that will be our moment to strike."

Mina scrunched her face. Were they plotting against Lord Klodian? She quietly stepped closer to the doorway and tried to get a glimpse of who the voices belonged to. Unfortunately, they weren't within eyesight.

"We mustn't make any moves until we receive word. Lord Klodian will be replaced, but it must be at the appropriate time."

"What of the spy? I don't trust her. She isn't loyal by choice. You didn't hear me say this, but I think he made a mistake in sending her. He should have entrusted the task to someone else."

The weight of the sword was taking its toll on her, and Mina lowered it from her shoulder, trying to rest the tip on the floor. It scraped against the stones, and she winced.

"What was that?" the man asked.

Mina heard footsteps. She fled to the next room and slipped inside, hoping nobody was within. The room was empty, and she gently closed the door. She pressed her ear to the wood and listened intently.

"I don't see anyone," the woman said. "Still, we should probably continue this later."

There was more said, but it was muffled and Mina couldn't make out the words. She ground her teeth in frustration and waited until she no longer heard anything. Pulling the door open, she glanced out and saw the hall was clear. She hurried to her own room and locked the door, then placed the sword back on the wall.

She had so many concerns. Who were those people? And why were they plotting against Lord Klodian? Judging by their conversation, they were pawns to someone else, someone more powerful. They'd also mentioned a spy. She considered going to Lord Klodian immediately, but aside from what she'd overheard, she had nothing else to provide.

Mina frowned. She would have to figure out who those people were. It would also be helpful if she could find the spy. Although her new position had brought some attention to her, she'd spent years being ignored. Like the servants, she'd been privy to many secrets simply because people overlooked her. She was certain she could use that to her advantage, but she couldn't steal the dragon egg *and* uncover a coup.

She was going to need help. If Caden were still here, she could ask him. He'd been her only friend, and now that he was gone, she was alone again. She could ask one of the servants to watch the comings and goings of the noble's hall, but she didn't know if she could trust any of them. It had quickly become apparent that they were jealous of her new position, and if one of them could find a reason to sabotage her, she knew they would take the opportunity.

Mina paced her room. There had to be someone she could enlist, but who? Her mind continued to draw a blank, so she turned her thoughts to the egg. If no guards were watching over it, she could easily sneak it out of the castle and deliver it to Copper. However, if there were eyes on it, she'd have to have a backup plan.

If only there was a guard she could trust to help her get inside and avoid any trouble. Her face lit up. She knew just who to turn to.

6

It took less than a full day for Caden to realize that the Dracan Dominion operated much differently than the Thophate. Aside from the assassination he'd performed the night previous, it was also evident in the way the Runesmen were organized. Since there were so many of them, they were divided into groups commanded by captains. The captains reported to Angus, who in turn reported to Lord D'Lance.

"Which company will I be assigned to?" Caden asked as he followed Angus through the castle.

"That depends on how your conversation with Lord D'Lance goes. If it goes as well as I think it will, you'll report directly to me."

"I'm afraid I don't understand."

"You will," Angus replied.

They arrived at a circular room that was lined with wooden benches. The room was packed with people that had bored expressions on their faces.

"This is the Coterie. Anyone who wants an audience with Lord D'Lance must come here and wait. If he has the time to hear their cases, they are summoned into the Cathedra."

Caden glanced around the room, counting at least fifty people. "Lord D'Lance is going to see all these people today?"

"No. Depending on his other priorities, he might accept five of them."

As Angus approached the large double doors that led into the Cathedra, the crowd of people parted to allow him access. Two guards dressed in ceremonial armor and armed with halberds bowed their heads and hurried to open the doors. A few of the waiting people groaned, and Angus snapped a glare at them.

"Apologies, milord," one man said. "I've been here for the last three days waiting. I was told I'd be next."

"My business with Lord D'Lance will be quick," Angus said. "It shouldn't impact your meeting."

"Thank you, milord."

Angus nodded at Caden, and they walked through the doors and into a much larger chamber, though this one was rectangular in shape. A plush purple rug at least thirty feet in length covered the floor, and guards were lined up along the walls. The room was lavishly decorated, and Caden felt as if he was walking in the court of the High Prince rather than a Dominion Lord.

Angus stopped at the edge of the rug and clasped his hands behind his back. Caden wasn't sure of the protocol, and so he mirrored Angus's posture. At the other end of the room, an enormous throne sat atop a raised platform. Caden squinted to see Lord D'Lance, but the lighting was dim and he was hidden within the shadows.

Standing at the base of the platform was a woman. She was petitioning Lord D'Lance to send soldiers to find her son.

"He's been missing for a week, and it isn't like him. I fear something may have happened to him near the abandoned temple," she said.

A man Caden hadn't noticed before leaned close to the throne as if listening, then stood straight and spoke with a loud voice.

"My Lord D'Lance has taken note of your concern, and he will be sure to have some Runesmen investigate your son's disappearance. Please go in peace."

The woman bowed low, then turned and made her way to the doors. Caden saw her face as she passed. She looked exhausted, and there were dark bags under her eyes. Once she had left the Cathedra and the doors were closed, the man beside the throne beckoned.

"My Lord D'Lance welcomes his faithful servant Commander Morin and his guest."

"Don't speak until Lord D'Lance acknowledges you," Angus whispered.

"Yes, sir."

Caden stepped onto the rug and was amazed at how soft it was beneath his feet. Even with his boots on, it felt as if he was walking on the clouds. At the end of the rug, Angus knelt on one knee and bowed his head. Caden did the same, and he watched from the corner of his eye for the commander to rise. He remained bowed for a long moment, then lifted his head.

"Rise," the man said.

Caden stood, glancing from Angus to the throne. Despite being only a few feet away from it, the shadows still hid Lord D'Lance from view.

"How goes the task of finding the dissenter?"

It was the herald again. He was of average height, bald, and without facial hair. Caden took note of his face, which was thin and clearly hadn't seen the sun much.

"He has been found and eliminated," Angus replied.

"Who is your guest?"

"This is Caden Davtyan, a Runesman from the Thophate Dominion."

Silence settled over the group, and a new voice spoke, one that made Caden's skin crawl.

"Leave us."

The herald bowed and hurried off without another word. Lord D'Lance stood and stepped into the light. He looked nothing like Caden had imagined. He was tall and thin, with long black hair that flowed down past his shoulders. He wore purple robes trimmed in gold, and his facial features reminded Caden of a hawk. Pointed, pronounced, powerful.

"This is the Runesman you told me about, is it not?"

"Yes, my Lord. I sent him to deal with Terlamin last night."

"And he was successful?"

"Yes. I verified that it was his body myself."

Lord D'Lance turned his icy gaze on Caden, and it seemed as if the man had the uncanny ability to see straight into his soul, slicing through the layers of his being like a hot knife through wax.

"My commander tells me that your former Dominion Lord did not cut your rune before you left. Is this true?"

"Yes, my Lord," Caden answered.

"Tell me, Caden, what do you aspire to be? What are your wants? Your needs?"

The look in Lord D'Lance's eyes made Caden uncomfortable. There was something about the man that set off warnings in his mind, but other than his demeanor, there was nothing visible that justified the discomfort.

"I want fame and fortune."

"A man after my own heart." He smiled. "I assume that is why you've come to my Dominion. My arm stretches farther than any other … aside from the High Prince, of course. How do you seek to find these things?"

"I'm a Runesman, my Lord. I am willing to fight to earn it. Literally."

"I see why you brought him to me, commander. He is ambitious beyond his reach. And loyal, it seems. Commander Angus gave you a task your first day here, and you completed it. I need a man of your strength and character. There are many enemies on the prowl, and I fear I do not have enough people that I can trust to aid me. Can I trust you?"

"With your life, my Lord."

"Perhaps one day you will earn that privilege," Lord D'Lance said. "How would you like to serve me directly, Caden? Doing so will earn you the fame and fortune you seek."

"It would be my honor."

Lord D'Lance looked back at Angus. "He doesn't know what he's getting himself into, does he?"

The two shared a knowing smile, and Caden began to ponder that very question.

"I'm sure you've heard that war is brewing on the horizon. Lord Culver in the Toren Dominion has been breathing threats against the High Prince. Not openly, of course, but his words have reached my ears. It is my duty to protect the High Prince from all enemies. I have men gathering the evidence I need to remove him from his seat of power, but until then, my attention is upon other things."

Caden wasn't sure where Lord D'Lance was going with all of his words, but he suspected that it would involve him somehow.

"How well did you get to know Lord Klodian?"

"Not very well, my Lord," Caden replied.

"A pity. I have reason to believe he's involved with Lord Culver's plot against the High Prince. If someone could give me information that swayed me in one direction or another, it would be most helpful."

"I know that he's obsessed with hunting dragons, but that's about all I learned before I was transferred."

"Dragons, you say? Intriguing. I, too, have an interest in dragons, but it does not involve killing them. Some people are just barbarians."

Lord D'Lance stared at Caden for a moment.

"I have a task for you. Commander Angus will give you the details, but there is another enemy that has come to my attention. If you can successfully handle this task, you will have my full and unwavering trust."

"Consider it done, my Lord."

Lord D'Lance smiled. "We shall see."

7

"You're insane," Thais said.

"That makes two of us."

Thais glared at her, but Mina didn't shrink away.

"You want me to help you steal something from Lord Klodian, and you don't see a problem with that? Your promotion must have gone to your head."

"It is a risk, I'm not denying that, but it's for the greater good."

"How so?"

Copper hadn't sworn Mina to secrecy, but she doubted anyone would believe her tale of talking dragons. People considered them nothing more than mindless animals, and she knew the world wasn't ready to accept the truth.

"I can't say. You'll just have to trust me."

"You seem to forget who you're talking to. I don't trust anyone."

Mina knew it was going to be difficult to convince Thais to help her, but she had to try. There were no other options.

"I don't need you to physically take the thing, I just need a diversion. If the guards can be lured away somehow, I'll do the stealing."

"Like I said, you're insane."

"What if I told you there's a spy here from another Dominion?"

Thais's eyes narrowed. "What spy?"

"I overheard two people talking about it," Mina replied. "I didn't see who they were, but they were talking about overthrowing Lord Klodian."

"Keep your voice down," Thais warned, glancing around the barracks. "Talk like that will get you strung up on the gallows, no matter who you are."

"Sorry," Mina said lowly. "I need help. Now that Caden is gone, I have no one else to ask. I can't do this on my own."

Thais frowned, but she leaned in close. "I won't have to go anywhere near this thing you're stealing, right?"

"No."

"I'll help you on one condition. I want to know who these people are that were talking about getting rid of Lord Klodian."

"I told you I don't know who they are," Mina said.

"Would you recognize their voices?"

"I think so."

"Then your task should be easy. Wander around the castle and listen for their voices. When you find out who they are, tell me. Once that's done, I'll help you with your theft."

Mina wanted to argue that they might run out of time, but she couldn't without explaining how. Copper had threatened to bring a host of dragons upon Klodian Keep, but when she agreed to steal it for them, it had satisfied his anger. She hadn't given the dragon a firm timeline, but she feared that if it took her too long, Copper would rescind his end of the bargain.

"Fine," Mina agreed.

She left the barracks, planning to go find Copper and tell him that she was working on getting the egg for him. She felt like she was being stretched too thin. Between stealing the egg and figuring out who the traitors were, she had a full plate. Still, the prize at the end of it all was worth it. She would finally be free of the scale and could make a new life somewhere else.

A gust of wind stirred up the dust of the courtyard, and Mina turned her gaze toward the gates. Dark clouds were on the horizon, and they flickered with lightning.

"Great," she muttered.

If she was quick enough, she should be able to reach Copper and get back to the castle before the storm struck. Mina hurried to the stable and found Aram laying fresh hay in the stalls.

"I need to take Tempest," she said. "Can you saddle her for me?"

"I'm afraid not," Aram said. "There's a storm coming, and you don't want to be caught out there in it, believe me."

"It'll be quick," Mina protested. "I promise."

"I'm sorry, my Lady, but it's Lord Klodian's rule, given the recent disappearance of patrols. Unless you have written permission?"

She shook her head. "I don't."

"Then you'll have to wait until after the storm passes."

Mina stepped out of the stable and looked at the gates. She considered going on foot, but there was no way she would be able to reach the mesa before the storm hit, let alone get back safely. She returned to the castle, hoping that Copper didn't get impatient enough to bring an army of dragons.

Since Thais wouldn't help her until she found out who the traitors were, she decided to start with that task first. She'd overheard them in one of the rooms in the noble's hall, so it made sense to start there. Mina navigated her way through the maze of halls and reached her room. She paused at the door, listening for the sound of servants. If any of them were working in the hall, she didn't want them to see her sneaking around.

All was silent.

Mina moved along the hall, keeping her steps light. She went straight to the room she'd heard the two people conversing in. The door was closed. She turned the handle slowly and pushed the door open, peering inside. It appeared to be empty, so she stepped across the threshold and shut the door behind her.

The room was similar to her own chamber. An enormous bed covered by a sheer canopy was up against the wall. Side tables were on either side of it, and a long dresser that doubled as a desk rested opposite the bed. Mina walked to the dresser and began going through the drawers. They were full of expensive clothing, jewelry, and other useless trinkets.

Mina assumed that if this was their room, there should be something incriminating to be found. As she continued to search, however, she didn't find anything that gave her any clues. She knew it was possible that the two conspirators could simply have been using the room for their conversation, but she didn't think that was the case.

"Where would *I* hide something if I was a spy?" she asked aloud.

She spun in a circle, looking around the room. Nothing was out of the ordinary, but she knew there had to be something. The window rattled, startling her. She walked to it and looked out. The storm had already reached the castle. Even if she had taken the horse, she would have been caught in it. She silently thanked Aram for refusing her. With the disappearance of the patrols, people had begun to whisper that there was some sort of creature or spirit responsible.

Mina wasn't so sure of that, but she did find it curious that the patrols had vanished without a trace. Outside of the castle, the wind howled like a demon from the underworld. It was so loud that she didn't hear the door open.

"What are you doing in here?"

8

As Caden walked with Angus out of the throne room, he wondered if he was going to have to kill again. Captain Eduard's words echoed in his mind.

There's more to being a warrior than killing someone.

It was his duty to protect the Dominion Lord, true, but he felt more like an assassin than a soldier. Sneaking around and murdering people in the dark wasn't what he had in mind when he'd become a Runesman.

Yet if he wasn't willing to do it, someone else would. Someone else would gain the fame he sought for himself. Caden didn't like feeling dirty, but he supposed the path to what he desired would require him to get his hands bloody on occasion. Once they had left the Coterie behind, Angus filled him in.

"The enemy Lord D'Lance mentioned is extremely dangerous, but you won't be alone. We'll be transporting her to a place outside of the castle where she won't pose a threat to anyone."

"She, sir?"

"Yes. This enemy is a female."

Caden frowned. "We have to kill a woman, sir?"

"No, we won't be killing her. That's easier said than done, I'm afraid. We're just going to neutralize the threat."

Relief washed over him. He didn't know that he would have been able to carry out that task. Whether this woman was dangerous or not, he wasn't confident that his nerve wouldn't fail. Then he thought of Thais. He could harm her, but that's because it was personal. He didn't know this other woman.

"You'll be assisting Captain Burke and his Runesmen," Angus continued. "She'll be delivered to a makeshift prison and left there. If all goes well and you return alive, Lord D'Lance will be very pleased."

Caden's curiosity about the woman grew the more Angus talked about her. How could one person be so dangerous that it required an entire contingent of Runesmen to handle them?

"You seem distracted," Angus said.

"My apologies, sir. I'm trying to wrap my mind around the fact that one person can pose such a huge threat. I'm finding it difficult to believe."

"You'll learn why soon enough. Get yourself some food and go see Burke. He'll give you some new armor."

"What's wrong with my armor?" Caden asked.

"It's antiquated compared to what we have here. Keep it if you feel you must, but for this mission, you'll need to wear what Burke gives you."

"Yes, sir."

Angus left him, splitting off and turning down a different hall. Caden was glad that he could grab a meal before going back out on the road. His stomach felt empty, a reminder that he hadn't eaten dinner the night before. He got turned around while trying to get out of the castle and ended up roaming a corridor that seemed abandoned.

There were no tapestries adorning the walls, no rugs on the floor, and no guards. There were no people at all, which made the atmosphere eerily quiet. Caden had the feeling that something bad must have happened here. He was about to turn around when he heard something that caught his attention.

He stopped walking and listened. The sound was coming from somewhere further down the hall. Caden trod lightly, curiosity driving his steps. The closer he got, the more he was convinced that the sound was a muffled cry. He reached the door where the noise was coming from and pressed his ear against the wood.

It sounded like someone was in pain, but it was muffled as if they were gagged. Caden tried the handle. It was locked. Was someone being tortured? He supposed the room could be the dungeon. That would explain the lack of decorations and people, but if prisoners were being kept inside, there should at least be guards.

He tried the handle again, more forcefully this time, but it didn't budge. Whatever was going on behind the door didn't seem good. He felt that he needed to do something, but if he couldn't open the door, there wasn't much he could do.

"I need to tell Angus," Caden muttered.

Frowning, he backtracked his steps and eventually recognized his surroundings. He exited the castle and returned to the barracks. Angus wasn't in his office, so Caden made a mental note to ask him about the abandoned hall. Breakfast was being cooked on the first level, and the smell made his mouth water as he headed down the stairs.

A line of soldiers had formed near the kitchen, and Caden joined them. He overheard a few soldiers talking about the trouble brewing in Lord Culver's Dominion. Lord D'Lance had mentioned Lord Culver making threats against the High Prince, but if he wasn't making them openly, how did lowly soldiers know about it?

Caden received a tray packed with enough food for two meals. A glance at the other Runesmen around him revealed that they had been given the same treatment. Lord Klodian hadn't scrimped on food back in the Thophate, but Lord D'Lance took everything to the next level. Caden took his tray upstairs and sat on his bed, eating by himself and thinking about what the rest of the day held.

Once he was finished, he returned the tray to the kitchen. Since he didn't know what Captain Burke looked like, he picked someone at random and approached them.

"Excuse me, but I'm looking for Captain Burke. Can you point him out to me?"

"You'll know Captain Burke when you see him," the man replied with a grin. "He's probably the shortest one around here. He's got a bushy red beard, too."

"Are you talking about me behind my back?" The voice was deep.

Caden turned to the newcomer and had to hide his surprise. Captain Burke barely reached five feet in height. His shoulders were wide and his stocky frame was thick with corded muscle. He walked with a confident bearing and stalked over to them.

"No, sir," the soldier said. "I'd never speak about you behind your back, only above your head."

Captain Burke burst out in roaring laughter.

"You're hilarious, Halber. I think your joke just earned you kitchen duty tonight."

"I'm sorry, sir. I didn't mean to upset you."

"Oh, you didn't upset me. You just haven't learned your place here yet. It's my job to rectify that." Burke turned his gaze on Caden. "Were you in on the short jokes, as well?"

"No, sir. Commander Morin told me to find you. He said I'll be working with you to escort an enemy somewhere."

Burke grinned and stroked his beard, eyeing Caden up and down.

"I'm always glad to have help," he said. "Are you a Runesman?"

"Yes. I just transferred from the Thophate."

"Good! That means I don't have to train you. Judging by the looks of you, I'm guessing you have a strength rune?"

Caden nodded, impressed.

"Even better," Burke said. "We've lost a lot of strength Runesmen recently, so I'm glad to have you. You'll need different armor if you expect to come along, though. What you're wearing isn't going to hold up if things go south."

"What do you mean?" Caden asked.

"Did the commander tell you what we're escorting?"

"He told me we were escorting a woman. A dangerous one."

"Aye, but dangerous isn't the half of it. She's a wily one, and she don't take kindly to our kind."

Caden's face scrunched with his confusion. "I don't understand."

Captain Burke shook his head. "The commander didn't tell you, I take it?"

"Tell me what?"

"The prisoner is a dragon."

9

MINA WHIRLED AROUND, HER HEART dropping into her stomach, but relief washed over her when she saw it was Kera.

"I was looking for … them," Mina said.

"Who?"

"The lord and lady who reside here."

Kera folded her arms and stared at Mina. "What for?"

"That's not your concern," Mina replied.

"Spoken like one of the nobles. If you were really looking for them, you'd know they are with Lord Klodian right now. So, do you want to tell me what you are doing in here, or should I let Lord Klodian know you're riffling through his court member's personal effects?"

Mina decided to bluff.

"Lord Klodian already knows what I'm doing. He sent me here."

Kera's suspicious demeanor faltered. "He did?"

Mina nodded.

"Why didn't you just say that?"

"I was told to keep quiet about it. Court politics."

Kera rolled her eyes and dropped her hands to her sides. "It's always something around here. One would think that being out here so far from the bigger Dominions that all that political nonsense wouldn't be an issue."

"It's worse than you know," Mina said. "But you didn't hear that from me."

"I'm sorry that you have to be involved in their games now. Freedom isn't really freedom, is it?"

Mina shrugged. "Most of my life has been this way, so it's not much of a change for me. I don't think I need to mention that you didn't see me in here and we never had this conversation."

"Of course not, my Lady. I'll just leave you to it, then."

"I do have a question. Whose room is this?" Mina's face flushed and she knew she was pressing the boundaries. "I wasn't told which room specifically to check, so I may not even be in the right place."

"I'm not surprised that no one gave you any sort of direction. The nobles like to assume we know everything even though they keep us in the dark. This is Lord and Lady Burgess's chamber."

"Then I am in the right room." Mina smiled, but inside she was a nervous mess.

"Anything else?"

"No, thank you."

Kera offered a nod and left the room. Mina rubbed her hands over her face, sighing in relief. That had almost gone disastrously wrong. She continued searching the room, but there was nothing she could find that proved the two she'd heard talking were planning to overthrow Lord Klodian. She suspected they were working for someone, which meant there had to be a letter or something incriminating. Mina checked the same drawers again but turned up nothing.

Despite that, she had learned who they were. And since she had a name, that meant Thais would help her with the egg. The wind rattled the windows again, interrupting her thoughts, and Mina knew she would have to wait for the storm to pass to speak with Thais. She made sure to put everything back the way she'd found it and hurried to her own chambers, flopping onto her bed.

The day was still young, so Mina decided that once the storm was gone, she would speak with Thais and then ride out to let Copper know of her progress. She hoped that if she kept him apprised of things, he would keep his word. Then again, she didn't know that the dragon would honor what he said at all. He was a dragon, and she had a lot of trouble trusting him, but she didn't have much choice. He was her best chance of removing the scale from her leg, so she *had* to trust him.

That was the last thing she remembered before she awoke. Mina sat up and looked to the window. The storm was gone, and the sun shone brightly through the glass. She found it odd that she'd fallen asleep because she hadn't even been tired, but perhaps the stress of everything had taken its toll on her.

Mina slid off the bed and left her room, leaving Vhan's sword behind. She went to the barracks and found Thais and several other Runesmen sweeping dirt from the floor. Thais looked at her quizzically.

"I found out who those people are," Mina said.

"That was quick," Thais replied.

"Well, it was pure luck. I went snooping around in their room and one of the servants walked in on me. Anyway, she told me that they are Lord and Lady Burgess."

"Burgess?" Thais frowned. "I've never heard that name before."

"That makes sense. Considering what they are plotting, I doubt they would use their real names. Burgess is probably a fake surname."

"If that's true, then we're still at the beginning. Find out more about them."

"No," Mina said. "You told me to get you a name. I did that. Now it's your turn to help me. Besides, I didn't find anything in their room that seemed suspicious."

"Did you look for false drawers or hidden compartments?"

"No, why would I?"

"These people are spies," Thais replied. "They aren't going to leave things out in the open."

"How would I know that? I don't unravel nefarious plots every day. In case you forgot, the most I've done until recently is clean things and lead Lord Klodian to dragons. You said you would help me, so unless you're going back on what you said, I need you to meet me tonight."

"*Tonight?*" Thais asked incredulously.

"Time is slipping away, and the danger grows with every hour that passes."

Thais looked around the barracks. "Fine. Where should I meet you?"

"Outside around midnight. The servants will be asleep by then, and I can sneak you into the castle without anyone noticing."

"Do you have a plan?"

"Yes. You'll cause a distraction, and I'll steal the e—item," Mina said, correcting herself at the last moment.

"How is that a plan? What kind of distraction am I creating?"

Mina shrugged. "Figure it out. I'm doing all the risky work."

"I don't like your attitude. I've got half a mind to wash my hands of all this."

"It's your duty to protect Lord Klodian and the Dominion. If you don't help me, you'll be shirking that duty."

"If we're in as much danger as you say, why don't you tell Lord Klodian? Wouldn't that simplify things?"

Mina wanted to tell Thais everything, but she didn't trust the woman. Not yet, anyway. Once this was all over with, maybe she would let her guard down a little.

"Lord Klodian doesn't need to be involved unless we fail. And by then, it'll be too late anyway."

"Do you know how to answer a question without being cryptic?" Thais asked.

"Yes, but as I said before, I can't tell you anything. If we manage to pull this off, then I'll reveal everything. Until then, you just need to do as I ask."

Thais chuckled. "You're an odd one, you know that? I'm still going to help you, but only because I'm curious. I don't believe we're in any danger, but if that's what drives you, so be it. Now get out of here before I get in trouble for not cleaning. I'll see you tonight."

Mina left the barracks and headed for the stable. It was time to go see Copper.

10

"A DRAGON?"

Caden didn't think he heard the captain correctly.

"Aye, a dragon. You ever seen one up close?"

"No, thank the gods. My previous lord liked to hunt them for fun, but I'd rather avoid them."

"You can stay behind if you want," Burke said. "But I wouldn't suggest it."

Caden knew that if he didn't go, his chance of earning Lord D'Lance's trust would be gone. He was afraid of dragons, but who wasn't? Burke didn't seem to be. Caden knew he would have to push through the fear, but he wasn't sure how.

"I'm going," he said.

"Good. First things first. We need to get you some armor."

"That's what Commander Morin told me."

"You'd be dead within seconds if a dragon flamed you, but we've got something that'll stand up to dragon fire. Come on, we'll get you fitted."

Caden followed Burke through the barracks, ending up in front of a steel door with several locks. Burke pulled a small ring of keys from his belt and methodically unlocked each one, but he didn't go in any specific order.

"This is the armory," Burke said. "Only those with the rank of captain or higher can get in, so if you need anything, you come to me."

Burke pushed the door open, motioning for Caden to go first. Caden stepped through the doorway and immediately noticed the large rectangular window that filled the space with plenty of natural light. A dozen or more racks of finely crafted swords were lined in orderly rows, and shelving units held breastplates, helms, and boots. One entire wall was covered with chainmail shirts that hung on hooks. Caden stared at them longingly.

"Those don't offer much protection against dragons," Burke grunted. "You'll be wearing full plate armor."

"I've never worn plate armor," Caden admitted. "Is it heavy?"

"Yes. It's also hard to maneuver in, but you won't have to worry about that. The dragon won't be walking around freely. The armor is just in case she escapes."

Caden didn't find much comfort in the man's words. His job as a soldier was to fight humans, not dragons. If the dragon escaped, he doubted any of them would live to tell the tale.

"What's so special about the armor?" Caden asked.

Burke grinned. "It's one of a kind. It'll protect you from dragon fire so long as you're wearing it properly."

"How? Doesn't dragon fire melt metal?"

"Aye, but this metal is different. It withstands high heat, acting as a buffer between you and the fire. A dragon could stand directly in front of you and blast away with its fiery breath, and you'll only feel a little warmth."

Caden stared at the armor dubiously until he remembered a conversation with Thais. She'd proposed a wild theory about someone using metal from some sort of creature that lived in volcanos. Was it possible that Lord D'Lance had actually pulled it off?

"You've seen it work?" Caden asked.

"I've got first-hand experience," Burke replied. "Find a breastplate that fits you snugly. You don't want any gaps at all."

Caden stepped over to the tall shelf and grabbed one that he thought would fit him, but when he slid it over his head, it was too big. He struggled for a moment to remove it, then set it back on the shelf and selected another. It fit perfectly.

"We've got a few helm styles. Pick the one you like best and grab a pair of boots."

"What about my arms and legs?" Caden asked.

"There are a few different bits that will piece together. Trust me, once you're fully suited up, there won't be an inch of you visible. Our blacksmiths have removed every possible flaw from the design."

"Sounds like the perfect armor."

"Lord D'Lance wouldn't accept anything less," Burke said. "We lose enough Runesmen as it is, so he spares no expense when it comes to protecting his soldiers."

"I appreciate that," Caden replied.

Burke turned and whistled, then waved someone over. Another man joined them in the armory.

"This is Kennet. He'll help you get the rest of the armor on because it's nigh impossible to do it on your own. Once you're done, meet me in the courtyard. We're leaving as soon as you're ready."

"Where are we going?" Caden asked.

"To escort the prisoner. Lock the doors when you're done," Burke said to Kennet, then marched off.

"I'm Caden. Thanks for helping me."

"It's no problem at all. Captain Burke isn't messing around when he says it's impossible to put this armor on alone."

"Are you a captain as well? He said only captains and above have access to the armory."

"I'm in training, so it's not official yet, but I do everything a captain does. I'll be taking over Captain Tayfur's position once Commander Morin signs off on me."

"Is Captain Tayfur retiring?" Caden asked.

"No. He was killed last week."

"Oh, gods. I'm sorry."

"Don't be," Kennet said. "He fell in battle during a border skirmish with Lord Culver's men. Culver's been slowly encroaching on Lord Veisi's Dominion for years, but it's become more aggressive recently. The commander has been sending a steady stream of Runesmen to Veisi's Dominion to deter any further action from Culver, but it hasn't seemed to make an impact."

"Sounds like a war is brewing."

"I don't know about that, but Lord D'Lance will have to do something before the High Prince learns about what's transpiring. The last thing anyone wants is for the High Prince to march his armies across Dominion lines. He'll let them ravage everything just to show his strength."

The more Caden learned about the politics of the Dominions, the less he wanted to know. He wanted wealth and fame, but he didn't want to be involved in the political sphere of things. That would only complicate his life, and he preferred things to be simple. His mind roamed as Kennet began strapping on pieces of armor to his arms.

By the time Kennet had finished, Caden felt as if his weight had doubled. The armor was considerably heavy, and even his boots had heft to them. Walking became so difficult it was a chore.

"Gods, how does anyone fight in this stuff? I can barely move."

"It's more for protection against dragon fire," Kennet said. "For battle, you'll probably wear chainmail. Since you're going with Captain Burke, you shouldn't have much to worry about. He's a competent man. It's pretty much assumed he's in line to become commander once Angus retires."

"Or dies?" Caden asked. It seemed to him lots of people died in this Dominion.

"I don't think Angus can be killed," Kennet said with a laugh. "That man has lived longer than most and seen more battle than anyone I know. Death herself will have to personally take him from this world. Let me tighten the strap on this vambrace, then you're all set."

Caden felt pressure around his left arm as Kennet pulled on the strap. Between the weight and the tightness of everything, he felt like he was being constricted to death.

"My suggestion is to leave the helm off until you get outside the walls. It traps in all your body heat, so I try to delay it as long as possible."

"Thanks," Caden said, gripping the helm with his right hand.

"You better hurry. Captain Burke isn't known for his patience."

Caden left the armory and exited the barracks, walking as quickly as he could manage. Halfway to where Captain Burke was waiting, he realized he'd forgotten to bring his sword. He dared not turn back and keep the captain waiting, so he continued around to the front of the castle.

"I forgot to grab my sword," Caden said as he approached Burke. "Do you want me to go back and get it?"

"No, we're already running behind schedule. I doubt we'll encounter any trouble. We're just taking this blasted creature to a new location and leaving her there to rot. The cage should hold her, but just in case, you may want to keep a wide berth of it."

Caden looked to where Burke indicated and swallowed hard. The cage was enormous, standing ten feet in height and at least twice that in length, not including the wheeled platform it was built upon.

"You ready for this?"

"As ready as I'll ever be," Caden answered.

"Good answer. Let's move out!"

11

Mina rode Tempest out into the desert, marveling at how the landscape had been changed by the storm. Typically, the dunes had flowing lines that made it seem as if they were rippling, but the wind had laid the sand down smooth and flat. She silently thanked Avera that Aram hadn't allowed her to leave earlier. The storm had struck quicker than she'd expected.

The scale in her leg alerted her to Copper's presence. He was on the same mesa that he'd been on the other day where she'd finally encountered him. Mina was dreading the climb to the top and was surprised when the dragon's voice resonated inside her mind.

Come to the base and I will bring you up.

How will you do that?

With my mighty wings. You humans are not very intelligent, are you?

We're smart enough to kill your kind, Mina fired back.

Copper's indignant snort gave her a bit of satisfaction. So, dragons had feelings and emotions about hurtful words just as humans did. That was interesting. She reigned the horse to a stop when she reached the mesa's looming walls.

Leave your horse and walk one hundred paces from it.

Why? Mina grew suspicious, wondering if the dragon intended on killing her.

Although, if you prefer, I can frighten your mount away, but then you'd have to walk back to your castle.

Mina hadn't considered that. She dismounted and patted the horse on its neck. Tempest nudged her, and she fished an apple from the saddlebag and offered it to the animal. It took a bite and chomped loudly, then finished off what remained.

"Did you even taste that?" Mina asked, shaking her head. "Stay here and wait for me. I'll be back shortly."

She counted her steps as she walked away from the horse, following the mesa wall. When she reached one hundred exactly, she stopped and looked up. A shadow fell over her as Copper leaped off the top of the mesa, his wings outstretched. He spiraled around in circles, descending slowly. Despite her hatred for dragons, Mina found herself admiring the majestic beauty of Copper.

Sand billowed into the air in small clouds as the massive dragon's wings flapped to stop his descent. He landed a few feet away and Mina stared in silence.

Are you going to gawk all day?

Sorry.

Mina tentatively walked toward Copper, but she didn't feel terrified of him.

The other day, I was frozen with fear, but I don't feel afraid now.

That's because I'm not projecting my pheromones.

What do you mean?

The dragon watched her intently as she approached. His slitted pupils remained fixed on her, unblinking.

We dragons can project a chemical into the air that lets other dragons know we're present. The fear you experience is a side effect. I think it's because humans don't know how to handle the pheromone.

Mina stopped in front of Copper, her eyes roaming over his scales. Here and there she spotted imperfections, knicks and scratches mostly, but a few scales were damaged and missing pieces entirely. His underbelly was the same color as the rest of his scales, and his claws were enormous. Talons as sharp as swords dug into the ground.

Why do you look at me so? Copper asked.

I've never seen a dragon up close before, Mina replied.

You saw me up close not long ago.

That was different.

She realized for the first time that the scale embedded in her leg didn't pain her. In the past, she'd have flaring pain that would cripple her anytime she got close to a dragon. Yet now, standing directly in front of one, she didn't feel that pain at all. And it had been the same the other two times she encountered him.

Are you ready?

Mina swallowed hard and nodded. *Should I climb on your back?*

Copper made a chortling sound that reminded her of laughter, and the scent of roses filled her nostrils. There were many things that she didn't understand about dragons, and she wondered how many of their secrets Copper would divulge to her.

Absolutely not. I'm going to grab you with my claws. Stretch your arms out. And don't squirm, else your flesh will slice off.

The dragon flapped his wings and rose into the air, then moved forward and extended his claws toward her. Before she could rethink her decision, Copper's front claws wrapped around her arms and he lifted her off the ground.

Mina clenched her jaw, fighting her instinct to scream. She watched the ground fade below her as the dragon rose higher and higher, the wind from his wings whipping at her hair and clothing. The top of the mesa became visible, and he set her down, then flew higher into the sky before streaking back down. He spread out his wings at the last moment, his upper body jerking upward while his rear legs touched the ground. She could hardly believe that a dragon could be so agile.

Can all dragons fly?

Yes. Can all humans walk?

Yes, Mina replied. *Well, most can.*

Most?

Some of us are born broken and cannot do certain things.

The same is true of dragons, Copper said. *But if a dragon cannot fly, it will not live long.*

Why not?

If the mother does not kill a hatchling before it leaves the nest, it will be prey for many creatures until it grows larger. Flying gives us the advantage of avoiding predators, and therefore killing a flightless dragon is a mercy.

What kind of animal hunts dragons?

Besides humans? Many things when we are small. Sand wyrms, mostly.

Mina's curiosity was piqued. *What's a sand wyrm?*

You have never seen one?

I don't think so.

You would know if you had. They do not come close to the places humans inhabit. They are found out here among the mesas sometimes. The further into the desert you travel, the more likely you will encounter them.

Mina didn't plan on going deep into the desert, so she hoped she had nothing to worry about. Copper tilted his head to the side.

How goes the hunt for the egg?

That's why I came out here, Mina said. *I am going to try to take it tonight. I'll have help, so I should be able to deliver it to you tomorrow.*

That is good news. I hope that the egg is not damaged.

How long does it take for one to hatch? Lord Klodian has had the egg for a long time, but the egg remains unchanged.

Copper made a humming sound, and Mina smelled the faint hint of lavender. She didn't know why she smelled the aromas, but she had her suspicions that it had something to do with dragons.

Dragons can wait for years to hatch. The circumstances must be right, and the dragon will know whether it is safe to come out of its shell.

How many dragons are there?

Too many to count, Copper replied.

Do you get along with the other colors of dragons?

Many of them, yes.

How many colors are there?

Ten.

I've only seen five.

The metallic colors, I assume? We prefer the solitude of the sand and heat. Our brethren, those whose colors are chromatic, do not.

Mina remembered the black dragon she'd seen on her trip with Lord Klodian when he'd taken her to test the scale's ability to sense magic.

Actually, I've seen six colors. One was black, but I saw him in the desert.

Truly? Copper's nostrils flared and his tail swished behind him. *I have not seen one of our brethren in many years.*

Why not? Mina asked.

They are the ones we do not get along with.

Care to explain?

It is a long story.

I've got some time.

Copper eyed her in silence for a moment.

Very well. The tale begins a thousand years ago ...

12

IT WAS LATE IN THE evening when Captain Burke called a halt.

Caden pulled his helm off and breathed in deeply of the cool air. His entire body was drenched in sweat, and he couldn't wait to take the heavy armor off. Including himself, there were just over two dozen Runesmen. The massive wheeled cage that carried the dragon was pulled by ten Clydesdales, giant beasts that made normal horses seem minuscule in comparison.

The cage was really a boxcar, crafted of the same metal as their armor. There was a single door on one end that was reinforced with steel and covered with padlocks. Caden didn't know a lot about dragons, but he had the feeling that if the creature really wanted to get free, the meager defenses of the boxcar wouldn't be able to contain it.

"Gather round!" Burke shouted.

Everyone crowded in around the captain, forming a chaotic circle.

"We'll set up camp here. There's a hill not much further ahead where we'll be leaving her, but we'll need daylight, so we don't get the cage stuck on anything. I want two men on watch at each corner of the camp. If anyone on watch is caught sleeping, you'll answer to Commander Morin. Any questions?"

No one spoke.

"Good. Sabir and Lorn, you've got the east corner. Erik and Quinn, west corner. Dirk and Finnis, south corner. Asa and Boris, you're on the north corner. After two hours, wake someone to replace you. It should be a quiet night, but if you see anything, alert the camp. The dragon has been sedated and should be knocked out until after we're long gone, but keep away from the cage regardless."

The soldiers who had not been called for watch began retrieving bedrolls from the wagon that had followed behind the boxcar. None of them removed their armor, though, and they laid down with only their helms removed. Caden grabbed a bedroll for himself and looked for a place to rest. Most of his fellow soldiers had scattered out, but a few had grouped together.

He picked a spot near the wagon and rolled the bedroll out, but it did little to provide any comfort. The breastplate jabbed into his lower back, causing lances of pain to shoot through him with even the smallest movement. He forced himself into a sitting position and glanced around.

The camp was at the edge of a wooded area, and the landscape was mostly flat. Caden got up and carried his bedroll over to the tree line and placed the bedroll against one of the trees, then sat down and leaned back against it. While it still wasn't comfortable, it was better than lying flat on the ground.

His body ached from exhaustion, but he had difficulty falling asleep. The night sky above reminded him of the last time he'd seen Mina, and his thoughts grew dark. He'd spent a night in the dungeon and been forced to another Dominion because of Thais's actions. He had believed that she had feelings for him, but perhaps that was how she'd deceived him into letting his guard down. Eventually, his eyes grew heavy and he dozed off.

A scream startled him into wakefulness.

He clambered to his feet confusedly, rubbing his bleary eyes. It was still dark. The clash of steel echoed across the camp, and Caden realized they were under attack. He put his helm on and ran to the wagon, ducking behind it when he spotted two people outfitted in black armor. Emblazoned on their pauldrons was a clawed paw print surrounded by a blazing sun.

"Fall back!" It was Captain Burke. "To me, Runesmen! To me!"

Caden peered around the wagon and saw the captain was at the front of the boxcar. A handful of Runesmen was already with him, but everyone else was engaged with their attackers. He rushed to where Burke was and struggled to stop his momentum.

"What's going on?" he asked.

"Isn't it obvious? We're under attack."

"Yes, but by who? And why?"

"They're wearing the crest of Lord Culver," Burke answered. "The fool has gone too far this time. Lord D'Lance will have his head."

"Only if he finds out," Caden replied.

"What's that supposed to mean?"

Caden pointed ahead, and Burke turned his gaze to the direction he was pointing. A host of men in black armor bearing the same red crest of Lord Culver came rushing down the hill.

"Here," Burke said, handing a sword to Caden. "I trust you know how to use one?"

"I do."

"Good. If they release the dragon, we're dead for certain. We need to keep them from letting her out."

Caden gripped the hilt tightly and nodded. Despite the gravity of the situation, he couldn't help but consider how this would elevate him even further with Lord D'Lance should he survive. Excitement and fear flooded his senses in a confusing mix, just as it always did before a battle.

He lowered the sword and waited until one of the approaching men was close enough, then he stepped forward and swung his sword in an upward sweeping motion. The blade screeched against his opponent's breastplate and hit his helm, bouncing off and sending powerful reverberations through Caden's arm.

"We're outnumbered, but we won't go down without a fight!" Burke screamed.

The words bolstered Caden's spirit, and he pushed ahead, latching onto his opponent's arm and wheeling him around. He kicked the man in the chest, knocking him backward into the door of the boxcar. The force made the padlocks knock repeatedly against the metal frame, and Caden likened the sound to the clash of arms.

He spun back to face another enemy and saw one of his fellows get cut down. The man wasn't wearing his helm, and his head split open as a dark armored figure struck him from the side. Caden couldn't believe how many enemies there were. It seemed as if their ranks swarmed endlessly down the hill, decimating Burke's entire company of Runesmen.

"Things aren't looking too good!" He yelled at Burke.

The captain didn't reply, he just kept fighting, cleaving through the horde of shadowy men. Something bright flared ahead, illuminating the darkness. Caden turned his attention to the light and his eyes widened. The silhouette of a robed man was at the top of the hill, and a ball of flame swirled in front of him. The figure flicked his wrist and the flames soared down the hill, striking the wagon next to the cage.

"Forbidden magic," he whispered.

If things had looked bleak moments ago, they were doubly so now. Caden had never run from a fight before, but he'd only been in a few insignificant battles. If he stayed and fought, he was as good as dead. He backed up a few steps, every instinct telling him to turn and flee. But he didn't. For some unfathomable reason, he just stood there watching. Burke was struck down, and the remaining Runesmen fell quickly after him.

Run! He screamed within his mind, but his legs wouldn't obey him.

Caden watched the enemies turn from the corpses of his fellows and trudge back up the hill. They disregarded him as if he weren't even there, as though his presence was so insignificant, they didn't need to worry about him. The truth quickly became apparent, though, as the robed figure crafted another ball of flame and sent it hurtling through the air.

Caden's legs finally moved, and he stepped back and was about to turn around when the fiery globe struck the boxcar's door. There was a loud explosion and something hard and heavy struck the back of his head. He crumpled to the ground and fell into an ocean of darkness.

13

Mina sat on the ground with her legs crossed, staring up at Copper as he related the events of the past. His words swirled around her, creating images within her mind as if she had been there herself.

In those days, the relationship between humans and dragons was much different than it is today. We were allies, friends even. Dragon and man were bonded closely, sharing their minds.

Truly? Mina asked.

Indeed.

I've never heard that before. Until I met you, I always thought dragons were mindless animals.

There's a good reason for that.

Which is?

Copper growled, a rumbling sound that resonated from deep in his chest. Mina felt the ground tremble beneath her.

There are some things better left forgotten, he said. *And yet, there is a reason we met that day inside the mesa.*

What do you mean?

I am hesitant to reveal too much, but I feel that I must tell you things that you may not be ready to hear.

Mina's face creased. *If you think that I am weak, I'm not. I can handle anything you have to say.*

I do not think you are weak. If I did, I would not have let you find me. You'd still be wandering in the desert. No, girl, you are strong. Stronger than you know.

Mina caught the scent of lemon and clove.

Then tell me.

What you are about to learn must be kept a secret. You cannot share it with anyone. Give me your oath.

I promise I will keep the knowledge to myself, Mina said.

Good. Long ago, when our two kinds were friendly, division arose when a king among the humans named Maël decided to invade other lands. He tried to use us in his plot. The elders among the dragons refused, and a feud began.

Mina knew from her experience around Lord Klodian and the other nobles that they were always vying for supremacy over one another. It was almost as though it was human nature to want more for the sake of having it.

Did dragons and humans go to war?

Almost, Copper replied. *My kind was able to avert such a catastrophe.*

How?

We used magic.

Dragons can use magic?

Yes. We were formed of magic at the beginning of time, and so we can use it. The greatest and strongest of every color gathered and sacrificed themselves to power a spell so potent, that it is still in place today.

What was the spell?

I do not know the name of it, but it caused all of humankind to forget that dragons were allies. That was all it was supposed to do, but it also caused humans to forget that we were intelligent creatures.

What about me? Mina asked. *How is it that I haven't forgotten that you can speak?*

Once a human learns the truth, the spell no longer has sway over them.

Mina considered Copper's tale. She found it difficult to believe that dragons and humans were once friends. The unintended effect of the spell did answer a lot of questions, but it also left many more.

You are confused about something. What is it?

I don't understand why the dragons wanted us to forget about our alliance.

We didn't want to be used as weapons. We are much more than that.

You say 'we.'

Yes.

Why?

There was a pause, and Copper exhaled a long breath through his nostrils.

I was there when it happened.

Mina's eyes widened. *How is that possible? That would make you ...*

Over a thousand years old.

I was going to say ancient.

Mina giggled, but Copper growled in annoyance.

I have lived a long life and seen many things, but I have never seen a human with a dragon scale in their flesh. I have thought long and hard about how it might be removed, but I fear I have not come up with an answer. Perhaps my brethren will find the solution.

Were you friends with any humans back then?

I was. One of my closest friends was a human.

What happened to him?

He died fighting against tyranny. When Maël began his invasion, he slaughtered innocent people. Those dragons and humans that were bonded fought against him. That was what led to the division between dragon colors as well. The chromatic dragons sided with Maël, claiming that he was just in expanding our kingdom.

Copper snorted.

There is no justice in murder, only darkness and evil. After the spell was cast, the chromatic dragons ceased to speak with us and disappeared. The rest of my brethren and I came to the desert to try and forget the past. Until Lord Klodian began hunting us down, we had found peace and solitude.

Mina didn't know what to say, so she remained quiet. Dragons and humans had once been friends. The thought still boggled her mind. She had despised dragons for most of her life. The idea that one could be her friend seemed so … foreign. Blasphemous, even.

You were bonded to your human friend, weren't you?

Yes. We shared our thoughts and desires with one another. We were a team with no rivals. We fought together until the day he fell.

What was his name?

Lucius. Copper blinked, and Mina swore she saw his eyes water. *It has been many years since I have spoken his name.*

I'm sorry, Mina said.

The emotion behind Copper's words was so strong, it was as if it were a palpable thing that she could touch. She didn't know why she apologized to the dragon. Perhaps it was the feeling of sadness he instilled in her. Or perhaps it was the feeling of losing someone close that resonated with her. She'd lost her parents, her friends, and her entire life when she'd fallen into that dragon's nest years ago.

Dusk is approaching. You should go. The desert is not a safe place during the night.

Your concern is touching, but I can take care of myself.

That remains to be seen, but I don't doubt your confidence. I must meet with my brethren regardless, so I cannot stay with you.

It's fine. I need to get back to the castle so that I can try and get the egg. With any luck, I'll have it for you tomorrow.

Copper extended his wings and stretched.

I hope you are successful, but if you are not, you are welcome to return empty-handed. I promise not to flame you into ash.

I appreciate that, Mina replied with a smirk.

Come, I will take you to the bottom of the mesa.

Just try not to rip my arms out of their sockets, will you?

I make no guarantees.

Mina stood and brushed the back of her pants off, then lifted her arms. Copper flapped his wings, ascending into the air a few feet above her. His claws encircled her arms and he carried her off the mesa. Mina's stomach dropped, but she found the quick flight exhilarating. Once she was safely on the ground again, she pulled her hair from her face and looked up at the dragon.

Good luck, Copper said.

Thank you. I'll need every bit, I think.

They sat in silence until Mina felt it was awkward. She cleared her throat.

I'll see you tomorrow, then.

Farewell, Mina.

Copper launched himself into the sky, gaining altitude before turning to the south and disappearing over the top of the mesa. Mina returned to Tempest. The horse was stomping the ground impatiently.

"I'm sorry," she said. "I didn't intend to take so long. Here." She reached into the bag on the saddle and pulled out an apple and offered it to the animal. Tempest nickered softly and ate it, licking her hand in the process.

"Yuck." She wiped her hand on her pant leg and climbed into the saddle, then turned Tempest around and urged the horse onward. As she rode, she thought about Copper's story. If he could help her find a way to remove the scale, then perhaps she would change her mind about dragons.

Perhaps she just might befriend one.

14

WHEN CADEN CAME TO, HE did so with stars bursting across his vision and the worst headache he'd ever experienced. Dawn was cresting on the horizon, and he wondered how long he'd been unconscious.

He was lying face-down on the ground, his left cheek pressed against the dirt. A few rocks were jabbing into his skin, and he could tell his mouth had been open for a while based on the dryness. As he struggled to get up, pain flared across the back of his head and neck.

"Gods," he gasped.

Caden got on his feet and looked at his surroundings. Bodies littered the area, a mix of both friend and foe. The horses that had been attached to the wagon and boxcar were gone. His immediate thought was to search for survivors, but first, he needed water. He walked unsteadily to the remains of the wagon and sifted through the debris until he found a canteen.

Popping the lid off, he drank ravenously. The cool liquid satisfied his parched mouth and throat, but his headache persisted. Caden leaned against the boxcar and waited for his vision to become fully clear, then set about searching the destroyed camp. Their enemy had struck hard and fast, but they hadn't pilfered any of their supplies.

That told Caden that their intent had been solely to kill. He drank some more water and trudged up the hill. There were more bodies at the top, but they were all Lord D'Lance's men. A few hundred feet ahead, an old stone building jutted up from the landscape. It was abandoned, and judging by the overgrowth, nature was doing its best to reclaim the space for itself.

He assumed that's where they were going to leave the dragon, but it didn't make any sense. Nothing did at this point. Caden stared at the structure in silence, trying to piece things together. Movement in the trees caused his heart to leap in his chest. Had the enemy returned to finish him off?

A horse stepped into view, whinnying softly. The leather straps that had bound the creature to the boxcar were present and dangled loosely at its sides.

"A small blessing," Caden whispered.

Lord D'Lance needed to know what had happened here. Another group of men would need to secure the boxcar and get the dragon to her prison. Caden approached the horse and grabbed onto one of the leather straps, then guided the horse down the hill. Oddly, he found it more difficult going down the hill than it had been to go up it.

He looked at the boxcar and paused. The door was lying on the ground, and the interior was empty. The dragon had escaped. Caden hurried as fast as he could the rest of the way down and tied the horse to the tandem pole that was still attached to the boxcar. He realized the door must have been blown off by the ball of flame that had struck it. That was probably what had hit him and knocked him unconscious.

It seemed suspicious to him that their enemies had known they would be here. Had they known they were transporting a dragon? And if so, had they taken it back to Lord Culver's Dominion? The latter thought seemed unlikely. They would've taken the boxcar. There were too many questions, and they only aggravated his headache.

A groan drew his attention and he moved toward the sound. Partially covered by the door of the boxcar was Captain Burke. Caden pulled the metal sheet off the man and looked him over. The captain was wounded. While his injuries didn't appear to be fatal, he wasn't going to be able to walk on his own. Caden knelt beside him.

"Sir? Can you hear me?"

Burke nodded slightly, flinching in pain.

"I found one of the horses, and I'm going to put you on it. It's probably going to hurt."

"Just get it over with," Burke hissed.

"Yes, sir."

Caden slid one arm under Burke's neck and lifted him into a sitting position. Burke's jaw was firmly clenched, and Caden hurriedly removed the man's armor and set it aside. He wasn't sure if his own armor would hinder him, but he took off the breastplate anyway and heaved the captain off the ground.

Despite his short stature, the man was heavier than he looked. Caden's muscled burned as he carried Burke over to the horse. He wasn't sure how he was going to get him on the animal, so he grunted an apology to the captain and essentially threw him into the air. Burke helped by grabbing onto the saddle horn, and between the two of them struggling, managed to get him on the horse's back and somewhat into the saddle.

With Burke situated, Caden turned his attention to the boxcar's door. It wasn't overly heavy, and he had an idea. He cut some of the leather straps from the tandem pole and lashed them together, then tied one end to the saddle and the other to the door. He set Burke's armor on it, as well as his own, and pulled the body of one of their enemies onto it. Now they had proof of who had attacked them, and Lord D'Lance could do as he wished with the information.

All the exertion intensified his headache and he had to rest for a moment to keep from passing out. He steadily downed the water from the canteen he'd found until it was empty, then grabbed the reins and began the trek back to the castle. Burke flitted in and out of consciousness, which forced Caden to rely on his vague memory of the route they'd taken.

His strength gave out on him several times, and he slumped to the ground and waited until his muscles felt rested enough to continue. Caden lost all sense of time, but he knew that he was making progress as he started to recognize landmarks that he'd seen. By the time the castle came into view, the sun was high overhead.

"We made it," Caden said, barely recognizing his own hoarse voice.

He looked over his shoulder and saw that Burke was slumped forward in the saddle. A trail of blood ran from his leg down the side of the horse, and Caden feared that the captain might be dead. Burke's eyes cracked open.

"Find Angus," he said weakly.

Caden wanted nothing more than to lie down and close his eyes, but he knew they would probably both die if he did that. He pushed himself onward, counting his steps as a way of focusing on something other than the pain. They reached the gates and the guards on duty rushed to their aid, one of them sprinting off to find the commander.

Before long, the courtyard was swarming with activity. Leaders were demanding to know what happened, promising retribution. Caden tried to relay the events, but the chaos was too much. He collapsed from exhaustion and was taken to the infirmary. Thankfully, the healers kept anyone from bothering them and Caden was able to rest both his body and his mind. He continuously dozed in and out of sleep until he heard the powerful steps of booted feet.

Commander Morin had arrived, and Lord D'Lance was with him. They spoke with the healers first, then came to stand by his bed.

"Tell me everything," Lord D'Lance demanded.

15

MINA ARRIVED BACK AT KLODIAN Keep just as the sun was descending. She dismounted Tempest and led the horse to the stable. Aram was still working, and when he saw her, he took the reins from her and led the animal inside.

"I was beginning to get worried," he said.

"You were worried about me?"

"No, I was worried about Tempest. Once the gates close at dark, there's no getting in. I didn't want her being stuck out in the elements all night."

"I wouldn't let that happen," Mina replied. "And even if it did, I would take care of her."

"Be that as it may, I would like all of my horses accounted for before nightfall. I don't ask questions of anyone, but if you can't abide by my rules, I'll have to inform Lord Klodian about your ventures outside the castle. Where do you go, anyway?"

"I just ride around. It relaxes me."

Aram eyed her, and she thought he was going to pursue the conversation. Instead, he shrugged and shooed her out of the stable. Mina went inside the castle and stopped at the dining hall to see if there was any food left. She managed to scrounge up enough scraps to make a full meal and took it up to her room.

She was supposed to meet Thais at midnight, and she was thoroughly exhausted. She was tempted to send word to the Runesman that they would try tomorrow night instead but getting the egg to Copper was too important. It guaranteed that he would help her find a way to remove the scale, and she wanted that above all else. Sleep would have to wait.

Mina entered her room and sat on the bed as she wolfed down her food. She wondered if Thais had come up with a suitable diversion. If not, then they would simply have to improvise. And then there was the issue of the mysterious couple intent on overthrowing Klodian. Mina decided to leave that problem to Thais. She had enough on her plate with stealing the egg.

After she finished eating, she laid down and stared up at the ceiling. Her stomach was full, and her exhaustion seemed to intensify. She yawned and fought to keep her eyes open but fell asleep anyway. She startled awake from a nightmare and looked to the window. It was dark.

"Blast it," she muttered.

A glance at the water clock revealed it was just after midnight. Mina cursed and clambered off the bed, rushing out of the room and through the halls. The castle was quiet, and Mina didn't encounter anyone except a few guards who were walking their rounds. They took an interest in her until they realized who she was, then they ignored her and went about their business.

Mina left the castle and looked around the courtyard. She didn't see Thais. The woman had probably gotten tired of waiting on her and returned to the barracks.

"Over here!" A voice whispered harshly.

Mina peered at the shadows that veiled the side of the castle. Hidden among them was Thais. She stepped into the light and frowned.

"You're late."

"Sorry. I fell asleep."

"Must be nice. Are we still doing this or what?"

"Yes, of course. I like the servant's robes you're wearing. That should help us avoid any unwanted attention. Does it have a hood?"

In reply, Thais reached back and pulled a hood over her head, hiding her face.

"Follow me," Mina said.

She led Thais into the castle, keeping her pace quick. Instead of going forward through the maze of hallways, she turned to the left and headed down the stairwell that led to the lower level of the castle.

"Have you been to the dungeon before?"

"No," Thais replied.

"The room we need to get inside of is just before the dungeon, so there will probably be a few guards. What did you come up with as a diversion?"

"I'm still working on that. You didn't give me much time to prepare, and my thoughts have been preoccupied with my duties."

"As long as no one sees me go into the room, everything should be fine. You just need to get the attention off me."

"For how long?" Thais asked.

"A few minutes. I know the egg is in there, I just don't know exactly where it's kept."

"What egg?"

Mina sucked in a breath, realizing her mistake. She ignored the question and continued down the stairs. They reached the bottom and Thais looked at her expectantly.

"I told you before, I'll explain everything if we pull this off."

"Yeah, yeah. Which way?"

Two hallways branched off from the landing, one to the left and the other straight on.

"I'm not sure where that leads to," Mina said, motioning to the left corridor. "We're going this way."

They continued onward and Mina froze when she heard voices. There was no sign of anyone ahead, and she quickly realized the voices were coming from one of the rooms. Mina motioned for Thais to follow her, and the two walked quietly.

"Changes are coming to the Thophate, whether you like them or not. If you want to be included in those changes, you would do well to align yourself with the right people."

Mina recognized the voice as the man she'd overheard speaking about overthrowing Klodian. Her heart started racing, and she turned to Thais.

"That's one of them," she whispered.

"Who?"

"The two people I told you about that mentioned the spy. That's the man."

"Who is he talking to?" Thais asked.

"I don't know."

Mina stepped closer to the doorway and slowly tilted her head to look inside. The door was ajar, but not enough for her to see the man who was speaking.

"You said that Lord D'Lance has evidence of a crime. What crime are you talking about?" It was Captain Eduard's voice.

Mina and Thais exchanged looks.

"Treason against the High Prince," the man answered. "Lord Klodian is involved in a plot with Lord Culver. They seek to start a war."

"What is he talking about?" Thais scowled. "Lord Klodian isn't potting anything."

"Not that we know of," Mina said. "He's been absent for a while now."

"He's not in the castle?"

"He is, but he's been in his personal chamber, sealed off from everything. I haven't seen him since he gave me my freedom."

"That doesn't mean he's involved in anything nefarious."

"Not necessarily, but who's to say?"

"My loyalty lies with the Dominion," Captain Eduard said. "Who rules from its throne doesn't matter to me."

"I'll take that as a promise of support, and I'll be sure that Lord D'Lance rewards you for your service. In the end, keeping the High Prince safe is the ultimate goal. I will call upon you when the time is right. Until then, it's business as usual. I appreciate your time, captain."

Mina grabbed Thais's arm and pulled her toward the door on the other side of the hall. They entered the room and Mina kept the door cracked, peering out into the hall. She saw Captain Eduard exit the room and close the door behind him. He headed for the stairs, a troubled look on his face.

"I don't think the captain is happy about what he's been told," Mina said.

"That's not surprising. He's loyal to the Dominion, but he's also loyal to Lord Klodian. I don't know what our mystery man is up to, but it can't be good."

"He's going to overthrow Lord Klodian, but it sounds like someone else is behind it. Who is Lord D'Lance?"

"He's the top dog among the Dominion Lords. He commands more soldiers than anyone other than the High Prince himself. Is there anyone else in that room with him?"

"I'm not sure," Mina replied. "I only heard Captain Eduard."

"We should confront him, find out what's going on."

"No. We need to keep to the plan."

"Plans change," Thais said, her tone giddy. "We can unravel all of this right now."

Before Mina could argue with her, Thais opened the door and strode across the hall.

"Stop!"

Thais didn't pay her any heed. She pushed through the other door and went inside. There was a shout, followed by a crash. Mina swallowed hard and peered down the hall toward the dungeon, fearing that the guards would come to investigate. Silence settled over the hall, and no guards came. Thais appeared in the doorway.

"Get in here," she said.

Mina hurried across the hall and followed her into the room. A man was sprawled on the floor, unconscious.

"What did you do?" Mina demanded.

"I'm protecting Lord Klodian. If this man is a spy, we can get the answers we need from him."

"How?"

Thais smirked. "By torturing him, of course."

Mina looked from the prone man to Thais and back again. She had the sinking feeling that she wasn't going to get her hands on the egg tonight.

"His friend will know he's missing. The woman."

"Then we'll leave a note for her to find that says he needed to leave. This is important. More important than your egg, whatever that is. Unless you care to reveal the details about that now?"

Mina chewed on her lower lip. She needed Thais's help to get the egg, but she didn't trust the woman enough to tell her anything. There was also the fact that despite Copper's friendly demeanor, he could just be using her. And there was Lord Klodian, the only man strong enough to kill a dragon on his own. There was too much going on.

"I'll help you if you swear that we'll get the egg tomorrow night."

"We will. On my word as a Runesman."

"Fine." Mina looked down at the man. "What do we do with him?"

16

After Caden had relayed what little he remembered about the attack, Lord D'Lance and Commander Morin left him to rest. A healer approached his bed, smiling warmly. She was dressed in white robes and had striking blue eyes.

"How are you feeling?" she asked.

"My head is pounding," he replied.

"You do have some head trauma. And you were also burned. It's a miracle you even survived, let alone were able to make it back to the castle."

Caden was surprised by her words. He'd felt rough, but he hadn't thought that his injuries should have killed him. He considered himself lucky.

"I've got a salve that will help with the burn, but it's going to cause you some pain when I apply it."

"I think I can handle it."

The healer helped him to roll onto his side, and then her soft hands gently touched his skin. A wave of pain washed over him, and his eyes rolled into the back of his head. When he awoke, he was lying on his back again. The pain of the burn had lessened, but his headache remained the same, a constant throbbing in the back of his skull.

"Soldier." It was Burke.

Caden sat himself up and saw that the captain was a few beds down, on the same row as himself.

"Sir?"

"Thank you for saving my life."

"I was just doing my duty, sir."

"Maybe so, but not many men have the fortitude you displayed. I saw the back of your head and thought you were going to die on me. I'm glad to see you're still here."

"It'll take more than a headwound to take me out, sir," Caden said.

Burke chuckled, then went silent for a long moment.

"You've done more than I could expect, but I'm afraid I must ask more from you."

"What do you need me to do?"

Burke glanced at the healers in the room. "I'll tell you tonight."

Judging by the captain's demeanor, Caden knew it must be something secretive. Now that his curiosity was piqued, he was impatient for the time to pass. He laid back down and tried to rest, but his mind was too alert. He replayed the events of the night before. The robed man who had thrown the fireballs had been using magic. Magic that was banned by decree of the High Prince.

If Lord Culver was truly trying to cause a war, his actions last night would certainly be the catalyst. Caden remembered what Thais had told him, about her father being killed in battle. Lord Culver called him a failure and banished Thais and her mother from his Dominion. The man was a lawless monster.

The hours passed monotonously, aside from the healers who came to apply salve to his burn or bring him food. His headache eventually faded to a minor pulsing, and he spent some of the time cleaning the dirt from under his nails. As the sunlight flowing through the windows began to dim, one of the healers came to see him.

"Given the nature of your wounds, we're going to keep you here for the night. We don't expect you to have any issues, but there will be someone on duty. If you start to feel bad in any way, ring the bell by the door."

"Thank you," Caden said. "Do you think I'll be able to leave in the morning?"

"That remains to be seen. We don't want you to aggravate your injuries, so we're going to take it one day at a time."

While Caden didn't like the idea of lying around for days on end, he also didn't want to disrupt his healing. He watched the healer leave the infirmary, then turned his attention to Burke. The captain had his eyes closed and appeared to be sleeping. Once nightfall had fully descended, Burke called his name.

"Come over here."

Caden eased himself off the bed and slowly walked to where Burke was. The captain's midsection was wrapped in bandages. A spot on his ribcage had blood leaking through, but it wasn't enough to cause worry.

"I can't move around much," Burke said. "Are we alone?"

Caden didn't see anyone, but he walked around the room just to be certain.

"All clear."

"Good. I need you to return to the site of our attack and look for anything out of the ordinary."

Caden's scrunched his face, which caused a brief lance of pain to shoot through his neck.

"I need you to trust me. Something isn't right about that ambush."

"What do you mean? Hasn't Lord Culver been trying to start a war? Attacking us would bring Lord D'Lance's wrath down on him, which will probably lead to war. He's signed his own death warrant."

"That's the problem," Burke said, lowering his voice. "I don't think Lord Culver is behind this."

"Why not?"

"I served under Lord Culver for a while before transferring here a few years ago. Lord Culver is one of the most honorable men I've ever known. When I saw his emblem on the armor of the soldiers who attacked us, it didn't sit right with me."

"People change," Caden replied. "He may not be the man you once knew."

"People *can* change, but I don't think Lord Culver would become a tyrant. His Dominion is closest to the High Prince and has long been coveted by the other Dominion Lords."

He didn't name off anyone specific, but Caden took the hint.

"Why would Lord D'Lance want Culver's Dominion? He's got more soldiers and land here."

"It's not about the size, but the location. Lord Culver's Dominion is the only thing that stands in the way of an army and the High Prince."

"If someone was going to attack the High Prince, they would have to come through all of the Dominions first," Caden argued. "They wouldn't make it very far."

"Unless the attacker is a Dominion Lord."

Caden opened his mouth to reply and paused. The captain had a valid point.

"You think Lord D'Lance is trying to make it look like Lord Culver is stirring up trouble so he can take over his Dominion?"

Burke nodded mutely.

"For what purpose?"

"Who knows, though I have my suspicions," Burke replied. "Our loyalties are with our Dominion lord, but ultimately they rest with the High Prince. If there is nothing at the ambush site to indicate what I'm saying is true, then we have nothing to be concerned about. However, if there is, then I fear we must get word to the High Prince immediately."

Caden agreed that the picture Burke painted was troubling.

"Is there something specific I should be looking for? And what about the dragon? What if it's still out there?"

"The dragon will be long gone, I'm sure. Just check the bodies. If they truly are Lord Culver's Runesmen, they'll bear his rune. That's the only thing that I can think of."

"I'll go first thing in the morning," Caden said.

"No, you must leave tonight. If I'm correct, then time is something we don't have enough of."

"Tonight? I barely walked in a straight line to your bed. There's no way I can make it to that far on foot."

"You won't have to."

Burke extended his hand and held up a small pin. It had Lord D'Lance's emblem engraved on the front.

"This will give you access to everything I have as a captain, including a horse. That will allow you to get there and return before morning."

Caden felt as though he were somehow working behind Lord D'Lance's back. The man had accepted him and even offered him the opportunity to earn the fame and fortune he wanted.

"I don't know if I can do this," Caden said.

"There is no else. We were the only ones who saw what happened and lived. I can't walk at all, so it must be you."

Caden wanted to say no. He wanted to forget everything Burke had told him and serve Lord D'Lance without question. But he couldn't, not until his mind was eased of the doubts Burke had instilled.

Caden took the pin.

<h1 style="text-align:center">17</h1>

After Mina and Thais had bound and gagged their prisoner, they'd snuck him into one of the cells in the dungeon for safekeeping. Thais had penned a letter since she knew how to write, and Mina had delivered it to the man's partner, slipping it under the door of their chamber.

Mina wasn't sure if the woman would believe that her co-conspirator would suddenly be called away, but Thais had convinced her that it was the most logical excuse for his absence. She then helped Thais out of the castle and returned to her room and managed to get a few hours of sleep.

A faint light shone through her windows as dawn arrived, and she forced herself out of bed. She didn't have to visit Copper this early, but she wanted to be certain she'd return before nightfall. Thais had mentioned interrogating their prisoner, but Mina refused to do anything until she had the egg in her hands.

She went down to the dining hall and ate a quick breakfast, then headed for the stable. Aram was absent, but a younger man was there shoveling out the stalls. Mina asked for Tempest, and the man handed the horse over without any questions. It was curious that Aram wasn't working, but she assumed he needed a break as much as anyone else.

Mina left the castle behind and guided Tempest toward the mesa where she'd been meeting with Copper. She had grown accustomed to constantly feeling his presence through the scale. Regardless of the distance between them, he was always there. It was another mystery that she hoped to unravel.

Tempest slowed as they reached the mesa and began to whinny, jerking her head against the reins. Mina patted the horse's neck comfortingly and scanned the sky. Atop the mesa, she could see Copper's head as he peered down at her.

I see you have returned without the egg, his voice rumbled in her mind.

Yes. Things didn't go according to plan.

Do you want me to bring you up here?

Mina hesitated. It was certainly quicker than climbing, but it was also terrifying. She debated back and forth with herself before Copper's chortling laughter interrupted her thoughts.

What?

I had forgotten how humans think. It's quite entertaining, really.

You can hear my thoughts?

Sometimes, Copper answered. *When you are close as you are now. It is more difficult when you are further away.*

Mina abruptly felt self-conscious. Had he heard all of her thoughts during their last encounter? Was he hearing them now? She shook her head, trying to clear her mind, and guided Tempest to a stop. She slid out of the saddle and walked around the mesa wall until Tempest was no longer visible.

A whooshing sound filled the air and Copper landed on the ground ahead of her. His wings were stretched out, and as Mina approached him, she could see the light shining through the membrane of his wings, highlighting veins and small punctures.

Do those holes affect your ability to fly? she asked.

No.

How did you get them?

Battles, mostly.

With other dragons?

A few of them, yes.

Mina extended her arms and tried to remain calm. Copper leaped into the air and flapped his wings, grabbing hold of her and lifting her into the air. The instinct to scream clawed at her mind as it had the first time, but she kept her mouth clamped shut. Her feet touched the ground again and she heaved in a relieved breath. Copper's wings stirred up the dust, causing Mina to cough as it got into her nose and mouth. Once it settled, Copper stared at her intently.

What happened with the egg?

The person I had asked to help me ruined my plan. She was supposed to draw attention so that I could get into the room and steal it.

Does she know what you are after?

No. Mina remembered her slip-up and corrected herself. *Well, I don't think so.*

Did she try to sabotage you?

Not intentionally. There is something I didn't mention yesterday. I overheard two people talking about overthrowing Lord Klodian. They also mentioned a spy being in the castle, and when I told her about them, she wanted to find out who they are. When we went down to get the egg, one of them was down there, a man. Thais knocked him out and now we have him in the dungeon.

It seems she has different priorities. Is she the best suited to help you?

She's the only one who can *help me,* Mina said. *I'll have to help her before she'll help me, but she wants to interrogate the man.*

What's the problem?

She's a soldier and she isn't allowed in the castle. I had to sneak her in last night, but if she gets caught, she'll be in trouble and I'll lose my help.

Copper hummed. The sound sent gentle vibrations through the ground that reached Mina's toes despite her boots, and it tickled her. She shifted her stance and clenched her feet against the feeling.

Perhaps I can help you, he finally said.

How?

I can search his mind.

Truly?

We dragons can do many things. The scale in your leg will provide the means, but you must touch the man.

In the back of her mind, Mina wondered if Copper was telling the truth. She trusted Thais more than she did the dragon, but if he was able to do what he said, then whatever he learned would hopefully placate Thais.

It's worth trying, she admitted.

When can you speak to this man? I will need to be close to you for this to work, and if I am seen near the castle during daylight, there are bound to be problems.

I can go at night. Will that work?

Yes. It will be easier to hide in the darkness.

Then it's settled, Mina said. *I'll go at midnight. Most of the servants will be asleep, and there shouldn't be many guards on the walls.*

Very well. Copper lifted his head and sniffed the air, growling lowly.

What is it?

A sand wyrm is nearby.

Mina tensed and looked around.

You are safe up here, Copper said. *They cannot burrow through the rock. It is curious that one is so far from the deeper area of the desert.*

What about my horse?

Copper turned his gaze on her.

You should go.

Mina swallowed hard, a wave of fear washing over her. She had no idea what a sand wyrm was, nor what one looked like, but her instincts told her she needed to run.

Will it follow me?

If it catches your scent. You'll need to ride fast.

I had hoped to spend more time with you. I have so many questions.

Your questions will have to wait, though I will answer one on the way down.

Copper launched himself into the air and Mina held her arms out, and then she was dropping toward the ground. She struggled to get her thoughts in order but managed to decide on the most pressing question.

Why can I feel you in the scale at all times?

They swooped down the side of the mesa, and Mina watched as the wall sped past. She was on the ground before she had time to realize it.

As you put it, there is something I haven't told you, Copper said. *I recognize the scale in your leg now.*

You know whose it is?

Yes.

Tell me!

The scent of lavender filled her nostrils, and she wondered why the dragon was afraid. He couldn't be afraid of her, could he? Or was he afraid that she would lead Lord Klodian to the dragon?

It is mine.

Mina was speechless. She stared at Copper with wide eyes. How was that possible? Her family's farm was many miles from Lord Klodian's castle. If the dragons resided among The Long Sands, how would one of Copper's scales have gotten in the nest near the farm?

You must go! Now!

The ground shook beneath Mina's feet, and she heard Tempest cry out in alarm. She sprinted around the mesa and saw the ground heaving up as something under the sand approached. Tempest's eyes were wild with terror.

"Please don't run," Mina prayed as she ran toward the horse.

She got her foot in the stirrup and was swinging her leg up over the saddle just as Tempest bolted. Mina held onto the reins as tightly as she could and tried to situate herself. Copper took to the air, causing Tempest to change directions. They were now in between the dragon and the sand wyrm.

Go left! Copper shouted in her mind.

She jerked the reins in reply, hoping the horse would obey. Tempest followed her lead and adjusted course. The sand wyrm also changed direction and broke the surface of the sand. The creature rose up, up, up into the air, the muscles of its long body undulating. It had no eyes that Mina could see, but it had an enormous circular mouth filled with serrated teeth. It twisted in the air toward her and Tempest.

Mina screamed.

18

CADEN THUNDERED ALONG THE ROAD astride a well-muscled destrier. The horse was doubtless more valuable than he was. When he'd asked the stable hand for a quick horse, he hadn't expected to be given such a magnificent animal. He *had* anticipated questions, but when he flashed the pin, no one asked him anything.

The lack of security was both a blessing and a concern. Regardless, he continuously questioned himself about why he was going through with Burke's request. A part of him argued that it was because Burke was a captain, and since he was a superior, Caden had to oblige the man.

And yet, there was something about Burke's words that bothered Caden. If the captain was right about the ambush, and Lord D'Lance's ulterior motives toward Lord Culver, then Caden was going to be drawn into something he wanted no part of. Saving the High Prince from being overthrown, or worse, would surely get him a reward, but nothing worth doing was ever easy, at least in his experience.

The distance flew by quickly, and when he reached the campsite, he was confused. There were no bodies, no boxcar, nothing. He dismounted from the horse and walked around the area. Overhead, the sky was clear and the moon shined brightly, giving him plenty of light to see by. Perhaps he was in the wrong spot? Everything looked familiar, though, even the burn marks on the ground and the trees.

Caden walked up the hill and saw the stone building. He was in the right spot. Why had everything been cleaned up already? He supposed Lord D'Lance wouldn't want word of what happened to get out, but if Burke's suspicions were true …

"I've got a bad feeling about this," Caden muttered.

He spent some time searching the area, looking for anything that may have been missed by whoever had cleaned the place. His headache returned, and he decided to go back to the castle. It was suspicious that there was nothing that remained, but he would let Burke know and let the captain decide what he wanted to do. Caden had done his duty, and he was going to wash his hands of the situation and pretend he didn't have his doubts.

The sun was creeping over the horizon when he arrived at the castle. He returned the horse to the stables and hurried toward the infirmary, but paused when something occurred to him. He'd brought back one of the enemy's bodies. If there were any clues to be had, perhaps he'd find them on the body. There was just one problem. He didn't know where it had been taken.

Caden turned away from the infirmary and backtracked, returning to the main entrance. Despite the early hour, many people were coming and going through the castle. He stopped someone on a whim, flashing the pin nonchalantly.

"Perhaps you can help me. Two Runesmen returned this morning with a tale of being ambushed. Do you know what I'm referring to?"

"The attack perpetrated by Lord Culver? Yeah, I heard about it. Who hasn't?"

"They brought back a body with them of one of the attackers. Do you know what they did with it?"

"It was paraded around the grounds earlier. Commander Morin said that was all the proof we needed to end Lord Culver's attempted campaign against the High Prince. Lord D'Lance has practically declared war."

"Do you know where the body is now?"

"At the chapel, last I heard. Though if you ask me, no enemy of ours deserves a proper funeral."

"Where is the chapel?"

"It's on the west side of the castle, near the barracks for the regular soldiers."

Caden thanked the man and rushed through the halls, frantically looking for the chapel and praying that the body hadn't already been buried. He entered a section that was separated from the main castle, though connected structurally by a covered walkway. The morning air was chill, and it drove back the heat that Caden felt flushing his face.

The chapel doors were propped open, and he stepped inside. The interior reminded him of the infirmary. Everything was white, crisp, and clean. Clergy members wearing white robes were offering prayers and speaking with people privately. The pews were empty, and Caden doubted that the morning service had begun yet.

He approached one of the clerics, a young woman with short brown hair. He'd confused her for a man at first and almost called her 'sir' before catching himself.

"Good morning," she greeted. "How may I help you?"

"I was told the body of a soldier was brought here. Is it still here?"

"Do you mean Lord Culver's soldier or another?"

"Yes, that's the one. Is it still here?"

"It is. If Lord D'Lance has sent you to tell us to dispose of it, tell your lord that the Church will not be bullied into submission. We will perform the necessary rituals, and then we will bury him."

So, Lord D'Lance had told them to get rid of the body. Why would he do that unless there was something to hide?

"I'm here of my own volition," Caden replied. "I need to check the body for … something."

"What is the reason that you must disturb the dead? There is enough suffering in life that the dead should be left alone."

"I wouldn't ask if it wasn't important. Please."

The woman stared at him in silence for a long moment, then nodded. "Very well."

She led him to the back of the chapel and through a door that opened into a large vaulted room. A number of bodies were laid out on stone slabs, covered with thin white shrouds.

"You are lucky that the prayers for the dead have not begun, else we would not allow you in here. This is the one," she said as they stopped at one of the slabs.

Caden pulled the shroud back. The man's armor had been removed, revealing a young face. The man couldn't have been much older than himself. His eyes had been closed, and his expression was one of peace. Caden lifted his head, but he couldn't get a good look at the rune, so he turned the man onto his side. The rune was the same as the one he'd seen on the emblem. A clawed paw print surrounded by a blazing sun.

Caden breathed a sigh of relief. Burke had been wrong. This was indeed one of Lord Culver's men. He started to roll the body onto its back when he spotted something covering the bottom of the rune. He leaned closer, but he couldn't determine what it was, so he rubbed his finger across it and held it up.

"What is it?" the cleric asked.

"I think it's ink," he replied. "Do you have a cloth?"

"No."

Caden grabbed the edge of the shroud and wiped the rune with the material. To his horror, the ink came right off, revealing a different rune underneath. Lord D'Lance's rune.

"You're certain this is the same body that was brought here this morning?"

"Yes."

"How certain?"

Her look of disapproval told him everything he needed to know. He pulled the shroud back over the body and left the chapel, heading back into the castle. Why was one of Lord D'Lance's Runesmen wearing a fake rune? The answer hovered in the back of his mind, but he didn't want to accept it. Burke had been right.

Caden rushed into the infirmary, ready to tell the captain what he'd discovered. A group of healers had gathered around Burke's bed, but he couldn't see what they were doing.

"What's going on?" he asked.

"There you are," one of them said. "We've been looking all over for you."

"I'm fine. What's wrong with Captain Burke?"

The healer cast her eyes to the floor forlornly. "He's dead."

<h1 style="text-align:center">19</h1>

Tempest reared back on her hind legs and Mina almost fell out of the saddle. She wrapped her arms around the horse's neck and prepared to die.

An unearthly roar split the air, and Mina watched in awe as Copper dropped from the sky. His talons raked along the sand wyrm's fleshy body, rending deep wounds that quickly filled with black blood.

The creature issued a horrendous shriek that made Mina think her eardrums were going to burst. Copper dug his talons into the wyrm's body and flapped his wings, pulling the behemoth away from Mina and her mount.

Flee! Copper shouted.

Mina released Tempest's neck and pulled on the reins, urging the horse to move. At first, she thought Tempest wasn't going to obey her, but the animal backed up a few steps and then hurtled in the direction of the castle. Mina rode hard, not daring to look back, even after they reached the castle. She knew it was irrational that she would see the two monsters battling at this distance, but she was terrified.

She returned Tempest to the stable and rushed through the castle, escaping to her room where she let tears flow freely down her face. Her emotions mingled together, overwhelming her, and she sat on the floor near her bed and sobbed. She had nearly died, out in the middle of the desert where no one would have seen anything except Copper.

Copper.

He'd saved her life. A dragon, of all things. And then she remembered what he'd said. It was *his* scale in her leg. She considered the implications and began to suspect that their meeting in the mesa that day with Lord Klodian might not have been a coincidence. That didn't explain why Vhan had been killed by his brethren, but it gave her something to consider.

Her focus switched from the sand wyrm to Copper, and she managed to calm herself. Mina wiped the tears from her face and stood, glancing to the window. She touched the scale in her leg and could feel Copper's presence, though she couldn't hear his voice. Perhaps later, when he was close enough, she would get answers to some of her questions.

For now, she would have to let Thais know that there had been a change in plans. Mina checked her appearance in the mirror and fixed her hair, then left her room and made her way to the barracks. The place was empty, so Mina walked the courtyard searching for Thais, but the woman was nowhere to be found. She looked at the gates, wondering if she was out on patrol.

"Mina."

Although she was no longer a slave, Lord Klodian's voice still had the same effect on her. Her heart skipped a beat and she turned around. He was walking with Captain Eduard and he motioned for her to come near.

"It is good to see you, my Lord. I've been wondering when you would come calling for me."

"I've been busy dealing with some things," he replied.

"Are we going on a hunt?" she asked.

"No, I don't have time for that right now."

Mina was relieved to hear that.

"We have a problem. Lord Burgess has gone missing, and his wife is distraught. She said she received a letter saying he was being called away, but it wasn't in his handwriting. Have you seen or heard anything?"

"No, my Lord. Perhaps he had one of the servants write it for him?"

"We've questioned the servants," Eduard said. "All of them. Unless one of them is lying, no one was asked to pen anything for him."

"I'll let you know if I hear anything," Mina replied.

Lord Klodian nodded, but Mina noticed that he appeared to be distracted. He started to walk off, then looked at her.

"The stablemaster told me you've been borrowing a horse?"

"Yes, my Lord. The rides help to clear my mind."

"Of what?"

"The dragons. I feel as though I sense them all the time lately, ever since Vhan …" Mina trailed off, hoping he would change the subject.

Lord Klodian cleared his throat. "Yes, it was unfortunate that he was killed. The dragons responsible will pay with their blood." Lord Klodian swept his gaze across the courtyard. "Keep your ears open and let me know if you hear anything about Lord Burgess's disappearance."

"I will, my Lord."

The two men left and she returned to her room. Thais wouldn't like being left out, but Mina was just going to have to go through with letting Copper probe Lord Burgess's mind. Now that his absence had stirred suspicion, she needed to hurry. In the back of her mind, the question of what to do with him after interrogating him continued to berate her. She would simply have to figure things out, as she always did.

When evening came, Mina was pacing her room. She could hear people in the hall retiring for the night, and her impatience was hard to contain. It wasn't just about getting the egg. She wanted to speak with Copper.

The clouds are thick tonight, his voice said, interrupting her thoughts. *That will help hide me.*

I wondered if you were still going to come, Mina replied.

I said I would, and I am a dragon of my word.

Are you all right? Did the sand wyrm hurt you?

Copper laughed. *No, it did not hurt me. They might be bigger, but they are slow, lumbering creatures compared to us dragons.*

I thought I was going to die.

You could have.

You saved me … why?

Copper fell silent, and Mina wondered if he would refuse to answer.

I don't know how, but I believe you and I are bonded. I felt it first in the mesa with my brethren, but I wasn't sure if I imagined the feeling. Each time we talk, I feel it more strongly. When I saw the sand wyrm coming for you, I couldn't allow you to die. It would have been easier that way, but it would not have been right.

When you say bonded, what do you mean? Like the humans and dragons before?

Yes.

Mina paused mid-step in her pacing. She couldn't believe it. She didn't want to, and yet, it explained her ability to sense dragons. It wasn't the scale itself, but the bond between her and Copper that enabled it.

I fell on this scale near my parents' home. How is it that your scale would end up there if you live in the desert?

When we mate, we leave the desert to find more hospitable areas for our eggs. The heat is too much for the unhatched to handle. You must have fallen into one of my old nests.

Copper was the dragon responsible for the way her life had changed. She had spent so many years full of hatred, and now that she knew who the scale belonged to, she found it difficult to hold onto that hate. What was wrong with her? What had changed?

Is that why you were afraid?

Dragons fear nothing.

Mina smiled. She knew better than to believe that.

Are you near the prisoner? He asked.

No. I'm waiting for the servants to retire. It should be safe to see him shortly. While we wait, can you answer some questions?

I will try.

Since we are connected by this bond, will I be able to speak to you if the scale is removed?

Yes, though I am not sure how the bond was created in the first place. I spoke with my brethren about removing your scale, but there is no clear answer on how it can be done. I fear that it may kill you to do so.

Mina didn't want to risk her life to remove it. And there didn't seem to be much point in removing it now if she would still be able to sense dragons. There had to be a way to block them out somehow.

There is, Copper said. *I can teach you if you want.*

I would like that, Mina replied. *It would be nice to keep you from hearing my personal thoughts. Some things are just private.*

She looked at the water clock. The servants would be done with their duties now.

It's time.

20

CADEN WAS CONFUSED. "DEAD? HOW?"

"He succumbed to his wounds not long ago."

Burke had been wounded, but he didn't think the wound hadn't been life-threatening. He watched as the healers lifted the captain's body off the bed and onto a stretcher, then they carried him out of the infirmary. The host of healers dispersed, and Caden stood alone staring at the empty bed.

Something wasn't right. Burke had been fine earlier. He walked over to the bed and noticed a piece of parchment sticking out from under the pillow. Scrawled roughly on it was written the words:

Don't trust anyone.

He crumpled the paper and looked around the infirmary. If Burke had been killed, it was probably at Lord D'Lance's command. At least, that was his suspicion. Perhaps his mind was clouded by Burke's words … but that wouldn't explain the false rune on the dead soldier. Everything that Burke had said appeared to be true, and that meant he had no one to turn to. Before he could decide his next steps, Commander Morin strode into the infirmary.

"I just got word about Captain Burke. To say I'm surprised would be an understatement. His wounds didn't seem that serious."

Caden nodded silently.

"How are you feeling?"

"I still have some pain, but I'll recover."

"Good, good. Lord D'Lance has requested to see you in the Cathedra."

"Now, sir?" Caden asked.

"Yes, unless you aren't feeling up to it. Should I call one of the healers for you?"

"No, I'm fine. I just have a lot on my mind, sir."

"Looking death in the face can be traumatic. It leaves you questioning things. Don't be afraid of those questions, embrace them. It'll make you stronger." He paused. "We should get moving. Lord D'Lance is waiting."

Angus escorted Caden in silence to the Coterie, where a small host of people were waiting to get an audience. The guards let them pass without question, and they entered the Cathedra. Lord D'Lance was sitting on his throne listening to two men dressed in extravagant clothing. Upon seeing them, Lord D'Lance held up his hand and the men fell silent.

"I apologize, gentlemen, but we will have to reconvene. I have pressing matters to attend to."

The men bowed low and left, whispering to one another. Angus waved for Caden to follow him and they approached the throne, stopping at the edge of the purple rug. Caden didn't wait to follow Angus's lead. He knelt and bowed his head.

"Rise," Lord D'Lance said.

Caden stood up and turned his gaze upon the Dominion Lord. He remained sitting, and the gold trim of his robes shimmered in the light that slanted in through the myriad of windows that ringed the top of the Cathedra.

"How are you feeling?"

The question was innocent, but his voice made Caden squirm uncomfortably.

"I was wounded, but it's nothing I can't push through, my Lord."

"I'm glad that you were able to deliver the news of the attack to us. It couldn't have been easy riding through the night while helping Captain Burke. You are to be commended for your fortitude."

"Thank you, my Lord. I was merely doing my duty."

Lord D'Lance turned his attention to Angus. "What of the captain? Is it true?"

"Yes, I'm afraid so."

"I see. It seems we are in need of a new captain. Any candidates in mind, commander?"

"Only one that I can think of."

They both turned their eyes on Caden. He swallowed hard to clear his throat which had suddenly become constricted.

"What do you say, Caden? You came here seeking fame and fortune, and you've proven yourself a capable Runesman. How do you feel about a promotion?"

"I'm not sure that I'm ready for that yet," Caden replied. It was a lie, of course. He was ready to lead, but he didn't know what to do with the information he'd learned from Burke. He couldn't trust Lord D'Lance, or Angus for that matter.

"Those meant to lead usually aren't ready, but it's not about being ready," Angus said. "It's about taking the opportunity."

"I've received reports that Lord Culver has an army at the border," Lord D'Lance said. "He's preparing to enter the Dracan Dominion at any moment, and I need someone capable to lead the Runesmen I'm sending there. Do you want the promotion?"

Caden considered the offer. It would allow him to confirm whether Lord Culver was truly responsible for everything, but it also posed a risk. If it was a trap like the dragon escort was, then he might not make it out alive. Though if it was a trap, he'd be prepared this time and he could flee to Lord Culver's Dominion and tell him everything Lord D'Lance had done.

"If you think I am the best suited, then I accept," Caden said. "When do we leave for the border?"

Lord D'Lance rose from his throne. "In a few hours, so you'll need to get some rest. Before you do, you need to take my rune." He snapped his fingers and one of the guards standing beside the throne stepped forward. "I need a scribe."

The soldier saluted and rushed off.

"Will having two different runes be a problem?" Caden asked.

"It shouldn't. Lord Klodian is too far from here to utilize the magic, so it won't interfere with my rune."

"If Lord Klodian was within distance, what would happen if both of you tried to use your runes at the same time?"

"It would probably kill you," Lord D'Lance replied. "Don't concern yourself with such things. I only use my Runesmen if it is important. And as I said, Lord Klodian is too far away. The chances of both of us trying to borrow your strength at the same time is slim."

Slim, but not impossible, Caden thought. The soldier returned a moment later, and an older man with gray hair followed quickly behind him. He carried a wooden tray that was covered with utensils and vials.

"My Lord," the scribe greeted, stopping to kneel.

"Please put my rune on him," Lord D'Lance instructed, motioning to Caden.

The scribe eyed Caden for a moment, then turned to Lord D'Lance. "Strength rune, yes?"

"Astute, as always master scribe. You are correct."

"Come over here and sit on the floor," the old man said.

Caden did as he asked, moving off the rug to sit on the stone floor. The scribe had him move around until the light from the windows was just right, then he told Caden to remove his shirt. He obeyed, and the scribe cleared his throat.

"He has a rune already, my Lord."

"Yes, I'm aware. Put mine below it."

"Very well. I assume you want me to cut this other one?"

"No. Leave it be."

Caden noticed that the scribe hesitated, but he nodded and began his work. The pinprick of the scribe's utensils didn't hurt much, but the hunched position he was sitting in made his back ache. When the scribe was finally done, Caden groaned in relief as he sat up straight and stretched his muscles.

"Let me see it," Lord D'Lance said.

Caden stood and turned around.

"Perfect. You are dismissed."

The scribe placed everything on his tray and left. Caden gingerly put his shirt back on.

"Return to the barracks and get some rest. Commander Morin will fill you in on the way."

"Yes, my Lord."

Caden left the Cathedra and headed for the barracks, slowly forming a plan in his mind. This would be the perfect opportunity to find out what was really going on.

<h1 style="text-align:center">21</h1>

THE HALLS WERE EMPTY AS Mina made her way into the lower part of the castle. The door to the room where Thais had waylaid Lord Burgess was wide open, but there was no one inside. Mina walked quietly, constantly looking over her shoulder.

If you are no longer a slave, why are you afraid of being caught? Copper asked.

It's hard to explain.

She reached the dungeon and paused outside the door, listening for voices. She could hear people talking, but they didn't sound close. Mina pushed the door open and slipped across the threshold. Only a handful of torches provided light, and the air felt heavy.

They had left the door to Lord Burgess's cell unlocked, seeing as how they didn't have the keys, but he'd been bound tightly so that he couldn't move. Mina crept up to the cell and peered into the darkness. Lord Burgess was still there, but he wasn't moving. She had the sudden fear that Thais may have killed him, but as she stepped into the cell, she heard his low moans.

What do I need to do? she asked.

Touch his head and clear your mind. I'll do the rest.

Mina knelt beside Lord Burgess and he looked up at her. He struggled against his bonds and tried to speak, but the gag in his mouth made the words come out as muffled groans. Mina hesitantly placed her hand on his forehead and closed her eyes. She allowed the darkness to envelop her, and she emptied her mind.

Copper's presence passed through her, different from anything she'd felt before. Fragments of images flashed before her eyes. Lord Burgess speaking to a woman with long blond hair and green eyes. A dark cave filled with dragons and a shadowy figure. Dread washed over her, but she didn't know what it was from. And then there was searing pain. Mina gasped sharply and Copper's presence retreated.

She pulled her hand away from Lord Burgess and sat down, feeling weak and dizzy. The feeling quickly passed, and she turned her thoughts to Copper.

What did you see?

The scheme against Lord Klodian is true, he replied. *Does the name Kristofel D'Lance mean anything to you?*

Yes, he's the lord of the Dracan Dominion.

Lord and Lady Burgess work for him. He's plotting to overthrow the High Prince by making it seem that Lord Klodian and a man named Lord Culver are sowing rebellion. He wants to start a war.

So it is true, Mina said. *Before Vhan died, he said something about rumors of war. This must be what he was talking about. What else did you see?*

Many dark things that I cannot tell you yet. I must speak to my brethren and make sense of them first.

What should I do with him? If I leave him here, he'll starve to death. But I can't release him or he'll report back to Lord D'Lance.

I can erase his memories, Copper said. *It is not something to be done lightly, but the things I saw tell me this man is dangerous.*

Mina wavered in her decision for a moment. *Do it.*

She put her hand back on Lord Burgess's forehead and waited, but she didn't feel anything.

It is done.

That was fast, Mina replied. *What memories did you erase?*

Everything dealing with Lord D'Lance. The only thing he will remember is that he is loyal to Lord Klodian. Will that suffice, or should I create some new memories for him?

That should be fine. I'm going to release him and let the guards find him. He's not my problem after that. I need to tell Thais everything we've learned.

Don't forget the egg, Copper said.

I won't. I'll bring it to you tomorrow.

Very well. I will leave you now. I smell a storm coming.

Mina waited until she no longer felt the closeness of Copper's presence before she untied Lord Burgess. She pulled the gag from his mouth and leaned in close to him.

"You've been missing for an entire day," she said. "Lord Klodian has been looking all over for you. Tell the guards who you are and they will help you."

She stood and stuck her head out, glancing down the row of cells. There were no guards visible, so she sprinted to the door she'd entered through and escaped into the main hall. The room that held the egg was down here, she just had to figure out which one it was. She tried the handles of each one she passed and found they were all unlocked. Her luck couldn't get any better.

When Mina opened the third door on the left, she saw all sorts of trinkets. She stepped inside and walked around stacks of wooden crates filled with all manner of things. It appeared to be a storage room. She almost left, but a glint from one of the crates caught her eye. Mina removed a rug from the top of the crate and was rewarded.

The egg was inside.

But there was a problem. It was much larger than she remembered. How was she going to get it out of the castle without being seen, let alone up to her room? She stared at the egg for a long while as she pondered her options. It would be impossible to get it through the front gates without someone seeing her … unless she took it out there now. There were fewer prying eyes, but where would she hide it until she could deliver it to Copper?

This would require thinking on her feet. She pulled the egg from the crate and was surprised to find that it wasn't very heavy. She grabbed a cloak from another crate and used it to cover the egg, then peered into the hall to make sure it was still empty. All was clear, and she hurried up the stairs to the upper portion of the castle.

A few guards were making their rounds, but they didn't pay her any heed. She offered a prayer of thanks to Avera and reached the courtyard. The night air was cool, but it did little to ease her nervous sweating. Mina walked to the gates and stopped when she saw they were closed. Aram had told her they were being closed at night and she'd completely forgotten. She looked around the courtyard, but there was nowhere ideal to hide the egg.

Footsteps from behind her caused her to panic, but when she heard Thais's voice, she sighed with relief.

"What are you doing out here?"

"I need to hide this," Mina replied, lifting the cloak.

Thais's eyes widened. "Is that what I think it is?"

"What do you think it is?" Mina asked.

Thais locked eyes with her. "You said egg, and I didn't put it together. Gods, you *are* insane, aren't you? Lord Klodian will kill you if he finds out you've taken that."

"It was buried in a storage room, so I doubt he'll know it's missing for a while. Where can I put this? I'll get rid of it tomorrow."

"I have no idea," Thais said, glancing around.

"Can you get me outside the walls?"

"If I get caught doing this, I'll kill you. Follow me."

Thais led her to a side entrance and produced a ring of keys from her waist. She fumbled through them until she found the correct one, then unlocked the door. Mina stepped out into the open and set the egg down, then swiftly dug a hole in the sand with her hands. She kept the egg wrapped in the cloak and placed it in the hole, then covered it with sand. It wasn't perfect, but it would make due. She stepped back through the door and Thais locked it.

"We've got a problem," Mina said. "The High Prince is in danger."

<h1 style="text-align:center">22</h1>

After a few hours of fitful sleep, Caden got out of bed and prepared himself mentally for what lay ahead. He put on a chainmail shirt and strapped his sword at his waist, then headed to the bottom level of the barracks.

Angus was there, along with a contingent of Runesmen. They were all dressed for battle, and Caden looked questioningly at the commander.

"What's going on?"

"Lord Culver has attacked our settlements on the border, so Lord D'Lance has ordered me to go with you and your team to the front lines. The others will follow, but it's going to take some time to mobilize them."

Caden counted roughly thirty men, including himself and Angus. It certainly wasn't enough to defend against an army. His suspicion grew, but he kept his mouth shut. He needed to know the truth before he made his move.

"We should get moving, then," Caden said.

"You heard the captain. Mount up!"

The Runesmen filed out of the barracks to the stable where horses were already saddled and waiting for them. Caden chose a horse at random and climbed into the saddle. He waited until everyone was mounted, then he flicked the reins and guided the horse across the courtyard. Angus rode up beside him and they traveled side by side in silence for a long while.

"Lord D'Lance doesn't want to cause a panic, so we're to keep things nonchalant. Once we get past the surroundings towns, we'll need to pick up the pace."

"Yes, sir," Caden replied. "I've been wondering something …" He trailed off, waiting for Angus to press him.

"What is it?"

"Does Lord Culver employ banned magic?"

Angus subtly side-eyed him. "Who knows? The man is crazed with his lust for power. People like that are unpredictable. If he's using dark magic, it wouldn't surprise me."

"How else would someone create a fireball that can fly through the air at their command? That has to be magic, right?"

"Sounds like it to me."

Caden watched their surroundings with a critical eye, wondering what sort of ambush might be waiting for them. Burke's note told him not to trust anyone, but what about Angus? He was close to Lord D'Lance, that much was obvious, but was he aware of what his lord was plotting? And if he was, did he continue to follow the man out of loyalty, or fear? Caden decided it was too risky to say anything to the commander.

"We may be headed for trouble, then. I'm certain that Lord Culver has magic users in his arsenal. We have nothing to defend ourselves with against magic."

"Let us wait and see what lies ahead," Angus said. "It's possible the reports were exaggerated. At least, that's what I'm hoping. The last thing we need is a war on our hands."

If Angus was aware of Lord D'Lance's dealings, he played ignorant well. They continued along the dirt road, up and down hills, and eventually passed through the last sign of civilization for the next several miles.

"Time to speed things up!" Angus shouted.

His horse charged ahead. Caden urged his own mount, and soon they were thundering down the road at a break-neck pace. The scenery flashed by too quickly for him to take note of an ambush, so he kept his eyes on the road ahead. They rode as long as the horses could manage, then stopped to give them a water break. After a few minutes of rest, they were back on the road again.

It was late in the afternoon when they reached the border between the two Dominions. Caden slowed his horse down and surveyed the area. There was a walled city in the distance, on the other side of the border. It was surrounded by an open field of tall grass that swayed from a light breeze that had picked up.

"What is that place?" Caden asked.

"That's Yediff. It's one of Lord Culver's fortresses here on the border. He's got several of them."

"I don't see signs of an army."

"Neither do I, but we shouldn't let our guard down. They could be holed up in Yediff, waiting to attack."

Caden had a bad feeling in his gut. Something was wrong, just as it had been with Burke's death. He scanned the field, and though the grass was tall, it wasn't high enough to hide an army.

"What do you think we should do?"

Angus scratched his chin, his gaze glued to the city. "We should scout the area. I don't want the rest of our men walking into a trap with no escape." The commander turned his horse around to face the rest of the Runesmen.

"Split up and ride through the field. Look for anything out of the ordinary, but try not to draw attention to yourselves. If you find anything, alert the rest of us."

The men divided into pairs and rode across the border at a leisurely pace. Caden looked at Angus.

"I guess you're with me," he said, smiling.

"I guess so," Caden replied, flicking the reins.

The grass was golden yellow, and Caden realized it wasn't grass, but wheat. It stretched as far as he could see, and aside from Yediff, there was nothing else around.

"They've got plenty of crops," he muttered.

"The Toren Dominion has lots of ideal farmland," Angus said. "It's one of the reasons Lord Culver has gained his wealth. He exports the excess food to his neighbors."

"Everyone has to eat."

"Indeed."

Caden continued to search for signs of an army or even the presence of one that might have passed through, but there was nothing that caught his eye. He wondered for a brief moment if he was being paranoid about Lord D'Lance, but he quickly reminded himself of all the evidence contrary to that thought.

As they neared Yediff, he scanned the wall for guards. There were none that he could see, and he found it curious.

"If Lord Culver is encroaching on the Dracan Dominion, I'd assume this place would be crawling with his troops."

"Maybe it was a diversion," Angus replied. "Perhaps the real attack is coming from somewhere else."

Something heavy struck Caden in the back of the head and he fell out of the saddle, crashing hard on the ground face-first. He rolled onto his back, and the world spun around him. His headache returned with a vengeance. Angus slid out of the saddle and came to stand over him.

"What happened?" Caden asked, confused.

"You shouldn't have gone snooping, you blasted fool. Burke should have kept his mouth shut. It would have saved *your* life, at least."

"Burke's death wasn't an accident, was it?" Caden's vision returned to normal, and he reached for the hilt of his sword. Angus kicked his hand aside and pressed his foot onto Caden's chest, then unsheathed his own sword.

"Don't bother fighting," Angus warned. "You're a dead man either way."

23

"I thought Lord Klodian was the one in danger?" Thais asked.

"He is, too, but Lord Burgess was part of a bigger plot."

"Was?" Thais's face paled. "Is he dead?"

"No," Mina shook her head. She didn't know how to explain things without revealing everything that had happened with Copper. She wished Caden was here, but there was no changing that now. She would have to trust Thais, as much as it went against her instincts.

"I want you to swear that you won't repeat what I'm about to tell you."

"Won't repeat it to who?"

"Anyone. This stays between us."

Thais eyed her distrustfully. "Did you kill someone?"

"Don't be absurd. Just promise me before I change my mind. I'm offering to trust you with something."

"You don't have to be dramatic. I won't say anything."

Mina took a deep breath. "Dragons can talk."

Thais's left eye twitched, but she didn't say anything.

"I know it sounds crazy, but—"

"I believe you."

"—just listen … what?"

"I said I believe you."

They stared at each other in silence for a moment.

"You do?" Mina asked.

Thais nodded.

"Why?"

"I have my reasons. What does that have to do with the High Prince?"

Mina told Thais everything beginning with her talk with Copper on the mesa before the sand wyrm showed up to their interrogation in the dungeon. Thais listened intently and didn't seem to be surprised by any of it. Mina related most of the details but left out the part of being bonded to a dragon and the bit of history that Copper had told her.

"Should we tell Lord Klodian?"

"No," Thais answered almost immediately. "At least, not yet. We need to eliminate Lady Burgess before she reports to back to Lord D'Lance if she hasn't already."

"You don't mean kill her?"

"No, not if we can help it. Can your dragon friend erase her memory as well?"

"I can ask him," Mina said.

"After she's dealt with, we can take all of this to Captain Eduard."

"Can he be trusted? We saw him talking in secret with Lord Burgess."

"I don't think the captain is a traitor. He has access to Lord Klodian at all hours of the day. If he wanted to do something, he'd have done it by now."

Mina silently conceded the point. She didn't know Eduard very well, but she had decided to trust Thais, which meant that she needed to be confident in the woman's judgment.

"What if he doesn't believe us? If Lady Burgess's memories are erased, then neither one of them can attest to Lord D'Lance's plan."

"Then as one of Lord Klodian's advisors, you can tell him directly."

Mina didn't know if he would believe her wild tale, but as long as she told him, her conscience would be clear. She nodded.

"What do you plan on doing with that egg?" Thais asked.

"I'm taking it back where it belongs."

"To the dragons. Makes sense, but is it safe? What if you hand it over and the dragon eats you?"

"He won't," Mina replied.

Thais shrugged. "If you say so. What about that wyrm thing? Is it still out there?"

"I don't know. I didn't ask Copper if he killed it."

"Copper, huh? So they have names?"

"Yes. They aren't mindless animals at all. Everything we've ever thought about them might be wrong."

"What changed your opinion about them?"

The question gave Mina pause. She honestly didn't have a clear answer. She supposed it was lots of little things all tied together.

"I guess Copper changed my mind about them," she said. "It's difficult to explain."

Thais remained silent, but Mina thought the woman looked like she wanted to say something. She waited, but Thais didn't speak.

"Say it."

"Say what?"

"Whatever is on your mind," Mina said.

"I suppose I'm feeling guilty."

"About what?"

Thais sighed. "You're forced to trust me because you need my help. I shouldn't feel obligated, but I do. For the record, I don't enjoy the feeling. I've never relied on anyone before, and I don't expect to in the future."

Mina frowned, confused. "I don't understand whatever it is you're trying to say."

"I'll ask the same promise of you. What I'm going to say could get me killed by many different people."

"You can trust me."

Although they were the only two people present, Thais lowered her voice.

"I believe you about the dragons because I've seen it myself."

"You've seen me talking with Copper?"

"No. I've seen what Lord D'Lance is doing. I tried to tell Caden when he was here, but he said I was crazy."

Mina was more confused than before. She opened her mouth to say something, then pursed her lips.

"He didn't tell you?" Thais asked.

"If he did, I must have missed it."

"The attack on Slia was done by dragons, but it wasn't an accident. Lord D'Lance was behind it. He's a wicked man, and the things he's doing are evil. He found a way to unite humans and dragons, but it isn't natural."

"What do you mean 'unite?'"

"He's using dark magic to force dragons into some sort of bond with humans. They can share each other's thoughts and communicate telepathically. Slia was a test. He wanted to see how his creation would work as a weapon."

Mina remembered what Copper had said about how humans and dragons had once been allies, and about the bond they shared. Had Lord D'Lance learned of it somehow and tried to recreate it by force? She would have to tell Copper.

"So Lord D'Lance attacked Slia with dragons? How can he control them?"

"His soldiers control them through their bond. They are magically bound to follow their rider's commands."

"The soldiers ride the dragons?" Mina asked.

"Yes, and Lord D'Lance is building an army of them. He's going to use them to take the throne from the High Prince."

Things were starting to make sense to Mina. Lord Burgess's mission to overthrow Klodian was part of the bigger picture, and Lord D'Lance's ultimate goal was to take over as High Prince. He needed something to divert attention from himself, and making Klodian and Lord Culver appear to be forming a rebellion was the diversion. There was one thing she didn't understand.

"How do you know all this?"

"Lord D'Lance sent me here … as a spy."

<h1 style="text-align:center">24</h1>

Caden stared up at Angus, angry with himself for not being more vigilant.

"You could let me go. I won't come back to the Dracan. I'll go to my grave with what I know." He doubted the commander would believe his words. Caden glanced to his horse. If he could get on his feet quickly enough, he was confident he could reach the mount and get to the city before Angus could catch him.

"Lord D'Lance doesn't want to any loose ends. So long as you live, you pose a threat. But I'm not the one you need to beg. It's not my blade that will be your end."

Angus removed his foot and drove his sword down, stabbing the point through Caden's chainmail and into the ground, pinning him in place. They locked eyes, and Caden prayed the man would help him, but Angus turned away and mounted his horse. He grabbed the reins of Caden's horse and rode back across the border.

Caden struggled to pull the sword free, but the angle was awkward and he couldn't get the leverage he needed.

"Help!" He cried out.

Did the other Runesmen know what was happening? Would they come to his aid, or had they left him there to die? He continued struggling and eventually, the sword loosened enough that he was able to get up. Caden ran for the city, waving his arms around. The closer he got to the walls of the city, the more his eyes began to play tricks on him.

The stone rippled like water, and when he reached the gate, he passed right through it. The city was an illusion. It faded before his eyes, leaving only a black cloud behind. Caden spun around, looking in every direction. There was nothing but the expanse of wheat fields. A whistling sound filled the air, and he turned to look at the cloud. It was swirling and began to expand in a circle, leaving a hole in the middle.

Caden watched the cloud with uncertainty, knowing it was the product of magic but scared of what it might do. The cloud continued stretching until it encircled a large portion of the field, then it touched the ground and the wheat erupted in flames. The fire spread quickly, and Caden realized too late what was happening.

He looked to the border and saw Angus, along with a robed figure who was directing the cloud with his hands. Caden couldn't see the man's face, but he knew it was Lord D'Lance. He must have found out that Burke had discovered what he was doing, and once he knew that Caden was also involved, it only made sense that the Dominion Lord would want him dead, too.

Ash and gray smoke billowed into the sky, blotting out the landscape and obscuring his view. Caden knew he needed to warn Lord Culver and the High Prince, but if he burned to death here, the Dominions would end up engulfed in war. He jogged along the perimeter, looking for a spot where he could get through the flames unscathed. Unfortunately, the fire burned intensely and the heat drove him back.

As the flames consumed everything in their path, Caden's hope began to flee. There was no way to escape. He was going to die, burned alive. All of his dreams and ambitions flashed within his mind, and he cursed Lord D'Lance as a fool and a coward. He kept moving despite the knowledge that this was the end. The wind blew the smoke into his face, and he coughed, covering his mouth with the crook of his arm.

Something whizzed through the air, striking the ground beside him. Through blurry eyes, he saw it was an arrow. Another one struck the ground a few away from the first one, and another. The smoke was too thick for him to see anything, and he gasped in surprise when an arrow struck him in the chest. It pierced his chainmail shirt and cut through his flesh, hitting bone.

Caden slumped to the ground on his knees, clutching the arrow. He wanted to pull it out, but he knew it didn't matter if he did. Nothing mattered anymore. He saw more arrows zip through the smoke, but they missed him. Breathing became difficult, though whether it was the smoke or his wound, he didn't know.

He struggled to stay up, but his vision was spinning. Caden felt himself falling, and then he was on his back, staring up at the gray sky. Darkness began to fill the edges of his vision, and it slowly dawned on him that it wasn't the lack of sunlight. This was it. His life was slipping away. He pictured Mina in his mind and prayed that she wasn't mad at him for the kiss they'd shared.

The darkness beckoned him, and he followed it. As the shroud of death closed around him, he thought he heard a woman's voice calling his name.

Caden ... come to me ...

25

THE NEXT MORNING, MINA LAY awake in her bed, thinking about everything Thais had told her the night before. The woman had been forced into working for Lord D'Lance because he had her parents as captives. Mina considered telling Lord Klodian everything, but she knew it would lead to him asking questions that she wouldn't be able to answer, not without endangering Copper.

She forced herself out of bed, yawning and stretching. She was tired, but she wanted to get the egg to Copper as soon as possible. The only problem she faced was how to carry it. Due to its size, it would be difficult to transport on horseback, and she didn't want to go on foot. Mina mulled it over as she got dressed, then headed down to the dining hall and ate a quick meal.

While she was eating, she saw one of the servants carrying a baby. It was swaddled in a cloth that was wrapped around the woman's body, giving her the ability to use her hands. That gave her an idea, and she went to Klodian's seamstress and got a long swath of cloth cut. The seamstress waved away her money, telling her that Lord Klodian's advisors didn't have to pay.

It still felt odd for her to be in a position of privilege. She rolled the cloth up and went to the stable. Aram was working again, and he gave her a look that told her he wasn't happy to see her.

"If you're here for a horse, you'll have to take Vesper. Tempest has been taken already."

Mina was disappointed to hear that, but she nodded. "Very well."

Vesper was similar in size to Tempest, but he was a chestnut color and seemed temperamental. Aram struggled to saddle the horse, and once he was done, he handed Mina the reins.

"Good luck with this one," he muttered.

Mina led the horse out of the gate on foot and went to where she'd buried the egg. She was relieved to see it was still there. Unrolling the cloth she'd got, she placed the egg in the center and wrapped it, then wound the cloth around her upper body, cinching it tightly. It seemed firmly in place, but she jumped a few times to make sure. Satisfied it wouldn't come loose, she climbed into the saddle and guided Vesper into the desert.

As they approached the mesa, she looked for the body of the sand wyrm, but there was no sign of it. Mina wondered if the dragons had eaten it, but guessed that might not be the case as there were no bones left behind. She could feel that Copper wasn't on the mesa. His presence was still pulsing from the scale, but he seemed far away.

She guessed he was with his brethren, and so she left the horse at the base of the mesa and climbed her way to the top. It was more difficult than her first venture, mainly because of the added weight of the egg. Once she was safe atop the mesa, she untied the cloth and removed the egg, setting it down on the ground. Its surface was scaled like a dragon's, but the scales were smaller and more closely overlapped.

The color had dulled since the last time she'd seen it. It had once been copper like the scale in her leg, but now it was a light blueish-green. Mina looked over the edge of the mesa and admired the view. The desert was a harsh place, but it was also beautiful. Some people found comfort among the busy city streets, but not Mina. She enjoyed the peace that nature brought.

After an hour of walking around the mesa, she heard the flapping of wings and looked to the sky. Copper was swiftly approaching. She hurried back to the egg and waited for him to land. He swooped down and touched the ground on the other side of the mesa, then folded his wings behind him and walked over to where she waited.

You were successful this time, he said.

I was.

Mina lifted the egg and carried it to the dragon, placing it at his feet. Copper leaned down and inspected it, and Mina caught the scent of orchids. She tilted her head curiously.

What is it?

This egg will never hatch.

Mina's heart sank. *It's dead?*

Not completely, but there is not enough life in it to survive. Even now I can feel it slowly fading.

I'm sorry.

It is the way of life sometimes, Copper said. *Regardless, I am glad it has been returned to us. I spoke to my brethren about the things I saw in Lord Burgess's mind last night, and we are in agreement that what this Lord D'Lance has done is a perversion and must be stopped.*

Thais told me that he's forcing humans and dragons to bond using magic.

How does she know this?

It's a long story, but she has seen it with her own eyes. She said Lord D'Lance is building an army to use against the High Prince. He wants the throne for himself.

Copper growled. *What we sought to prevent is unfolding before us again. Perhaps we were wrong in our thinking. Perhaps humans will never stop.*

We aren't all bad, Mina said.

Copper regarded her in silence. *No, not all,* he said. *Yet those that are always seem to wield power. And they always want more of it. Humans do not know how to be content. I fear the time has come that dragons must wage war against the darkness.*

War? Do you really think it will come to that?

Yes.

A war between humans and dragons would be disastrous. There must be another way.

I'm afraid there isn't. The elders have already made their decision. They are making preparations even as we speak.

Innocent people will be caught in the middle, Mina protested. *Please, you must ask them to reconsider. If we can find a way to stop Lord D'Lance and free the dragons from the magic, that should be enough, shouldn't it?*

You are asking me to go against the stream, he said. *The elders have grown tired of seeing dragons killed, and what Lord D'Lance has done has pushed them over the edge.*

Then let me speak to them. Mina didn't know why she said those words. They just slipped right out of her mouth. She stared up at Copper, silently praying he would deny her.

There is much you will need to learn about being bonded to a dragon. As a bonded human, you are allowed certain privileges, such as an audience before the elders. I will take you to them, but I cannot guarantee they will heed your words.

Although she was afraid, Mina knew that she was probably the only person who might be bonded to a dragon. At least, not forcibly. If she could avert a war between their two races, then certainly she had to try.

I wish to speak with them, even if they won't listen.

Very well. It is a long journey from here, and we will go deep into the desert where it is not safe for you, but I will do my best to protect you. We will need to go now, else we may be too late.

Now? Mina's eyes widened. *But I'm not ready to go yet.*

In this matter, time is not on our side. If we don't go now, then war will come.

Mina looked over her shoulder in the direction of the castle. She couldn't see it from here, but she knew it was there in the distance. Why had she suddenly been thrust into the middle of this? It was partly because she didn't know how to keep her mouth shut, true, but she was a nobody. Who would listen to what she had to say?

You have more worth than you give yourself credit for, Copper said.

That's hard to believe when you've spent your entire life being told differently.

Perhaps, but the opinions of others should not influence how you view yourself.

She knew he was right, but that didn't change her mental struggle. Either way, her view of her worth wasn't important right now. There were much larger things at play, things that she potentially had the chance to sway.

If we must go now, then so be it.

Copper hummed in satisfaction and lowered himself close to the ground.

Climb upon my back, he said.

Truly?

Unless you want to go in my claws, but that will not be comfortable. Riding upon my back is one of the benefits I mentioned.

Mina took a few hesitant steps, then steeled her mind against her fears. She climbed up Copper's shoulder and sat upon his back, hardly believing that it was all real. Copper grabbed the egg in his mouth and flexed his wings out.

Hold on, he warned her.

She dug her fingers under the scales on Copper's neck and closed her eyes. Her stomach flipped and turned as she felt herself falling, and then the sensation was gone. She peeked her eyes open and saw they were flying above the mesas. It was both exhilarating and terrifying. Copper turned south, and the desert stretched as far as she could see.

I'm afraid, Mina said.

I know, Copper replied.

They continued over the landscape, toward the elders, the possibility of war, and many other things yet to be seen.

But mostly, Mina knew they were headed toward the unknown.

CALL

OF THE

DRAGON

1

When Mina arrived at the underground city that Copper called home, the first thing she noticed was the heat. It was located deep within The Long Sands, and she was drenched in sweat by the time they landed. A few dragons flew overhead, wheeling around in lazy circles.

What are they doing?

They are scouts, Copper replied. *They keep watch for sand wyrms.*

She thought about the one she had seen before and shivered at the memory.

You are safe here. Even if one got past the scouts, it would face an army of us.

What if more than one came?

They are not intelligent enough to band together.

His answer gave her some relief. That was one thing she didn't have to worry about. She slid off Copper's back and groaned. Her rear end was sore, as were her back and legs, and her fingers were cramped. She stretched them by making fists and releasing them, trying to work the stiffness out.

Many of the dragons here have not seen a human in centuries. I expect you'll not receive a warm welcome.

Will they try to hurt me?

No. And if they did, I would not allow it. You are bonded to me, and it is my duty to protect you.

Even from your own kind?

Yes.

Mina hoped for both their sakes that it wouldn't come to that.

Follow me, Copper said. *You can rest in my chamber.*

The dragon walked down into the sloped cave-like entrance, and Mina trailed behind him. Thick glass formed the walls and ceiling, and unnatural light flickered within it, illuminating their way as they lost the sunlight behind them.

Where did all this glass come from? Mina asked.

We made it.

With magic?

Copper laughed at the question. *With our flames. Sand turns to glass under extreme heat.*

Truly? I didn't know that. She paused. *Why did you use glass?*

Sand on its own is weak. We wouldn't be able to tunnel through it without something to keep it from collapsing. We dragons like to see our reflections, so glass was the logical choice.

Mina stared at the wall to her right and watched their likenesses drifting along beside them. Lord Klodian had ornate mirrors and windows, but they were nothing in comparison. The deeper they traveled, the cooler the air became. By the time they reached Copper's chamber, she was no longer sweating.

Inside, an enormous pool with crystal clear water drew her attention. She wanted nothing more than to bathe in it and wash the grime from her body.

Go ahead, Copper bade. *I must go and speak with the elders.*

You want me to stay here, alone?

You'll be fine so long as you don't venture out of my chamber. Until certain things are decided, you must stay in here.

That sounded like she was a prisoner, and Mina didn't like it. What could she do, though? She was a defenseless human surrounded by dragons.

How long will you be gone? she asked.

Not long. Wash yourself, and when I return, I will teach you some things that you will need to know before you go before the elders.

What kind of things?

Don't worry about that now. Go.

Mina walked to the edge of the water and looked over her shoulder, glimpsing Copper's tail as it swished out of view. She wondered how she was safe when the chamber had no door, but she pushed the thought away. If Copper said he would protect her, then she had to believe him. She stripped out of her clothes and tossed them into the pool, then stepped into the water.

The temperature was cool, but not cold. She submerged herself to her neck and sighed, feeling relaxed. Her clothes floated nearby, and she grabbed them and rung them out, setting them on the edge of the pool to dry. After Mina had washed the sweat and filth from her body, she left the pool and drip-dried.

There was nothing to warm her clothes with, and they were still damp when Copper returned. Mina hid from his view by holding the wet clothes against her body. He snorted in response.

I care nothing for your nakedness.

It feels weird letting anyone see me, whether we are the same species or not.

I forgot how sensitive humans were. It's no wonder that your lifespans are so short.

Mina rolled her eyes. *I'm not sensitive. I'm just ...*

Self-conscious? Copper asked.

Yes.

He snorted again.

Can you dry my clothes?

Sure. Set them on the ground.

Mina hesitantly did so, then quickly stood up and tried awkwardly to cover herself with her arms. Copper ignored her and opened his mouth, setting the clothes on fire with a gust of his flaming breath. Mina's eyes widened in shock.

Why did you do that?

You don't need those rags anymore. You are dragon-bonded, and so you shall dress appropriately. Your new chamber is beside mine. Do you see the cleft there?

Mina followed his gaze to a spot in the glass wall that was darker than the rest.

That is a passage that connects our chambers. When we first built this place, we added rooms for our bonded. We had hoped that the spell the elders cast would eventually fade and that we would bond with humans again. That never happened, but we kept the rooms anyway. This is your new home if you so choose.

What of the elders? Mina asked. *Won't they have a problem with me being here?*

That remains to be seen, Copper replied. *They have agreed to hear your petition, so get dressed. The clothes in there should fit you, but let me know if they do not. Once you are ready, I will teach you about the Enclave.*

The Enclave?

Go, Copper bade. *We have little time before the elders call upon you.*

Mina nodded and made an embarrassing dash to the passage. It was only about six feet in length, and then she found herself in more familiar surroundings. The room was decorated with human decor. There was a bed and a wardrobe, as well as a large rug and a manakin with a suit of leather armor.

She wandered over to the wardrobe and opened the double doors. Black pants and a blue shirt caught her eye, and she quickly put them on. Casting a glance at herself in the mirror, she saw that she looked different somehow. Perhaps it was an illusion, or perhaps she only thought she looked different.

Are you ready yet? Copper asked.

Yes.

Mina looked at the manakin and wondered if she would end up wearing the armor. She was not a warrior, but that didn't mean she couldn't become one.

Can you teach me to fight? she asked.

Perhaps. If you sway the elders, your potential is limitless.

Mina's eyes lingered on the armor a moment longer, then she went back into Copper's room. She was going to do whatever it took to impress the elders.

2

There was nothing.

He was nothing, just an ethereal thought floating amid the unknown. Something indistinct floated near him. As he stared at it, it became clearer, more defined. It was five letters arranged in a specific pattern.

Caden.

His name, perhaps? Yes, there was something about it that rang true within his spirit. He tried to reach for it, but he had no hands or arms. A voice spoke the name, his name, and it echoed all around him.

Come to me.

Caden's eyes snapped open and he gasped in a deep breath. He laid there, confused. What had happened? Where had he been? The memory was already vague, and soon it was gone completely. He was staring up at the sky, the blue vastness of it more striking than he remembered.

Rise, and come to me.

The voice sounded familiar to him, and yet he couldn't place it. A strange feeling, to be sure. Caden sat up and looked around. A blackened field stretched in all directions. He touched the black stuff with his fingers and inspected them.

Ash.

Slowly, the events came back to him. He'd been murdered. Or at least, they had *tried* to murder him. Strangely, he was still alive. Another mystery. He stood on shaky legs and wondered how long he'd been out. The smoke he'd breathed in must have caused him to lose consciousness. Not far away, he saw the bodies of horses and their riders. He didn't have to see them up close to know they were Runesmen. Lord D'Lance's cruelty and malice knew no bounds.

He had survived, which meant that he could take the knowledge of what he'd learned to Lord Culver. Once the High Prince learned of Lord D'Lance's treachery, there would be hell to pay. Caden ran his tongue across his cracked lips. He needed water and food, in that order. Shelter too, but that could wait. He'd slept under the stars plenty of times. As he turned to the east, he felt something pulling at him.

Go north.

It was that voice again. Caden turned to the north and stared ahead. If he went that way, it would mean going back into Lord D'Lance's dominion. He knew he should probably go east to Lord Culver, but the voice that called to him was so very strong. His curiosity was too much, and he walked across the field, following the pull he felt.

He walked for hours, crossing over rivers and open fields, and navigating through darker landscapes that were bereft of life. The voice guided him the entire way. His clothes became dirty, his feet blistered, yet he pushed himself onward until he reached the base of a jagged mountain. Clouds had gathered overhead, signaling rain. Lightning flashed, and thunder rumbled a moment later. He was close now. The source of the voice was up there somewhere.

Caden began climbing the mountain.

At first, it was easy. Then the rain started, pattering softly here and there until it became a downpour, forcing him to scramble on all fours up the treacherous terrain. The water made it more perilous. The voice was stronger here, filled with power, and he focused on it, ignoring the pain in his muscles.

His clothes became soaked and stuck to his skin, annoying and awkward. Caden didn't relent. He continued up the face of the mountain until he reached a plateau. As he pulled himself onto it, he saw the shadowy ingress of a cave. Crumbling pillars engraved with symbols lined the entrance, standing guard silently.

Glancing behind him, Caden realized just how far he'd come. The base of the mountain was lost far below, hidden by the clouds and the rain. The air was thinner up here, and it was colder. He shivered and turned his gaze back to the entrance, staring into the inky blackness.

Enter, the voice bade.

How could he refuse? He'd come this far. Inexorably, his feet took him into the shadows. Once he passed between the pillars, the darkness took his sight and it forced him to feel along the wall with his hands. The stones were smooth, and Caden somehow knew this wasn't a natural cave at all, but a tunnel built by mortal hands.

He followed it blindly for so long that he thought he would be forever lost, but the voice strengthened his resolve. Ahead, he saw a faint green light. It was coming from the moss that had grown along the walls and across the ceiling. The glow illuminated the way, and he walked with confidence.

The tunnel opened up into a large circular chamber. The remains of what Caden assumed was an old temple were scattered around the room. He had a vague feeling that he'd seen this place before, but he knew that wasn't possible. He had never been to this mountain before, never knew of its existence until the voice had called him there.

Still, it *felt* familiar to him somehow. Perhaps he'd dreamt of it.

Yes, Caden thought. *I've been here in my dreams.*

He made his way closer to the ruined structure and stopped when something in the shadows moved. Fear crept into the back of his mind, and he grabbed the hilt of his sword. He couldn't die here, not like this. Alone. Forgotten. The voice soothed those fears.

Come inside.

Caden hesitated for only a moment, then he stepped inside the open doorway. Judging by the hinges on the frame, it was obvious there had once been a door attached. Inside, there was an altar with a bowl that rested atop it. From the looks of things, a fire had ravaged the place. The floor was covered in a thick layer of gray ash, and the crumbling walls were black with soot.

Behind the altar was a tall chair that reminded him of a throne. And behind the throne, he caught sight of two glowing eyes. Caden's heart raced in his chest, but as the seconds slipped by and nothing happened, he calmed himself. There was nothing to fear. The voice would protect him, just as it had on his journey here.

Before, there had only been the voice in his mind, but now, there was a presence. It loomed in the shadows behind the throne.

"Who are you?" Caden asked. He kept his hand on the hilt of his blade.

You don't recognize me?

"No."

Mankind has forgotten me, the voice mused. *I was worshipped by men long ago. One goddess among many. I was here in the beginning. I owned the skies before men walked the earth, before their greed drove them to hurt me. You wouldn't hurt me, would you?*

Caden wondered why anyone would hurt her. She offered comfort and peace, provided protection where nothing else could. He had an epiphany, then. It was she who had kept him from the brink of death. Lord D'Lance had betrayed him, but she had saved him.

"I will never hurt you," Caden vowed.

That is good. We must have trust, you and I.

The eyes behind the throne blinked lazily.

I grow weary of being forced here. There is something you must do for me.

"What is it?" He would do anything for her.

The man who imprisoned me is the one you call Lord D'Lance. He is a wicked man, a foe to all of my kind. There is a room in his castle where he performs his dark deeds. Do you know of it?

"I'm afraid not," Caden replied. "But I will find it."

I trust you will. Inside the room, there should be a gemstone. It was created by Lord D'Lance to hurt me and keep me here in these ruins. Even now, its power sears my very being. I need you to destroy it.

"I will destroy it," Caden swore, removing his hand from the hilt and placing it on his chest. "And I will kill Lord D'Lance."

No! The voice hissed. *His death will come at my claws when I am ready.*

"You can trust me. I will spare him for you."

He will try to stop you. He will say many things to dissuade you from this course. You must not believe them.

"I will not believe his lies," Caden said.

The glowing eyes twinkled with satisfaction.

Once you have the stone, I will tell you how to destroy it. It will not be easy, but the cost will be worth it. You will be my general, and I will gather many to our cause. You will lead them all.

"I am not worthy."

I will make you worthy.

Caden could feel her power pulsing, expanding throughout the chamber. Ripples in the air drifted toward him and he held out his hand to touch them. Electricity touched his fingertips, filtering through his body. Caden could feel the raw power coursing through him, and it was exhilarating.

A tremor shook the mountain. Loose rocks clattered on the ground, joining the chittering of bats and other subterranean creatures that awoke from the disturbance. The voice spoke a single word.

Go.

3

TELL ME AGAIN.

Mina forced her eyes closed and tried to be patient. Copper was trying to get her to memorize an abundance of facts about the elders and dragons, but it was just too much information for her to take in all at once.

There are seven elders that rule the desert, and all of them are from the metallic colors.

Good. Keep going.

Every 100 years, they switch places with another set of elders. They do this for many reasons, but mainly to prevent keeping the brethren stuck in their ways. Every group of elders leads differently. They are all to be respected because they are both wise and powerful.

Copper stared at her with slitted eyes and nodded his head. *When you are standing before the Enclave, what must you remember?*

That I should not speak out of turn, Mina replied.

And?

Mina huffed in a breath. *And I should address the elders as Tiarna.*

I think you are ready.

I don't feel ready.

Movement near the cave entrance caught Mina's attention. A silver dragon looked at Copper and bowed his head, then left.

We're out of time, Copper said. *The elders have summoned us.*

You'll be there with me?

Yes, but I will remain silent. The petition is yours, so you must speak for yourself.

I'll do my best.

That is all anyone can ask. Come.

Mina walked behind Copper as he led her through the glass tunnels, twisting and sloping deeper underground. They paused outside two towering glass doors, but Mina wasn't able to see anything on the other side. Her reflection stared back at her, and she took a deep breath to steady her racing heart.

Copper pressed the top of his head against one of the doors and closed his eyes. A few seconds passed, and then a creaking sound echoed off the walls as the doors slowly swung open. On the other side of the threshold was a massive cavern. Seven dragons were there waiting, all of them as large as Copper.

He walked inside, but Mina stood rooted in place. Dragon fear had consumed her. She trembled uncontrollably, her eyes fixed ahead where a silver dragon sat. The dragon returned her stare unblinkingly. It was a female. Mina could sense her through the scale. The dragon was probing her mind. Hundreds of memories of her past flashed before her eyes within seconds.

The dragon's presence receded from her mind, taking the fear with it.

Mina swallowed hard and stepped into the cavern, taking her place beside Copper. All the elders were watching her, and they filled the chamber with a chaotic wave of scents, but two stood out the strongest: vanilla and freesia.

Why do your emotions have smells to them?

Copper tilted his head to the side, flicking his gaze at her. *We will talk about that later.*

She could feel his astonishment through the scale. Why was he surprised? She turned her attention to the silver dragon in the center. The platform she rested on was taller than the others, and Mina assumed she was the leader of the Enclave.

Step forward.

Mina hesitantly stepped in front of Copper. She was tempted to cast her eyes to the ground, but she forced herself to keep her head up. She could feel all the dragons through the scale, their various presences unique and distinct from one another.

Tiarna, she greeted. *Thank you for honoring me with an audience.*

She felt odd talking like a noble, but Copper had stressed the importance of her words. She bowed at the waist and held the position, counting to three in her mind before rising back up.

It has been a long time since there has been a rider among us, the silver dragon said. *I hope that this is a good thing.*

The other dragons echoed their agreement, their voices swirling together within her mind.

Your bonded tells me you wanted to speak to us about something important?

Yes, Tiarna.

Speak your mind, rider.

Mina wasn't sure why the dragon was calling her a rider. She'd only rode on Copper's back once, and it wasn't something she thought she would do again. She was getting sidetracked, and she knew it.

Copper told me you are going to war against Lord D'Lance. I have come before you to beg you to reconsider. I know that he has perverted the bond, forcing humans and dragons together using dark magic, but many lives will be lost if you take this course.

The dragons remained silent, so she continued.

I learned that we used to be allies. If that is true, do you not think that war is too harsh a punishment? One man's crimes should not weigh upon the innocent.

Collateral damage is always a problem with war, the dragon admitted. *Yet what would you have us do? He must be stopped. Not only has he corrupted the bond, but he is also performing twisted experiments with dragon eggs.*

Mina grimaced. *I did not know that. What kind of experiments?*

The silver dragon looked at Copper. He lowered his head, and they shared a knowing look. The dragon looked back at her.

He is using his magic to manipulate the eggs, combining their life force with humans. He is making himself an army of monsters.

Why didn't you tell me that? Mina asked Copper.

Would it have mattered?

She supposed it wouldn't have, but she didn't like being surprised.

Please, Mina begged the silver dragon. *I am afraid that war will cause more problems than it will solve. If you do this, there's no telling what might happen. People might band together and hunt down dragons.*

Do you think this is something new? It is not. Humans have hunted our kind for ages. You yourself have been responsible for the death of many of my brethren.

Mina's throat constricted and her heart felt like it plummeted into her stomach.

You are right, she said. *I led death to the door of many dragons, but I was naïve and didn't know what I do now. I can't take back my actions, but I hope that I can repair the damage I've done in some way.*

We shall see.

Do not go to war, Mina begged again.

Lord D'Lance must be stopped.

I will stop him.

Her mind went silent. The dragons kept their eyes on her, but their words and emotions eluded her. Their faces were impassive, devoid of any telltale signs that she could decipher. The silence stretched until she thought she'd gone deaf.

What makes you think you can stop him? Powerful men surround him, and his magic is as dark as the night. Are you a warrior, that you will raise a sword against him? No. I have seen your memories. You are not a fighter.

Then I will learn to be one.

Who will teach you?

I'll find someone, Mina said.

The dragon growled and looked at the other elders. They grumbled back and forth, speaking to each other in a way that Mina didn't understand. Finally, the rumbling ceased and the silver dragon looked at her.

We will hold off our attack. You will have two weeks to learn to be a warrior, and then you must deal with Lord D'Lance. If you fail, then we will have our war.

And if I don't fail?

We shall see.

4

CADEN SAT BESIDE A STREAM, his bare feet in the water. The temperature was frigid and numbed his skin, which eased the pain of his blisters. Now that he had put some distance between himself and the source of the voice, the entire encounter felt like a dream. If it wasn't for the constant presence of the voice in the back of his mind, he would believe it *had* been a dream.

His stomach growled, reminding him that he needed to find food. He had no idea how long he'd been lying in the burned field before gaining consciousness. Had it been hours or days? Judging by how empty his stomach felt, he guessed the latter. He was in the heart of the woods, so finding game would be easy. Catching it, however, would be the challenge.

The smell of something cooking reached his nose, and he pulled his feet from the water and slipped his boots back on. He stood, strapping his sword belt on, and listened for sounds. At first, there was nothing, and he assumed that the smell must have been the workings of his imagination.

Then he heard voices.

Caden rested his hand on the hilt of his blade and slowly stalked along the trees, following the sound of hushed conversation. Water squished between his toes, making a wet sucking sound with every step. He slowed his pace as he came around a thick cluster of bushes.

A group of men were gathered around a fire. He counted five of them, all wearing armor and armed with a range of weapons. They also had hooded cloaks on, and Caden wondered why they would wear them with the heat. It wasn't as hot as the desert, but wearing a cloak in this weather was still too much.

As he listened, he realized the men were Lord D'Lance's. They spoke low, but he made out the man's name a few times. One of them was tending to an animal that was cooking over the fire. His stomach rumbled again, and the smell tempted him to join them. It was unlikely they would know who he was, especially since he was thought to be dead, but he didn't think it was worth the risk.

Caden turned to leave and found himself cornered by three men. At least, their stature implied they were men. Their faces proved otherwise. They had long snouts like a lizard, and their flesh was scaly. Caden blinked, not sure if what he saw was real. The one closest to him stepped closer.

"What'sss are you doings here?" His tone was low, almost like a whisper.

"I was just passing through," Caden replied. He couldn't take his eyes off the man's face.

"He's lying," another said.

"A spy," chimed the third.

"Comes to see what our master has done? You sees now, don'ts you?"

Caden took a step back, but the lizard man quickly grabbed onto his arm, pulling him close. Caden tried to break away, but the man's grip was solid. The other two closed in and they subdued him, forcing his arms behind his back and binding his wrists.

"Stops yer fighting," the leader-apparent snapped, punching Caden in the stomach.

The blow forced the air from his lungs, and he gasped, falling limp. The lizard men grabbed him by the arms and lifted him, carrying him to where the others were and dropped him to the ground. They began talking to one another in a harsh-sounding language. Caden fought to breathe, temporarily ignored as his captors talked among themselves. Finally, the one that punched him knelt at his side and looked him in the eyes.

"We're goings to eats you," he said.

"You can't," Caden huffed.

"We cans and we wills."

"I'm one of Lord D'Lance's Runesmen. You can't eat me."

The lizard man frowned and rolled Caden onto his stomach, his clawed hands scratching at his neck as he searched for the rune. The creature made a noise that sounded like a curse and began talking with his fellows again. Another of the creatures came and checked the rune for himself, then snorted.

"Two runes. He isss a spy. We will eats him."

"Lord D'Lance will punish you severely if you eat me," Caden said. "He's waiting for me to return to the castle."

The two lizard men exchanged glances, and for a moment, Caden held onto the hope that they were going to release him. The one that noticed both of his runes drew a dagger from a sheath at his waist and pressed the blade to Caden's neck.

"We eats him. Lord D'Lance won'ts knows."

That seemed to excite the entire lot of them, for they began whooping. Caden cursed his luck, and in the back of his mind, he found their existence difficult to fathom. They were like something out of a nightmare, a mix between giant lizards and humans.

A horn blared, and the creatures drew their weapons and looked around worriedly. Caden offered a silent prayer of thanks, thinking that a patrol had found them. Several figures rushed into view, and the clash of arms filled the air. Caden tried to roll away from the fighting, but he only managed to get stuck on his back.

He watched the two groups battle it out and realized that his rescuers weren't human either. They were the same lizard-like men as his captors. Why were they fighting with each other? Was he in more trouble now than before?

The attackers made quick work of his captors, and bodies littered the makeshift camp. Caden closed his eyes and laid still, hoping these new creatures would think he was dead. He felt one of them standing over him, and curiosity drove him to peek his eyes open.

"He's alive," a rumbling voice said. "You're safe now, my Lord."

Caden was confused. Was the creature referring to him? It knelt and rolled him over, untying his bonds, and then easily pulled him to his feet.

"Our master told us you were in trouble," the creature said.

"What are you talking about?"

"The master that we both serve. She resides in the mountain and has given you authority over her forces. We are small in number now, but we are growing daily. I am Bast."

The voice. That's who he was referring to. The creature spoke flawlessly, unlike the ones who'd captured him.

"Thank you for helping me, Bast."

"It is my duty and an honor, my Lord."

"Just … call me Caden."

"As you command."

"Our master has given me a task that requires entering Lord D'Lance's castle. Is that something you can help me with?"

Bast's lips curled into what looked like a snarl, but Caden realized he was smiling.

"I know of secret entrances. We will get you inside."

"Excellent."

They stared at one another in silence. Caden had many questions, but he didn't know how to ask them without offending the creature.

"You do not need to fear us," Bast said.

"I'm not afraid, just curious."

"You want to know what we are?"

Caden nodded.

"We were once men like you … until Lord D'Lance changed us."

"How did he change you?"

Caden's stomach grumbled.

"Food first. While you eat, I will tell you what happened."

5

Who was going to train her?

The question plagued Mina as she sat on the floor of Copper's chamber, waiting for him to return. The Enclave had dismissed her and asked him to remain behind, which only added to her worries.

She doubted Lord Klodian would educate her on how to be a soldier, and Thais was questionable. Caden would be her ideal teacher, but he was in the Dracan Dominion now. Did he know that he was serving such a wicked man? That was another fear added onto her already full plate.

Mina was pacing the cavern when Copper finally joined her. She looked at him questioningly.

Your doubt surrounds you like a thick cloud, he said.

I can't help it. I have no idea how I'm going to learn enough in two weeks, but the biggest problem is I don't know anyone who can train me.

Then it is a good thing I do.

You do? Who is it?

Me.

Mina waited for him to laugh, but he only stared at her in silence.

How will you train me to be a warrior? Do dragons use swords and armor?

No, but my previous rider did. We dragons have an excellent memory, and I am confident that I can teach you what you need to know to fight and survive.

She didn't like it, but at this point, it was her only choice. She nodded.

It looks like I'll have to trust you.

As well you should. We are bonded, and therefore we must have trust in one another. You gave me your word that you would not lead Lord Klodian to any more dragons, and you have kept it.

Your trust only stretches so far, Mina said. *I don't even know your real name.*

Copper snorted. *When you prove to the Enclave that you are a warrior, I will tell you my name.*

I won't fail. I can't.

I believe you. In your chamber, you will find a suit of armor and a sword. Get them and we will begin your training.

Now? Mina asked.

Yes. Two weeks isn't much time, so every moment counts.

He had a point. Mina got up and hurried through the tunnel into her room. She stood before the manakin that had the armor, her hands trembling. Was she ready for this? She wanted to believe that she was, but doubt assailed her. Even if she could learn to use a sword, would she have the fortitude to strike someone down with it?

She didn't know the answer to that. Not yet, at least.

It took her a moment to figure out how to put the armor on, but once she did, she felt different somehow. Stronger, if that made any sense. Copper had mentioned there was a sword as well, but Mina didn't see it. She scoured the room and finally found it atop the wardrobe. A thin layer of dust covered it, and she brushed it off with her fingers, careful not to cut herself.

The blade was smooth and gleamed as if it were new. She strapped the sheath around her waist and returned to Copper's chamber.

You remind me of Lucius, he said.

Was this his armor?

No, but the design is similar. How does it fit?

It's perfect, I think. I've never worn any before. It feels weird.

You'll get used to it. For now, the only time you'll remove it is when you sleep.

And what about later? she asked.

That depends on what happens with Lord D'Lance, but you'll probably have to wear it at all times to be safe.

Mina couldn't imagine trying to sleep in the armor. It wasn't uncomfortable, but it was tight and somewhat constricting.

Do I really need the sword right now?

Yes, Copper replied. *We're going to do some practice while flying.*

Wouldn't it be easier to learn on the ground?

It would, but if you can learn to fight from my back, then fighting on the ground will be a breeze under your wings.

Mina lifted her arms and flapped them playfully. Copper chortled in response, and it made her giggle.

Come, he said. *We're going above ground.*

She followed his lead, admiring the sights as they walked. The large tunnels were much less confusing than the maze of Klodian Keep, and she was confident that she would memorize them quickly. Thinking about the castle made her feel oddly homesick. It was a strange emotion, considering she'd grown up as a slave there. She supposed it was the familiarity of the place, the certainty of what was expected of her.

Here among dragons, she didn't know what to do. Copper was her only friend … if that was what she could call him. He was a stranger to her as much as Thais was, if not more so. Mina watched the dragon as he walked. His stride reminded her of a cat, particularly the way his shoulders rose and fell, and his leathery wings rustled with every step.

As they stepped out of the cave and into daylight, the sun momentarily blinded Mina. She blinked several times until her eyes adjusted.

Sit on my back the way you did when we came here, Copper said.

Is there a saddle we could use? It would be safer with one, wouldn't it?

Nothing about your training is going to be easy.

Mina hesitated. She wanted to learn, but at what cost? Pushing her doubts aside, she climbed onto Copper's back and situation herself. The dragon flapped his wings and leaped into the air, gaining altitude. Once they were high above the ground, Copper wheeled around in large circles.

You will learn the basics first, he said. *While we are flying, you must be aware of the wind. Gusts can spring up suddenly, and they can push you off of my back. If you fall, there's no guarantee I'll be able to catch you.*

That's comforting, Mina replied glumly.

Are you afraid of heights?

I don't think so. Flying here didn't bother me.

Good. Draw your sword.

Mina awkwardly pulled on the hilt of the blade until it came free of the scabbard. It was heavy, and she wondered how she could swing it accurately, let alone wield it in a fight.

Take a practice swing, Copper said.

What if I hit you?

I'll be fine.

Mina stretched her arm out and swung the blade in a forward chopping motion. Her eyes widened as the hilt slipped from her fingers and the sword went tumbling end over end through the air.

I dropped it, she said.

Copper laughed and dove, streaking through the sky until the ground drew close, then he stretched his wings to catch the air. He landed in the sand and Mina jumped down, running over to where the sword was. It had landed tip down and stood up out of the ground like a relic of bygone days. She pulled it free and carried it back to Copper.

Sorry. It was heavier than I thought.

There's nothing to apologize for. You'll build the strength necessary to keep your grip on it.

Mina doubted she'd be able to make that much progress in two weeks, but she didn't want to give up. She got back on the dragon and waited until they were airborne to try swinging it again. Just as before, the blade jerked free and went spinning to the ground.

It was going to be a long day.

6

CADEN WATCHED THE LIZARD MEN with a wary eye as he chewed on some meat. Bast had cut him a piece from the animal that had been roasting over the fire. The creatures were a lot like normal men with their mannerisms and personalities, but their scaled flesh and elongated faces defied that assumption.

"What do you know of dragons?" Bast asked.

"Not much," Caden replied, shrugging. "They're just wild animals."

"I thought that once, too. I can tell you with certainty that nothing could be further from the truth."

"What do you mean?"

"They aren't mindless creatures. They have intelligent thoughts and they can speak."

Caden rose his left brow. "They can speak?"

"Yes," Bast answered. "I see the doubt on your face. How is it that you can see me and my brethren and know that our existence shouldn't be possible, yet you balk at the idea that dragons can communicate?"

"You make a good argument."

"You don't know, do you?"

"Know what?"

"Our master … she is a dragon."

The image of the glowing eyes behind the throne came to the forefront of his mind, and Caden realized Bast was telling the truth. It made sense looking back now, especially since the source of the voice hadn't come into the light.

"I believe you," he said.

Bast's nostrils flared as he breathed in sharply. "Her scent is on you. Did you get to stand in her presence?"

"I did."

"You hold a high honor. I have not seen her with my own eyes. I have only heard her voice in my mind."

"You said you were all men like me. What happened?" Caden wanted to know more about these lizard men and what their purpose was. If Lord D'Lance was doing more than staging a rebellion, the High Prince would have a much bigger problem on his hands.

"We were not Runesmen like you, but we were loyal soldiers. He came to us with a proposition, one that he wasn't entirely forthcoming about. After we agreed, he changed us. I didn't know it then, but he practices dark magic. The stuff outlawed by the High Prince. He melded us with the energy from dragon eggs. We are both man and dragon. A chaotic existence. Our master calls us draman."

"That's horrible," Caden said. "Why did you agree to it?"

"That is the part that Lord D'Lance left out. He promised us strength and power without the need of a rune. He never told us *how* he would manage the feat."

"What about the ones you attacked? They didn't seem as bright as you."

"My brethren and I were among the first that he transformed. Once we realized what he'd done, we rebelled and fled the castle. We've been hiding in the woods, slowly growing as our master collects more of us. Lord D'Lance started making his newer creations less … intelligent."

"You keep saying brethren. Are you related, or do you consider yourselves family?"

"My apologies. That's the dragon part of me speaking. All dragons are brethren, or family, if you will. The different colors don't get along, but that is a trivial issue when it comes to eradication."

Caden frowned. "Lord D'Lance wants to kill off the dragons?"

"No," Bast replied. "He wants to use dragons as his slaves. He's forcing them to bond with humans while stealing their eggs and making more soldiers. Dragons don't lay many eggs and it can take years for them to hatch. If he isn't stopped, he might cause the extinction of dragons."

You must not let him succeed.

The voice echoed in Caden's mind. He nodded to himself and stood, wandering over to the stream to wash his hands. For some reason he couldn't explain, there was a horrible feeling in the pit of his stomach when he thought about his master dying. He knew nothing about her, certainly not enough to warrant concern, and yet he felt it as surely as he felt the water on his hands. But why?

It was something he would have to think about. He returned to his spot next to Bast and let his hands air dry as he considered the task before them. If Bast could get him into the castle unnoticed, he was confident that retrieving the stone would be relatively easy.

"How many men do you have?" he asked.

"Just under two hundred."

Caden blinked. Two hundred men did not equate to much of an army. Still, it was better than nothing.

"You look disappointed," Bast said.

"It's an obstacle we'll need to overcome."

"Our master is gathering dragons who are not enslaved by Lord D'Lance, and they will bolster our forces greatly."

Caden didn't doubt that, but unless their headcount grew exponentially, it would be a suicide mission trying to battle directly with Lord D'Lance's forces. Their situation was dire, and unless some miracle presented itself, he didn't know how they would succeed. The presence of the voice whispered in the back of his mind, comforting him.

"We need a way of getting more of your brethren to join us. Why are they defecting?"

"The newer ones aren't as smart, but they still know that they aren't natural creations. And I've heard that he is harsher with his punishments when it comes to their failures. No one wants to be brutalized."

"Perhaps we can use that to our advantage," Caden said, the wheels in his mind turning. "If more of them see what he's doing, they might break ties with him."

"I think you're right," Bast replied. "What are you thinking?"

"It'll be risky, but we can send the newest defectors back to the castle. They can cause a scene, something that will get them punished. If I know Lord D'Lance, he'll want to parade them through the street before executing them publicly."

Bast's eyes turned to slits. "He will kill them, but not in the open. He doesn't let us mingle with anyone. I dare say that none of the nobles are even aware of what he's doing."

"That poses a problem. What about the patrol that captured me? They were in the open."

"He lets us patrol the countryside freely. We don't wear his emblem, therefore no one can tie us back to him if we're seen."

"What if the defectors reveal themselves? They show their faces and start telling everyone what he's doing in secret. He'd have to take action then."

"That is risky," Bast said. "I will talk to my brethren and see if any of them are willing."

Caden nodded. "Good. If we have volunteers, then this should work. They can cause a raucous and gather a crowd. When Lord D'Lance sweeps in and tries to kill them, we'll bring everyone we've got to stop him. The only problem I foresee is that unless your brethren see him using force against the defectors, they won't know the extent of his cruelty."

"Leave that to us. We will spread the word that something big is coming. My brethren will find a way to watch it, and when they do, it should sway them to join us."

"I need to get inside the castle before all of this happens. Our master requires something that he has, so we'll need to make sure we have it in hand first. The sooner, the better."

"We can go tonight. It will give my brethren time to consider the risks, but I'm confident I know what the answer will be."

Caden had the feeling that what they were plotting could very well start a war. That was what Lord D'Lance wanted anyway, but would he still want it if he had to fight dragons?

7

MINA'S FINGERS WERE SORE, AND her hand throbbed painfully, yet Copper pushed her onward. The wind plucked at her clothes as she stood on his back, knees bent to keep her low. Her lips were chapped from the wind and sun, and her eyes were so dry that she could barely keep them open.

When can we take a break?

When you can swing the sword correctly, Copper rumbled.

He wasn't being harsh with her, but she was exhausted and his persistence was irritating her. Although they had only been practicing for a few hours, her energy level was flagging. Her stomach felt hollow and her throat was parched. If she lived long enough to get some food, it would be no minor miracle.

Don't be so dramatic. As a rider, you will often go long periods without food or water. You must acclimate your body because things will not always go smoothly.

Mina gritted her teeth against the pain and focused on the image that Copper pushed into her mind. It was of Lucius, his previous rider. He was in a crouched stance, sword at the ready. She was in the same position, but whereas he appeared comfortable and practiced, she felt awkward. The image became animated, and Mina replicated Lucius's movements.

She twisted her wrist, bringing the blade forward. Her grip on the hilt was as tight as she could get it, and the sword remained in her hand. A wave of excitement washed over her. She did it!

Good, Copper said. *You didn't drop your weapon. Let's try something different. Run along my back to my tail.*

Why?

Just do it.

Mina tightened her grip on the sword and slowly turned around. The ridges and spines on his back provided an uneven terrain, but she reminded herself that she needed to trust him. She inhaled a deep breath and sprinted, her ankles jerking sharply with each step. As she reached his tail, she slowed her pace.

What now?

Keep going!

She did as Copper said. As she reached the thinnest part of his tail, he undulated it, sending her flying into the air. Her eyes widened as she rose higher, and she windmilled her arms, letting go of the sword. Time stilled as she hovered in the air. Copper's tail faded from view, and then she was falling. She screamed in terror as her stomach flip-flopped.

The wind whipped violently, buffeting her as she streaked toward the ground. Mina closed her eyes and cursed Copper, wondering why she had allowed herself to trust him. Suddenly, her fall broke. The air was forced from her lungs and she opened her eyes, struggling to breathe. She had landed on Copper's back. Or rather, he had caught her. Instinctively, she grabbed onto his scales and held on. Copper spiraled in wide circles as he slowly descended.

You tried to kill me!

I did no such thing, Copper retorted. *It was a lesson.*

A lesson in near-death experiences?

The dragon laughed, but Mina didn't find the situation funny at all.

I wanted to show you what can happen if you fall off my back. I was able to easily catch you, but if we were battling in the sky, it would be almost impossible. Now that you know the feeling of free falling, you will remember the importance of keeping your balance.

Mina thought it was an incredibly dangerous way to teach such a simple lesson. She silently fumed until they landed, and then she leaped off his back and trudged across the sand to the cave entrance. Copper didn't follow her, for which she was thankful. She made it to Copper's chamber with little difficulty and stripped her armor and clothes off, then climbed into the pool of water.

Judging by the sting of her flesh, she'd received a decent sunburn. The water cooled her off, and she sighed with relief. She was tempted to drink some of it, but she didn't think that was a good idea. Who knew what sorts of germs were floating unseen, especially in a dragon's cave.

She got out and air-dried, then put her clothes back on. She left the armor on the ground and went back above ground. Copper was basking in the sun, his wings outstretched.

I did not intend to upset you, he said.

He *had* upset her, but she shrugged in reply. Serving under Lord Klodian, she'd learned many things, such as how to control her emotions. Her wall of stoicism had cracked and her anger had slipped through. Guilt assailed her.

I'm sorry for overreacting, she said.

You didn't overreact. It is natural for your emotions to affect you in such ways. You felt that I put you in danger. Your anger was justified. I will give you more warning next time.

Mina stared at him for a moment before nodding.

I'm hungry, she said, changing the subject.

You will find food in your room. Two meals will be prepared each day.

Only two?

Yes. Humans are frivolous in their consumption. You will only eat what is necessary.

What about water?

Copper's eyes glinted in the sun as he tilted his head.

I will show you where to drink. I think you will find it ... interesting.

He retracted his wings and walked past her, leading the way back into the cave. They followed the tunnel that bypassed their chambers and continued. The ground sloped under Mina's feet, and she could tell they were going deeper underground. At one point, the light that flickered within the glass walls faded.

Grab hold of my tail, Copper said.

Mina did as he asked and trailed blindly behind him. The darkness was impenetrable, but despite her discomfort, she wasn't afraid. They walked a few hundred feet before a faint glow appeared ahead. Mina released Copper's tale and moved beside him. The light was coming from a giant green stone that was lodged in the ceiling. It was multi-faceted and smooth.

What is that?

It's a crystal, Copper replied. *We found it when we were building our home here.*

Does magic make it glow like that?

Not everything is magical. It glows naturally.

The tunnel opened up to a crescent-shaped ledge. High above, but below the crystal, a waterfall cascaded down the left wall, filling a large pool with clear liquid.

This water is safe for you to drink, Copper said. *It is filtered by the sand and rocks.*

Mina knelt at the ledge and cupped her hands, dipping them into the water. She brought them back up quickly and drank. The water was cold and refreshing. Copper waited patiently while she drank her fill, and when she was finished, they trekked through the tunnel and returned to his chamber.

You can eat now, and when you are ready, we will practice with the sword again.

I dropped it when you tossed me into the air, so I'll have to find it.

I retrieved the weapon when you stormed off.

Oh. Thank you.

Mina left Copper's chamber and went into her own. A tray of steaming food was waiting for her. As she dug into it, she paused to wonder who had made it. A shuffling sound came from the shadows, startling her. She peered in the direction of the noise and saw two glowing eyes. Copper was only a few feet away if she needed him, so she wasn't too worried.

"Who's there?" she asked.

"It me," a soft voice replied. The tone was light, almost musical.

"Me who?"

"Me. It me."

"Step out of the shadows so I can see you."

The shuffling sound repeated, and a diminutive creature stepped into the light. It was roughly three feet tall, and at first, Mina thought it was a child. As she took in the creature's appearance, it became clear that it wasn't. In fact, it wasn't even human. It had a pale complexion, a bald head, and pointed ears.

There's something in here, Mina told Copper.

What is it?

I don't know.

Mina felt Copper's presence within her mind intensify.

Ah. That's Areg. Don't be afraid of him. He's harmless.

"It me," Areg repeated, pointing to himself.

"Your name is Areg?"

The creature nodded.

"What are you doing in my chamber?"

"Bring food. You eat."

"Oh. Thank you."

"Me serve you. If need, pull rope."

Areg pointed to the doorway that led into the hall, and Mina realized there was a rope that hung down from the ceiling.

"I will let you know if I need anything."

Areg attempted a bow, but it looked more like he was about to fall over. He righted himself and then hobbled out of the room.

What is Areg? He walks on two legs, but I've never seen anything like him before.

Areg is an elf, Copper replied.

Mina had heard of them before, but only in stories. She never thought that they could be real. With each new thing she learned, it became more and more apparent that the world of dragons was much different from what she ever imagined.

8

THE MOON GLOWED OVERHEAD AS Caden followed Bast through the woods toward Velbridge. A few stray beams of light penetrated the canopy, but Caden still found it difficult to see the way ahead. Bast, on the other hand, strode with sure steps.

"You have some good eyes," Caden said.

"There are some benefits to what Lord D'Lance has done to me, but they are few."

"I still can't believe he's done something so unholy. No offense."

"None taken," Bast replied. "Some days are harder than others, but it's a constant struggle to know who I am. The humanity battles against the dragon, and they are never at peace."

Caden couldn't imagine an existence like that, and he admired the man's fortitude. They trekked for a few hours, and by the time they reached the outskirts of the city, it was past midnight. Bast led him along the eastern wall, stopping at a large grate that covered a tunnel. A thin rivulet of sickly green water streamed out of it and into a trench that directed it away from the city. Caden wrinkled his nose.

"The sewers?"

"It's disgusting, but it's the safest way inside the city without attracting attention. Guards don't patrol them, so we'll have little trouble until we come back above ground. I'll need your help to open the grate."

Between the two of them, they were able to jerk the rusted grate open enough to get inside. It was rectangular in shape, and the tunnel was low and narrow.

"We'll leave this open," Bast said.

"Won't that draw attention?"

"I think that's unlikely. We need to have a quick way of escape in case something goes wrong. There are too many guards to risk going out of the main gates."

Caden didn't like it, but he didn't have a better idea.

"How close can we get to the castle?"

"There's an exit on the western side that will bring us into Lord D'Lance's private garden. From there, we can use a secret passage to get inside. The only problem is that because of its proximity to Lord D'Lance's personal quarters, they usually pack the place with soldiers. We'll have to use caution to ensure we aren't caught."

"If we're able to get that close to his quarters, why not just sneak in and kill him in his sleep?"

"That would not be prudent," Bast said. "Our master desires to spill his blood herself."

Caden remembered that she'd told him not to touch Lord D'Lance. He nodded. "We're going to need a torch."

"No, we won't. I can see as plain as day in the darkest room. Just follow me."

Bast stepped into the tunnel, and Caden trailed after him. A few feet in and the darkness was absolute. Caden's steps were hesitant, so Bast grabbed his hand and pulled him along. He felt awkward holding hands with the draman, but he forced the feeling aside. They had a task to complete, and he would not let a minor discomfort get in the way.

Caden assumed the sewers would be a quiet place, but that was far from the truth. The sound of flowing water and scurrying creatures echoed off the walls. Every time they splashed through a puddle, he was glad he was wearing boots. The thought of that water touching him made his skin crawl with revulsion.

The sewer tunnels were a confusing labyrinth and reminded him of the interior of Lord Klodian's castle, but it wasn't long before they stopped. Overhead, faint light shone through a circular grate.

"There are rungs in the wall," Bast said, guiding Caden's hand to one. "They are slippery, so climb slowly. I'll go up first to make sure it's clear."

Bast ascended them quickly. In the dim light, it looked to Caden as though the draman was scaling the wall itself rather than using the metal rungs. He reached the top and pushed the grate aside, then stuck his head into the open.

"All clear," he whispered.

Caden made his way up slowly. Condensation had collected on the rungs, making them slick, and he had to be meticulous with how he placed his hands and feet. Bast had already exited the tunnel by the time Caden reached the top.

"Over here." Bast waved.

Caden spotted the draman hiding in some tall shrubs that rested against the castle. He cast a glance around the garden and didn't see any guards, so he climbed out and hurried to where Bast was.

"Step lightly and try not to jostle the bushes."

Bast pressed his back against the stonework and began sidestepping through the slim space between the shrubbery and the castle. Caden did the same thing, doing his best to creep without noise, but it was difficult because loose stones covered the ground. It seemed to take an eternity, but finally, Bast held up his left hand and placed a finger from his right one to his lips.

"Two guards," he murmured. "They are in front of the entrance."

"Do they know it's there?"

"I don't think so. We need some way of getting them to leave."

"I've got an idea," Caden said.

He knelt and felt around blindly with his hand until he found what he was looking for: a palm-sized rock. He hurled it up through the bush and, a moment later, it clattered in the distance.

"What was that?" one of the soldiers asked.

"How should I know? It's my turn to roll, so go check it out. It's probably a critter."

The first soldier grumbled and headed in the direction of Caden's stone. The other was sitting on the ground in front of a small wooden square. Behind him, a lantern hung upon a post and offered a small amount of light to see by. The soldier held his hand over the board and dropped two dice onto it. He cursed under his breath and looked for his fellow, then flipped the dice over and grinned.

"We need them both gone," Bast whispered.

Before Caden could reply, the other guard returned.

"I didn't see anythin'. Hey! What's this, then? There's no way you rolled a double six. Are you cheating?"

"I ain't never cheated a day in my life," the other guard sputtered.

"I doubt that!"

"Are you callin' me a liar?"

"Well, I ain't calling you a truth teller. Roll 'em again while I'm watchin'."

"Bah! Fine."

He picked the dice up and rolled them again. This time, he did roll two sixes.

"Ha! See? I wasn't lyin'."

"We don't have time for this," Caden said.

Bast stared at him. "We can kill them, but we'll have to hide their bodies."

Caden considered the option for a moment and sighed. "No. I don't want to kill innocent men. They probably know nothing about what Lord D'Lance is doing."

"Then what?"

"Do you hear that?" the first guard asked.

"Hear what?"

They both went silent, and Caden and Bast barely breathed.

"I don't hear nothin'. Are you losin' your mind now, too?"

Bast motioned for Caden to stay put and sidled his way through the bushes until he was behind the soldier sitting on the ground. Caden had no idea what the man was up to, but he hoped he wasn't going to kill either of them. Bast rustled the bushes, and the second soldier peered suspiciously into the shadows.

"There's somethin' in there."

"Where?"

"Behind you."

The guard stood up and turned around, retrieving the lantern from the post. He held it out in front of him and shined the light into the bushes. Bast held perfectly still, and neither soldier saw him.

"Must be the wind," the soldier said. He turned back around, and Bast made his move. He rushed forward and wrapped his arm around the soldier's neck, putting him in a chokehold. The other soldier's face went pale, but he drew his sword and took a step toward Bast.

"Let him go or I'll gut you!"

Caden slipped out of the bushes and stealthily moved in behind the man. Bast bared his teeth in a nightmarish grin and released the guard, who crumpled to the ground, unconscious.

"You killed him! Demon spawn!"

Caden kicked the back of the soldier's right leg, buckling his knee. He went down and Caden placed his hand over the man's mouth, pinching his nose closed. The man struggled to get free, but Bast took his sword and pressed the tip to his throat.

"Hold still," he said.

The lantern had fallen to the ground, and the light it cast shined on Bast's face. The guard stopped fighting, and a moment later, Caden laid him on the ground.

"They won't be out long," he said.

"We should hurry, then. Where is the item you seek?"

"I'm not sure, but I know where we can check first."

9

Her eyes cracked open. Had someone called her name? She waited a moment, but she didn't hear anything. It must have been one of the servants. Her eyelids slowly descended and she was about to drift back to sleep when she heard it again.

Mina rubbed the sleep from her eyes and sat up, glancing around the room. She frowned in confusion. This wasn't her room. Where was she? And then it all came flooding back, hitting her like a bolt of lightning.

Copper?

Get your armor on and meet me in the hall.

She frowned, not remembering how she'd fallen asleep. Then again, the dragon had pushed her beyond exhaustion. Mina groggily slipped out of bed and was about to retrieve her armor from Copper's chamber when she saw it was on the manakin beside her wardrobe. She paused, her tired mind trying to remember when she'd brought it into her room.

Shrugging, she put the armor on over her clothes and buckled her sword belt around her waist, then stepped into the hall where Copper was waiting.

I'm awake, she said, stifling a yawn. *Well, mostly.*

Copper laughed. *You fell asleep early. I'm surprised you slept so long. I would have been concerned, but your mind was still present.*

I haven't worked that hard in a long time.

Today won't be any easier. How are you with a bow?

I've never used one, Mina admitted.

Then you shall learn today. An effective rider must know how to wield more than just a sword.

Shouldn't I master one weapon before learning another?

In an ideal situation, yes, but time is not on our side. You must learn many things quickly.

She knew he was right, but she wasn't feeling confident in her ability to learn what was needed.

Come, Copper bade.

They went above ground and Mina realized the sun hadn't quite risen yet. The morning air was cool, and she shivered, rubbing her hands along her upper arms. Areg was there, holding a bow and a quiver of arrows. Dotting the desert landscape around them was a multitude of manakins.

We will fly past the targets, and you will attempt to hit them with an arrow. Are you ready?

Mina rubbed her eyes, still not fully awake. *I suppose I am.*

"Here go."

Areg held the bow out to her and she grabbed hold of it. The wood was a pale honey color and smooth to the touch. The elf handed over the quiver next, and she noticed that each arrow had a thin red ribbon attached.

What are those for? she asked.

In case you miss. It'll be easier to find them. Since you are shooting from my back, that strap on the quiver will go across your chest. If you are on foot, it'll go around your waist.

What's the difference?

Pulling arrows from the quiver on your back is clumsy and only suitable when riding. It's easier and quicker to pull them from your waist when you're on foot. And unless you're wearing strong leather boots, you'll want to be barefoot when firing, otherwise you won't have firm footing.

I'll remember all of this somehow, Mina lamented.

Mastery comes with time. For now, you just need to know the basics. Climb up.

Mina slipped the quiver strap over her head and adjusted it across her chest, then climbed onto Copper's back. She braced herself as he flexed his wings out and leaped into the air, rising quickly. He flew a fair distance away from the area where the targets were before turning back and slowly descending until he was roughly ten feet above the ground, then leveled out.

Ready your bow, he said, projecting an image of Lucius into her mind.

She pulled an arrow from the quiver, almost dropping it as she tried to fit the end on the bowstring. Copper glided effortlessly over the landscape, but the wind pushed against her, making her unsteady. They were approaching the first target. She took aim and fired. The arrow shot forward a few feet and then whipped away in the opposite direction.

You must pull back on the string harder. More tension.

Mina grabbed another arrow, but before she could nock it to the string, the next target zipped by.

Too slow! Copper grumbled.

I'm trying, Mina retorted.

She caught sight of the third target and aimed again. When it was only a few feet away, she released the string. The arrow flew straight and struck the manakin in the leg.

I did it! Mina shouted excitedly.

Copper remained silent, but she could smell lemon and clove coming off of him. As the rest of the targets came and went, she fired off more arrows as best as she could, but missed all the shots. Copper landed near Areg and Mina jumped down to the ground.

Retrieve the arrows.

Mina jogged across the sand to each target and collected the projectiles, then returned, panting.

Areg will show you how to fire accurately.

Mina looked at the elf and he took the bow from her, along with one arrow.

"Watch."

In one fluid motion, he nocked the arrow, aimed, and let the shaft fly. It whizzed through the air and struck one of the furthest targets.

"Go get," Areg said.

Mina did as he asked and saw that he'd struck the manakin dead center. Her eyes widened in surprise. Areg was so … small. How had he shot the arrow that far? She pulled the arrow free and walked back to where the elf was.

"How did you do that?" she asked.

Areg smiled. "Me do it before."

"What do you mean?"

The elf shook his head and gave her the bow back. He motioned at her, and she nocked the arrow to the string, then looked at him expectantly.

"Now what?"

"Kneel."

She did so, and Areg smacked her elbow.

"Twist," he said, then placed his hand over hers and put his index, middle, and ring finger on the string, keeping the arrow between his index and middle fingers.

"Keep here. No squeeze."

"Don't squeeze the arrow. Got it."

Copper projected another image of Lucius into her mind, and she mirrored his stance. She drew the arrow back to a comfortable spot on her face, at the corner of her mouth.

"Focus," Areg said. "Small."

"I don't understand."

Focus on something small, Copper clarified. *A blemish or something specific on the target. The smaller the better. Keep your eyes on it until everything else becomes a blur, then relax your fingers and let the string slip past them.*

Mina followed the instructions and focused on an odd patch of color on the manakin's shirt. She released the string and the arrow struck the target exactly where she'd aimed. Areg clapped and Copper emitted lemon and clove again.

Very good. Now try to hit every target from here.

She knew it wasn't possible, but tried anyway. Two arrows hit, and the rest were way off mark.

That was impossible.

Perhaps, but you learned how to aim. Let's try from the air again. You don't get breakfast until you can strike all the targets in one go.

Mina gathered the errant projectiles and climbed onto Copper's back. He flew past the targets again, and this time, she didn't hit a single one. He landed so she could collect the arrows again, and she stalked back to him.

Let's go again, she huffed.

10

CADEN WASN'T VERY FAMILIAR WITH the castle's interior, especially in the dark. He described the door he'd seen previously, and Bast guided him through the halls. They encountered a few soldiers making their rounds and had to duck into a darkened doorway to avoid being seen. After they guards passed, they continued onward until they reached an empty hall.

"This is it," Caden said. "It's the door at the end."

"I know this place," Bast replied. "I think it is where my transformation happened."

"You're not sure?"

"I was in and out of consciousness, but this area feels familiar. I don't have any memory of it before that point."

Caden strode to the door and tried the handle, but just as it had been before, it was locked.

"You don't remember anything about a key, do you?"

"No."

Nothing could ever be easy, could it? Caden frowned as he stared at the door. They could try to search for a key, but the chances of finding one were so remote it didn't seem worth the effort. It was impossible to know if any of the guards had a key, and if one of them did, who?

"Step aside," Bast said. "Hopefully this isn't too loud."

Caden moved out of the way. Bast took up a stance in front of the door, placing his shoulder against it. He grabbed the handle and jerked it. It broke, and he cast it aside. It clattered along the floor and slid to a stop.

"That didn't go as expected," Bast said. He pushed on the door, but it didn't budge.

"How did you break the handle?"

"I didn't mean to."

"No, I mean *how* did you do it? It's metal."

"Fusing with the dragon egg has increased my strength. Sometimes I use too much force."

"Can you break the door open?"

"Yes, but it may draw the guards on us."

Caden knew he was right, but they had little time. "Do it."

Bast took a few steps back and kicked the door. The wood where the handle had been splintered, and the rest of the door flew inward, slamming loudly against something on the inside. They hurried into the room, and Caden froze at what he saw.

Lying atop a table was a body. The top half was human, but from the waist down, it had scales like Bast's. Strange utensils were laid out next to it, including a vial of black liquid. The human portion had pale skin and a sunken face. It was obvious the person was dead.

"This one didn't survive the process," Bast said, standing next to him.

"What causes them to die?"

"Lord D'Lance hasn't fully mastered the dark magic he uses, and dragons are powerful, even as an unhatched egg. If the dragon fights back, the spell is disrupted and it can kill the person involved. I saw a few survive the failure, but they ended up dying within a couple of days."

"He's more of a monster than I realized."

"He has deceived many, but now is not the time to discuss that. What is it that we are looking for?"

"A gemstone," Caden replied.

"What kind?"

The image of a bright green jadeite formed within Caden's mind. He could sense it was coming from his master, and it impressed him that she could still communicate with him despite their distance.

"It's green, but it's not like an emerald. It's murky looking."

"I don't remember seeing anything like that, but as I said, my memories from the transformation are not cohesive."

"You check this room. I'll look in that one."

He pointed to the doorway at the far end of the room. Bast began his search, and Caden went to the other room. Inside, there were a dozen tables with the same grisly scene. Half transformed bodies were laid out, their flesh in the beginning stages of decay. Caden pinched his nose against the stench and glanced around.

There was a long table against the back wall that held dragon eggs. At least, he assumed that's what they were. He walked over and inspected them. They varied in size and color, but they were all covered with a dark shade of red, similar to rust. He didn't dare touch them. Aside from the bodies, there wasn't much else to see, so he returned to the room where Bast was. The draman was looking closely at the body on the table.

"Any sign of the stone?"

"No," Bast answered. "But this corpse looks different from the others I've seen. I think Lord D'Lance is experimenting."

"There are eggs with some sort of red dust on them in there."

Bast's reptilian eyes turned to slits, and he growled. "He's up to something."

"We can deal with that later. Right now we need to find the stone, and it doesn't seem to be in here."

"What does this stone do?"

"Our master said that Lord D'Lance is using it to keep her trapped in the mountain. She wants me to find and destroy it."

"If it is valuable to him, he will keep it close. He likely has it in his personal quarters," Bast said.

"We can't leave without it."

The two exchanged looks.

"If the master needs it, then we shall get it. Are you prepared to die if it comes to that?"

"I will do what I must," Caden replied.

"Follow me."

Bast took the lead again and they headed back the way they'd come. Instead of going back out of the secret passage, they turned right and ended up in a large chamber that resembled the Coterie. A plush rug rested in the center of the room and benches lined the walls. The room was dark aside from the meager moonlight that streamed through the windows. A single door offered the only path ahead, but as they approached it, a guard stepped out of the shadows to intercept them.

"What are you two doing in here?"

"Apologies, sir. We've got urgent news for Lord D'Lance," Bast said.

"You can tell me what it is, and I'll inform him personally."

"I'm afraid it's for his ears only, sir."

"Then I'm afraid it will have to wait until morn—" His words turned into a gurgling sound and Bast removed a dagger from the guard's neck. The man clutched at the wound and collapsed to the floor.

"I'm sorry," Bast said, turning to Caden. "I know you said you didn't want to kill anyone, but this one deserved it. He's as cruel as Lord D'Lance."

Caden didn't say anything. He stepped over the body and opened the door. It swung open silently, and the first thing he saw was an enormous bed. Sheer curtains draped the entire thing. Caden crept into the room and quickly rummaged through the drawers of an ornate dresser. Bast went to the desk on the other side of the room, and after a few minutes of searching, he joined Caden.

"Nothing," he whispered.

"Blast our luck," Caden replied. "It must be here somewhere."

He saw a side table beside the bed and hurried over to it, but it was empty. Lord D'Lance was in the bed, his breathing rhythmic and steady. Caden put his hand on the hilt of his sword. It would be so easy to end the tyrant's life. He wanted to, and deep down he knew that he should, but the invisible presence of his master kept him at bay.

His life is mine. Your task is to find the stone.

Forgive my weakness.

Caden was about to continue looking through the room when he saw a silver chain around Lord D'Lance's neck. Pushing the curtain aside, he leaned closer and saw the gemstone. It was encased in a pendant that was affixed to the chain.

"I found it," he whispered, looking at Bast.

"Take it and let's go."

Caden didn't see the clasp, which meant that he either had to pull the chain free or get the gemstone out of the pendant. Neither option was ideal, considering the situation.

"Get ready to run."

Caden gently lifted the chain enough to get a firm grip, then yanked it free. Lord D'Lance's eyes opened and he sat up. He looked from Caden to the pendant, and his brow furrowed.

"Come on!" Bast shouted.

Caden turned to flee, but his legs wouldn't move. He looked at Lord D'Lance and saw the man had ensorcelled him. His hand was balled into a fist, and he was chanting something under his breath.

"I can't move!"

Bast rushed over and tried to pull him, but his legs remained where they were, as if rooted in place. The draman leaped onto the bed and punched Lord D'Lance in the face, breaking his focus on the spell. Caden lurched forward a few steps, but then he was thrown to the ground as Bast crashed into him. They both grunted in pain and struggled to untangle themselves.

"Guards!"

Caden got on all fours and crawled for the door, but an unseen force slammed it shut. He clambered to his feet and looked for another way out. Lord D'Lance was out of his bed, his face twisted with rage. He made a motion with his hand, and the pendant was ripped from Caden's grasp. It flew across the room and Lord D'Lance snatched it out of the air.

"Tell that sniveling dragon that she'll rot in that mountain. She will never be free again."

"She will be free," Bast shouted. "And she'll flame you into oblivion!"

The door burst open, and armed guards filed into the room. Caden and Bast retreated to the window.

"Kill them," Lord D'Lance ordered.

The guards drew their swords and rushed toward them. Bast grabbed Caden and shielded him with his body as he crashed through the glass of the window, stumbling onto a balcony that overlooked the garden.

"Bend your knees and roll," Bast said, then tossed Caden over the edge.

Caden landed on his feet and used his momentum to spring forward, rolling into a bed of flowers. He quickly got up and sprinted for the sewer entrance, Bast right behind him. They reached the hole and climbed down into the sewer, escaping into the night.

11

MINA WAS AWAKE WELL BEFORE dawn. She paced her chamber anxiously, continuously running her hands over the front of her armor as if to smooth it out. Her nerves were on edge. This day was probably the most important that she'd ever waited for. The last two weeks of training had been arduous, miserable even. It felt like months had passed.

But it was over.

Almost.

She took a deep breath and continued pacing. Copper was recounting his time with her to the Enclave, and upon their approval, they would test her to prove if she was a capable warrior.

A warrior.

Mina almost laughed. Her life was so foreign now. She'd been raised from the position of a slave to a height that she'd never dreamed of.

Copper had pushed her beyond what she'd thought possible. Every day, she woke up before dawn and practiced with the sword, then with the bow, then back to the sword. She had no time to relax, had barely received any personal time to reflect on what she was doing. Now that she had a small amount of free time, she didn't know what to do with herself. And so she paced, her thoughts full of turmoil.

What would happen if she failed? War, obviously. But what about her? What did her fate look like? Scarier still, what did her future hold if she succeeded?

You dwell on things you have no control over, Copper said, his voice invading her mind.

I can't help it. What did the Enclave say?

They want to see what you have learned. Grab your sword and come with me.

Mina's sword was already strapped around her waist, so she stepped into the hall. Copper regarded her in silence.

What troubles you? he asked.

I'm afraid of failing.

Do not fear failure. It is a fire that refines you. Give everything you have in these tests. Whether you fail or succeed, you have done your duty in trying.

I will do my best, Mina swore.

They headed above ground, where the Enclave was waiting for them, as well as a host of other dragons. Mina's breath caught in her throat. There were so many of them, and they were all different colors. Their shiny scales glinted in the sun, creating a myriad of miniature rainbows.

Why are they all out here?

You are the first rider in a thousand years, Copper replied. *It is a momentous event.*

The invisible weight of their judgement and expectations suddenly fell on her shoulders. She hadn't expected so many witnesses. Still, the stakes were clear in her mind. She cast the doubts aside and walked with as much confidence as she could muster.

Mina, step forth and kneel before the Enclave.

It was the silver dragon, the one who'd probed her mind when she'd first arrived. Mina left Copper's side and approached the group of leaders, then knelt in the sand.

Today, we will see what you have learned. Put forth your best efforts. Not only to convince us, but because you are a rider. We are in a unique predicament, and I trust that there is a reason for the bond between the two of you. Do not disappoint us.

Yes, Tiarna.

A tremor shook the sand beneath her feet, and Mina glanced at the members of the Enclave. The dragons looked at each other, and she could smell vanilla drifting off of them. She wrinkled her nose.

Prepare for your trials.

Mina lowered her head briefly and rose to her feet, returning to Copper's side. Areg handed her a bow and a quiver of arrows. She slipped them both over her shoulder and climbed up Copper's foreleg and onto his back.

Did you feel that a moment ago? she asked.

Yes.

What was it?

I don't know.

I smelled vanilla on the elders. What does that mean?

Can you truly smell our emotions?

Yes, Mina answered.

You are one of only a few humans who've been able to do so. I don't know why you have the ability, but it will help create a stronger bond between us. Our emotions release pheromones to other dragons, much like the pheromone that lets us locate one another. In this case, you don't get overwhelmed with fear, but can smell our emotions.

Mina scrunched her brow.

What emotion is vanilla?

Curiosity.

So the elders are curious about the ground tremor?

Possibly, or they may be curious about you. If you cannot decipher the object of their emotion, then you will never know.

Can't you tell me?

I could, but I'm not going to.

Why not?

You need to be focused on the trials you are about to face. Do not worry about these things now.

Mina sighed. *Very well.*

The silver dragon nodded, and Copper leaped into the air. The silver dragon's voice penetrated her mind.

Your first test is archery. You must hit every target.

Mina unslung the bow and grabbed an arrow, readying herself. As Copper gained altitude and the ground below grew distant, she wondered how she would hit the targets at this height. And then she noticed there were other dragons joining them, each one wearing a target on their back.

What's going on? she asked. *What are they doing?*

My brethren bear the targets you must hit.

I have to hit moving *targets? But I've only trained on stationary ones!*

You can hit them, Copper said. *If I didn't think you were capable, then you wouldn't be tested.*

She thought that his confidence was misplaced, but she'd gone through too much to give up now. She inhaled a deep breath and lifted the bow.

I'm ready.

The dragons flying around them broke away, wheeling in different directions. Copper flapped his wings and turned left, following after the closest one. The wind pummeled her, drying out her eyes. She clenched her jaw and kept her legs pressed tightly against Copper as she took aim.

Her first target was on the back of a sleek gold dragon. Mina wasn't sure, but she assumed it was a female judging by the smaller stature of the beast. She drew the string back and held herself as steady as she could, keeping her eyes fixed on the center of the target. The dragon did a barrel roll, causing her to lose focus.

I can't get a good aim because she keeps moving!

Calm yourself, Copper admonished. *Patience is key. Wait for the right moment.*

She refocused on the target and waited. Time slipped by, and she lost count of the seconds. The gold dragon swooped up, and Mina saw her opportunity. She released the bowstring and the arrow whizzed through the sky. It was faint compared to the wind, but she heard the arrow strike the target. The dragon tilted to the side and fell below them, returning to the ground.

A perfect strike. Very good, but don't let it go to your head. You've got plenty more targets, and you must hit them all.

Do I have to hit them on the first try?

Yes.

Mina grabbed another arrow and knocked it. She leaned low as Copper turned and closed in on the next target: a brass dragon twice the size of Copper. His bulk would make it harder for him to maneuver, but it also made the target on his back seem much smaller.

Can you fly over top of him?

Yes, but you won't be able to see the target.

I meant upside down.

She sent an image of what she had in mind through the scale. The brief scent of freesia hit her nostrils, followed by lemon and clove.

Hold on, Copper replied.

Mina clenched her legs against his neck and prepared for the riskiest thing she'd ever attempted.

12

THE MASTER WANTS YOU TO stay behind.

The words echoed within Caden's mind, a reminder of his failure to retrieve the gemstone two weeks earlier. He assumed it was a punishment, and he berated himself daily. If only he'd been more prepared.

Lord D'Lance was hosting a public celebration for the High Prince, and Bast had spent the last few hours finalizing their plans to disrupt the event.

"You seem depressed."

Caden looked up at the draman and laughed. "Disappointed is more like it. I can't lead our master's forces if I'm not with them. I failed the task she gave me, and I know this is my reward."

"I think you misunderstand her," Bast said. "She wants you to stay behind for your safety. If you are killed tomorrow, then we suffer a significant loss. Our numbers have doubled since you arrived, and my brethren are beginning to see that there is hope."

"I hadn't considered that. I suppose I'm being too hard on myself."

"Everyone fails at some point. What you do after that determines your character."

The two of them sat near a small fire, one of many scattered around their camp. Caden was warm and relaxed, and he watched the flames dance about. Perhaps Bast was right. The master wanted him to stay behind to keep him safe, not to punish him. The thought did comfort him, at least until he dwelled on his men going into a possible death trap alone. How could he call himself a leader if he wasn't in the thick of danger with them?

"What's the point of hosting a party for the High Prince if he won't even be attending?"

"To the people, it's a show of support," Bast said. "And to the High Prince, it's a sign of loyalty."

"I've heard it said that the High Prince has eyes and ears everywhere. What are the chances that Lord D'Lance's plot has already reached him?"

"It's possible. If he does know, I wonder why he hasn't marched his army out to destroy Velbridge."

Caden had wondered about that, too. There were many answers, but he feared it was because either the High Prince was too proud to admit one of his lords would betray him, or that Lord D'Lance had become too powerful to stop. The latter idea was the most concerning.

"So far, Lord D'Lance has kept his dragons and draman a secret, but I don't think that's going to last much longer."

"Especially not after tomorrow," Bast said with a grin.

"You're still leaving before dawn?"

"Yes. My brethren are ready. I will leave some men behind to guard you while we are away. A line of messengers will also be in place to alert you if something happens. You'll have plenty of time to escape to the mountain if we are compromised."

"You're a capable leader," Caden complimented. "I have no doubt you'll be fine."

"Thank you. As long as Lord D'Lance's dragons do not make an appearance, I think all will go according to plan. We've been spreading the word, and I am confident that the rest of our brethren will see the truth and join us."

"Let us hope so. You should get some rest. Tomorrow is an important day."

"I am excited, but you are right." Bast stood and stretched, his scales shimmering softly under the firelight. "We shall meet again tomorrow after the dust has settled."

Caden stayed by the fire after he left, battling with his own thoughts. Their master hadn't told him directly to stay behind, so if he followed his men to Velbridge, he wouldn't be disobeying her orders.

Technically.

And it wasn't like Bast was his commander. They led the band of draman together. He laid down and got comfortable, staring up at the dark canopy. The more he thought about it, the more he convinced himself to tag along in secret. He wouldn't get involved … he would just keep an eye on things.

He awoke early in the morning as the draman were preparing to travel to Velbridge. They weren't a quiet lot, and it was impossible for him to go back to sleep even if he wanted to. Bast bid him farewell and led the men away from the camp.

Caden waited as patiently as he could, allowing them a head start before going after them. The few guards left behind weren't paying him any heed, and he grabbed a discarded cloak and a torch, then snuck off into the woods. He kept a fair distance behind Bast and the others, and once Velbridge was in sight, he turned to the east and used the sewer entrance Bast had showed him to enter the city.

He used the torch to light his way, and since he wasn't familiar with the tunnels, he decided to keep straight until he reached a fork, then turned right and climbed up the first set of rungs he found. The grate slid aside easily and he exited into an empty alleyway.

Cheering echoed off the walls, and Caden realized the celebration was already underway. He pulled the hood of the cloak over his head and doused the torch, tossing it aside, then stepped into the street and made his way toward the festivities. The streets were normally crowded, but with the event happening, he only encountered a handful of people, stragglers who were going the same direction he was.

It was only midmorning, but it amazed him to see how big the crowd was that had flocked to the front of the castle. The people were packed close together, all trying to get a good view of what was happening. Caden scaled the side of a building and got on the rooftop. A parade of sorts was passing through the primary thoroughfare, blocked off by guards with halberds.

Trumpets and other instruments were being played, adding to the cacophony of sounds that drifted through the air. Caden spotted a few cloaked figures among the crowd, and he suspected they were some of his men. The people around them weren't affected by their appearance, and when one of them turned around, he saw why. They were wearing masks.

"Clever," he muttered to himself.

Bringing up the rear of the parade was a group of Runesmen decked out in armor. Commander Morin walked with them, and Caden was surprised to see that Lord D'Lance was present as well. He knew the man was wearing the pendant, despite the fact that he couldn't see it. If he thought it was valuable enough to sleep with, then he surely carried it on him now. Excitement welled within him. This was his opportunity to make amends for his failure. He just needed to wait until Bast and the others—

A commotion broke out near the guards blocking the main street when a group of draman cleared the area, forcing the city folk aside. The guards called for reinforcements, but before their help could arrive, the draman subdued them. The crowd surged away from the creatures, screaming about demons. Horns blared, and the Runesmen in the parade quickly made their way to the scene, but by then, a fight had broken out.

Soldiers and draman engaged in full battle, swords clanging. The city folk scattered in every direction, their screams and stampeding only adding to the chaos. Commander Morin joined the fray, swinging his blade with a fury that seemed impossible for a man his age. Caden watched it all from the roof, biding his time.

Lord D'Lance strode into the midst of the fighting and shouted for more soldiers. Caden couldn't wait any longer. He returned to the street and pushed his way through the throngs of fleeing people. All he needed to do was get near enough to steal the pendant, and then he would abscond with it back to his master.

He kept his sword sheathed as he neared the soldiers, dodging between the press of bodies to get closer. Lord D'Lance was only a few feet away and he was facing the other direction. Caden lunged forward, right hand reaching for the man's neck. His fingers grazed the chain at first, but he managed to grab hold of it and yanked it free. Lord D'Lance whirled around, and the two men locked gazes.

"You again. I'll have your head!"

Caden turned to flee and felt pain lance up his ribcage. He grunted and staggered, something wet slicking his skin. He knew without looking that he'd been stabbed. His vision grew hazy and he fell to the ground, the pendant skittering across the cobblestones.

13

COPPER FLAPPED HIS WINGS, LIFTING them higher. Mina's stomach churned uncomfortably as the dragon looped up and over the other beast, but she fought through the fear and fired her arrow, and then quickly wrapped her arms around Copper's neck, the bow dangling around her wrist as they flew upside down.

She couldn't see if the shot had struck the target, but once Copper leveled out, the giant brass dragon trumpeted at her and began to descend. Sitting dead center in the target he carried was her arrow. Mina whispered a prayer of thanks to Avera and sat up, looking for the next target.

There were three more, each one on the back of a silver dragon. They were gliding side by side, their scales shimmering brilliantly under the sun.

Are those the last targets?

Yes, Copper answered. *Silver dragons are quick, and they will be difficult to keep pace with. You'll need to strike as soon as we're within range.*

Mina prepared another arrow as Copper tried to catch up to them. The wind whipped her hair about wildly and she had to shield her eyes to keep them from drying out again. The nearest of the three dragons flew lazily, and once they were within range, the dragon zipped ahead, easily outdistancing Copper.

You weren't lying. They are fast!

Of course I wasn't lying. Dragons never lie.

Mina leaned forward as Copper flapped his wings faster, setting the bow in her lap. Copper's chest heaved with his breaths and his shoulders bumped her up and down.

Can you catch them? You seem to be struggling.

He growled in reply and flapped harder. Mina felt as if it took a while, but soon they were gaining on the dragon. It would occasionally slow down, then speed back up, and she realized that the creature was toying with them. It added fuel to the fire of her determination, and she readied her bow.

The other two are behind us, Copper said. *You might be able to get them both if you shoot fast enough.*

One target at a time.

Get ready. I'm going to close the distance, but as soon as she knows what I'm doing, she'll speed ahead.

I'm ready.

Copper shot forward suddenly, putting them within firing range. Mina took aim and fired, quickly pulling another arrow from the quiver. The projectile struck the very edge of the target, almost missing it.

That was close.

Too close, Copper replied. *I'm going to let the other two get ahead of me. Once we're behind them, you'll have to fire two arrows as fast as you can manage.*

At the same time?

No. That would be impossible.

Mina thought knocking two arrows back-to-back and hitting the targets would be impossible, but she had to try. Copper was too slow to match the silver dragons' speed, and if they lost this opportunity, she would never pass the test.

Hold on. It's going to get rough.

Mina pressed her legs into Copper's neck and grabbed two arrows from the quiver. She placed one in her lap and held onto the other, then braced herself. Copper lifted his wings up to catch the wind, and his bulk jerked backward. The two silver dragons continued past, and Mina lifted the bow and fired off the first arrow. It struck the target on the outer edge of the dragon to the left. Her fingers fumbled with the second arrow, and she almost dropped it. She struggled to knock it, her frustration adding to the hindrance. She got the arrow on the string and aimed, but the last target was just out of reach.

Hurry! Copper urged.

She swallowed hard and tilted the bow up a few inches and let the arrow fly. It soared through the air. A gust of wind blew it off mark and it missed the target, striking the wooden leg that supported it. Mina's heart sank into her stomach. She'd missed. The last two weeks had been for nothing. She bit her lip in anger and tried to keep her eyes from welling with tears. Copper descended slowly, but she lost focus on everything. Despair reared its ugly head.

They landed on the ground where the Enclave waited. Mina climbed down from Copper's back and walked over to stand before the elders. She kept her face as stoic as she could, but internally, she was screaming. She paused a few feet from the Enclave members and knelt.

Rise, the silver leader said.

Mina stood and waited to hear the crushing news.

You did well. The final target proved to be a challenge, but your arrow did strike it.

It did? Mina knew it had struck the leg, but she didn't think that counted. The dragon stared at her, and she realized she didn't use the proper title. *Apologies, Tiarna. I'm confused.*

Your task was to hit every target. You did so. What is there to be confused about?

I ... She cleared her throat. *I didn't think hitting the leg of the target counted.*

It is a technicality, but the Enclave has agreed to let it count. Prepare for your test with the blade.

Yes, Tiarna.

Mina turned around and walked back to Copper, a smile encompassing her face.

You did well, but two of those arrows came close to missing. Keep your mind focused. If you let your guard down now, you won't make it.

I'm just happy that I didn't fail, she replied. *I thought for sure that last arrow wouldn't count as a strike.*

The Enclave is being generous, but do not expect the same leniency with the sword.

Mina drew her sword from the sheath and took a few practice swings.

How will they test my skill with a blade?

You will fight an opponent.

I have to fight a dragon?

No. You will fight Areg.

Areg? But he's ... she wanted to say dull, but she bit her tongue. *He's so small.*

Do not mistake his odd speech and size for a lack of intelligence. There is more to him than you know.

What do you mean?

I will tell you after your test. You need to remain focused.

The crowd of dragons closed in around them, forming a large makeshift ring. Areg stepped into the circle, wearing chainmail armor and carrying a sword. Mina wondered at the training Copper had given her. He'd trained her to use the bow on the ground, yet they tested her on dragon back. Now she was going to fight on the ground, but she'd trained in the air.

A hint of distrust washed over her, and she entertained the brief thought that he was trying to sabotage her. She looked at him and immediately pushed the thought away. Copper could have killed her long before now. And despite learning the bow on foot, she had managed to hit moving targets with his guidance. No, he wasn't trying to sabotage her.

How will one of us win? she asked.

You will battle until one of you has scored three hits. You should not seek to do mortal harm, but a little pain is acceptable. I'll let you know if the strike counts. The first to land three hits is the winner. Go and take your place.

Mina left Copper's side and walked to where Areg was.

"It me," he said.

"I hear you have some skill with these things." She shook the blade.

"Yes."

"Well, don't take it easy on me. I want a fair fight."

Areg smiled at her. "Me fight good."

"Let's see what you've got then."

He bowed to her, she mirrored the movement, and then he came at her with a ferocity she'd never seen before.

14

Caden scrambled ahead on all fours, grabbing the pendant and getting to his feet. Lord D'Lance was shouting incoherently behind him, but he ignored everything and ran along the street, turning down side alleys and zig-zagging his way through the city until he reached a random sewer grate.

His side throbbed painfully, and he spared a few seconds to look down. Whatever had struck him had cut right through his chainmail. Blood soaked his clothes, and judging by the amount of blood that trailed behind him, he knew the wound was deep. He knelt and pulled the grate aside, clenching his teeth against the pain. He just needed to reach the camp alive and one of the draman could get the pendant to their master.

Caden climbed down into the tunnel and walked blindly in the darkness, wandering in the direction he assumed would lead outside the city. As the minutes passed and his strength failed, he paused and leaned against the wall. He was losing too much blood.

Keep going.

His master's voice penetrated the veil of pain and weakness, energizing him. He forged ahead, keeping a quick but cautious pace. A rumbling sound reverberated through the tunnel, and the ground shuddered under his feet. What was going on above him?

The tunnel curved to the left, and daylight became visible. Caden exited the sewer and continued into the woods, but his vision was blurry and he struggled to put one foot in front of the other. He tripped and fell; the ground seeming to spin him round and round. He closed his eyes to ease the dizziness and the next thing he knew, he was on the back of a dragon, flying through the sky over The Long Sands.

Caden looked around, confused as to how he got there. Was he dead? Or if not, then why was he riding a dragon? He was also holding a bow, and he took aim and fired an arrow at another dragon. The projectile struck something on the creature's back, but he couldn't discern what it was. Suddenly, the scenery changed and he fell off the dragon, hurtling toward the ground.

Just as he was about to hit the ground, his eyes opened. He was lying on his back, staring up at the green canopy of the woods. The face of a draman looked down at him.

"You live," he said. "Good. The master would be furious if you died."

Caden touched his side. The wound was closed. He sat up to look and saw a long scar line, but otherwise, there was no sign that he'd been injured. His chainmail and sword had been removed and were lying nearby, but the pendant was missing.

"Where's the gemstone?"

The draman nudged the armor with his foot. Caden grabbed the edge of it and pulled it over, lifting it. The pendant fell to the ground. He breathed a sigh of relief and picked it up.

"How did you close my wound?"

"It wasn't us. It was our master."

Thank you, Caden said, mentally pushing the words through the connection he felt with the dragon. She didn't respond, but he could sense her presence was still with him. He got to his feet and glanced around the camp. Bast and the others hadn't returned yet.

"Any word from the messengers?" he asked.

"No, sir. It's been silent."

That didn't sit well with Caden, especially considering how the events had unfolded before he escaped the city.

"If we don't get a report soon, send someone to investigate."

"As you command."

Caden slipped his chainmail back on and retrieved his sword sheath, strapping it around his waist. He wandered around the camp, killing time. He didn't want to leave while Bast was gone, but if he didn't return soon, Caden wouldn't have a choice. His master wanted to be free of her prison, and the gemstone in his possession was vital to achieving that freedom.

The smell of smoke reached his nostrils, and he looked in the direction of Velbridge. The woods were too thick for him to see anything, but he was confident the scent wasn't from the campfires.

"Sir!" One of the draman flagged him down. "They've returned!"

Caden rushed across the camp. Bast and about twenty others marched through the trees. They were covered in blood and ash and looked exhausted. Bast met Caden's gaze and shook his head slightly.

"Let's speak in private," the draman said.

Caden walked with him until they were away from everyone else, and even then, Bast kept his voice low.

"We suffered heavy losses. Lord D'Lance brought out one of his dragons and it all went downhill from there."

"How many got out of the city?" Caden asked.

"I'm not sure. Those who returned with me are the only ones I can confirm."

Caden did his best not to let his expression reveal the alarm he felt. Out of four hundred men, only a handful returned to the camp.

"Where is the dragon now? Were you followed?"

"I think he lost control of it. It started burning the city. That's when we fled. I doubt he cared enough about us to give chase. His attention was diverted to a new crisis."

"Hopefully nobody was killed. The people have no idea what kind of monster rules over them. The fact that he lost control of the dragon is a surprise, possibly a good one."

"Why is that?"

"It shows the creatures are fighting against his magic. If they can break free of his control, we could use that to our advantage."

"Our master is going to be upset when she learns that our forces are scattered and possibly dead."

"Maybe this will help." Caden held up the pendant.

Bast's eyes turned to slits. "Is that the stone she seeks?"

"Yes."

"How did you get it?"

Caden rubbed his chin, offering a slight grin. "I went into the city. Lord D'Lance was there, and I had the opportunity to take it, so I did."

"It will not please the master that you disobeyed her orders."

"She may already know. Either way, I had to redeem myself in her eyes. She gave me a task, and I needed to see it through to completion."

"I admire your determination, but you could have been killed."

"I nearly was," Caden said. "I took a deep cut to my side, but our master healed it. Here, you should take the gem to her. I'll stay here and work on regathering our men … if they are still alive out there."

"No. She will expect you to deliver it. You should take it to her now. Lord D'Lance will be looking for you, for all of us, and the further away you are from here, the better."

Caden looked across the camp at the other draman. He would feel guilty leaving them here, injured and alone.

"We were doing fine before you came, and we'll be fine without you," Bast said as if reading his mind. "Go."

"Very well. With any luck, I'll return with our master."

"It will be an honor to see her in the flesh."

Caden clapped a hand on Bast's shoulder and nodded, then walked to where he slept and gathered a few rations of food into a leather satchel. It would take a few hours to get to the mountain, and he was already feeling the pangs of hunger. He slung the bag over his shoulder and headed east, the pendant firmly in hand.

Lord D'Lance was going to pay dearly for his tyranny and slaughter.

15

MINA STAGGERED BACKWARD UNDER THE fierceness of Areg's attack, almost tripping in her haste. The elf's diminutive size and unassuming nature deceived her, but now that she knew he was a trained warrior, she would not let her guard down. Mina brought her sword up to deflect his strikes, and their blades clanged loudly. The steel vibrated in her hand, sending an odd sensation along her arm.

I didn't train to fight an opponent this skilled!

You will not always be prepared for what you encounter in the world, Copper replied.

He always had an answer for everything she complained about, but it was never a resolution to her problem. She tried to remember what she'd heard Captain Eduard teach when Lord Klodian would visit the Runesman training grounds, but there was little she could recall. At the time, it hadn't seemed like information she would need to know.

She was so wrapped up in her thoughts that she didn't notice Areg was slowly pushing her into a corner until it was almost too late. The crowd of dragons watched intently, silently judging her progress. Areg outmatched her, but that didn't mean he was invincible. Mina dug her heels into the sand grabbed the hilt of her blade with both hands, driving the pointed end straight for Areg's chest.

The elf twirled aside, slapping her sword up high as he did so. She couldn't believe how graceful his movements were. They were in a battle, but he was so nimble that he seemed to dance more than anything. His feet capered over the sand, barely leaving an indentation at all. How was that possible?

Her thoughts shattered into a thousand pieces as stinging pain erupted along her wrist. Areg slapped the flat of his blade across her flesh, and he was already gone by the time she tried to jab at him.

That's one point for Areg.

Mina rubbed her wrist with to soothe the sting and watched the elf warily. He'd put some distance between them, and she took the brief respite to evaluate her lack of strategy. She had no doubt that she couldn't beat Areg, which meant that she would fail the test. Was this the Enclave's way of telling her that she wasn't fit to be a rider?

Focus, Copper's voice rumbled.

Sorry.

She shook her head as if that would dispel the thoughts from her mind and rolled her shoulders. Areg was staring at her, waiting.

I will do my best, she told herself.

Mina rushed toward Areg and swung her sword in an overhand chopping motion. She assumed she must look clumsy to everyone watching. Her movements were nowhere near as beautiful as Areg's. Yet again, he easily evaded her. As she passed him, unable to stop her momentum, he flashed her a grin and smacked the back of her knees with his sword.

Her legs buckled and gave way, sending her sprawling face-first into the sand. She got a mouthful of the gritty grains and spat repeatedly as she struggled to get back on her feet. Had this fight been in front of humans, there would be loud cheers and people heckling her. Instead, there was only silence as the dragons watched impassively.

I'm failing miserably, she complained.

Keep going. The tide can always change.

Mina wiped her mouth on the back of her hand, brushing the sand off. The ground trembled beneath her like it had earlier, and she looked around. Dragons glanced among themselves, and the smell of vanilla was overwhelming. She wished that their thoughts were available to her mind, as she could only wonder what they were saying to one another. She looked back at Areg, and he nodded at her.

"Fight," he said.

"I am."

He came at her like a flash of lightning, quick and terrifying. She barely brought her sword up in time to parry his strike, and the force ripped the hilt from her hand. The sword landed in the sand, and she threw herself to the ground to retrieve it. Areg was next to her immediately, his small foot landing a kick to her ribs. Despite his size, the blow was powerful and sent her rolling onto her back.

Mina could feel the ground still trembling, but now it was a constant vibration. She ignored Copper's announcement of the points as Areg placed his foot on her chest, preparing to land his final strike. She rolled away from him, latching onto the ankle of his other leg. Areg grunted as he fell on his back, temporarily stunned. She scrambled on all fours to her blade and snatched it out of the sand, then struck Areg's leg before he recovered.

Two to one in favor of Areg.

At least I finally hit him, but he only needs one more point. It's impossible for me to win.

Keep going, Copper repeated.

Mina got to her feet, chest heaving. Sweat was rolling down her arms and legs, and sand clung to her flesh. This type of fighting was harder than she thought. Areg stalked around her like a predator, and she turned with him, keeping her eyes locked on his. Copper was right, there *was* more to him than she knew.

As if reading each other's minds, they lunged toward one another at the same time. Their blades clashed as they fought in close proximity, and for a fleeting moment, Mina thought she might hold her own against Areg.

The elf dropped to his knees and jabbed his sword upward, hitting her in the stomach with the tip. Her armor kept the sword from impaling her, but pain still flared through her abdomen at the strike. Mina clenched her jaw against the pain and stumbled backward.

Three to one in favor of Areg, Copper said.

I lost, Mina mentally gasped.

Yes, but you did well. Areg is a skilled warrior, and you lasted longer than I expected.

Mina found that difficult to believe, but it eased the sting of her loss until she realized that she'd failed the test. The Enclave would deny her request to hold off the war, and humanity would burn under their wrath.

You did well, the silver dragon's voice entered her mind.

I lost. How is that doing well?

Your small amount of training has proven that you do have what it takes to be a warrior. You could never have defeated Areg, even if you had trained for years rather than weeks.

Then why did you put me against him?

We have our reasons, the dragon vaguely replied.

Since I failed, will you go to war?

You might have lost, but you did not fail. We will not go to war against the humans.

Mina had never felt more relief in her entire life.

Thank you for trusting me. I will do whatever I must to stop Lord D'Lance.

Good. You must kill him, else he will never stop.

I will do what must be done, Mina said. She didn't agree to kill him, but if that's what needed to be done when the time came, then she would do it. She sheathed her blade and knelt, embracing Areg in a hug.

"Where did you learn to fight like that?" she asked.

"Story long."

Before she could say anything, there was an unearthly roar that hurt her ears. She clasped her hands over them and snapped her gaze to Copper.

What was that?

One of the scouts, he replied. *We're under attack.*

From who?

Sand wyrms.

16

CADEN FOUND THE CLIMB UP the mountain less arduous than the first time, but it still proved to be an exhausting task. The sky was clear, a vibrant blue, and the sun beat down directly on him. Sweat seemed to come from his every pore, but unlike the first journey, he stopped periodically to rest and eat the provisions he'd brought.

As he topped the ridge where the abandoned temple's entrance was, he had a sense of foreboding. Now that he knew the voice that had called to him belonged to a dragon, he was unsure about many things. Still, he reminded himself that she had brought him back from death, healed him, and given him charge over her army of draman.

Caden inhaled a deep breath to calm his nerves and entered the cave. The darkness was thick, but he remembered there should be light ahead. When he encountered the glowing moss, he knew that he was getting close. His steps were sure, despite the thundering pace of his heart. The tunnel brought him into the abandoned temple, and the glowing eyes of his master peered at him from the shadows. He swallowed hard and drew as close to her as he dared.

Caden, my devoted servant. I sense something different about you.

"I'm not sure what you mean," he replied.

There is something keeping your thoughts from me. You haven't betrayed me, have you?

"No, of course not. I owe you my life. I could never forsake my oath."

Good, she hissed. *Why have you come here?*

Caden retrieved the pendant from his satchel and held it up for her to see. The dragon growled, low and dangerous.

That is why you feel distant. That cursed stone is the bane of my existence. You must destroy it for me.

"Gladly," Caden said.

He dropped the pendant to the ground and drew his sword, then struck the portion holding the stone with all his might. He inspected his work, but the stone wasn't even scratched.

Your enthusiasm is commendable, but normal weapons cannot destroy the stone.

"Then how?"

You must take it to where it was created and use words of power to unravel its magic.

"I am not a sorcerer, so I do not know what words would be used. Should I seek one out?"

No. I will teach you the words needed. They do not need to come from a sorcerer, they only need to be spoken.

"Where do I need to take the stone?"

At the pinnacle of the mountain. Lord D'Lance crafted his dark magic there and tricked me, imprisoning me and stealing my eggs. You will go there and speak the words I teach you. When the gemstone is broken, I shall be free.

Caden put the pendant back into the satchel and sheathed his blade. The air was thin at this altitude, and he wondered if he had the fortitude to make it further up. He would try regardless, because he had given his word to her.

The wind is strong up there, so take your steps prudently. If you fall, you will perish.

"I will heed caution. If I die before you are free, then I have failed in my duties."

Good. Remember these words: Cealaigh an draíocht seo agus oscail an méid atá curtha faoi ghlas. When you reach the top, speak them and it will undo the dark magic binding me here. Repeat them.

Caden stumbled over them a few times, but on the sixth try he spoke them perfectly.

Now go. I want to be free of this place before the sun sets.

He offered a slight bow and left, making his way back out to the ledge. His gaze roamed the upper portion of the mountain. Rocks jutted up everywhere, enormous and jagged, and the peak seemed so far away.

"I can do this," he muttered to himself.

He started making his way up, picking the route carefully. The higher he climbed, the more powerful the wind whipped. The temperature dropped as well, and the sun did little to warm him. Caden was making good progress before he tripped. A small, flat rock shifted under his weight and sent him careening backward. His arms rotated in circles as he fell, but there was nothing for him to grab ahold of, and he tumbled for twenty feet until he roughly came to a stop, wedged between two boulders.

His mind hadn't fully comprehended what had happened, and he sat there unmoving for a long while. Pain lanced through his chest with every breath, and he knew that something was broken, likely a few ribs. He tried to communicate with his master, but then he recalled what she'd said about the stone blocking his thoughts.

Caden refused to die, at least not here, and he forced himself to get up. His right side was the source of his pain, and he gingerly pressed a hand onto his ribcage. He sucked in a sharp breath and used his other hand to steady himself as he grew lightheaded. Once the weakness passed, he continued his ascent.

It took him a long time to reach the area where he'd fallen, and even longer to find a safe path ahead. The mountain was a veritable death trap, and he cursed Lord D'Lance in his thoughts with every setback. The man had done well to ensure no one would be foolish enough to seek the place where he'd created his spell. Perhaps Caden was foolish, or just brazenly insane, but he forced himself to continue the trek.

The peak was only a few hundred feet away now. He wasn't sure if it was the lack of oxygen or his imagination, but he thought he could see something glowing. It was a translucent pale shade of blue, and whatever it was, it cast its light around the entire mountaintop.

"I'm losing my mind," Caden said, unsure exactly why he was talking to himself. He laughed at the thought, causing his ribs to flare with agony, but the pain brought a semblance of clarity. He was almost there, and while he wasn't truly losing his sanity, he was being affected by the thinness of the air.

Caden's movements became sluggish, and his vision was blurred. He jostled his side, and the pain brought his focus back, but only for a short time. Eventually, even that did nothing to help him keep his wits. At one point, it startled him to realize that he was sitting on a rock and hadn't been walking at all.

His satchel was on the ground at his feet, open. The rations were gone, and his canteen was empty. When had he partaken of them? His mind was muddled. He spotted the pendant on the ground and picked it up, standing on unsteady legs. There was a reason he had this, a reason he'd come up here to begin with. What was it?

Then he remembered, though the memory was foggy. He needed to take it to the top of the mountain … for some reason or other. He continued up the steep slope, finally reaching the base of the plateau where the glowing light was coming from. Caden staggered up the last few feet and found a pool of water. It bubbled, wisps of steam rising from its surface.

It was a hot spring. The water looked warm and inviting. He'd made it, so he deserved a break, didn't he? He tried to step closer, but the pale blue light turned out to be a magical barrier, keeping him from going any further.

Now what was he supposed to do?

17

THE HOST OF DRAGONS AROUND Mina and Areg took to the air, creating a mini sandstorm in their wake. Mina buried her face into the crook of her arm and waited until she could see, then ran to Copper.

You said sand wyrms aren't smart enough to band together.

They're not.

Then why are they attacking?

I'm not sure, but I suspect it has something to do with Lord D'Lance. Get on my back. It's not safe being on the ground.

She climbed up onto his back and looked at Areg.

Will he be safe underground?

Yes, but I doubt he'll willingly go down there.

Mina motioned to him. "Come on!"

The elf rushed over to them and easily clambered up Copper to sit behind her. He wrapped his small arms around her and held on tightly. Copper launched into the air and ascended high above the ground. Mina scoured the landscape and spotted the approaching sand wyrms. The ground heaved upward as they tunneled through the sand, heading for the dragon cave.

There are so many of them.

Something has driven them here, Copper replied. *There is nothing natural about this.*

The other dragons were circling in the air, roaring challenges at the wyrms. Mina was worried. If Lord D'Lance was controlling the creatures, what was he trying to accomplish?

He probably knows we're aware of his scheme.

How would he be controlling them, though?

Magic. The same kind he's using to force bonds with.

One of the wyrms broke free of the ground, rising into the air like a monolith. Its thick flesh rippled, and Mina scowled in disgust. The dragons attacked it with fury, clawing and biting at its exposed body. It screeched in pain, and two more wyrms ascended from the sand nearby.

Are there enough dragons to drive them back?

Yes.

There was something about the way he answered that made Mina think he wasn't entirely confident. She could smell a hint of lavender. Copper was afraid.

How can I help? she asked.

You can't. They're too strong for you to injure. Driving a sword into one would be useless, and getting that close would get you killed. We will stay in the air and wait for them to flee.

As more wyrms continued to breach the sand, Mina feared that Copper was wrong about the strength of the dragons' numbers. They hadn't killed one yet, and none of the wyrms were trying to escape the wrath of tooth and talon.

How can Lord D'Lance be controlling them from so far away?

Copper hummed in thought. *He may be out here somewhere, though I doubt it.*

One of the wyrms began bleating, but it didn't seem to be a cry of pain. Mina watched it, wondering what it was doing. The other wyrms joined it, producing a chorus of deep rumbling cries.

Something is coming.

More wyrms?

Copper didn't answer, but a moment later, the ground erupted as a wyrm twice the size of the others broke free. Black spines lined its body, and its maw was full of razor-sharp teeth. It roared like a dragon, its eyeless face swishing back and forth as if searching for an enemy to battle.

"Wyrm king!" Areg shouted from behind her.

"What's that?"

It's trouble, Copper answered. *They are harder to kill than the others. The heart is its only weak spot, and it's encased in a thick layer of bone and muscle and buried too deep to be reached by dragon claws.*

Then how do you strike its heart?

It must be done from the inside.

You don't mean ...

Yes, Copper confirmed. *The one to kill it must be swallowed.*

That's certain death!

For some, yes. But there are a rare few who have survived to tell the tale.

Have you?

Copper chortled. *No, but Areg has.*

Mina twisted awkwardly to look back at the elf.

"You've killed one of those?"

He grinned. "Me kill two."

Two. Areg had killed two wyrm kings. He was an expert swordsman and a phenomenal shot with the bow. She couldn't help but wonder who the little elf truly was.

"Take close," he said, a gleam in his eyes. He patted the hilt of his sword.

I'm going to fly over the wyrm so Areg can deal with the beast.

Mina slid her fingers under Copper's scales and gripped them tightly. Copper turned in the direction of the wyrm king and sped straight for it. A host of dragons had swarmed the creature, and Mina gasped in horror as the spines on the wyrm's body shot free, impaling several of the dragons. Their broken bodies fell from the sky.

Stay low, Copper advised.

Mina leaned forward, practically laying on his neck. The wyrm roared as they flew over it, and despite their altitude, Mina could feel the warmth of its breath on her skin. Areg released her and she saw him leap off Copper's back from her peripheral. She winced as the elf disappeared into the mouth of the wyrm.

I hope he survives.

It will take more than a sand wyrm to kill him.

Copper continued, wheeling around and ascending higher into the sky. Mina looked from wyrm to wyrm. The dragons had numbers on their side, but they were smaller in size than the bulky wyrms.

You said you would tell me about Areg after my tests. Who is he? How is he so good with weapons?

Areg is an elf, and they have a natural gift when it comes to agility and speed, but that is not what makes him different. He was once a rider, bonded to a dragon like you.

That took Mina by surprise. She struggled to wrap her mind around the information.

You said he was a rider. He's not now?

No. Sadly, his bonded passed away many years ago. He's remained with us ever since, pledging his life to help us however possible.

Why does he talk so odd?

Areg aided in the battle against Maël, and he was struck by a spell that damaged his mind. He's spoken that way ever since, but otherwise, he is the same as he was back then. I have never known a braver elf than Areg.

That explains a lot, Mina said. *When you said I was the first rider in a thousand years, I thought that meant there weren't any other riders alive.*

Areg is the only one.

Mina didn't understand why the elf chose to live with the dragons instead of his own people, but she guessed he had his reasons. Her attention returned to the wyrms and the unfolding battle. The situation looked grim. More dragons had fallen, and no wyrms were dead. She saw the silver dragon who led the Enclave leading a group toward the wyrm king.

Looks like she's got a plan.

Copper swiveled his head and Mina felt him tense.

She's going to get herself killed. I need to stop her.

I go where you go, Mina replied.

She could sense his hesitation through the scale. That was a new experience.

Go, she urged. *We must protect her.*

Copper dived toward the wyrm king, roaring thunderously. Mina was afraid and excited all at the same time, and she held on to Copper as firmly as she could. The wyrm king released more spines, and one of them flew directly at Copper. He swerved sharply to avoid it, and Mina's eyes widened as his scales slipped free of her sweaty hands.

She fell off his back and tumbled through the air.

18

CADEN STARED AT THE FLICKERING blue barrier and considered his options. The reason he brought the stone up here still eluded him, so it likely wasn't too important. Was it something he wanted to do, or someone else? The answer hovered at the edge of his mind, but it was clouded with uncertainty.

He looked back the way he'd come and considered going back down, but he couldn't find a reason to do that, either. It was as if he were in a battle of tug-of-war, the two opposing thoughts vying for control of his mind, and the pressure made him tired. Caden wanted nothing more than to rest, but a strange force wouldn't let him.

"Please," he begged. "I can't do it."

The force increased, and he dropped to his knees, the pain in his ribs causing him to cry out in agony. The two forces continued to clash in his mind, and one gained control.

Touch the gemstone to the barrier.

The voice was familiar. It was … his master? Yes, that seemed right. He lifted his hand and pressed the pendant to the barrier. At first, the blue light intensified, blinding him. A sizzling noise filled his ears, and the barrier blinked out of existence. Warmth washed over him, driving back the chill in his bones. He crawled forward and reached the bubbling pool. The water stank of rotten eggs, making him gag.

Get in the water. That is the source of the magic.

He didn't want to, but he would obey her regardless. Rising to his feet, he hesitantly stepped into the pool. The water was blue, a much different shade from the barrier. Its color was deceiving, though, given its smell. The temperature was hot, uncomfortably so, but he pressed on at the urging of his master.

Go to the center. It will be the deepest spot.

The water grew too deep for him to reach the bottom, and it forced him to swim. He reached the middle and treaded the water to keep his head from going under.

Now speak the words I told you.

Caden tried to remember them, but the fog in his mind hadn't fully lifted yet. His muscles ached, and his ribs burned fiercely. It was all he could do to keep from sinking, and when he went under, he sunk like a sack of rocks. Water flooded into his mouth and he panicked. His feet touched something solid, and he kicked off of it, splashing above the water's surface. He coughed and sputtered, fighting to stay afloat.

Say the words!

He was trying not to drown, and his master wanted him to speak some magical words he could barely recall. Fear flooded him. He was going to fail. He was going to *die*. Despite his brush with death on the plains, Caden was still afraid of the unknown.

Say them!

Caden went under the water again, but this time he was prepared. He held his breath and touched the bottom, springing himself above the pool's surface again. The words came to him then, and he shouted them as loudly as he could.

"Cealaigh an draíocht seo agus oscail an méid atá curtha faoi ghlas!"

He fell beneath the water, and the pendant in his hand shivered. The gemstone shattered, and an invisible force escaped from it, sending ripples through the water. The fragments of the stone fell free of the pendant and drifted down to the bottom of the pool. Before he could try to get out of the water, it churned in a circular motion, quickly becoming a maelstrom.

The current swept Caden along, spinning him around and around. He tried to grab onto the edge of the pool, but his hands kept slipping off the slick surface. The maelstrom spun faster and suddenly shot up into the air. Caden was pushed aside, and he struck the ground with a grunt and laid on his back, watching the geyser of water rise into the sky, pain shooting through his chest.

As it came back down, it spread out and landed everywhere but in the pool, disappearing into the soil or rolling down the sides of the mountain. Caden couldn't believe he'd succeeded. The entire situation felt unreal, more like a dream than anything.

My shackles are free!

His master's voice was filled with emotion, a mix of excitement and relief tinged with anger. The ground under him trembled, reminding him of being in the sewers under Velbridge. The pain in his ribs subsided, and a wave of strength invigorated him. He sat up and looked around, wondering where the tremors were coming from.

You have kept your oath and freed me. I am most pleased with you, and you shall be my right hand among my forces. I shall lead my brethren to war, and you shall lead my draman.

"I am honored!" Caden shouted, his words echoing into the sky. "You saved me from death, and I shall serve you for the rest of my days!"

His master's pleasure pulsed through him, filling his veins with fire. He could also feel her rage boiling under the surface of all of her other emotions, kept in check ... for now. Lord D'Lance had made a grave mistake by trapping her in the mountain.

The tremors in the ground strengthened, and in the distance, one peak crumbled, spilling boulders and dirt down the slopes below. Caden hurried to the edge of the plateau and looked down. Avalanches of stone tumbled down the mountain, obliterating the path he'd taken. It seemed as if the entire mountain was going to split in two. He needed to get to safety, but there was no way he could climb down without being crushed.

Stay where you are, his master said. *I will get you.*

Far below, an explosion rocked the ground, and debris scattered from the ridge where the temple was. A massive form as dark as the night sky came forth, swatting the boulders aside as if they were nothing more than small bugs. She turned and winged her way toward him, and Caden was overcome with fear and awe.

He fell to his knees in reverence but kept his eyes locked on her beauty. Her scales were black as ebony, her wings easily twice the size of Lord D'Lance's castle grounds. She was massive in every regard. She opened her mouth and breathed fire, huge gouts of orange flames ripping through the sky. Even from this distance, he could feel the heat of them.

She landed on the peak where the pool of water had been, and she raked the ground with her claws, tearing the rock apart and flinging it away. When she finished, he couldn't tell that anything had been there at all. She roared, the sound louder than anything he'd ever heard before. He clapped his hands over his ears. The dragon narrowed her gaze on him and snaked her head forward, emerald eyes blazing as hot as her flames.

Now this world is going to burn.

19

Mina screamed in terror.

Above her, Copper weaved back and forth, dodging the black spines. A hundred thoughts passed through her mind, but mainly she feared that Copper didn't know she'd fallen off of his back. She maneuvered herself face-down toward the ground and immediately regretted it. Seeing the desert landscape speeding toward her was like looking death straight in the face.

Before she could prepare for her untimely demise, a massive claw grabbed ahold of her, breaking her freefall. Her body whipped harshly to a stop, but she was alive. She looked up to see the large brass dragon from her test.

Thank you. She pushed the words through the scale, but the dragon didn't respond. He ascended higher and Mina saw that the dragons were falling back, retreating from the wyrms. Had they lost?

Dragons don't give up that easily, Copper said. *We're regrouping.*

He swooped in below her, matching the brass dragon's pace. The dragon released her, and she fell a few feet down onto Copper's back.

I thought I was going to die.

You're lucky that Gavar saw you fall. He was the only one close enough to catch you.

Mina watched Gavar as he flew toward the horde of dragons gathering near one of the wyrms. She expressed her gratitude again through the scale, but she didn't know if he heard her.

I'm glad he helped me. I don't think I've proven myself enough yet, and I want to live long enough to do so.

If Gavar didn't think you were worthy of being a rider, he wouldn't have saved you.

The group of dragons were circling above the wyrm, staying high enough that it couldn't reach them. That didn't stop it from trying, and it screeched in frustration.

What are they planning?

We've lost too many of our brethren to divide ourselves, so we're going to attack them one at a time, Copper replied. *Once Areg kills the wyrm king, the others should flee, regardless of the magic being used on them.*

I hope you're right.

Copper joined the other dragons, and together they descended and began breathing fire on the wyrm. The heat washed over Mina, heavy and thick like a weighted blanket, forcing her to shield her face in the crook of her arm. Just when she thought it would become too much to bear, Copper broke away and the heat subsided.

Are you all right?

The heat is intense, but I'm fine.

The wyrm's cries of pain drowned out everything else, and Mina shuddered at the sound. Dragons swarmed the beast a second time, their fiery breath blistering and burning the wyrm's flesh, and the third attack silenced its cries forever.

Mina didn't know which was worse, the heat or the stench. With the first wyrm dead, the dragons turned their attention to the next one and began attacking it the same way. Mina was awed by the power of the dragons. Working together, they seemed like an unstoppable force. This wyrm fell quicker than the first one, and as they flew toward the third, a shrill keen came from the wyrm king.

The giant monster's body went limp, and it crashed down onto the sand, sending shock waves rolling across the desert. Mina couldn't believe that Areg had been successful. If what Areg told her was true, then he had now killed three wyrm kings. It seemed to her an impossible feat, something she could never accomplish.

The rest of the wyrms immediately began burrowing back into the sand, fleeing the area. It relieved Mina to see them go. Copper joined the silver Enclave leader and they landed near the body of the wyrm king. Mina had thought the creature massive before, but as she stood on the ground next to it, she felt like a grain of sand next to a mountain.

Are you sure it's dead? she asked.

As if in reply, a slit appeared on the beast's side and the flesh ripped open. Areg staggered out, wiping blood and entrails from his face and casting the gruesomeness to the ground. The dragons roared, a cry of victory rising to the heavens.

"It me," Areg said.

Mina laughed. She felt as if it had been an eternity since the last time she'd done so, and it eased the stress from her. The silver Enclave leader joined them, and she fixed her gaze on Mina.

This attack on our home cannot go unpunished.

You said you weren't going to war.

And I will keep my word, but I am going to send a small force of dragons to harass Lord D'Lance. They will travel with you and your bonded as protectors, but their first duty is to exact revenge for this affront.

I thought you wanted me to kill him?

The smell of lemon and clove hit Mina's nostrils.

I do, but I doubt that Lord D'Lance will be an easy target. My hope is that when my brethren are attacking his castle, he'll put himself in the open where you can strike. And if you die, then we will have our war.

I understand, Tiarna.

Mina desperately hoped that she could do what was needed to avoid a war, but her confidence was shaken. If Lord D'Lance could control beasts as large and powerful as the sand wyrms, what else was he capable of?

We will feast tonight, and in the morning, you shall deliver our wrath to that wretched man.

Yes, Tiarna.

—

By the time Mina tiredly stumbled into her chamber to get some sleep, it was late into the night. She removed her armor and flopped onto her bed. The sounds of dragons still celebrating their victory over the sand wyrms echoed faintly off the walls, but her exhaustion ensured that wasn't a problem, and she fell into the darkness of sleep.

When she awoke, the first thing she noticed was the soreness in her muscles. A groan escaped her lips as she sat up and looked around. Her armor was on the manakin again, and she suspected it was Areg who had placed it there.

I wondered if you would sleep all day, Copper said.

How late is it?

It's morning, but the sun has been up for a few hours now.

Mina rolled her eyes and got out of bed. She'd eaten so much the night before that she wasn't hungry for breakfast. She donned her armor and put her boots on, then headed into Copper's room. Despite the oddity of living with dragons in an underground cave for the last few weeks, she was going to miss the place.

I get to keep the armor and sword, right?

Yes, it is a gift from the Enclave.

I suppose I'm ready to leave if you are.

There is one more thing I must give you.

What is it?

You asked my name, and I told you that I would give it to you when you earned my trust.

Mina sucked in a breath. The silence seemed to stretch unendingly until he finally spoke.

My name is Gedrith.

I'm honored that you have come to trust me, Mina said, full of emotion.

And I am honored that we are bonded, Copper, now Gedrith, replied.

They stood quietly for a moment, and then Mina rushed forward and wrapped her arms around his leg, hugging it tightly. She had once only known hatred for dragons, and now she called one friend.

So am I, Gedrith. So am I.

The two of them went to see the Enclave to wish them farewell, and then they took to the air, heading for the Dracan Dominion. Mina was soaring over the clouds, literally and figuratively. She wanted nothing more than to see Caden, to tell him of everything that had happened to her since he'd left. She just needed to survive her encounter with Lord D'Lance, which didn't seem likely.

You will not die at his hands.

Why are you so sure?

I'm not. But if you do, I'll scorch him from existence in vengeance.

Mina smiled. Having a dragon at her back was all she needed. Gedrith was right. She would survive.

And then she would be free.

WRATH

OF THE

DRAGON

1

Mina took a drink from her canteen and stared at the castle in the distance. It had only been two weeks since she'd left, and yet it felt like an eternity had come and gone since she'd last seen Klodian Keep. Gedrith and the other dragons wanted to go straight to the Dracan Dominion, but she asked them to stop here first.

Are you sure about this? Gedrith asked.

I think so. Lord Klodian needs to know what is happening.

Was it foolish of her to warn him? Possibly. The man had used her ability for his own gain, but he had also provided her with shelter and food. That wasn't a justifiable reason for her slavery, but she felt an odd sense of obligation toward him.

I'll be back as quickly as I can.

If you run into trouble, call for me.

I will.

Mina returned the canteen to her pack at Gedrith's feet and walked across the sand. She mulled over how Lord Klodian would react. Given her hasty departure, he probably thought she was dead. Thais probably did, too. And there was also the unresolved issue with Lady Burgess and the plot to overthrow Klodian. Had Thais handled that on her own?

The gates were open, and Mina walked into the courtyard. A quick look around showed nothing much had changed. She headed for the castle and was almost at the main doors when a voice called out behind her.

"Mina?"

She turned around to see Thais. The woman and had an astonished expression on her face.

"Where have you been? I thought you'd been taken by Lord D'Lance's spies."

"It's a long story," Mina replied.

"You can tell me later, then. Are you all right?"

"I'm fine. I need to speak with Lord Klodian. Is he here?"

"He is." Thais eyed her up and down. "You look like a soldier. Why are you wearing armor?"

"I don't have time to explain. Has anything odd happened around here?"

"Aside from your disappearing act?" Thais smirked and lowered her voice. "Actually, we might have a problem."

"Lady Burgess?"

"Yes. She left back to the Dracan Dominion after her husband reappeared with a strong sense of loyalty to Lord Klodian. He's still here, by the way, doting on Lord Klodian's every whim. She seemed deeply disturbed before leaving, but nothing has come of that situation that I'm aware of."

"Good. I had planned to help you with her, but I ... got sidetracked."

Thais looked around to make sure nobody was nearby. "Does it have to do with that dragon you mentioned?"

Mina nodded.

"How did you escape?"

"As I said, it's a long story."

Thais glowered at her. "What's going on? You were trusting of me before you disappeared, and now you're being vague about things again."

"I'm sorry. There's a lot going on, and I don't have much time before I have to leave again. Lord D'Lance is doing more than just plotting against the High Prince. He's building an army of dragon riders."

"I know."

"You do?"

"I told you about why I'm here," Thais replied. "And there's a reason I believed you when you told me that dragons could talk. I've seen what he's done."

"Do you also know what he's doing with the dragon eggs?"

"Dragon eggs? I know nothing about that."

"It's bad, Thais. The dragons wanted to go to war with him, but I convinced them not to."

"How did you do that?"

"I have to kill him."

"Him who? Lord D'Lance?"

"Yes."

Thais laughed harshly. "Do you know what you're saying? Lord D'Lance is powerful beyond belief. If someone could kill him, they would have done it by now. And since when are you an assassin? You don't even know how to wield a sword."

Mina felt her face flush with warmth, but she kept her anger under control.

"Don't worry about me. Lord D'Lance may be strong, but I've got some mighty friends to help me."

"The dragons?"

"Listen to me, Thais. If I can stop Lord D'Lance, there won't be a war. With the dragons or the High Prince."

"If you want to commit suicide, go ahead. I won't stop you. You've changed, Mina. I don't know if that's a good thing."

Thais turned and walked away. Mina watched her go, wondering why she was so upset. If Lord D'Lance died, her parents would be free. Isn't that what Thais wanted? She pushed the thought away and entered the castle. Servants were going about their tasks, and the smell of fresh food drifted on the air.

It was such a busy atmosphere compared to the dragon cave, which was normal for Klodian's court, but it was something that Mina had never considered before. She navigated her way through the maze of hallways, pausing outside the door of Klodian's personal chamber. There were two muffled voices engaged in conversation on the other side, and she was about to turn and leave when the door swung open.

"Keep me informed," Lord Klodian said to Captain Eduard.

Upon seeing her, they both froze. Mina offered a shy smile and offered a bow.

"My Lord," she greeted.

"I'll be on my way." Captain Eduard stepped around her and left.

"Am I seeing a ghost?" Klodian asked. "The last thing I heard was that you rode into the desert and your horse came back alone."

"I'm sorry if I caused you to worry. Can we talk in private?"

Klodian eyed her curiously and pulled the door open completely, motioning for her to enter. She stepped inside and waited to speak until the door shut.

"I must go to the Dracan Dominion."

"What are you going on about? You disappear for a fortnight and show back up, only to leave again? Do you know how many resources I used searching the desert for you?"

"May I speak plainly?"

"Please do."

Mina cleared her throat. Despite how strong she felt in her armor with a sword strapped to her waist, his presence was so imposing it felt as though she were still a slave under his control.

"Lord D'Lance is plotting to overthrow you."

Klodian's left brow rose, but otherwise, he didn't react.

"Explain."

"It's a lot to tell, but I overheard Lord and Lady Burgess talking. They mentioned that Lord D'Lance was going to request soldiers from the other Dominions and that you would refuse the request. That would give him what he needed to replace you as the ruler of the Thophate."

"And why would he want to replace me?"

"Because his goal is to take the throne of the High Prince."

"You've swayed my interest. Keep going."

"He's spreading rumors that Lord Culver and you are working together to cause a war that will divide the Dominions, and he's doing a good job of leaving convincing evidence."

"So you learned of this information two weeks ago and decided not to come to me directly?"

Mina flushed under his intense gaze. "I needed proof," she said. "I didn't want to make an accusation without it."

"Fair enough. Where is your proof?"

"I don't have anything physical to show you, but I trust the source who confirmed that it's all true."

"Who is this trusted source?"

Mina hesitated. This was where things were going to get tricky.

"Gedrith told me. He's a dragon."

2

CADEN STOOD WITH HIS ARMS folded, watching the draman as they erected a line of new tents. Bast had done well with rallying their forces that had fled Velbridge after their failed attack. More of them had survived than Caden initially thought, and the presence of his master and her brethren continued to bring more draman to their ranks every day.

Lireth had been a constant presence in his mind ever since he'd freed her from the mountain. She listened to his every thought, but he didn't mind. The bond between them was stronger than anything he'd experienced before.

At her order, they had moved the camp further away from Velbridge to ensure Lord D'Lance's men didn't find them. Scouts had also reported that Lord D'Lance was no longer keeping it a secret that he had several dragons under his control. His patrols in the region had tripled, and there had even been sightings of his dragon riders keeping watch from the sky.

"It's impressive, isn't it?" Bast said. "I never expected to see so many of my brethren in one place, united under one cause."

"It is," Caden agreed. "But I can't help but wonder if it will be enough. We have Lireth and the others, but Lord D'Lance has more men in his army than the next two Dominions combined. Even without his dragons and the draman still loyal to him, we're outnumbered."

Bast stared at him, his pupils becoming thin slits.

"We may be outnumbered, but we have something more powerful than magic or steel, or even dragons."

"What's that?"

"Hope."

Caden shook his head. "Hope doesn't win wars."

"How do you know?"

"I've been in battle before. Skill and luck are the only reason a man walks off the battlefield alive."

"Do you go into battle wanting to die?"

"Of course not."

"You want to live, yes? You want to see more of this world, go home to your family?"

"Yes."

"None of that is a certainty. It's hope. Hope drives us more than anything."

Caden hadn't considered that before. He remained silent for a moment, then cracked a smile. "You are right. Forgive me. It is hard to see the sky for the clouds sometimes."

"We all have our moments of weakness."

"Leaders don't have that luxury," Caden replied.

"They should."

"I don't disagree, but not everyone views things the same way." Caden scanned the camp. "How many do we have now?"

"One thousand at last night's count, but we've probably had a hundred or more arrive just this morning. The idea of leaving secret messages that only the draman can see was a clever one."

"Sometimes I'm hit with genius."

They both chuckled. Caden felt his master's presence in his mind before she spoke, and he turned his gaze to the edge of the woods.

Come and speak with me.

"The master calls?" Bast asked.

"Indeed."

"Best not keep her waiting, then."

Caden left the camp behind and crossed out of the woods. Lireth and the other dragons kept to themselves, choosing to bask in the sun away from the trees. Considering how long she'd been a prisoner in the mountain, Caden understood her desire to be in the open.

He paused when he saw her. She was lying atop a pile of rocks, her massive wings outstretched. The sunlight glittered off her scales, a myriad of rainbows shimmering in and out of existence as her body moved with her breathing. Caden approached her and knelt a few feet from her head.

"I am here," he said.

I know. I can smell you even when you are in the woods. Humans have a particular odor to them I find hard to stomach. Yours, however, is manageable. Since we are joined, the scent is muted.

Caden wasn't sure what she was talking about. Joined? He shrugged the thought aside.

"What did you want to speak with me about?"

Straight to the point. That's one reason I chose you. Since you lead my draman, we have something to discuss.

"I'm listening."

Many in this world who seek to do me harm. Lord D'Lance is the focus of my wrath for now, but there are others. I have received word from those in The Long Sands still loyal to me that there are rumblings among the Enclave. They know of Lord D'Lance's crimes against my brethren.

"What is the Enclave?"

They are the self-proclaimed leaders of the dragons. The metallic ones these days, anyway.

"So they are on our side?"

Hardly, Lireth hissed. *They are a worse enemy than Lord D'Lance, but I had not expected that I might need to deal with them now. If they come for Lord D'Lance, we will have to be quick.*

"I'm sorry, but wouldn't it be good to let them deal with him? If they are strong in number, they could clear out his defenses and leave him vulnerable."

Lireth retracted her wings and snaked forward. She snatched Caden up in her claw and brought him close to her face.

He will die by my flames!

Caden could feel the heat from her rage radiating off of her scales. He swallowed hard.

"Forgive me."

I must remind myself that you are a human, weak and unwise to the ways of dragons.

She snorted, her warm breath ruffling his hair, and set him down.

The Enclave is my enemy. They took many of my brethren captive, and hold them against their will even now.

"Do they know you are here? If so, their attack on Lord D'Lance may merely a ruse."

Now you are thinking like a dragon, Lireth said. *While I trust my servants, I also know that the Enclave may be feeding them information. We will keep our guard up and prepare for their arrival, but even if they do not come, we will face them in battle. Once I have killed Lord D'Lance, we are going to attack the Enclave.*

"You want to take the draman into the desert?"

Yes, and you will lead them. Together, we will tear down their archaic way of life and forge a fresh path. We will make this world bend its knees to us.

"You give me too much honor," Caden replied. "I will do my best to live up to your expectations."

If you don't, your end will come swiftly. I may have saved you from death, but I can give you back with a single breath.

Caden remembered the flames she'd spouted when he freed her. She was terrifying even when she was calm, and even more so when she was angry.

"I understand."

How many draman fill our ranks?

"Just over a thousand. We're growing so rapidly we're having trouble finding space for everyone."

That is a good problem to have.

"What of your brethren? Have any more of them agreed to come out of hiding?"

Lireth growled and scraped her claws on the stones beneath her.

Not yet. They fear the Enclave more than me. I will have to change that.

"Perhaps when they see Velbridge fall, they will change their minds."

That remains to be seen. Either way, they will fall into line or fall under my flames. Consider what I've told you and devise a plan for getting the draman to The Long Sands in one piece.

"I will."

Caden bowed to her and left, making his way back to the camp. Lireth was full of rage. He understood why, but he feared that the path she was on would only lead to ruin.

Even so, he would follow her.

3

Lord Klodian's face creased with surprise, and then confusion.

"Did you lose your mind in the desert? Dragons can't speak."

"I didn't think so either, but I heard them in the mesa. The ones that attacked you and killed Vhan. They aren't wild animals at all. They're just like us."

"I'll admit, you had me in the beginning. The idea that Lord D'Lance would want the throne isn't outside the realm of possibility, but the rest of your prank borders on the imbecilic."

"This isn't a prank," Mina protested.

"Then you have lost your sanity, especially if you expect me to believe something so outlandish."

"I've been with them in the desert. They have an entire cave system underground that serves as their home. The things I've seen … you wouldn't believe me. But I assure you, my Lord, my wits are still intact. The scale in my leg belongs to Gedrith. He and I share a bond that allows us to communicate with our minds."

Lord Klodian's expression turned to one of scorn.

"You sicken me," he said. "If what you say is true, then you are worse than a slave." His fists clenched at his sides.

"Whether or not you want to hear it, it is the truth. And I'm telling you because I felt that you should know what Lord D'Lance is plotting. Do with the information as you will, but know that I am going to kill him."

He laughed at her, just as Thais had.

"You won't get within a hundred yards of him before his Runesmen tear you apart."

"If I don't succeed, then the dragons will go to war against him and ravage everything in their path."

Lord Klodian shook his head.

"Get out."

Mina wasn't completely surprised by his reaction, but she had hoped that he would be more receptive. She gave him a nod and left the room. There was nothing else to be done. He knew of the threat that Lord D'Lance posed. What he chose to do about it wasn't her concern. She went to her room and found her belongings were still there. It surprised her that the servants hadn't thrown everything out.

Her clothes were old and tattered, so she didn't bother packing them. She slid the chest of dragon horns out from under the bed and opened it, gazing at them. Each one came from a dragon that had lost its life because of her. Knowing what she did now, the collection gave her an ill feeling in her stomach. She closed the lid and hefted the chest. It was the only thing she was going to take.

As she walked through the castle, the servants and nobles gave her looks of curiosity. They probably all thought they'd lost her to the desert. A smile crept across her lips. Let them talk. Let them wonder.

She exited the castle and walked through the courtyard, taking a last look at everything. She'd grown up here, and she had a bittersweet feeling about leaving for good. Of course, she didn't know if it was permanent, but she suspected that once she reached the Dracan Dominion, her entire life would be different. If she survived her encounter with Lord D'Lance, anyway.

Gedrith watched her approach and she could smell freesia. She dropped the chest onto the sand and looked up at him.

This is a mark of shame.

Gedrith snaked his head down near it and sniffed the air.

It stinks of death.

Mina swallowed hard and nodded.

It's the horns of the dragons who've died because of me.

Why do you keep them?

It was a way to make myself feel better about being a slave. Every dragon that died was one step closer to being free. Or so I thought, before I met you. I brought them out here because I want you to burn them.

Do you think that will absolve you of your guilt?

No, she answered. *Nothing ever will. This is going to haunt me forever.*

Gedrith hummed in reply, his tail swishing across the sand.

Move away.

She did as he asked, moving to stand beside him. He opened his jaws and released a stream of flames that set the chest on fire. Mina watched it burn, and in a way, she felt as though it was her past that was burning.

Did you speak with Lord Klodian?

Yes.

I assume it did not go well.

No, it did not.

Are you ready to leave, then?

Mina grabbed her pack off the ground and climbed up his shoulder, settling onto his back.

Let's go, she said.

Gedrith launched into the air and flapped his powerful wings, taking them high above the landscape. The other dragons joined them, flying in formation behind Gedrith. Once Mina could no longer see Klodian Keep, her mind eased.

Have you been to the Dracan Dominion before?

Yes, though it has been a long time.

How long?

It was before Maël's betrayal.

Then you are going into this as blind as I am.

Humans like to expand and build, so I am sure it will differ greatly from what I remember.

We'll need somewhere to stay that is away from prying eyes, Mina said. *If anyone sees you or your brethren, they could alert Lord D'Lance.*

I know of a place that should be safe. It was once home to a dragon I knew before the colors turned on one another. It should serve our needs.

How do you know they don't live there anymore?

A hint of saffron hit her nostrils, but it quickly faded before she could pinpoint the emotion behind the smell.

I know because she abandoned it. The last time I came to the Dracan Dominion, it was to capture her.

Why would you capture another dragon?

She was the one responsible for the division between the colors. She gathered the chromatic dragons and sided with Maël. When the elders learned of her betrayal, they wanted to imprison her. When I came to get her, she was gone. The cave hadn't been lived in for some time. Not even her scent remained.

Is she still alive?

I don't know, Gedrith replied. *I never found her. She was a mighty dragon even then, so it is likely that she is not dead.*

You said you knew her. Was she your friend?

There was a long pause before he answered. *Yes. Once.*

Mina could sense a wall of turbulent emotions behind his words, so she didn't press for more information. They flew in silence for a long time, so long that Mina's eyes began to droop. She jolted several times, startling herself into wakefulness.

Are we almost there?

Yes. Do you see the castle to the right?

Mina squinted and saw a gray splotch, but the details evaded her.

Somewhat.

That is Lord D'Lance's fortress. The cave we will use is a few hours' walk from it. We could get closer, but we might be seen. If we haven't been already.

Mina looked down and watched the scenery speed by. If anyone was down there looking up, she couldn't see them. Trees came into view, and Gedrith began his descent. He glided over the canopy until the treetops thinned out to a clearing, then he swooped down and landed. Mina climbed down and stretched her muscles.

Where's this cave at?

That way. He nodded toward the other end of the clearing. He sniffed at the air, his head swaying from side to side.

What is it?

I'm not sure. I've smelled nothing like it before. Stay here. My brethren and I will scout ahead to make sure there's nothing to worry about.

Gedrith launched himself back into the air, joining the other dragons who had yet to land. They circled over the clearing, then broke formation and each headed in a different direction. Mina rolled her neck, trying to work the kinks out. She scanned the tree line and saw something metallic flash.

A moment later, a monster stepped into the clearing.

4

"WE HAVE A FEW PROBLEMS," Bast said to Caden as he returned to the camp. "We're running out of supplies. The last of the tents have been assigned, and we still have two dozen draman that need shelter."

"Divide them across some of the others until we can get more," Caden replied.

"We're also running out of food."

"How? The woods are full of deer and other animals."

"It seems our growing presence here has driven the wildlife away. I've sent scouts further out, but they aren't having much luck."

Caden frowned and ran his hands over his face, scrunching his eyes closed in thought.

"We could send some men to Velbridge to buy supplies."

Bast snorted, his reptilian nostrils flaring wide. "It will take a lot of coin to feed this lot."

Caden was well aware of their lack of funds. It seemed as though their problems continued to grow just as quickly as their numbers did. He knew this day would come, but he hadn't expected it to happen so soon.

"Do you remember what we discussed about Lord D'Lance's caravans?"

Bast grinned. "Yes."

"It's time to set that plan into motion. Put together a group of draman, no more than ten or twelve. You and I will lead them on a trial run. It'll give us the supplies we need and give him a few headaches."

"As you command." Bast walked away to gather their crew.

Do not draw him down upon us, Lireth warned. *We are not ready yet.*

"I won't," Caden said aloud, unsure if she could hear him. He wished he could communicate with her as she did with him, but so far, the ability eluded him. Still, she could read his every thought, so he visualized the words in his mind.

Within an hour, Bast had gathered a group together and he and Caden led them through the woods to the nearest road. Scouts were posted at strategic points, providing updates on the movement of shipments coming and going from Velbridge, and they had noticed a pattern.

"You're sure that it's today?" Caden asked.

"Yes," Bast replied. "And always at the same time."

"Good. Make sure everyone is hidden. I'll get the wagons to stop, and at my signal, that's when they should reveal themselves. Keep an archer ready in case any of the drivers try to make a run for it, but they shouldn't shoot to kill. We want to send a message to Lord D'Lance and we can't do that if everyone dies."

"We'll be ready."

Caden sat on the ground beside the road and waited. Eventually, the clopping of horses and raised voices reached his ears. He waited until the wagons came into view and counted three of them. They rolled along the road, no guards visible.

Good, he thought. *This should be painless.*

As the wagons drew closer, he stood up and moved onto the road, raising his hand to the lead driver. The man was looking off into the woods, and for a moment, Caden thought the driver had spotted the draman.

"Hail!" Caden shouted.

The driver snapped his gaze forward and jerked on the reins, forcing the wagon to a halt.

"Get out of the way! I could have run you down!"

"Sorry about that. I'm in need of some help. Are you headed to Velbridge?"

"Aye, but we don't have any extra room. You're welcome to join us on foot, though you could walk there yourself without us."

"You're right about that, but I haven't had a meal in days," Caden lied. "Do you have anything to spare?"

"A beggar, then? Move aside. I don't have time for this."

Caden whistled. A moment later, Bast and the others stepped into view. They all had their hoods down, leaving their reptilian faces in plain sight.

"Apologies, friend, but we'll be confiscating your goods. You can keep your wagons, we just want what's in them."

"Lord D'Lance will hear of this!"

"By all means, let him know. And also tell him that Caden Davtyan sends his regards."

The draman moved in and started rifling through the wagons. Terrified cries filled the air, and Caden heard the words "demon spawn" mentioned several times. Bast approached him, shaking his head.

"There's more here than we can carry."

"We'll unload it and carry what we can back to the camp. Two draman will stay behind with what remains and we'll come back for it."

"Is that wise? Lord D'Lance may have his patrols out here by then."

"Good point," Caden said. "We'll hide the rest and come back when it's safe, then."

"I'll let them know what to do."

Caden turned back to the lead driver, who stared daggers at him.

"You must know that you serve a tyrant."

"Lord D'Lance is a generous man with a heart for his people," the man replied. "The only thing you're doing is hurting me and my family. You're stealing from *me*, not Lord D'Lance."

"Are you not taking these goods to Velbridge for Lord D'Lance?"

"I am."

"Then we are stealing from Lord D'Lance."

"It's only theft if it's paid for," the driver retorted. "I don't get paid until I deliver. When I show up empty-handed, I won't get anything for my trouble. So again, you are stealing from *me*."

Guilt assailed Caden. He didn't want the innocent to suffer, and surely not by his hands. He looked at Bast. The draman was helping the others unload sacks from the last wagon, stacking them in a pile. He was torn. His men needed to eat, but this man's livelihood was at stake.

Steel your emotions, Lireth bade. *There is no room for a conscience during war.*

His first instinct was to argue, but his discontent was pushed aside, suffocated under the weight of her presence. Caden gritted his teeth and reached for the bag of coins at his waist.

Don't.

Lireth's word was a command. If he defied her, she would kill him. He didn't want to disobey her, but his morals battled against his loyalty. Caden clenched his hand into a fist and turned his back to the driver. He tried to tell himself that what he was doing was more right than wrong, but he wasn't convinced.

"We're done," Bast said. "Everything has been unloaded. We'll be able to feed the camp for a few days with all this."

Caden's eyes roamed over the pile of stuff they'd taken. There were sacks of grain and rice, as well as wicker baskets full of fruits and vegetables.

"Leave," Caden said, turning around to face the driver again. "And be sure to tell Lord D'Lance what I said."

The man shook his head and flicked the reins. The horses pulled forward, and the wagons continued toward Velbridge. In the back of the last wagon, the head of a small child peered out from the covering.

"This is wrong."

"Is it? We're able to feed ourselves. Seems well and right to me."

"I suppose," Caden grunted, but it still conflicted him. "Let's get this stuff off the road."

He helped the draman carry everything into the woods and they covered what they couldn't transport with brush and leaves. By the time they returned to the camp, Caden realized that Lireth's presence seemed far away. He handed his supplies off to one of the draman and looked around the line of tents.

"Sir," a breathless draman rushed over to him.

"What is it?"

"Dragons have been spotted."

"More of Lireth's brethren?"

"No, sir. They are the metallic colors of her enemy."

Caden sprinted out of the woods to where Lireth had been earlier.

She was gone.

5

MINA WATCHED THE CREATURE IN disbelief. It walked on two legs like a human, but its appearance was reptilian. She remembered what the Enclave leader had said about Lord D'Lance mixing dragon eggs with humans to create an army. Although she knew the dragon hadn't been lying, it still shocked her to see one of the things up close.

She was in the open, and before she could try to hide, the creature spotted her. It shouted something and ran toward her. Mina drew her sword and took a defensive stance. She sidestepped the creature as it reached her, his sword cleaving the air harmlessly. The facial features looked masculine, and she assumed it was a male. He struggled to stop his momentum, and Mina stepped behind him and landed a blow to the back of his knee with her foot.

It surprised her when the creature didn't fall. His leg didn't even buckle. He whirled around, snarling. She backpedaled and swung her sword at him, but he blocked the strike with his arm and her blade clanged as if striking metal. Her brow creased in confusion and the creature took advantage of her surprise. He grabbed the blade of her sword with his clawed hand and jerked it free, tossing it aside.

Mina made a dash for the weapon, but the creature crashed into her, the two of them landing on the ground in a tangle. He was larger and stronger than her, and he quickly gained the upper hand and pinned her down.

"Yous is mines now," it said.

Help! Mina pushed the plea through the scale.

The creature leaned in close, and she could smell his foul breath. It stunk like rotten eggs. She turned her head to the side, struggling to break free. The creature laughed, droplets of saliva landing on the side of her face.

Gedrith!

A shadow passed overhead and the creature looked up. Mina tried to pull her arms free, but the creature gripped her flesh tighter and growled. He stood, pulling her to her feet and wrapped his right

340

arm around her neck. Mina scanned the sky, but there was no sign of Gedrith or the others.

The creature drug her backward toward the tree line. She stared at her sword, wishing she could magically command it into her hand. A roar split the air, and she jerked her head in the direction of the sound. She still didn't see any of the dragons, but Gedrith's presence was strong, which told her he was nearby.

A glance over her shoulder revealed the creature's uneasiness. His eyes were wide, and he kept growling lowly. He was distracted. Mina did a silent countdown and then broke free and ran for her sword. The creature chased after her, but she managed to grab her sword before he reached her. She jabbed the blade forward, striking the creature in the chest, but it did no harm. Was the beast impervious to weapons?

A whooshing sound filled the air as Gedrith swooped down out of the sky and snatched the creature up in his claws, crushing him. He flung the body into the trees and landed.

Are you hurt?

No, I'm fine. What was that thing?

They call themselves draman. Neither human nor dragon, but a mix of both.

How do you know what they are?

My brethren and I just killed an entire group of them. One was so frightened, he babbled on about many things before I silenced him. There are more of them out here, so we need to be vigilant.

Mina sheathed her blade and tucked her hair behind her ears. She was about to say something when a deafening roar echoed across the clearing. She clapped her hands over her ears, looking to the sky. An enormous black dragon landed in the clearing, snarling with fury. Dragon fear washed over Mina and she fell to her knees, but she managed to crawl behind Gedrith.

The copper dragon wrapped his tail around her, keeping her in place as he turned to face the black behemoth.

So, it is you *that slaughters my children. I should have known the Enclave would stoop to murder.* The dragon's voice echoed in Mina's mind.

Those abominations are yours? Gedrith replied. *Have you sided with Lord D'Lance as well?*

The black dragon snorted. *Do not mention that name to me. I will burn his castle and everyone in it.*

Mina gasped at the thought of Caden being burned alive.

Who's the welp?

She is my bonded. The first rider in a thousand years.

I wouldn't be so sure of that.

The only true rider, Gedrith clarified. *Those twisted bonds that Lord D'Lance has created were not forged willingly.*

Who said that's what I was talking about? But it does not surprise me that the Enclave knows about his dealings. They've never kept their snouts to themselves.

You allied with Maël knowing his course was only about greed. Do not defame the Enclave because you made a foolish decision.

What do you know about me, Gedrith? Nothing. Did I want more for our brethren? Yes. Count me guilty of that desire, but you are confused when it comes to what is right. Was it right for the Enclave to imprison our own kind?

They made their choice to join you in your folly, Lireth. They are just as guilty as you.

Lireth growled. *What are you doing here? Are you leading the Enclave to war against the humans?*

There will not be a war with humans. My bonded will slay Lord D'Lance and put an end to his blasphemous acts.

That scrawny human is going to kill him, is she? Not if I get to him first. He and I have history, and my vengeance is coming.

Then we are united in our cause. Perhaps if you help us against Lord D'Lance, the Enclave would forgive your past deeds.

Do not waste your words on me, Gedrith. Once I have killed the human, I am coming for the Enclave. No one is safe from my wrath, least of all our brethren.

I cannot let you leave knowing that you are going to attack the Enclave.

Are you challenging me?

Gedrith released Mina.

Go into the woods, he said.

Mina nodded and sprinted for the trees, dragon fear weighing heavily on her. She reached a tree with a thick trunk and stood behind it, peering out cautiously. The two dragons circled one another, their tails flicking back and forth behind them. They were equal in size, though Lireth's wings were larger.

The other dragons that had come with them appeared over the clearing, dropping down to surround Lireth. The Enclave had sent five dragons with them to terrorize Lord D'Lance's forces, and all of them were silver. Gedrith had told her silver dragons were the fastest of the metallic colors, and having seen them in flight herself, she knew it was true.

Mina's heart thundered in her chest as she watched. She expected to smell the scent of lavender from Lireth, but instead, she only caught hints of rose and saffron. They outnumbered her. Why wasn't she afraid?

A battle cry erupted from the other side of the clearing and a host of draman swarmed forth from the trees. A man was with them, a human, and Mina's eyes widened in surprise. No, it couldn't be. She gasped.

It was Caden.

6

"SHE'S JUST UP THERE!"

Caden led Bast and a contingent of draman into a clearing where he spotted Lireth. As soon as he'd been told that they had seen her enemies in the area, he knew there was trouble. He couldn't explain how, but he knew exactly where to find her. As they entered the clearing, Caden skidded to a stop.

There were six other dragons. Five were silver and one was reddish copper. He was just as monstrously large as Lireth, and the metallic dragons had surrounded his master. The sight of so many of the beasts made his knees go weak and fear paralyzed him. He watched helplessly as the draman swarmed forward, attacking the enemy dragons. It was like watching ants try to take down a tree.

The copper dragon swatted the draman aside and rushed toward Lireth. She roared and backed up, swiping her massive claws at him. She missed and the two of them clashed. Caden remained frozen in place. He screamed at himself within his mind to do something, to help his master, but what could he do against dragons? He would surely die. And yet, he would rather die defending his master than watch her fall to her enemies.

Caden used every ounce of mental strength he could muster and pushed through the fear. He staggered forward a few steps and drew his sword, then paused. Would steel even pierce the scales of a dragon? Probably not. He sheathed the blade and ran to a draman that was lying on the ground. It wasn't moving. Caden looked into the draman's open eyes and there was no life in them. He glanced around and saw that several others were also dead.

Lireth and the copper dragon were still fighting, a rolling ball of vicious talons and snapping teeth. The silver dragons stood by impassively, ignoring Caden and his men. Bast was helping a limping draman to the tree line, and he glanced over his shoulder at Caden. Once the draman was out of danger, Bast returned and joined him.

"Our master is outnumbered."

"We need more men," Caden said.

"No," Bast replied. "We do not have enough to defeat a single dragon, let alone six."

"We have to help her."

"Yes, but how?"

Caden didn't have an answer. How indeed?

"What's a dragon's vulnerable spot?"

Bast remained silent. The copper dragon gained the upper hand and pinned Lireth down, clamping his jaws around her neck.

"Hurry!"

"Without a weapon crafted of magic, the only weak spot is the eyes," Bast answered. "You'll be burned alive before you get close enough to try anything."

"What about arrows?"

"No. Even if you had the marksmanship to hit a dragon in the eye, arrows are too frail to puncture the membrane that covers the eyeball. A sword could do it, but as I said—"

"Save your words, my friend. They'll not sway me. You're in charge. If I die, do whatever you can to save her."

Caden sprinted toward his master, dodging between the silver dragons that surrounded her. He climbed up the copper dragon's tail and ran along its back. The beast jerked and Caden almost slipped, but he grabbed onto the dragon's scales and forged ahead. The dragon flexed its wings, trying to push him away, but Caden dropped on all fours and kept going. He reached the dragon's neck and stood, quickly drawing his blade. If he could just strike the creature in one of its eyes, his master could get free.

Before he could take another step, the dragon released Lireth and rose into the air, standing on its back legs. Caden scrambled to grab ahold of the dragon, but his hands slipped off the scales and he fell, landing hard on the ground. The impact forced the air from lungs and stars burst before his vision.

Free of the copper dragon's jaws, Lireth got up and leaped into the air, escaping. The silver dragons started after her, but the copper dragon roared at them and they stayed put. As Caden fought to gain his breath, the look in Lireth's eyes flashed within his mind's eye. She was afraid, but of what? The copper dragon, or of being imprisoned again?

The thought fled his mind as the copper dragon turned to face him, its clawed hand clamping down around him. He was going to die. There was no doubt about that. But he had ensured his master escaped, and so he had done his duty. He closed his eyes as the dragon's face drew down upon him.

"Stop!"

It was a woman's voice. Footsteps approached, but he dared not open his eyes. He waited expectantly to feel pain, but nothing happened. A few seconds passed, and the dragon's weight lifted from his body. He cracked his eyes open and saw a woman standing in front of him. She was facing away from him. Her hair was long and blonde, and she wore armor and carried a sword at her side.

She finally turned around, and his eyes widened. It was Mina! His excitement quickly faded. She couldn't be here, not really. Either he was hallucinating, or … he was dead. Yes, it had to be the latter of the two. Mina knelt beside him and peered into his eyes.

"Caden? Can you hear me?"

Her voice was the same as it had been in life. He smiled at her.

"I know this isn't real," he gasped. "But I don't care."

"What's not real?"

"You. This. Everything."

Mina laughed. "It's all real," she said.

"Even you?"

"Yes. Here, let me help you up." She offered her hand. Caden accepted it and she pulled him into a sitting position, then onto his feet. The dragons towered over him, death in their eyes. He spotted his sword on the ground and made a move to grab it, but the copper dragon's growl stopped him.

"He will not hurt me," Mina said, casting a look behind her. "Here." She retrieved the sword and handed it to him. Caden hesitantly accepted it and sheathed it.

"What's going on? Are these creatures keeping you against your will?"

"Hardly. They are my protectors. Well, these ones are." Mina waved at the silver dragons, then thumbed behind her. "This one is my friend."

"Friend?"

"Yes. His name is …" She paused. "Copper. He and I are bonded."

"I don't understand."

"You hit your head pretty hard when you fell. You should probably sit back down."

"I'm fine," he said. "I'm just confused. You said you were bonded to a dragon. What does that mean?"

"We can talk to each other using our minds, among other things. I know, it's a lot to take in."

Caden looked from her to the copper dragon. They could communicate using their minds? That was how Lireth spoke to him. The similarity startled him. Did that mean that he was bonded to Lireth? He could feel her presence, but she wasn't close by.

"What are you doing here?"

"It's a long story," she replied. "Why did you attack Copper?"

"Because he attacked my master."

Mina's forehead creased. "Your master? Do you mean Lord D'Lance?"

"No. That tyrant can burn for all I care. I'm talking about Lireth."

"The black dragon?"

"Yes."

Mina's expression fell. "Oh. I have some bad news."

7

Mina stood beside Gedrith and watched Caden as he paced the clearing. The other dragons had gone into the cave after Gedrith told them not to pursue Lireth, and Mina told Caden about his master's history with Gedrith and the Enclave. She supposed he was feeling conflicted about where his loyalty resided.

He cannot be saved, Gedrith said.

Why do you say that?

Lireth is the most deceptive dragon I have ever known. If she has bonded to him, she is fully ingrained in his mind.

Can a bond be broken?

I have never known one to be severed except by death.

Mina had a sinking feeling in her stomach. Caden was her friend, and she previously entertained the idea that they could be more than that, but if what Gedrith said was true, then she didn't know how their paths would end up.

When you lost Lucius, how did it feel?

Like I had lost a part of me, Gedrith replied.

Does it feel the same for humans?

Yes. I think that is why Areg has stayed with us all these years. Being with us must bring him solace from the pain. It is said that time heals all wounds, but that is not always true. Some wounds never heal.

The pain behind his words tore at her heart. She rested a hand on his foreleg comfortingly. Caden stopped walking in circles and turned toward her, striding purposefully.

"Can I speak with you?" he asked. "Alone?"

Gedrith growled.

It's all right, Mina reassured him. *Caden would never hurt me.*

So you say. You don't know Lireth or what she's capable of.

I'll be fine.

Mina joined Caden, and they walked together through the woods until Gedrith was no longer visible.

"I want to apologize," he finally spoke.

"About what?"

"For kissing you at Klodian Keep."

Mina's face flushed with warmth at the memory. He'd left her breathless and confused that night, and then she had used her newfound status to have Lord Klodian send him to the Dracan Dominion. It all seemed so long ago, and yet, standing with him now, it felt as though he'd only been gone a few days.

"You don't have to apologize for that," Mina said. "It was nice."

They stared at each other in silence for a moment, and Caden drew close and placed a hand on her neck, rubbing his thumb along her cheek. Her heart began racing, and she leaned toward him. He met her, their lips pressing together. Fire coursed through her, burning under her skin. It gave her desires she never knew she wanted. When Caden broke away from her, it was like waking from a dream.

"I'm glad you weren't upset with our first kiss. I must admit, the fear that you hated me for it has kept me awake many nights. After Thais betrayed me to Captain Eduard and had me sent out here, I thought I'd never see you again."

"What do you mean? What did Thais tell Captain Eduard?"

"I found something in the ruins of Slia, a stone. I didn't know it at the time, but it's a piece of armor that Lord D'Lance's men used to protect them from dragon fire. Lord D'Lance destroyed that city with his dragon riders. Thais wanted me to tell Captain Eduard what I had found, but I refused. The next thing I knew, I was being locked up in the dungeon."

Mina could feel her throat constricting. He thought Thais was responsible for his departure from the Thophate? "Did Thais tell you she said something?"

"No, but she must have. There's no other explanation for why I was sent here."

"I thought you wanted to earn fame and riches? Didn't you say you wanted to transfer to a Dominion where you could go into battle and make a name for yourself?"

"I did, but after I met you and Thais, I changed my mind. I'll meet her on the battlefield one day, and only one of us is going to walk off of it alive."

"Caden, there's something I need to tell you," Mina said, her tone lowering.

"What is it?"

"Thais isn't the one who got you sent out here. It was me."

Caden frowned, his brow creasing.

"I'm sorry. I thought it was what you wanted. After I saved Lord Klodian's life out in the mesas, he asked me how he could repay me. I asked him to transfer you to a Dominion where you would get time on the battlefield. You were transferred because of me."

The look on his face made her stomach drop. She knew what he must be thinking. He probably hated her now and regretted ever kissing her in the first place.

"I'm a fool," he whispered. "All this time, I thought …" His eyes met hers, and she felt as if he was searching her soul somehow.

"I'm sorry," she repeated.

"Don't be. I'm not mad at you, just … surprised. I had no idea. Thank the gods that Thais doesn't know the things I've said about her beneath my breath since then. She'd want to pummel me for sure."

Relief washed over Mina like a soothing wave of cool water.

"Thank you for not being mad. I thought I was doing the most unselfish thing because I didn't want you to leave."

"Things could have gone better, but it seems to have all worked out. We're both here now, and we both have dragon companions."

"Except yours is a murderous lunatic," Mina said.

"You don't know her as I do. She hasn't murdered anyone."

"Yet."

"Our forces should ally against Lord D'Lance. We're stronger together. I know they have a turbulent past, but uniting against a common enemy for the greater good is hard to argue with. This might be the best way for the dragons to mend their differences."

"I don't think the Enclave would agree. What Lireth did was unforgivable, even after all this time. If there is truly a bond between you two, you know her thoughts. She isn't simply misguided, she's evil. The Enclave will never ally with her, and she's made her feelings clear. She plans to go after them once Lord D'Lance is dead."

"She has said the same thing to me," Caden replied. "Perhaps the Enclave deserves to fall."

Mina pulled away from him, scowling.

"You don't know what you're saying. I've seen the Enclave. They want what's best for their kind. Lireth wants only death and destruction. Surely you see the problem with that?"

"New things will rise from the ashes. It is the way of life."

"You've changed," Mina said, backing away further. "Our destinies may be entwined, but they are not united."

Caden stared at her in silence. She silently prayed that he would see reason and make the right choice. His facial expression turned to one of anger.

"You are the one who has changed. You think to lecture me? Only one person standing here is responsible for the death of dragons, and it isn't me. I can see why Lireth hates your dragons. They have allied themselves with a murderer."

His words stung her deeply. She could feel Gedrith's presence in her mind and allowed his strength to flow through her. Mina steeled her emotions.

"Leave," she said.

They stared death at one another until Caden snorted and stormed off. She watched him go, and he didn't look back once.

It was the second time she watched him leave as her heart broke.

8

CADEN STOMPED THROUGH THE UNDERGROWTH, fuming with anger. He couldn't believe that Mina had refused to ally with him. She thought he had changed, but she was wrong. Or if he had, it was only that he wasn't blind anymore. He had purpose, *real* purpose. Fame and fortune were the things he wanted before, but now he wanted to ensure Lireth succeeded in every endeavor.

He reached the camp and went straight to her usual spot. She was there waiting for him.

"Are you all right?" he asked. "I tried to help you, but there's not much I can do against a dragon."

I am fine, but I see you aren't. What happened? Anger radiates from you like the sun.

He debated not telling her, but he knew she would probe his mind and find out, regardless.

"The girl with the dragons … her name is Mina. I know her from the Thophate Dominion. She said she is bonded to the red dragon." Caden was still curious about the bond, but he wasn't sure how to broach the subject.

I am familiar with Gedrith. We have much history together. It's a shame that he's given his loyalty to the Enclave.

"So has Mina. I offered her a place among our forces, and she refused."

The Enclave has a way of distorting the innocent and making them into zealots of their cause. Once I burn their world to ash, their slaves will be free to think for themselves. I can sense your feelings for the girl are strong. You mustn't let your emotions cloud your judgement. There may come a day when you must kill her.

Caden was angry with her, true, but that didn't mean he wanted her dead. He was mostly convinced that she would come around, he just didn't know if the red dragon would hinder that.

Will you be able to kill her if it comes to that?

"I don't know."

352

Then I will make it easy for you. You are to kill her if you see her again, Lireth said. *That is my decree.*

Caden knelt before her and bowed his head. He kept his mind clear so that she couldn't discern his true feelings about the order.

"As you command," he said.

Good. Your loyalty is stronger than that of my brethren. You've done something very few have done before. You've impressed me.

"I am honored to do so. Are we safe here, or should we move the camp again?"

We will stay where we are. If Gedrith thinks to intimidate me, he is wrong. I do not fear him. It is he who should fear me.

"Should we take the fight to them? I can gather our forces and lead them there under the cover of night."

No, Lireth growled. *I need more of my brethren at my side first. Lord D'Lance is your only concern for now. We will deal with Gedrith after Lord D'Lance has fallen. I am leaving and will return tonight.*

"Is there anything you want done while you are away?"

Must I instruct you in everything?

"No, of course not."

Good.

Lireth stretched her wings out and took to the air, flying north. Caden watched until she was no longer visible, then he returned to the camp and found Bast.

"I need a few scouts," he said. "Two or three draman at the most. They need to be stealthy."

"Is this for something the master wants?"

"No, it's something for me."

Bast nodded. "What is the task?"

"I need them to keep an eye on someone."

"The girl?"

"Yes."

"Very well. I'll post them at the cave. If she goes anywhere, you'll know."

"Thank you, my friend. Did we get the rest of the provisions from the raid earlier?"

"Yes," Bast replied. "We have enough rice and grain to last us a week, maybe longer. It helps, but we still need more supplies."

"If Lireth gets her brethren to join her, then we'll have all we need when Velbridge burns. I hope she will give us a rest before marching us to the desert."

"The desert?"

"I forgot to tell you. Lireth wants to attack the home of the metallic dragons after we've dealt with Lord D'Lance."

Bast's left eye twitched, but he said nothing.

"Is that a problem?"

"No, but we will need many things for a journey that long. And what of the other Dominions? We may find trouble waiting for us, especially as word travels. And if word has not reached the other Dominions, what will the other lords think of an army marching through their territory? There is much to consider."

"I agree," Caden replied. "We'll need to start planning soon. If Lireth has her way, we'll be marching to the Long Sands before the embers of Velbridge have cooled. I'm going for a walk. Let me know when the scouts have something."

"As you command," Bast replied.

Caden left the camp and wandered through the woods on his own, trying to clear his mind. Mina had him wound up with anger and frustration. Now that Lireth had ordered him to kill her … he mentally felt along his mind to see if she was present. Her presence was there, but it was faint.

Good, he thought. He rarely had time for his own thoughts, and while he didn't normally mind the lack of privacy, he had tumultuous feelings about her new orders. Could he really kill Mina? Of course he *could,* but *would* he? Did he have the conviction to? Caden was glad Lireth was away. If she knew that he had doubts about her command, she'd be furious.

And what of Bast? His reaction to the news that they would march to the desert to battle the Enclave didn't bode well. Were the draman as loyal as Lireth assumed they were? Bast had once said that the humanity in him battled against the dragon. Perhaps they all suffered from that internal battle. And if they did … well, who knew what would happen if the human part won.

If the draman rebelled against Lord D'Lance, there was nothing to keep them from breaking ranks with Lireth. They revered her as though she were a goddess. While he admitted she was awe-inspiring and intimidating, she was mortal just like he was. She was no goddess, no matter how the draman worshipped her.

"Stop it," Caden muttered to himself. His thoughts were straying too far for comfort. Perhaps it was a good thing that Lireth stayed in his mind so much. He couldn't be trusted otherwise. It seemed he had an internal battle going on as well. He'd never doubted his master before. Why was he doing it now? The answer was obvious.

It was Mina.

She was the reason he'd been sent away from the Thophate. She was also the reason for everything he'd been through. If he'd remained under Lord Klodian's command, none of the terrible things that had befallen him would have happened. Yes, the blame resided with her. She was reckless and untrustworthy. Perhaps Lireth was right. She wasn't clouded with bias, after all.

Mina had to die.

9

MINA SAT IN THE CAVE'S entrance in front of a small fire, staring off as her thoughts led her on a wild ride, her dinner long since cold. She wasn't the only one bonded to a dragon now. The thought didn't sit well with her, but only because Caden's dragon was evil. The thing that bothered her the most was that he'd tried to convince her to join the wrong side.

Was it her fault? She had been the one to get Lord Klodian to send him away, after all. Yet, while that was true, she didn't control his thoughts and actions. He had chosen to follow Lireth, to align himself with darkness. No, she decided, it was not her fault. Gedrith told her that Lireth was deceptive, and Mina was convinced that the dragon had bonded with Caden without his knowledge.

I believe you are correct in that line of thinking, Gedrith's voice entered her thoughts. *He may not even be aware that she's influencing his thoughts.*

Mina sighed and tossed her food into the fire, then rose to her feet. Her appetite was gone. She put the fire out and walked further into the cave. It was dark for a few feet, but glowing moss spider-webbed across the ceiling of the cave, giving the impression that the stone was cracked.

It doesn't seem fair that Caden doesn't know what she's doing to him, she said, sitting beside Gedrith.

Life is rarely fair.

I know that more than anyone. My point is that I don't think it's fair that a dragon can have so much power over another being.

It is the natural order of things. Some species are more powerful than others.

Mina leaned her back against Gedrith and stared up at the glowing moss. If she was going to kill Lord D'Lance, then she needed to familiarize herself with the layout of Velbridge and, if possible, find a way into the castle.

What do we do about Lireth? She asked. *She may disrupt our plans.*

I will deal with her myself, but I must wait for the right opportunity. In the meantime, my brethren are going to give Lord D'Lance a few headaches. They plan to attack some of his outposts on the border. Since he's using his draman and dragon riders to patrol the area near the castle, it is the safest option to avoid an open battle.

Good idea. Mina stifled a yawn, her exhaustion much stronger than she realized.

Sleep while you can, Gedrith said. *Soon we will not have time to rest.*

Mina had a feeling he was right. She fell asleep, and the next thing she knew, slanted rays of sunlight were shining into the cave. Gedrith was still asleep, so she quietly rose to her feet and slipped out of the cave, casting a backward glance over her shoulder. Rubbing the sleep from her eyes, she stretched and surveyed the forest. Birds were chirping overhead, so she knew there weren't any draman nearby. At least, she hoped not.

Her dreams had fueled an idea, and she wanted to carry it out before Gedrith knew what she was doing. Her stomach was empty, but she didn't have time for breakfast. Velbridge was calling her name.

Mina turned northwest and began the trek to Lord D'Lance's city. If she was going to kill the Dominion Lord, then she needed to know the layout of his domain, and she figured it would be easier to do alone. It wasn't like Gedrith could go with her, anyway. The sight of a dragon flying toward the city wouldn't just cause a panic, but it would draw Lord D'Lance's attention. The longer she could keep the element of surprise, the better her chances of success.

The woods soon gave way to open flatlands, and in the distance, Mina spotted the walls of Velbridge. With the city in view, she quickened her pace. By the time she reached the gates, droplets of sweat had collected on her forehead. A multitude of guards were keeping a watchful eye on everyone coming and going through the gates, but otherwise, they didn't harass anyone. Mina held her breath as she passed them, praying to Avera that they wouldn't stop her.

Relief washed over her and she relaxed a little once she was inside the city. Patrols were everywhere, composed of both humans and draman. It surprised her to see the creatures walking about freely, and the city folk shied away from them whenever they approached. The tenseness in the air was obvious, and Mina couldn't help but wonder what had caused it.

She wandered along the main road before turning down a side street and entering a tavern. The place had a light crowd, and Mina took a seat at the bar.

A plump, bald man rushed over and smiled warmly.

"What can I get you?" he asked.

"What kind of food do you have?"

"The usual fare. How does eggs and sausage sound?"

"That sounds delicious."

"Perfect! And an ale to wash it down with?"

"Do you have water?"

The man laughed. "We do, but we don't get many requests for it. I'll have it to you shortly."

Mina watched him bustle away and glanced around the room. Most of the patrons were drinking ale, and she couldn't believe they were partaking of it so early in the day. At the nearest table, a group of men were talking about the increased patrols within the city. Mina pretended to mind her own business, but she listened intently to their conversation.

"All these creatures are bad for business," one of them said. "Everyone's afraid to leave their homes, and I can't sell anything if I don't have any customers."

Another man nodded. "My business has dried up completely within a matter of days. I don't know about you, but I blame whoever was behind that failed attack. Lord D'Lance may have had those foul beasts this entire time, but I'd rather he kept them a secret."

"I hate to admit it, but I might have to pack up and move somewhere else if things don't change quickly. I've got a family to feed."

Mina frowned. A failed attack? She wondered if it had to do with Caden. The clatter of a plate made her turn around and she saw the barkeep had delivered her food along with a wooden mug filled with clear liquid.

"That'll be two silvers."

Mina reached down at her waist and realized she didn't have any money. The look on her face must have given the barkeep a clue because he smiled again.

"First time customer?"

She nodded.

"It's on the house, but next time, you'll have to pay."

"Thank you, but I can't accept—"

"You can and you will," he replied. "Enjoy!"

He rushed away to another customer before she could argue any further. She stared at the plate of steaming eggs and considered leaving, but hunger won over and she devoured them ravenously. The water was cool and quenched her thirst.

Where are you? Gedrith's voice startled her.

Velbridge. I wanted to learn the layout of the city.

Did you see the draman?

Yes. The city is crawling with them. There was an attack recently, and Lord D'Lance has heightened security everywhere.

Not those draman. The ones that were in the woods.

Mina's brow creased. *What do you mean?*

You're being followed.

10

CADEN WAS UP BEFORE THE sun rose. The sound of flapping wings had woken him. Not that he'd been in a deep sleep, anyway. His dreams had been dark and kept him from being able to rest. He stretched his muscles and trekked across the camp, heading to Lireth's usual spot.

It surprised him to see that she had returned with more than a few dragons. There were a dozen of the creatures, most of them as ebon scaled as she was, but there were four exceptions. Two green dragons, a blue, and a white. The green ones were thick and bulky, but they weren't as large as Lireth. The white one was the smallest of them all but looked just as fierce. Of them all, the blue one caught his attention the most.

It was the largest of the newcomers, dwarfing the green duo. Many of the scales on its face were chipped or missing completely, giving the dragon an ominous appearance. Where entire scales were absent, the flesh was scarred and mottled. He tore his gaze away before the beast looked at him.

"I see you were successful," Caden said to Lireth.

Their numbers are less than I wanted, but I will take them. More will come when they see the devastation I unleash upon Lord D'Lance's domain.

"They will certainly bolster our forces, but he will know we are coming long before we reach the castle. A dozen dragons in the sky would be hard to miss."

That is why we will take down his scouts.

"The draman can manage that, but they'll need to find a way to sneak into the city. The place has guards everywhere. We can send them ahead of us, but their task will be a challenge."

I am speaking of the dragons that patrol the skies. There are only a few. With them out of the way, he will be defenseless against our onslaught.

"You are as clever as you are awe-inspiring," Caden complimented.

You speak the obvious. Inform Bast that he is in command until you return.

"Return from where?"

You and I will be the ones to take down the scouts.

"What good will I do? I can't injure a dragon, nor could I attack one from the ground even if I could."

You will ride on my back. Lireth snorted derisively. Tendrils of smoke drifted out of her nostrils. *Use your brain before I find another use for you.*

Caden bowed to her. "My apologies," he said. "I didn't realize you were going to grant me the honor."

It is a privilege I give you for being joined to me.

"Is that the same as being bonded? Mina mentioned being bonded to Gedrith. Do you and I share the same connection?"

Lireth regarded him in silence for a moment.

Yes, but our bond is different. When I feel you are ready, I will teach you about it.

"I look forward to proving myself worthy in your eyes."

Caden returned to the camp and found Bast eating breakfast. He was sitting beside the glowing embers of a fire from the night before. Their eyes met, and the draman rose to his feet.

"What is it?"

"You're in command while I'm gone. I'm going with our master to clear the skies of enemies."

"How many men do you need?"

"None," Caden replied. "It's just the master and me. Her orders, not mine."

He could tell by Bast's scowl that the draman didn't approve.

"Keep the men here in the camp except for the scouts. They need to be prepared for battle. I have a feeling that when we return, she'll want to attack Velbridge."

Bast's expression brightened.

"We're still vastly outnumbered, but the men will be ready."

"That shouldn't be a problem. Some of our master's allies have joined her."

"We may yet have our revenge," Bast said.

"Indeed. Any word from the draman in the woods?"

Bast looked past Caden, toward Lireth.

"Nothing yet, but I've instructed them to report in every twelve hours. I should have something for you when you get back."

"Good. She wants to kill Lord D'Lance as much as any of us, but I doubt she'll get near the castle gates before she's caught. She's not a soldier, so I don't understand why she thinks she'll be successful."

"There's no telling. Perhaps she has a sickness of the mind. It can make people do strange things."

"I can only hope that's true. I'll return as soon as possible."

Caden went to his tent and slipped a chainmail shirt on. He didn't want to be weighed down too heavily, especially if things went bad and he was forced to escape on his own. He also belted on his sword, though he didn't know why he bothered. It wasn't like he could strike down a dragon with one.

He stopped by the chef's tent and grabbed some cheese and rice, scarfing it down as he walked back to Lireth's position. She was with her brethren, and they were all gathered in a circle. Caden waited nearby, taking in the details of the other black dragons. Lireth was longer and larger than all of them. He suspected that had something to do with her age, but that was only an assumption. The dragons broke away from each other, and Lireth looked at him.

Come. The blood of our enemies shall rain upon the ground.

Caden climbed onto her back, feeling overwhelmed and unworthy. He sat between her shoulders and grabbed onto the scales of her neck. She stretched her wings out and took to the sky, the wind buffeting him violently. He held on as tightly as he could, but he was no match for the forces of nature. He lost his grip and whipped back, crashing against Lireth's back and knocking his head.

Your grip is too weak. If you can't hold on, you'll fall to your death.

Her dire words gave him the push he needed to force himself up, and he grabbed hold of her scales again. He found it helped to lean low, practically hugging her. The wind still battered him, but it was no longer threatening to send him tumbling off her back. It wasn't long into their flight before Caden heard a roaring sound ahead. He lifted his head and blinked rapidly, trying to keep his eyes from being ripped out of their sockets.

A dragon was coming toward them. He wasn't sure, but it looked like someone was standing on its back. Lireth bellowed and angled herself into its path. If Caden hadn't emptied his bladder earlier, he was certain he would have pissed on himself now. He could see the ground below, but something about not having his feet firmly planted on it made his stomach queasy.

He watched helplessly as the dragon steadily got closer. Once it was almost upon them, Lireth barrel rolled to the right, forcing a scream from his lips. His arms and legs felt like they were slipping, and just as he thought he was going to fall, Lireth leveled out and breathed a fiery torrent at their enemy as they passed one another.

The flames streamed over the other dragon harmlessly, but the rider on its back screamed as they overcame him. The fire sizzled from existence, and Caden saw there was nothing left of the person. Lireth wheeled around and went after the dragon. She extended her forelegs and flexed her claws wide. As she dropped, Caden held his breath.

11

WHY WOULD THEY BE FOLLOWING me? Mina asked.

I'm sure they are associated with your friend.

He's not my friend. Not anymore.

It stung her to admit that. Caden had been the first and only person to befriend her despite her deformity. To see him walking toward destruction beside Lireth was heart-wrenching, but she'd tried to dissuade him from the path. She had done her part. The decision to turn away from evil was his alone.

Mina's hand drifted to the hilt of her blade, and she scanned the room. Two draman were sitting at a table by the door. She hadn't noticed them before, but she wasn't paying much attention to the surrounding people, either.

You need to be more alert, Gedrith said.

I was just thinking the same thing. No one other than Caden knows who I am, and I wasn't expecting him to keep eyes on me.

You should come back to the cave. They won't dare try anything with me and my brethren beside you.

I have something else in mind. If Caden thinks he's the only one with things up his sleeves, he's about to be surprised.

Mina left the tavern and headed toward the castle, keeping a brisk pace. As she turned onto another street, she casually looked behind her and spotted the two draman from the tavern. Gedrith was right, she *was* being followed. The creatures kept their distance, and Mina decided she wasn't in danger.

She reached the walls that separated the castle from the city and wandered along the perimeter, looking for a stealthy way across. Heavily armed guards were posted every few feet, and they eyed her distrustfully as she walked.

Lord D'Lance has the castle protected like it's full of treasure, she told Gedrith.

He holds dragons and eggs captive. Those are more valuable than gold and gems. Both give him more power than money could ever buy.

I suppose you're right. He may not be afraid to let the world see his dragons and draman, but he's clearly afraid of losing the ones he hasn't converted to his cause.

They haven't been converted, Gedrith said. *They are bonded against their will. Whether they are locked in the castle or not, they are prisoners.*

Mina walked the entire length of the wall and turned down an alley. It was a dead-end, taking her to a wall too high to climb. A pile of trash was the only place to hide, and she grimaced as she hurriedly hid among the filth. She pinched her nose and waited.

A few moments later, the two draman stepped into view. It confused them when they didn't see her and they began talking to one another in another language. Mina held completely still, breathing as softly as she dared. The draman began arguing and then stormed out of the alley, turning to the right. Mina waited a moment longer before climbing out of the garbage. She ran to the end of the alley and peeked around the corner. The draman were still arguing.

She followed after them, ducking into doorways or blending in with crowds to keep them from seeing her. They returned to the tavern from earlier, and Mina looked for the nearest human guards. A group of them were marching along the street, and she intercepted them.

"Oh, thank Avera you're here! There are two of those creatures in the tavern."

"The draman are official guards in Lord D'Lance's army," one of them said dismissively, but the look on his face told Mina that he wasn't happy about it.

"They aren't Lord D'Lance's men, sir. They're defectors."

That caught the attention of all the soldiers.

"How do you know?"

"I overheard them plotting to hurt Lord D'Lance."

"You said there were two of them?"

"Yes, sir. They're armed with swords, too."

The man looked at his fellows and nodded toward the tavern. They broke formation and headed for the building.

"We'll take care of them," the soldier said.

Mina watched them converge on the place and storm inside. A commotion erupted within, and the two draman were escorted out forcefully. They were bound with shackles and the soldiers marched them toward the castle. Mina smiled. She could play Caden's game all day, and she would win. He might have an army with him, but he couldn't openly march them after her. He was stuck in the shadows while she could walk freely.

That was clever, Gedrith chuckled.

I learned many things while serving Lord Klodian, one of which was how to be petty. Caden doesn't know what he's getting himself into.

Be careful that the taste of hatred does not blind you. Some lines can never be uncrossed.

I'm not blind, she replied. *I'm teaching him a lesson. Just because he's gained power doesn't mean he can do with it as he pleases.*

Lireth will drive him into madness. She may already be doing so. It wouldn't surprise me if he tries to kill you.

Mina frowned. She wanted nothing to do with Caden, but that didn't mean she wanted him to die. If Lireth twisted his mind into making him try to kill her, would she be able to stop him? And if not, did she have the strength to kill him first? She wasn't so sure.

Hopefully, it won't come to that, she said.

Unless he leaves her, a battle between you two is inevitable. You are the champion of the Enclave, and he is hers. Once Lord D'Lance is dead, I do not doubt that there will be war among the dragons.

As long as that war doesn't spill over onto humanity, then let them fight.

There is no 'them' anymore. If there is war, you will be involved.

Mina didn't like the idea of being in the middle of a war with men, let alone one with dragons. If Caden didn't change his mind and find a way to sever his connection to Lireth, then deep down she knew they would end up in battle against one another.

And that scared her more than anything.

12

Caden clenched his jaw against the fear welling within him. Lireth crashed onto the enemy, her claws scraping against the dragon's scales. Raw anger filled Caden's mind, and he knew it was coming from Lireth. Her rage was overwhelming and it made him dizzy. He tightened his grip on her and tried to put up a mental block.

Fire. Death. Fury.

Images and emotions swirled chaotically before his eyes, real and yet imagined. A distant memory flashed briefly, a scene of dragons battling one another. Just as quickly as it entered his mind, it was gone, leaving him reeling.

Smoke. Bodies. Desolation.

Caden used all of his mental facilities to push the images away. With his mind clear, he saw Lireth had the other dragon at her mercy. With a mighty swipe, she tore through the dragon's wing membrane with her talons. The beast issued a roar of pain and plummeted toward the ground. Caden averted his eyes.

Traitors are sentenced to death.

Even if they are forced? Caden posed the question without knowing if Lireth would hear him.

You've learned to mind-speak on your own. I'm impressed. Regardless of whether Lord D'Lance has forced the bond or not, they are tainted by him and cannot be trusted. They are not fit to join us until he is dead.

When he dies, will the bonds be destroyed?

Yes. His magic will die with him.

Good.

There are a few more dragons on patrol to remove, and then we launch our attack.

Caden stiffened. *We're not ready. Our draman are still outnumbered, not to mention that we don't have enough supplies.*

My brethren and I will do most of the work. You and the draman will enter the city after we've ravaged it. You will concentrate your effort on the soldiers first, then the rest can be killed.

The rest?

Anyone living under Lord D'Lance's banner is subject to his punishment as well.

But ... what if they are innocent?

No human is innocent. This shall be a lasting lesson for anyone who thinks to harm and control dragons.

Caden's face creased with concern. How could she ask him to kill innocent people? In the back of his mind, a memory came to the forefront. The night he'd killed Lord D'Lance's potential assassin. If he'd known then what he knew now, he would have let the man live. Lord D'Lance was wicked and deserved his fate, but the people who lived in Velbridge were innocent, weren't they?

Perhaps not. Perhaps they were just as wicked as their lord, but they were better at hiding their atrocities. Even he had dark thoughts at times. He didn't act on them, but that didn't mean other people refrained. He supposed Lireth was right. These people needed to be punished. Obliterating the city would be a harsh lesson, but one that would never be forgotten.

Very well, Caden said. *Our forces will be ready at your command.*

I knew my trust was well placed in you.

Lireth wheeled to the west and sped over the landscape. Caden held on tightly, excitement brimming within him. All his life he'd wanted to show others that they didn't have to be a tyrant to have fame and riches, and now he was about to prove it. He would help Lireth wipe the evil from the Dracan Dominion, and the people would rejoice.

And if they didn't, then they too would be destroyed.

The next patrol they encountered was completely unprepared for Lireth's fury. He'd thought the lone dragon before had been easy prey for his master, but she proved that creature's death had been merciful in comparison. The patrol was a trio of dragons with riders, and they fell to her flames and claws with a violence he'd never witnessed before. When their bodies fell from the sky and struck the ground, she swooped down and tore their lifeless forms limb from limb.

Caden reveled in the power of his master. No one could stop her. She would have her revenge on Lord D'Lance, on the Enclave … the world would burn, just as she said. When they returned to the camp, they were both covered in blood.

Prepare the draman. Once the city is on fire and the castle falls, send them in.

As you command, Caden replied.

He strode through the camp shouting for Bast. The draman rushed into view.

"What is it? Are you all right?" He skidded to a stop and sniffed the air. "That's dragon blood." Bast looked past him to where Lireth normally stayed.

"All is well, my friend. Lireth has cleared the patrols from the sky in preparation for our attack. Gather the men. We're going to war."

"Now?"

"Yes. Once Lireth destroys the castle, we will sweep the city and deal with the others."

Bast hesitated, but he nodded, his reptilian pupils turning to thin slits. "I trust that she will lead us to victory."

"For her glory," Caden replied.

He left Bast and headed for the stream in the woods. The stench of the dragon blood was making his stomach queasy. He didn't bother taking off his armor as he marched into the water and began washing the blood off.

Cupping his hands, he brought some of the cold water to his face, sucking in a sharp breath as it splashed onto his skin. He removed most of the grime, but he didn't bother deep cleaning the armor. They would soon spill more blood, and he didn't want to waste his efforts. When he stepped out of the stream, Bast was waiting for him.

"We don't have enough men," the draman said.

"I know, but our master and the other dragons will reduce most of the city's defenses, so we won't have much to contend with. If Lord D'Lance's soldiers haven't fled by the time we arrive, they're either fools or insane."

Caden wiped the water from his eyes and face and looked at Bast directly. Judging by his demeanor, he could tell Bast was uneasy.

"If I wasn't confident in this, I wouldn't be asking this of you, or of them. Lireth can't be stopped by anything Lord D'Lance has in his employ."

"I was hoping more of my brethren would have joined us. Killing my own kind feels … immoral. Anyone under the influence of Lord D'Lance's magic will stay and fight as long as he's alive."

"I understand your reservations. I have my own, but this is the right path. Once that tyrant is dead, the world will be better off. If it were easy to stand up to injustice, everyone would do it."

Bast sighed. "I know you wouldn't lead us astray, but the human in me has doubts. I will trust our master's plan. If all goes well, we will finally have some peace."

"This is only the first step toward peace. The Enclave will fall next."

"And what about after that?"

Caden shrugged. "We will go where Lireth wants and do as she commands."

Bast bowed his head and left in silence. He may not have said anything, but Caden recognized the draman's conflict. It wasn't much different from his own, but whereas his bond with Lireth gave him the strength and wisdom to see past the doubts, Bast did not.

Perhaps the draman had outlived his usefulness.

13

MINA SPENT A FEW HOURS watching the castle gates, and she could now determine a definitive rotation of shifts among the guards. They changed out every hour, but as they made the switch, those being replaced waited until they were relieved. It was precise, leaving her with no opportunity to get into the castle grounds.

By the time Mina felt hungry, she realized it was already past noon. With no money to buy food, she decided to return to the cave and see if she could scrounge something up. As she navigated the streets, she noticed people were looking at the sky and pointing. She slowed her pace and glanced up. At first, she saw nothing other than a few sparse clouds.

"Are those Lord D'Lance's sky patrols?" someone asked.

Mina squinted and made out about a dozen splotches that steadily grew larger. Had the Enclave sent more dragons to harass Lord D'Lance? The crowd of people stopping to stare continued to swell, and they speculated what the shapes were. As the seconds turned to minutes, the truth became clear.

Mina's stomach churned, but it wasn't from hunger. The unknown shapes were dragons, but they weren't metallic like Gedrith and his brethren. They were chromatic dragons. And the one leading them was the black behemoth bonded to Caden. Mina's mind screamed at her to run, but her legs froze in place. The dragon fear was thick in the air, and she watched helplessly as the dragons descended on Velbridge.

They roared, their battle cries so loud that she thought she would go deaf. Lireth passed over the crowd of people and unleashed her fire. The flames bathed the buildings along the street, setting them ablaze. The heat singed her hair and burned her flesh. A scream pierced the air, and Mina felt sorry for the person before she realized it was her own.

Where are you? Gedrith's voice cut through the fear and she slumped to her knees.

I'm still in Velbridge. Lireth just attacked!

I'm coming to get you.

No! Even with your brethren, we are outnumbered. I'll try to get out of the city.

How many are with her?

Mina gingerly looked skyward and saw numerous black dragons, a couple of green ones, as well as a blue and a white.

Over a dozen, she said.

She has found allies, then. The city will be destroyed by the time the Enclave can send help. It is up to me and my brethren.

She'll kill you.

If I die protecting you, then I have done my duty. Get near the walls if you can't escape the city. I'm on my way.

Mina didn't bother arguing with him. She struggled to her feet and began jogging along the street, heading south toward the main gates. Thick smoke filled the air, burning her eyes and lungs. She coughed and buried her mouth in the crook of her elbow, trying not to breathe it in. The heat coming off the burning buildings drove her to turn down a side street, and she tripped over a prone body.

She fell, smashing the side of her face hard on the cobbled stones. The body she stumbled over was a woman, and a small child, a girl, was sitting nearby, tears streaming down her face. The girl was crying and moving her mouth, but Mina could barely hear her. She offered a quick prayer to Avera that she wasn't truly deaf now and crawled over to the child.

"Come with me," she said, not sure if she was yelling or not. She held her hands out and the child latched onto her. Mina held her close and got up, continuing her trek through the burning city. She passed more bodies, most of them charred, and eventually found her way back to the principal thoroughfare.

Small groups of people had gathered and they were trying to battle the flames, but Mina thought their pursuit was hopeless. Unless Lireth and the others were driven away, nothing would be left after their rampage.

A grizzled old man was gathering the more helpless to him, and Mina diverted her steps to him and handed over the child. She couldn't take care of the girl, even if she wanted to. With the child as safe as possible, she sprinted for the main gates. An inordinate amount of people fleeing the devastation blocked the way out, and they were all pushing and shoving against one another.

I'm near the gates, but I can't get out, Mina said.

The smoke overhead swirled and cleared away to reveal Gedrith. He landed atop the wall, his rear claws snapping onto the stone to keep him balanced. His head swiveled back and forth, enormous eyes scanning the sky over the city.

Mina spotted stairs leading to the top of the wall and ran to them, taking them two at a time. She hastily climbed onto Gedrith's back and looked out over Velbridge. A haze of smoke hid most of the cityscape, but she could clearly see Lireth and her minions flaming more parts of the city. The flames had yet to reach the castle, though.

We need to get help.

There isn't time, Gedrith replied.

Is there no way to get word to the Enclave?

I can send one of my silver brethren, but even with their speed, it will be too late before help arrives. Most of the city burns even now.

I'm less concerned with the city and more worried about the people, not to mention Lord D'Lance. Why hasn't he come out to fight Lireth? Where are his dragons?

Perhaps he doesn't have as many as we thought.

As if to reject that statement, a horn blared in the distance. A moment later, more dragons filled the air and a battle erupted.

We should help the people get to safety, Mina said.

No, we should join the fight. If my brethren and I are lucky, we can kill Lord D'Lance and Lireth at the same time.

Mina looked from the dragons to the city. She didn't know what to do. Either option held its own risks, but she didn't see how she could truly help against the other dragons.

You are my rider, and your place with me, Gedrith said. *You must stop doubting yourself and learn to trust me.*

He was right. She knew that, but she still had her reservations.

Fine, she replied. *Let's end this.*

She drew her sword and he leaped into the air, the wind from his wings pushing the smoke in all directions. Here and there she glimpsed ravaged sections of the city. It broke her heart to see so many bodies littering the streets. The three silver dragons that the Enclave had sent joined them, forming an arrow formation in front of them.

My brethren will target Lord D'Lance.

What about us?

We will deal with Lireth.

As they closed the distance to the battle, Mina saw Caden wasn't with Lireth. In fact, none of the Lireth's dragons had riders.

Wait. Something's off.

What is it?

If Caden's not with Lireth, where is he?

She scanned the ground and found her answer. He was on the ground, leading a force of draman to the city.

14

C ADEN STOOD WITH B AST IN front of their force of draman, watching Lireth and her brethren wreak destruction on Velbridge. Flames peaked over the walls, and billowing smoke drifted into the sky above the city, creating a massive gray cloud.

"Now?" Bast asked.

"Not yet."

He was waiting on Lireth to give the command, but it worried him that she was too caught up in her emotions. Violent joy filled his mind through their bond, and his skin tingled from the sheer power she displayed. Torrents of fire left her maw, incinerating everything below her, including portions of the stone wall.

"Our master will leave nothing standing," Bast said. "This place will be a sign of her vengeance for ages to come."

Caden didn't doubt that, but he did doubt Bast's loyalty, especially after their last conversation. He side-eyed the draman as he considered how to deal with him. Many of their forces would likely perish in the city, and he could use that as justification for Bast's absence. Lireth was so enveloped in her revenge that he doubted she was reading his thoughts.

"It's time," Caden said loudly. "To the city!"

A cheer rang from the draman behind him, and they began their trek toward Velbridge. Caden marched quickly, leading the charge to the walls. A wave of heat hit him before he was a hundred feet away. He halted and staggered back, but the draman continued, unfazed by the drastic temperature. Bast urged his fellows onward, but he stayed by Caden.

"Are you all right?"

"The heat is a bit much for me."

"I thought your armor protected from the heat of dragon fire?"

Caden watched the draman continue ahead of them, oblivious to the fact that their leaders were now at the rear. He grabbed the hilt of his sword and hesitated. What if Bast wasn't disloyal? What if

376

Caden had misjudged the draman's words? If that was the case, killing him would be wrong.

And yet ... if he was right, he'd be protecting Lireth and stopping dissension before it could spread to the others.

"What is it?" Bast stared him in the eyes.

"I'm sorry, friend."

Caden drew his blade and jabbed forward, aiming the tip of the sword for the vulnerable fleshy spot of the draman's neck that was unprotected by armor. Bast moved with a quickness that surprised him, and the draman brought his own blade up, knocking Caden's strike to the side with a clang.

"What are you doing?" he hissed.

"You've lost your trust in our master," Caden replied, circling to the left. Bast mirrored his steps to the right.

"I swore an oath to her. I would never go back on my word."

"How do I know that? You question her decision to march to The Long Sands. If you were loyal to her, you wouldn't have."

"Bah! You're blinded by something, but I don't know what it is. Just because I question something doesn't mean I have forsaken my oath. Lireth rescued me. She rescued all of us."

"She saved me from death," Caden said. "I see more clearly than you, it seems. I would never question her."

"We are marching to victory, and you attack me for nothing. Please, let us call peace and battle together as brothers in arms."

Caden knew the draman was trying to trick him. He lunged ahead, jabbing with his blade. Again, Bast blocked the strike, retreating from Caden's reach instead of launching his own attack. The draman was clever, but Caden wouldn't be fooled. He went on the offensive, slashing and stabbing. Bast was his equal, if not superior, and the draman deflected every blow, backpedaling instead of fighting him.

"Fight back, you coward!"

"You are mad," Bast said, his reptilian pupils nothing more than slits. "Stop this foolishness before ..."

"Before what?" Caden demanded.

"Before one of us dies untimely. Our master will not be pleased, regardless of who falls."

"She'll be glad to know that I have removed a traitor when you are dead." Caden could feel his anger building. The draman was playing stupid, trying to get him to lower his guard. He refused to believe that Bast was still a loyal servant of their master. Bast looked past him, up at the sky, and his expression hardened.

"The enemy is coming!"

Caden growled and swung his sword at the draman. Bast jumped backward out of range and Caden stumbled from his momentum, but he quickly recovered. Something large and heavy hit the ground behind him, but before he could look, something struck him down. Bast turned and fled.

"Your master has killed innocent people!"

It surprised him to hear her voice. He honestly believed he'd never see her again. Or maybe it was that he hoped he wouldn't, because that meant he would have to kill her. Caden roared in anger and got to his feet, retrieving his blade and whirling around to face her.

Mina had her sword drawn, and he could see the fury in her eyes. *Good,* he thought. It would make his task easier if she wanted to fight him.

"There are always casualties in war. Everyone knows this."

Mina pointed toward the city. "Look at that and tell me it's not wrong."

Caden kept his gaze on her, which only seemed to infuriate her further.

"Look at it!" she screamed.

He flicked his eyes to the side briefly.

"What do you want from me, Mina? You want me to betray her? She saved my life. I am indebted to her, and I will honor her until I die."

Mina's jaw tightened and he knew that only one of them was going to walk away from this fight alive. He gripped the hilt of his sword firmly and brought the blade up.

"No!" Mina screamed. "I will kill him myself!"

Caden assumed she was talking to her dragon. The copper beast loomed behind her, his bulk just as sinuous and muscled as Lireth's. Dragon fear tugged at him, but he channeled his master's strength to push it away.

"Try if you think you can," he said.

Mina rushed him, swinging her sword wildly. She had some skill, which impressed him, but her movements showed that she was still a novice. Caden parried her strikes and stepped closer when he spotted an obvious opening in her defenses. He swiped his blade along her forearm, slicing the skin open. She cried out in pain and drew back, cursing.

Guilt assailed him. He was more practiced with a sword than she was, and it was clear that he would win. Yet his master had ordered him to kill her if he saw her again. He was conflicted, his obligation warring with his emotions. Why did she have to be involved with Lireth's enemies?

Kill her.

Lireth was present in his mind, and her words compelled him. He attacked her ferociously, her weak attempts to block his strikes fueling his desire to see her die. Or was it his desire? It was hard to discern where he ended and Lireth began, but he supposed that was because of their bond.

Her dragon is here. If I kill her, he will kill me.

Not if I kill him first.

Lireth roared, and all eyes turned toward her approach.

15

GET DOWN!

Mina fell to her knees and Gedrith curled his body around her, shielding her with his wings as Lireth dropped among them, spewing fire in their direction. Mina clenched her eyes closed, expecting to be burned alive. When death didn't take her, she peaked them open and saw that Gedrith's body was unharmed.

When I open my wings, get on my back as quickly as you can.

I'm ready. Mina got into a crouch and sheathed her sword.

Gedrith removed his wings from around her and she stood, risking a glance at Lireth. Caden was mounted on her back and she leaped, taking to the sky. Mina hurriedly climbed up Gedrith's shoulder and had barely seated herself before he launched into the air. They chased after Lireth, flying over the city and into the smoke.

Mina lost sight of the black dragon in the haze, but Gedrith confidently wheeled left and right, and she assumed he could see better than her. He swooped down and Lireth's tail whizzed past her head.

Hold on!

Mina gripped Gedrith's neck tightly. He angled upward and flew higher and higher until they broke above the thick smoke that blotted out the city. Lireth was there as well, and she came straight for them.

Gedrith spread his wings out wide, catching the wind, and thrust his rear claws out to grab Lireth. She mirrored the maneuver and the two dragons locked their claws together, spinning in circles and falling toward the ground. The force of their spins was so strong that Mina lost her grip and flew backward.

Despite having fallen before, the feeling of sheer terror that enveloped her wasn't something she could ever get used to. Her stomach churned and she screamed, waving her arms frantically. As she fell, she watched Gedrith and Lireth claw and snap at one another as they continued to spiral.

Mina thought for sure that Gedrith was going to break free and come to her rescue, but that assumption was violently tossed aside when her fall was broken by the remains of a vendor cart. It collapsed under her and she gasped in surprise and agony as pain flared through every inch of her body.

She lay there unmoving for a long moment, afraid that if she tried to get up, she would discover that she'd broken some bones. Holding her breath, she sat up and was astonished to find that other than some cuts, she was unharmed. She looked up to see if the two dragons were still battling, but the smoke was thicker now than before.

I'm alive, Mina muttered as she climbed out of the wreckage and surveyed her surroundings. She was on a street filled with vendor carts and wagons, all of them blackened and a few still burning. Distant voices echoed off the charred buildings, but she didn't see anyone in the vicinity.

Without a clear idea of what she should do, she walked toward the sound of the voices. The intense heat had subsided a little, but the smoke still choked her and burned her eyes. She blinked rapidly and turned down a side street. The voices were louder now, and she knew she was going the right way. The street widened into an open spacious square and she saw the source of the voices.

A large force of draman. They were coming out of one of the buildings, and two of them were dragging a lifeless body behind them. They stopped when they saw her, and Mina froze.

"No prisoners!" one of them yelled.

The others shouted in excitement and rushed toward her. Mina turned and bolted. She was overwhelmingly outnumbered and had no doubts that they would kill her. She zig-zagged down random streets and climbed over piles of debris in her panicked flight.

Gedrith, where are you? I need you!

She could feel his presence in her mind, but he didn't respond. He was probably still battling with Lireth. Mina skidded to a halt when she reached a bridge that spanned over a canal. The center portion of the bridge was gone, and the distance to the other side was too far for her to jump across.

Mina looked back and saw the draman were closing in on her. She cursed the creatures and jumped into the water. Her sword and chainmail weighed her down, but she kicked and swam as fast as she could, following the canal's current. The draman didn't follow her, and she floated along until she encountered a shallow spot that offered a platform for fishermen. She pulled herself out of the water and slumped onto her back, panting heavily.

A roar shattered the momentary silence and Mina sat up. It sounded like it was right above her. Something was coming.

Gedrith?

Nothing.

She got to her feet and kept her eyes on the cloud of smoke. A few moments passed, and then one of the silver dragons broke through the haze and crashed into a building. Mina gasped. His neck was twisted at an odd angle, and he was obviously dead.

Gedrith!

I'm here, he replied.

Thank Avera! Is Lireth dead?

No. Lord D'Lance joined the fight on dragon back and she went after him. Where are you?

I'm not sure. There's a canal, and one of your brethren is dead.

I saw him fall, Gedrith said sadly. *I couldn't reach him in time to help. Stay where you are.*

The sound of flapping wings signaled his approach and he descended through the smoke, landing feet first in the canal.

Are you hurt?

No, Mina answered. *Well, not seriously. I'll be bruised tomorrow, I'm sure. What about you?*

Gedrith lifted his head to reveal some damaged scales on his neck. *More battle scars.*

Where are your other brethren?

Fighting. We need to take Lireth down, but that's going to be a hard task with Lord D'Lance and his riders in the air.

Maybe he will kill Lireth and save us the trouble.

Perhaps, but it will not be easy for him. And if she falls, those allied with her will scatter. Although I despise her, her actions will help us defeat him.

Is Caden still with her?

Yes.

Mina nodded. She looked at the cut on her arm. It wasn't deep and the wound had clotted, but it still stung when she moved it. Caden had intentionally injured her, but his expression afterward had been one of remorse.

Do you think there's a way to kill Lireth without killing Caden?

Maybe, Gedrith said. *The Enclave would rather imprison Lireth, but I fear that capturing her alive will be impossible without help. We're outnumbered and she won't be taken without a fight.*

Do you think Lord D'Lance will kill her, or do you think he'll try to force her into a bond as he did with the others?

I don't know.

Mina chewed her lower lip in thought. *I have an idea, but I don't know if it will work. It would rely on Lord D'Lance using his magic, and there's no guarantee he will.*

What is it?

If we can get Lireth's attention on us long enough for Lord D'Lance to use his magic on her, then we can kill him and take her captive.

The only way that plan works is if Lord D'Lance does what we want. How do we ensure he does?

We offer him something he wants.

What is that?

Caden.

16

CADEN HELD ON TIGHTLY AS Lireth sped through the sky toward the castle. Lord D'Lance had joined the fray, and he'd brought a host of his riders with him. Upon seeing him, Lireth immediately ceased fighting Mina's dragon and turned her focus upon the Dominion Lord. Caden didn't blame her. He hated Lord D'Lance as well, and the opportunity to see him fall was too tempting to pass.

Stay alert, Lireth said. *Lord D'Lance has learned to use dark magic and he does not hesitate to use it.*

Caden gritted his teeth, remembering how the man had tried to kill him. *I'm well aware of what he's capable of.*

Lord D'Lance rode on the back of a green dragon. He stood without support as if he were part of the dragon itself, and he wore black plate armor that covered him from the neck down. He didn't wear a helmet, and his long black hair whipped freely behind him. If his hair wasn't moving, Caden imagined he could be nothing more than a statue.

Lireth roared in challenge and flapped her wings harder, picking up the pace. Caden drew his sword despite not having the reach of hitting anything and watched the distance close between them. The green dragon issued its own roar and a billowing cloud of yellow gas poured out from its mouth. Lireth banked to the left and flapped her right wing, sending the cloud backward into Lord D'Lance. The yellow gas swept around an invisible barrier that surrounded the Dominion Lord and the wind blew it away.

What is that stuff?

Poisonous gas, Lireth replied. *It'll burn your flesh if it touches you.*

And I thought fire was bad.

Lireth circled to the rear of the dragon, but another rider swooped in the way. Lireth went up, cracking the rider's dragon in the head with her thick tail. The blow knocked the dragon's head to the side and it careened out of control. When she turned back toward Lord D'Lance, his dragon was on top of her. It grabbed onto Lireth's horns and jerked violently. Her neck undulated and Caden fell backward, slamming his back on her hard scales. He coughed and forced himself to sit up, then jabbed his sword at the dragon. He misjudged the distance and the sword stabbed nothing but the air.

Lord D'Lance looked down at him and glared. His hands moved in odd patterns and his mouth moved silently. The air rippled briefly and then lightning began flickering between his fingers. Before he could do anything with the magic, Lireth shook her head free and pulled her wings in, free falling a few feet. She unfurled them and caught the air, spiraling a few times before shooting back up at the green dragon.

She crashed bodily into the beast and used her front claws to latch onto the dragon's throat. Blood splattered Lireth and Caden both as scales and flesh ripped free. Lireth snapped her jaws onto the dragon's wound and jolted her head back and forth, tearing the flesh further. The green dragon gurgled an anguished cry and its wings slackened.

Watch out! Caden warned.

Lord D'Lance unleashed his spell. Several lightning bolts flashed forth from his hands, all of them striking Lireth. Her body spasmed as the projectiles hit her, but she didn't make a sound. That impressed Caden. Lireth unhooked her mouth from the green dragon and winged backward. The dragon plummeted to the ground, Lord D'Lance still on its back. Lireth dived, following after the dead beast.

Lord D'Lance leaped through the air before the dragon collided into the ground with a thunderous crash, landing unharmed atop the rubble of a building. Lireth opened her jaws and unleashed a torrent of flames, but they sizzled from existence as they struck his invisible barrier.

Caden gripped the hilt of his blade, preparing to take the fight to the ground. As he shifted his legs to jump down, a shadow passed overhead. He looked up in time to see Mina dangling from her dragon's claw, her right foot outstretched. It connected with the side of his head, and pain exploded from his brow down to his neck. The force pushed him off Lireth's back and he fell a few feet before slamming facedown onto the rubble at Lord D'Lance's feet.

He gasped, trying to force the breath back into his lungs. He heard Lireth roar and the sounds of battle, but they sounded faint, as if they were far away. Someone rolled him over and the darkness that threatened to consume him was held at bay.

Lord D'Lance looked into his eyes.

"You've done more to irritate me than most," he said lowly.

Above them, Lireth and Mina's dragon battled, but he didn't see Mina anywhere. Air filled his lungs, and he slowly became aware that things had taken a turn for the worse. His body sagged as his strength abruptly left. He'd completely forgotten about Lord D'Lance's rune.

"What were you hoping to accomplish, Caden? Did you think you could defeat me? You're nothing more than a cockroach meant for the bottom of my boot. You've destroyed my city for nothing. Now I'm going to destroy your dragon and make you watch."

"You can't kill her," Caden whispered harshly. "She's stronger than you."

"Who said I was going to kill her? There is more than one way to destroy a dragon."

Lord D'Lance gripped Caden's face, his fingers hard as steel.

"You do not want to miss this."

With his other hand, Lord D'Lance pointed to Lireth and began muttering words that made Caden's skin crawl. He tried to lift his arm to strike the Dominion Lord, but his muscles refused to obey. He watched helplessly as Lireth slowly became ensnared by Lord D'Lance's magic. Wispy white tendrils stretched from his hand and into the sky, wrapping around Lireth's body. As the tendrils touched her, her movements became sluggish. Caden could feel her strength flowing through him and into the Dominion Lord.

A group of Lord D'Lance's dragon riders arrived, forcing Mina's dragon to retreat. He fled, disappearing into the smoke above the still burning city. Lord D'Lance clenched his hand into a fist and Lireth began to descend. She roared and thrashed against the magic, but it didn't help. Lord D'Lance proved to be the more powerful of the two.

Caden's eyes watered. He did not know what Lord D'Lance had planned for her, but he knew it wasn't good. His own body refused to obey him, leaving him unable to help his master. Who knew where Bast was, and the draman were probably pillaging the city. Where were Lireth's brethren? Had they all died? Their plan seemed foolproof, but it shattered like broken glass in front of his eyes.

If only there was something he could do, or someone who could help. But there wasn't. There was nobody, and he was at the mercy of a maniacal tyrant.

"Just kill me and get it over with," he begged.

"Your fate will not be so easy," Lord D'Lance said.

By the time Lireth's body touched the ground, she was completely immobile. Lord D'Lance released Caden's face and walked over to the dragon, standing in front of her head. He laid a hand on her snout.

This was it. This was the end, and it was nothing like Caden had imagined it would be. Something caught his eye; a sliver of movement among the rubble. Was he seeing things, or was that …

Mina.

17

Mina crouched among the rubble of a ruined building. Her crazy idea had worked, for the most part, and now Caden was at the mercy of Lord D'Lance. What she had not expected, however, was that the Dominion Lord could deal with Caden and Lireth at the same time—all on his own.

He was more powerful than she expected, and now her plan was slightly astray. Instead of delivering Caden to Lord D'Lance and Lireth swooping in to rescue him, thereby taking over his focus, he had them both ensnared by magic.

This isn't going to work, she told Gedrith.

Why not?

Lord D'Lance has them both captive.

That is good. It will rid us of both.

Mina looked at Caden's prone form and couldn't help but feel a little guilty. She knew he was her enemy now, but that didn't mean she had to let him die.

If Lord D'Lance dies, does his magic fade?

I don't know, Gedrith replied.

I have a clear path to him, but if I kill him and his spells end, we may lose the chance to capture Lireth.

That's a risk we'll have to take. Our orders were to kill Lord D'Lance.

I know, but which of them is the bigger threat?

Gedrith didn't reply. She knew Lireth could wreak more havoc than Lord D'Lance, but the dragon technically wasn't her responsibility. She shifted her eyes between the two enemies, struggling briefly before deciding.

She was going to kill Lord D'Lance.

The laughter of Thais and Lord Klodian echoed in her mind, and it dawned on her that she might not be able to kill him, that she might not even be able to get near him before he ended her existence.

Trust your training, Gedrith said. *Stop listening to your doubts.*

He was right, she knew that, but it wasn't easy to ignore the thoughts. They were strong and persuasive. Mina tightened her grip on the hilt of her sword and took a deep breath.

Get ready, she warned, but she was also talking to herself. She flicked her eyes to the sky. Gedrith was nowhere to be seen. Mina emerged from the rubble slowly, careful of where she stepped. Lord D'Lance was in front of Lireth, his hand on her snout. White tendrils of smoke were wrapped around the dragon, keeping her from moving. Lireth's fiery gaze locked on the Dominion Lord, but Mina knew the dragon saw her.

With each step, Mina's heart hammered louder in her ears. Only a few steps away, she lifted her sword above her head and grabbed the hilt with both hands. Her strike needed to be precise, but her hands tremored. She'd never killed anyone before, at least not with her own hands.

Calm yourself.

Mina inhaled a deep breath and held it. Her hands steadied, and she lunged forward, driving the blade in a downward motion, aiming for Lord D'Lance's exposed neck. Time slowed, and she watched the tip of the blade as it drew nearer.

Without even looking back, Lord D'Lance swung his right hand behind his head, slapping her sword wide. Her momentum was thrown off and she staggered to the left, her sword chopping the air harmlessly. She quickly recovered and whirled around to face Lord D'Lance. He turned his attention to her and smiled.

"You're just as foolish as Caden, so you must be one of his. Do you not realize I have the power of a dragon flowing through my veins?"

He moved so quickly that Mina's eyes barely registered a blur of motion before agony exploded throughout her chest. She flew back several feet and crashed into something hard. It took her a moment to register it was the remnants of a stone wall. Lord D'Lance began laughing, a deranged look on his face.

Mina gritted her teeth against the pain and stood. Lord D'Lance strode toward her, Lireth and Caden still unmoving. Mina brought her sword up and stepped forward to meet him, but she knew she couldn't beat him. He was more powerful than her with his magic alone, and now that he had Lireth's strength, she had lost all hope. But she was still going to fight. Perhaps her sanity had left, or perhaps it had never truly been there to begin with.

She jabbed her sword at an angle, trying to hit him in the neck again, but he batted it away. Mina jabbed a second time with the same result. With her third attempt, Lord D'Lance grabbed the blade with his bare hand and snarled foreign words. The metal of her blade drooped and then turned to liquid, splattering on the ground. Mina's eyes widened in shock. She threw the hilt at him and it struck his chest plate, clanging loudly but doing no harm.

Mina blinked, and Lord D'Lance was directly in front of her. He wrapped his hand around her neck and squeezed, choking her. She gasped and tried to break free of his grasp, but his hold was firm.

Help me! She screamed through the bond. She could feel Gedrith's presence, and it was the only thing that kept her from giving up.

"I don't need you, but I want your dragon," Lord D'Lance said. "Tell him to come to me."

"No," Mina rasped.

"You will if you want to live. Call him here. Now." He squeezed harder.

I will not let him kill you, Gedrith's voice filled her mind. He sent an image to her, and she knew exactly what to do. She could hear the flapping of his wings, and she knew the moment he came into view, because Lord D'Lance's gaze looked up to the sky. Her throat was warm, quickly becoming hot. Mina could see Gedrith's reflection in Lord D'Lance's eyes, and she held on to consciousness despite the blackness closing in around her.

Her lips parted, and she whispered, "The Enclave … sends … their regards."

The burning in her throat overwhelmed her and she opened her mouth as if to shout, but instead of her anguished cry, flames spewed forth. A fiery torrent washed over Lord D'Lance and he released her, screaming and staggering backward. The sickly smell of burnt flesh stung Mina's nostrils, but the flames continued unabated, bathing the Dominion Lord so fully that she could see nothing but fire.

Finally, the blaze died and the burning in her throat faded. She fell to her knees, overcome with weakness. Lord D'Lance was lying on the ground, writhing and crying out. He was somehow still alive. Mina crawled over to Caden and took his sword, then got on her feet and stumbled over to where Lord D'Lance was and stood over him. The man's face was burned so badly he was unrecognizable.

With no hesitation, Mina swung the sword down, separating his head from his body, and then she promptly turned away and vomited. She wiped the back of her hand across her lips and looked at Lireth. The tendrils of smoke still bound the dragon in place, but she thrashed about, trying to get free.

His magic still holds, she said as Gedrith landed nearby.

I see that. It will make our task easier.

Are you really going to take her back to the Enclave? You could kill her instead. It would ensure she never poses a threat again.

Although you are right, I will not kill her. She will face the Enclave for her crimes and be imprisoned for the rest of her life. What do you want to do with that one?

Mina turned to look at Caden. For a moment, she thought he was dead, but then she saw his chest rising and falling and realized he was only unconscious.

If Lireth is as ingrained in his mind as I fear, then we must keep them separated. He will face the same punishment as his master. Imprisonment.

A wise decision. With Lireth in the desert and Caden here, the distance will be too far for them to communicate. It doesn't break their bond, but it is just as effective.

How will we get Lireth to the Enclave?

Only one of my brethren fell in battle, so we will carry her. We need to make haste while her forces are in disarray, lest her minions try to free her.

Mina nodded, still looking at Caden.

Where should we take him?

I know a place.

18

CADEN OPENED HIS EYES AND slowly became aware of his surroundings. He was in a dimly lit room with stone walls. An iron gate, a cell door, was closed and sconces on the walls outside of the cell illuminated the space. He groaned as he sat up and noticed he was on the floor. His wrists were shackled, the chains connected to rings in the floor, and he had little movement. As his mind was putting it all together, he realized he wasn't alone.

"I was beginning to wonder if you'd ever wake up."

There was no mistaking her voice. It was as rooted in his mind as Lireth was.

"Mina," he said. "Where are we? What happened?"

She was leaning against the wall to his left, her arms crossed over her chest.

"You lost," she replied. "And so did Lord D'Lance."

"Lireth killed him?"

Mina laughed scornfully. "Hardly. Thanks to your rune, Lord D'Lance was able to draw on Lireth's strength through you. He almost killed me. Probably would have if it wasn't for Gedrith."

"Your dragon?"

She nodded. Caden looked around the room, but there wasn't much to see. He could feel Lireth's presence in his mind, but it was muted, as if a thick cloth was covering their connection. If what Mina said was true, then his master was defeated. He hesitated to ask, but he needed to know.

"Where is Lireth?"

"She's being taken to the Enclave for judgement."

"Will they kill her?"

"No. Gedrith says they will lock her up. She'll die of old age in an underground cave."

At least she's alive, Caden thought. He held his hands up and jingled the chains.

"Any chance I'm getting out of these?"

"No."

"What is this place?"

"This is Lord Culver's dungeon. I told him Lord Klodian transferred you here for crimes against the High Prince. You'll never see daylight again."

Caden silently digested her words. He was a prisoner, and Lireth was being taken somewhere else. Whose cruel idea was it to separate them so far from each other? Would he be able to sense her from such a distance, or would her presence shrink until she was nothing more than a memory? The uncertainty was going to make him sick.

"I'm sorry for what I said before. I'm sure you regret aiding Lord Klodian with killing all those dragons now that you know they aren't mindless animals."

Mina pushed off the wall and approached, kneeling in front of him.

"If you were free and Lireth wasn't, would you try to help her escape?"

"If you and your dragon were in the same situation, would you?"

"Our situations are not the same," Mina said. "Lireth is wicked. She's brainwashed you into blindly following her. Do you not see that?"

Caden smiled at her despite the turmoil of emotions raging within him. "You don't know her like I do. You think she is evil, but I know she is kind. She saved me and gave me a place among her draman. No one has ever accepted me as I am like she has."

"I did."

"That's not what I meant."

"Then perhaps you should say what you mean. You'll have plenty of time to learn how to do that in here."

"Your dragon has changed you. The way you hold yourself, the way you speak … you are not the girl I met."

"Did you prefer that I stayed the same? A meek slave, always bending to the will of others?"

"No, never that. I just wish that things had gone differently between us. If I would have told you that I no longer wanted to leave the Thophate, you would never have asked Lord Klodian to send me away. Perhaps if I had never left …"

"I told you before that our destinies may be entwined, but they are not united. Whether or not you stayed would not have changed that. Avera had other plans for me."

Caden found it difficult to accept that she truly believed that, but he knew it was futile to argue the point.

"So you leave me here and go … where? What will you do now that Lord D'Lance is dead?"

"That's none of your business," Mina replied. She leaned closer to him. "You were a good man once. Maybe you will be again. Once Lireth is out of your mind, I hope that your sanity will return. If you can find a way to remove yourself from her bond, do it. That'll be the only way you get out of here."

Caden stared into her blue eyes and longed to touch her, but he didn't dare try. She returned his stare with equal intensity, but neither of them spoke. Finally, she leaned in and kissed him on the lips. He closed his eyes and savored the moment, which ended too soon. Mina pulled away from him and stood up.

"Goodbye, Caden."

And with that, she pushed open the cell door and walked away. A guard stepped into view. He closed the gate and locked it, then returned to his post. Caden sighed and laid back down on the floor, staring at the ceiling. Mina told him to end his bond with Lireth, but he would not do that. If anything, he was determined to strengthen it and find a way to escape.

One step at a time, he told himself. *One step at a time.*

—

As Mina left the dungeon, she had to force herself to ignore the pleadings of her heart. Caden was her enemy as long as he was bonded to Lireth, and she held no reservations about locking him up. It was for his own good as much as it was to keep the world safe. Still, the thought that she might never see him again gave her pause.

He'd asked what her plans were, but she didn't tell him because she didn't want him to know where she was in the unlikely event that he ever managed to get out of the prison. Now that the tyrant Lord D'Lance was no longer a threat, she was free to do as she pleased. Her odd relationship with Lord Klodian had ended on a sour note, so she could go back to the Thophate, especially not with a dragon.

Perhaps she would return to the Enclave and continue training as a rider with Areg. Or perhaps she wouldn't. Nothing was set in stone, and she liked the idea of having the free will to do anything she dreamed of … or nothing at all.

She left Lord Culver's castle behind and trekked into the grain fields where Gedrith and his brethren awaited her. Lireth was there as well, still magically bound, and Mina climbed onto Gedrith's back.

All is well? He asked.

Yes. We are all set to leave.

Good. I miss the desert.

Mina smiled and held on tightly as the dragon lifted off the ground. Between him and the remaining silver dragons, they were able to carry Lireth in their claws. They gained altitude and rose higher, then turned south toward The Long Sands, toward the Enclave. Mina closed her eyes and let the wind whip her hair about, enjoying the sensation of flying.

It felt good to be free.

SACRIFICE

OF THE

DRAGON

1

THE AIR WAS HOT AND dry, and Mina shielded the sun from her eyes as Gedrith flew above The Long Sands. A sand wyrm had been spotted on the fringes of the Enclave's domain, and as part of her continued training, the two of them had been tasked with scouting the area.

Mina watched the sand dunes, looking for the telltale signs that signaled the underground movement of the beast. She'd learned much in the two weeks since the fall of Velbridge, and yet she couldn't shake the feeling that she was still too ill-equipped to be a dragon rider.

"It there!" Areg shouted, pointing. He stood in the saddle behind her, his arm outstretched past her head.

She followed his fingers to the ground and saw it clearly. A bulge in the dunes that rose and fell, swaying side to side, like an enormous desert serpent. Mina swallowed hard and clenched her jaw.

Do you see it? she asked Gedrith.

Yes.

What do you think it's doing here?

I do not know, but it doesn't matter. We must kill it.

Mina was afraid he was going to say that. Her only encounter with sand wyrms had been terrifying, and they'd had the aid of many dragons then.

Should we alert the others?

There isn't time. If we leave, it may get away.

Is that a bad thing?

The only good sand wyrm is a dead one, Gedrith rumbled.

The smell of orchids filled her nostrils, and she knew he was disappointed with her fear and reluctance. She ignored the urge to apologize.

We need to draw it to the surface, she said.

Without offering a reply, Gedrith dove down sharply. Areg latched onto her shoulders, gripping her tightly with his small hands. Despite his diminutive size, he was much stronger than he looked. The air whipped past them, pulling at her hair and rippling her shirt wildly. The dry air stung her eyes, and she leaned forward and squinted.

When the ground was only a few feet away, Gedrith pulled up and leveled out, using his massive wings to catch the air and slow his descent. He glided over the shifting sand and raked his rear claws down deep. Catching on the flesh of the wyrm, Gedrith's bulk shuddered briefly, but it was enough force that Areg crashed into Mina and the two of them fell from Gedrith's back.

Mina gasped in surprise and pain as she tumbled along the dune. Once her body stopped rolling, she sat up and spat grit from her mouth. A glance at herself didn't reveal any injuries, but she'd probably be sore tomorrow. Staggering to her feet, she looked around for Areg. The elf was a dozen paces away, already on his feet with his sword drawn.

Are you hurt? Gedrith asked.

He flew over her, his shadow temporarily blotting out the sun.

I don't think so. Where's the wyrm?

Get to the top of the hill.

His lack of an answer told her they were in danger. She ran up the dune, pumping her legs furiously, but the sand pulled at her boots, slowing her down. Areg raced past her, his small feet skimming the sand so lightly he barely left any footsteps. If all elves were as agile, it was a wonder they weren't the only ones allowed to bond with dragons. Then again, he was the only elf she'd ever seen, which was curious.

By the time she reached the top of the hill, sweat slicked her skin and she had trouble pulling her sword from the sheath at her side. The ground trembled beneath her, and the sand vibrated, causing miniature landslides to pour down the dune. A moment later, Areg tackled her, knocking her on the flat of her back.

Before she could question him, the ground where she'd been standing erupted. The head of the sand wyrm, its maw opened wide, burst forth, showering her and the elf with sand and spittle. Areg had saved her life. She scrambled onto her feet and drew her sword.

"Thank you," she huffed.

Areg nodded, turning to watch the path of the wyrm. Mina did the same. The beast continued down the other side of the dune, disappearing back below the ground, though the bulge it left behind was a clear sign of where it was going. It made a wide turn and circled back.

"What do we do?" she asked, panic threatening to overwhelm her common sense.

"Kill," Areg replied simply, smiling.

"How?"

The elf shook his blade.

"Yes, with a sword, obviously. I mean, *how* do we kill it with a sword? What exactly do I need to stab?"

"Heart," he said.

Mina remembered Gedrith's words from their battle with the wyrm king.

"It's encased in bone and muscle, so how do I penetrate it?"

"No, wyrm king only. This easy."

At Mina's baleful look, Areg shrugged. "More easy," he clarified.

When the elf had killed the wyrm king, he'd been swallowed by the creature. The only way to kill them was from the inside. Mina shuddered at the thought.

"I'll draw its attention, and you get in there and kill it," she said.

Areg shook his head. "You."

"Me? No, I can't do it."

"Can. Hold breath. Stab heart. Easy."

Mina watched the swell in the sand as it drew nearer, and realization dawned on her. This was part of her training, another test of her abilities and what she'd learned. Why hadn't Gedrith warned her?

"If it's so easy, why did you push me out of the way?"

"Not prepared. Wrong place." Areg motioned with his hands, indicating she would have been dismembered by the creature. The trembling of the ground ran up the length of Mina's legs, drawing her focus back to the approaching wyrm. It was time to stop questioning herself. She was no longer a slave, but a dragon rider.

The first dragon rider in a thousand years. The only *true* dragon rider.

Mina gripped the hilt of her sword tightly and pushed the fear aside. The bulge in the sand came straight toward her. She centered herself with it and had to scream at herself not to flee. The wyrm broke the surface of the ground, and time seemed to still. The creature's mouth opened, revealing a torrent of saliva that dripped onto the sand.

Time returned to normal, and Mina brought her sword up in front of her, lunging forward into the wyrm's mouth. It swallowed her, plunging her into wet darkness. She ran ahead blindly, holding her breath as Areg had instructed. The fleshy walls inside of the wyrm pulsed and constricted around her. Her lungs burned intensely, and she feared she was going to suffocate.

Where is the heart? she cried out.

You will know it when you see it, Gedrith replied. *Keep going.*

Mina forced herself to put one foot in front of the other, hacking at the wyrm's insides as she did so. If the creature felt any pain from it, she couldn't tell. Her chest tightened and the burning in her lungs was almost too much to bear. Why did she have to hold her breath, anyway?

She gasped and heaved in a deep lungful of air. The foul smell of decay assailed her and she understood why Areg told her not to breathe. It made her eyes water, but she felt something thrumming ahead. It was powerful, and she assumed it was the heart. A few more steps forward, and a reddish-pink light became visible. The light pulsed in conjunction with the vibrations, giving her no doubt that it was indeed the wyrm's heart.

Mina pointed the tip of the sword at the light and spread her feet, bracing herself. She thrust the blade with all her might. It cut through the layers of flesh easily, and the sword sank in up to the hilt. The wyrm shuddered around her, and she was aware that the creature came to an abrupt halt.

The deed was done, and now she needed to escape. She remembered Areg had cut his way out of the wyrm king's side, and so she began hacking at the fleshy wall to her left. Warm, wet liquid coated her arms, and she assumed it was blood. Ignoring her revulsion, she swung the sword over and over until daylight was visible and she burst out onto the sand. From her periphery, she saw Areg running down to the dune toward her.

"Did it!" he shouted triumphantly. "Did it!"

A shadow passed overhead and a moment later, Gedrith landed nearby, his powerful wings stirring up the desert sand. Mina dropped her sword and fell to her knees, covered in blood and other things she'd rather not consider.

Very good, Gedrith said. *You have passed the Enclave's final test.*

Mina remained silent for a moment, her thoughts a scrambled mess. She looked from the dragon to Areg, then wiped some entrails from her cheek.

"I need a bath," she huffed.

2

Sunlight filtered into the cell from the narrow window near the ceiling. It was the only thing that marked the passage of time. Caden used the edge of his right shackle to scrape a line on the wall. It joined the other thirteen, and he stared at the lines in silence. It had been a fortnight since Mina had left him here to rot, but it felt much longer than that.

With the absence of Lireth in his mind, it was as though a fog had lifted. His thoughts felt like his own, and it was an odd feeling. It was almost as if he was experiencing things for the first time, yet he knew that was not true. Had Lireth taken control of his thoughts, or did he simply feel this way because of the distance that separated them?

It was impossible to tell.

The former would explain why Mina had turned against him, but it was her dragon that was evil. Wasn't he? It all made his head throb, and he pushed the thoughts aside. A guard must have brought breakfast at some point, for a wooden bowl filled with soup sat on the floor near the cell door. Caden crawled along the floor and grabbed it, lifting the bowl to his nose and sniffing its contents.

It was a sweet, earthy aroma, and he could smell hints of celery and carrots. The food was better than nothing, but he longed for eggs, fresh bread, and meat. He downed the soup and grimaced. It was cold, and the flavor was lacking. Whoever was cooking the food didn't know what they were doing.

Something *clinked* against the bars of the window, and Caden looked up. Nothing was there. He had lost Lireth already. Was he now losing his mind? A dark shape flew past the window, and a moment later, a dull thud echoed into the cell. Caden rose to his feet and stilled his breath. He could hear muffled voices on the other side of the wall, but he couldn't discern their words.

He took a couple of steps closer to the wall and froze, tilting his head to the side and listening intently.

"Give it to me, you fool. It isn't that hard."

405

Caden looked at the window again just in time to see a thin, cylindrical-shaped item come through the bars. Before he could think to move out of the way, it struck him across his right eye. He fell on his back with a gasp of pain and pressed his hand to his face. There was no blood, but it stung like fire.

He sat up and glanced around. The cylinder had rolled up against the wall. He grabbed it and held it up, wincing as a flash of pain erupted near his cheekbone. The pain lessened to a dull ache, and he ran his fingers over the smooth wood. At the top was a cap. He pulled it off and looked inside to see a rolled parchment. Sliding his finger in, he fished it out and unfurled it. There were only five words written on it:

Stand back from the wall.

Caden set the letter and container aside and massaged his face as he scooted back from the wall. Who was out there? And what did they want? A grinding noise filled the cell, and the sharp edge of a metal tool ripped through the stone wall. It cut a rough square shape, and someone on the other side pushed the stones into the cell. Daylight flooded through the opening, blinding Caden. He held his hand up to block the light and saw the outline of a figure climb through the hole in the wall.

"My lord," the figure extended a hand. "We've come to rescue you."

Caden accepted the help and looked into the reptilian face of Bast. A confusing swirl of emotions washed over him. The last time Caden had seen the draman, he tried to kill him, thinking he was a traitor. An unexplainable guilt filled his gut.

"Bast," he finally said. "I'm sorry."

"We must go before they realize you are gone."

Bast grabbed the shackle on his right hand and snapped it off, then did the same with the other. Caden rubbed his sore wrists, still confused.

"Why are you here?"

"I told you already."

"No, I know *why* you are here, but why are *you* here? I'm sure you despise me."

"I do not," Bast replied. "There was much on your shoulders. We can talk about these things later. Come."

The draman climbed back through the hole, and Caden glanced around the cell. He'd finally resigned himself to dying alone here in the dungeon, but now freedom was right in front of him. Did he deserve to be free? Lireth had saved his life and bound herself to him, yet he had failed her when she needed him most.

"My lord, please. Our mistress needs our help. She is being held captive by the Enclave."

"Our mistress," Caden repeated.

Perhaps she would show him mercy when he arrived with the draman to break her out. It was the only thing he could hope for, and it was certainly better than rotting in Lord Culver's dungeon. Caden slipped through the damaged wall and out into the fresh air. The warmth of the sun on his skin was a welcome change from the cold stones of his cell.

"Thank you," Caden said, looking from Bast to the dozen other draman who had aided in his rescue. "I failed you all, but I will do my best to restore your trust in me."

Bast waved his clawed hand. "We are all guilty of failure."

"Is this everyone?"

"No, the others are gathered in the woods where we were camped before the attack on Velbridge."

"How many?"

"Twelve hundred strong."

Relief washed over Caden. He was thankful they hadn't all died in the battle. "What of Lireth's allies? The other dragons?"

"Gone, I'm afraid. They fled when Lord D'Lance used his magic to stop her."

"And Mina, the girl, her dragon slew Lord D'Lance?"

Bast chuckled. "No. The girl did."

That gave Caden pause. Mina had killed Lord D'Lance? That meant she had … saved him. And Lireth. That was intriguing. And … unexpected.

"I see."

"We should get moving," Bast said. "We can discuss these things while we walk."

3

After Mina had thoroughly washed the grime and sand wyrm filth from herself, she walked along the corridors, the pattering of her bare feet echoing softly off the glass walls. Word had spread quickly among the dragons that she had single-handedly killed a sand wyrm. She still found it hard to believe she had succeeded.

Lost in her thoughts, she found herself standing outside the chamber that served as Lireth's prison cell. She stared through the glass, watching the dragon stalk back and forth across the cave. She was enormous, and the dragon seemed all the larger in the confined space. Her claws scraped the floor in her pacing, and the scent of saffron drifted in the air, reaching Mina's nostrils even through the cave wall. Lireth's fury had yet to abate. Although the wall was thin, it had proved to be impenetrable. The myriad of scratch marks on the other side was proof of that.

When Lireth's pacing brought her near, Mina turned away. She had watched the creature long enough. Firm steps echoed off the walls, and she saw Areg approaching.

"What doin'?"

"Nothing," she replied.

The diminutive elf still wore his leather armor and carried his sword at his waist. When she'd first met him, he'd startled her as she had never seen an elf before. His short stature and pale complexion differed from any human she'd ever met. His odd speech, the result of a horrific accident, added to his peculiar appearance. Despite all that, Mina found him to be cute in a platonic way, though she would never tell him that. He was a fierce warrior, his endearing appearance deceiving.

"Ready?"

"I need to get my boots," she replied, lifting her right foot and wiggling her toes.

"We go."

Mina nodded and walked with the elf to her chambers. She slipped her boots on and belted her sword around her waist.

"Do you think the draman will come for Lireth? I know she is too far away to speak with them, but they are still connected to her."

Areg shrugged his small shoulders. "Foolish. Dragons stronger."

"True," she said.

It had been two weeks since Lireth's imprisonment, two weeks since Caden had been locked away in Lord Culver's dungeon. Mina had thought about him every day since she'd left him there. They had been friends, and at one time, she even hoped it would blossom into more than friendship, but Lireth's bond with him had corrupted his mind and turned him against her.

She spent her days training with Areg and strengthening her bond with Gedrith. Again, she considered the inadequacy she felt, though slaying the sand wyrm had alleviated the feeling somewhat. She was the first dragon rider in a thousand years, but it was all a coincidental accident. She wasn't born a warrior, nor was she a leader. Until recently, she'd been a slave to Lord Klodian, leading him on dragon hunts so he could kill the creatures for sport.

Now, she was living among them as if her past wasn't full of blood and death. Gedrith had forgiven her, but the sins of her past still haunted her. She knew she needed to forgive herself, but she didn't know how.

She and Areg walked up the slope that led out of the underground caves and into the sunlight. The air was hotter and drier than earlier, if that were possible, and the smell of dust was overwhelming. The scenery wasn't much different from Klodian Keep, aside from the lack of human buildings. She wondered how Lord Klodian was doing, then pushed the thought from her mind. It didn't matter. *He* didn't matter.

Gedrith sunbathed while waiting for them, his massive wings outstretched. He lifted his head as they approached.

The Enclave is impressed with your victory over the sand wyrm.

Did they send you out here to tell me that?

No. I wanted to see your progress with the blade.

Mina unsheathed her sword and took a few practice swings.

I have learned many things, but I still don't think I am fit for battle.

You are too hard on yourself, Gedrith said.

I must be.

Why?

Mina inhaled a deep breath. *To atone for my sins.*

Is your name Avera now, that you have such power?

That gave her pause. *I do not fancy myself a goddess, if that's what you mean.*

Then let go of your past, for only the gods can erase history.

Mina stabbed the tip of her blade into the ground and knelt, grabbing a handful of sand. She let it sift through her fingers as she contemplated his words. Perhaps he was right. Her mistakes plagued her thoughts, but if she was the only one thinking about them, then it amounted to nothing more than self-torture. She stood and grabbed her sword, turning to face Areg.

What am I training for? she asked Gedrith. *Lord D'Lance is dead.*

Do you believe that he was the only force of evil in the world?

No.

Good, I would be worried otherwise. As a dragon rider, it is your duty to protect those who cannot defend themselves.

How is one person supposed to protect everyone else?

With help, of course. Mine, as well as the Enclave's.

Will there be more like me? More dragon riders?

Gedrith remained silent for a moment. *The Enclave has not decided on that yet. It will depend on you.*

Me? I thought I proved myself to them already.

You did, but it is not as simple as that.

What do you mean?

Focus on your training, Gedrith said.

Mina stared at him. There was something he wasn't telling her.

We are bound as one, are we not? If you expect me to trust you, then you must trust me as well.

Very well. I did not want to worry you, but I will not hide anything from you. The Enclave has been keeping an eye on things in the Dominions. Lireth's draman are slowly regrouping.

Regrouping? Are they plotting to come for her?

That remains to be seen, but it would not be wise for them to come here.

Yes, but we have already seen what madness Lireth can accomplish inside people's minds. Danger will not keep them from doing what is foolish. They need to be stopped before they do anything rash. What is the Enclave going to do about them?

As it stands, nothing, Gedrith replied. *They are not a threat to us.*

Mina wasn't so sure of that, but she didn't argue with him.

Unless something changes, you will stay here and continue learning.

And if something changes? Then what?

Then you and I will deal with it.

Mina nodded. *Very well.* She turned back to Areg. "Are you ready?"

Areg smiled. "Come on."

Mina lifted her blade and lunged forward.

4

A FLOOD OF EMOTIONS WASHED over Caden as he walked into the camp with Bast. Draman were working busily, some cooking and others moving supplies to large tents used for storage. He was glad to see so many of them had survived the battle in Velbridge. Bast led him to a pavilion that was modestly sized, though larger than most of the other tents.

"This one is yours," he said. Bast seemed to have genuinely forgiven him, but Caden couldn't help feeling guilty about his prior actions.

"I am sorry for questioning your loyalty," he said, looking at the draman. "My mind was clouded by many things."

"I do not hold any ill feelings toward you, my lord. Even if I did, our mistress has put you in charge of her forces, and I would never disobey her commands."

Caden nodded. He believed Bast, which made him again question why he thought the draman had been a traitor. An uncomfortable thought hovered at the back of his mind, but he dared not acknowledge it.

"What's left of Velbridge?" he asked.

"The fires destroyed much, and the people ransacked what remained before fleeing to safer places. We've already scoured the ruins for supplies, but there was little that was usable. What you see here is all we have."

"What of the other Dominions? Have any of the lords tried to claim the Dracan for themselves?"

"No. The High Prince sent soldiers to patrol the dominion and ensure order. We've kept hidden since they arrived."

Caden was unsurprised by the news, though he knew little about the High Prince. He suspected the man was collecting the details of what had happened, and once he discovered what Lord D'Lance had been plotting, he would probably be relieved the man was dead.

"What of the other dragons? Those who came to aid our mistress?"

Bast growled. "They fled north when the tides of battle shifted. Cowards."

"I don't disagree with that assessment, but we are going to need their help to find the Enclave. With our limited numbers, it will be impossible to find their home in The Long Sands."

"Do you want me to send some men to seek them out?"

"No," Caden replied. "I will do it."

"You've just returned to us, my lord. Is it wise for you to leave?"

Caden didn't like the idea of tracking down dragons on his own, but he felt by doing so would prove his devotion to Lireth. That, and perhaps she would be more merciful to him after she was free. He reached through the bond, but it faded into obscurity and there was nothing at the other end.

"I will return as soon as I can. In the meantime, focus on finding food and water. We'll need plenty of both if we're going to march through the desert."

"As you command," Bast said, bowing his head.

A realization dawned on Caden, and he frowned. "With Lord D'Lance dead, there will not be any new draman. We will need to find a way to strengthen our numbers."

"When the castle was destroyed, we found female draman that Lord D'Lance was keeping in the dungeon. It seems he did not limit his experiments only to the soldiers."

"What does this mean?" Caden asked.

"It is yet to be seen, but I believe we will be able to breed more of our kind in natural ways."

"I think Lireth will be happy to hear that."

"I would not want to give her false hope, my lord. As I said, it remains to be seen."

"You are right, my friend. Let us not mention it until we know for certain."

They stood in silence for a moment, and then Bast said, "It is good to have you back among us."

"It is good to be back. Thank you again for rescuing me, though I do not deserve your kindness after what I did."

"It is forgiven," Bast replied, waving a clawed hand. "Do not mention it again. It is in the past now. When will you leave?"

"Soon," Caden said. "I need something to eat, and then I will go. Lireth has been gone too long as it is, and I do not want her imprisoned any longer than is necessary."

"Until you return then, my lord." Bast bowed his head again and turned to leave.

"I told you before to call me Caden. Nothing has changed that."

"Very well. Until you return, Caden."

Bast left to attend to his duties, and Caden got some food from a group of draman who were cooking meat over a large fire. It was impossible to tell what sort of creature was on the spit, but when Caden put a piece of the meat into his mouth, he immediately recognized the taste of deer. He complimented the draman on the meal, then went to his tent.

Being back among them felt much like being home, though he supposed it truly was his home. They were all servants to Lireth, and in that shared bond, they were close. One could even say they were family, in a way. Caden's eyes roamed the camp as he considered his path forward. Searching out the other dragons was risky, especially if they flamed him before hearing him out.

For a brief moment, he almost lost his nerve, but he pushed his doubts aside. There was no sense in waiting. The quicker he returned, the quicker they could get to The Long Sands to free Lireth. It seemed an eternity since he had heard her voice or felt her presence. Something deep inside him stirred, and he wondered if she could feel him even if he couldn't feel her.

Caden turned away from his tent and went to the pavilion that served as an armory. He grabbed a chainmail shirt and pulled it over his head, then chose a sword that was sharp and well-balanced. They would do nothing against a dragon, but there was no telling what sort of trouble he might run into considering the dominion was still recovering. High Prince or not, people would resort to the darkest of deeds to ensure they could eat.

With that thought in mind, he also grabbed a short dagger and tucked it into his belt. Satisfied he was suitably armed, Caden strapped a leather satchel over his shoulder and returned to the draman who were cooking. They offered him enough rations to last a week, but he felt guilty accepting that much and refused, taking only a couple of days' worth instead.

Content he had everything he needed, he left the camp and trudged north.

5

MINA SAT ATOP A HILL, taking a break from sparring with Areg. She sipped water from a canteen and stared at the rolling dunes that stretched to the horizon. Gedrith joined her, and the two sat in silence until Mina voiced a question that had been on her mind since the battle in Velbridge.

How did I breathe fire?

Gedrith issued a deep rumble that shook the sand and sent a miniature avalanche down the hill.

When the bond is strong enough, riders and their dragons can share their senses and abilities. You needed help, and I gave you power over my flames.

Mina stood and opened her mouth. After a moment, she frowned and turned to look at Gedrith.

Nothing happened. Can I not breathe fire at will?

Yes, if I allow it.

What do you mean?

You have access to me and my power through the bond, but I must allow you to use it.

Let me use your fire, please. I want to see how it works.

Very well.

Mina turned away from the dragon and opened her mouth again. She focused on the bond and called on Gedrith's flames. Her throat grew warm, but only a small flicker of orange flew out of her mouth.

It will take time to master the ability, Gedrith said.

Then how did I do it so easily in Velbridge?

Desperation made the connection more powerful. It is difficult to recreate that urgency without genuine fear.

Some things took time. That was the way of the world, even with magic it seemed. Mina had plenty of time, as there was nothing to do but train. Unless a new enemy arose, anyway. She licked her lips and closed her mouth, then sat down in the sand and leaned back against Gedrith.

I feel out of place here, she admitted. *I'm surrounded by dragons.*

Areg is not a dragon.

I know, but he's not a human.

Do you miss being among other humans?

Yes.

Despite the way many of them are?

It sounds strange, I'm sure, but yes.

Even when Lucius was alive, I was always around other dragons. I cannot understand your desire because I have never experienced it myself, but I do not think it is wise for you to leave here.

Although she missed her own kind, Mina didn't want to leave. Not without Gedrith. He was as much a part of her as any of her limbs. She smiled as she thought back to the first time they had met. He was about to kill Lord Klodian, and she heard him speak. Much had changed since then, and some of it was for the better.

She shielded her eyes from the sun and looked down to where Areg was. The elf was still practicing his swordplay, whirling this way and that, his blade flashing under the sun with every slash. It was nice to have someone to learn from. It helped with the boredom, but it also took her mind off things, such as her loneliness.

Perhaps it would be beneficial for you to have human companionship here, Gedrith said.

The Enclave would allow that?

It will take some convincing, but I do not see why they would take issue with it, especially if it is someone open to bonding with a dragon.

Mina abruptly sat up and turned to look at Gedrith. *Another dragon rider? I thought you said the Enclave hadn't decided on that yet?*

They haven't. I do not speak for the Enclave, but they trust my wisdom. This could be an opportunity to show them it is time to rebuild the riders.

Is the world ready for that?

We shall see, Gedrith replied.

More dragon riders? Mina relished the idea of having others who could understand her struggles, but she also feared what would happen if the wrong person were to bond with a dragon. Gedrith sensed her unease.

The Enclave fears the same thing, but we must not let that keep us from the world. We are part of it despite how much we try to isolate ourselves.

The two were silent for a moment, and Mina wondered if the Enclave would agree to have another human here. She didn't think so, but it wouldn't hurt to ask. The question was, who would she want to come here? The obvious answer was Caden, but she pushed the thought from her mind. Having spent most of her life as a slave, she didn't have any friends. The only person she had ever slightly trusted was …

Thais wouldn't come here, would she? Mina hadn't thought about her since she'd left Klodian Keep. With Lord D'Lance dead, had her parents gained their freedom?

Do you have someone in mind?

Gedrith's question broke her reverie.

I may have someone. Her name is Thais. She's a soldier, but I don't know if she would want to come here.

Is there no one else?

No. She didn't hesitate with her answer. *She would make a good dragon rider. She's strong and smart.*

Gedrith hummed in thought. *Very well. I will speak to the Enclave. I cannot guarantee anything, but perhaps they will allow it.*

Mina stood and stretched, ready to continue sparring with Areg. She laid a hand on Gedrith's snout, feeling the rough texture of his scales against her skin.

Thank you. Will you keep the connection to your flames open for me? I want to practice breathing fire.

Yes, but take heed. Until you have learned to control the fire, you risk hurting yourself or others. Do it in the open when no one is around.

I will.

Mina turned and walked down the dune, returning to where Areg was. The elf raised his sword and shouted, "Ready more?"

She lifted her own sword in response, and the two clashed blades again. Gedrith's shadow passed over them as he left, and Mina hoped she would soon have another human around.

6

AFTER TWO DAYS OF WALKING through woods and crossing over small rivers, the landscape subtly changed to flat plains. The tall grass swayed under a gentle breeze, but the wind did little to ease Caden's discomfort. There were no clouds in the sky, and the heat was unbearable despite the sun slowly creeping below the horizon. The occasional groupings of boulders cast long shadows that stretched along the field.

His feet ached from the effort, and his throat was dry. Droplets of sweat dripped down his face, and his stomach growled with hunger. He'd been strict with his rationing, perhaps too strict. He pushed on, driven by the thought of Lireth's captivity. Occasionally, he scanned the landscape, shielding his eyes against the sun's fading light with his right hand.

There was no sign of the dragons, but he spotted a glimmer that could be water. Caden changed direction, angling his steps northeast. A few minutes later, he saw the glimmer was indeed water, and he collapsed on his knees at the edge of the pool. Reaching his hands into the water, he splashed some onto his face, wiping the sweat and grime away.

It was a welcome relief, but he was starting to worry that he wasn't going in the right direction. He should have seen something by now. After drinking his fill, he replenished his leather waterskin with as much water as it would hold and stood, ready to continue his trek. A rustling among the reeds gave him pause, and he drew his sword. A small fox emerged. It regarded him with curiosity for a moment before scampering off.

Caden sheathed his blade and couldn't help smiling. The animal didn't count much for company, but its brief presence was a break from the monotony. He pulled some dried meat from his bag and devoured it, then continued his trek.

He walked until the stars were the only light in the sky before stopping to make camp. It took a lot of effort to keep his eyes open, and he fell asleep almost as soon as he lay down. When he opened his eyes, he was aware that he wasn't alone. A fire burned a few feet away, the flames banishing the cool night air.

Not daring to move, he tried to see who was tending the fire, but the figure was just out of his line of sight.

"I know you are awake," a soft voice said.

Caden sat up and rested his right hand on the hilt of his sword.

"Who are you?" he asked, his voice gruff from sleep.

The figure turned toward him, and the firelight revealed it was a woman. She was tall and lithe, with long dark hair and eyes that seemed to pull the light from the fire. She wore a simple tunic and pants, and a bow was slung across her back.

"I am the guardian of these lands," she said. "It has been a long time since I've seen another human out here."

"What do you want?" Caden tightened his grip on the hilt. Was she a ghost or something worse?

"I want nothing."

"Then why are you here?"

"Curiosity, I suppose. I saw you marching across the plains and decided to keep an eye on you. This area is inhospitable at best, and you looked like you could use some help."

Caden relaxed the grip on the hilt but kept his hand in place. He studied the woman for a moment, trying to gauge the truth of her intentions.

"I appreciate the offer, but I can take care of myself."

"What are you doing out here alone? Civilization is that way." She nodded back the way he'd come.

"I'm looking for something," Caden said vaguely.

"Care to share what that is? I may be able to point you in the right direction. I know these lands better than anyone."

Caden hesitated. He knew nothing about this woman, but she seemed genuine. He was getting nowhere on his own. If she turned out to be a threat, he would handle it.

"I'm searching for a group of dragons," he answered. "They would have passed this way about two weeks ago."

"I've seen them. They've taken up shelter in the mountains there." She pointed in the distance behind her. They were nothing more than a clump of shadows in the darkness, but Caden nodded. At least he had a clear direction now.

"I can lead you there, but it won't be easy."

"I don't need a guide," he said.

"You may not think so, but if I let you wander there on your own, you won't make it back."

Caden highly doubted that, but if she truly knew the area, then perhaps he should trust her enough to listen.

"Very well. Lead the way."

"First, we eat. I've got some rabbit left from my earlier catch. Then you need to rest. We'll leave at first light."

Caden was impatient to get moving, but he nodded and accepted a skewer from the woman.

"I'm Caden," he said.

"You can call me Eira."

They ate in silence for a moment, and then Eira began advising him of the dangers in the area. A band of soldiers from the Dracan Dominion had fled and set up camp at the base of the mountains. In desperation, they had turned to worshipping the dragons, offering things like gold and other humans in exchange for their lives.

Caden's stomach twisted at the thought. Instead of staying to ensure the safety of the commoners in the aftermath of the battle, they had fled like cowards and were offering their fellows to the dragons.

Despite his mistrust, he was glad to have someone to talk with. Something skittered in the darkness, and he snapped his gaze toward the sound.

"That's just Rem," Eira said.

Before Caden could ask who that was, the same fox he'd seen at the water pool earlier came trotting into view.

"Is that your pet?"

The fox stopped and glared at Caden, baring its teeth.

"Rem is no one's pet. He's my companion."

Caden rose his left brow in curiosity but said nothing. The fox curled up beside Eira and watched the wavering flames of the fire.

"Get some sleep," Eira told him. "I'll keep watch."

"Wake me when it's my turn."

"There's no need. I'll be fine."

"Suit yourself," Caden replied. He laid down and eventually drifted back to sleep. When he awoke, it was still dark. He could see Eira's faint silhouette against the sky. She was sitting cross-legged in front of the fire. He was glad she hadn't merely been a dream.

"How long have I been asleep?" he asked, rubbing crud from his eyes as he got to his feet.

"Not long," Eira replied. "Just a few hours. Dawn is approaching."

Caden stretched and rubbed a sore spot on his neck. Sleeping on the ground wasn't very comfortable.

"I'm ready when you are."

Eira stood and brushed her pants off. She clicked her tongue, and Rem sprinted off toward the mountains. Caden looked at her questioningly, and she smiled.

"He's going to scout the way ahead."

Caden couldn't shake the feeling that there was something more to the fox. He had heard legends of people who could shapeshift into animals and wondered if Rem was truly a sorcerer in disguise.

"Come on," Eira said, interrupting his thoughts. "We've got a few hours before we reach the base."

Caden shrugged the thought away. As long as the two of them could lead him to the dragons, he didn't care what they were. Eira headed for the mountains, and he followed after her.

7

MINA SAW LITTLE OF GEDRITH over the next few days, though she felt his constant presence through the bond. Her training was going well, but she tired of the same drills. She was also impatient to know the Enclave's answer.

She put on her armor and strapped her sword around her waist, then headed aboveground. It was early, and Areg had yet to rise. The sun was only a sliver on the horizon, but the sky was filled with colors that made her stop and pause to admire them. The temperature was cool and refreshing, but it wouldn't last. The Long Sands was an unforgiving place, full of heat, sand, and creatures that wanted to kill her.

Mina scanned the rest of the sky and saw a few dragons gliding upon the air currents. They were keeping watch for enemies. Despite no sand wyrm ever getting near the cave system, the dragons remained vigilant. She turned away and strode up the nearest dune. As she reached the top, a lizard darted away, startled by her presence.

She watched the creature until it was no longer visible, contemplating how it feared her while dragons feared nothing. The species were two heads of the same coin, at least in her estimation. Inhaling a deep breath, she closed her eyes and focused on the bond. She sensed Gedrith's fire and coaxed it through the bond until her throat grew warm. Parting her lips, she urged the fire forth.

Nothing happened.

She bid it a second time, and a third, all to no avail. Frustration turned to rage, and she clenched her hands into fists and screamed. The warmth in her throat faded, and she opened her eyes. Gedrith had told her it would take time to master the ability, but she didn't care. She wanted to do it *now,* not later.

You sound like a petulant child.

The voice startled her, and she opened her eyes to see the silver dragon who led the Enclave. How had she arrived without notice? Mina dropped to one knee and bowed her head.

Tiarna, she greeted.

The dragon regarded her in silence for a moment, and Mina wasn't sure if she should move or stay as she was.

Rise.

Mina lifted her head and slowly stood. *How can I be of service?*

Do you believe you are fit to be a dragon rider?

No.

Why not?

Mina paused. *I am not a warrior.*

The ways of war can be taught.

My past is filled with the blood of dragons.

We have forgiven you of those deeds.

Mina remained silent, not sure what else she could say.

The dragon looked out across the landscape. *It seems you struggle with the power you hold.*

Mina felt a pang of guilt wash over her. She was struggling, to the point that even the Enclave had noticed. How could she explain the turmoil inside her? She had lived a life of servitude, where her will was not her own. The bond with Gedrith had given her a newfound sense of power and freedom, but with those also came fear. The fear of losing it all and becoming a slave again.

I can sense your emotions. They are like chaos, swirling around one another, feeding the fear that makes you doubt yourself. You are the first human to speak with dragons in centuries, the first to bond with our kind since the Severance. You believe it happened by chance, but I do not. Whether you or I know the purpose, there is a reason you fell into that cave and landed on dragon scales.

Mina wanted to disagree, but she dared not interrupt the dragon. She cast her eyes to the ground, feeling as though she were being reprimanded like a child. And in a way, she was being scolded, but the dragon's words were a refining fire, burning away Mina's many excuses and revealing the strength underneath it all.

You are no longer a slave, Mina. Those days are behind you. You are a dragon rider. Remove your doubts and be confident.

Thank you, Tiarna. Your kind words have helped me more than you know.

Good.

The two were silent for a moment, both staring out at the rolling hills of sand. Mina cleared her throat and looked at the dragon from her periphery.

Did Gedrith ... ask anything of the Enclave?

He did.

Mina waited impatiently, anxiously curling and uncurling her toes. There was sand in her boots, and the grit rubbed the skin between the cracks of her toes.

Has the Enclave decided?

The dragon looked at her, meeting her gaze. *We have decided we will not allow another human into our domain.*

I understand. She tried her best to hide her disappointment, but it must have been evident on her face.

Take heart. It is not for the reasons you likely think. We are not cruel, nor do we seek to be. The world is hardly ready for the return of dragons, much less dragon riders. That endeavor will take time.

Everything takes time, Mina complained.

It is the way of the world, as you know. A babe does not come into the world fully formed.

How will people come to accept dragons if you do not show yourself to them?

That is something the Enclave has considered. I believe the answer lies with you.

Me? What do you mean?

It will take years of training with Areg for you to be ready to go into the world, but if we want to ensure another Lord D'Lance does not arise, we cannot wait that long. We have decided that you and Gedrith will be sent out to patrol the dominions and provide aid where you can. As people come to see your deeds, you will gain their trust. That is the first of many steps that will allow us to return without meeting violence and confusion.

Mina repeated the words in her mind, surprised to hear them. *You think I am ready for that?*

Are you not?

Pushing her doubts and fears aside, she bowed her head. *I am. Thank you for putting your trust in me. I will do my best to prepare the world for the truth about dragons.*

I trust you will. There is another matter you must know, as it is something you will need to deal with.

What is it?

The one bound to Lireth escaped his prison.

Caden. Mina's heart leaped in her chest. *How?* she asked.

It was the draman. They've been regrouping since the battle at Velbridge, and now they have their leader back.

They're going to come for her, Mina said, a statement more than a question. She looked over her shoulder at the cave entrance.

So long as their bond exists, nothing will stop him from seeking her.

Mina knew what needed to be done. She'd always known whether she wanted to admit it to herself or not.

I will take care of it.

Be wary. Lireth's corruption knows no limits, and he will do whatever he must to eliminate obstacles in his path. The person you once knew is gone.

Yes, Tiarna. When do you want us to leave?

I will give you three days to prepare. Take anything you need.

Thank you. Mina knelt and bowed her head. *Tiarna.*

You have earned the right to call me by name. It is Silvara.

With that, Silvara stretched her wings and leaped into the air, returning to the cave. Mina remained where she was, her thoughts a whirlwind. She should have felt more honored to be given the right to call Silvara by her name, but she was too troubled by the other news.

Caden had escaped.

8

EIRA LED THE WAY ACROSS the plains, and as they reached the foothills of the mountains, the grass faded to more rocky terrain. The air was dusty, and Caden fought the impulse to frequently drink from his waterskin, knowing he needed to conserve his meager supply.

"Do you see the cave there?"

Caden squinted up at the mountain, trying to make out the details.

"That's where the dragons are," Eira said grimly. "We'll have to climb up there to get to them."

"We?"

"You didn't plan on going up there alone, did you? Aside from the climb, you'll also have to deal with the rogue soldiers. And, of course, the dragons themselves."

"I'll be fine," Caden said, though he wondered if the dragons were as loyal to Lireth as he was. If not, he probably wouldn't get far before they flamed him. As he considered it further, he decided to let the woman come with him. At the very worst, he could use her as a diversion to escape. "But you can come if you'd like."

"I don't have anything else to do out here, so why not?" She grinned at him.

"Aren't you afraid of the dragons?"

Eira shrugged. "I'm afraid of many things, but fear is nothing more than an emotion that needs to be controlled. Do you need to rest before we start?"

Caden was tired, but he didn't want to waste time. He shook his head and steeled himself for the climb, reminding himself that Lireth was likely in more dire conditions. They began their ascent. The rocks were jagged and unforgiving, and one misstep could mean a deadly fall. Caden struggled clumsily, but Eira's steps were sure and steady. He strove to keep up with her swift pace, refusing to fall behind.

"You're quite skilled at this," he huffed, baffled at how she seemed to glide up the mountain.

"I'm used to it," she called back, not even winded.

Finally, they reached a plateau just below the cave entrance. Eira put a dust-covered finger to her lips and motioned with her other hand. Voices drifted in the air, and Caden pressed his back against the mountain, glad for a break. His muscles ached, and he was parched. He drank sparingly from the waterskin, consuming just enough to rid the dust from his throat. He offered the skin to Eira, but she shook her head.

Rem skittered onto the ledge, and Eira knelt and scratched his head. She leaned in close and whispered something to the fox that Caden didn't hear, and the creature scrambled up to the ledge where the cave was. They waited in silence, and Caden stared at the vast plains that stretched out into the distance. He could see the pool of water he'd come across the day before and wished it were closer. He wanted nothing more than to dunk himself beneath its cool surface.

The fox returned, leaping down onto the plateau. It barked and yipped excitedly. Eira shushed him and scratched his head again, then looked at Caden and whispered, "Rem says there are six men up there, all of them armed. The dragons are sleeping."

Caden stared at Eira for a moment, trying to comprehend what she said. "That thing can talk?"

"All animals can talk. It's a matter of whether you're listening."

Again, he suspected magic was involved with these two, but that would be useful if things went badly with the soldiers. He shrugged in reply and started to climb up to the next ledge. Eira grabbed his leg and pulled him back down.

"We can't just rush in there," she said. "There may be traps."

"What do you propose?"

Eira smiled. "An ambush. We'll wait until they come out of the cave and catch them off guard."

Caden decided that was a better idea than trying to fight them in the darkness of the cavern. And if the dragons heard the sound of fighting, he may not have the opportunity to explain why he was there before they joined the fray.

"We'll need to give them a reason to come out here," he said.

"Rem can manage that, can't you, Rem?"

The fox chittered and brushed up against Eira, much like a dog.

"I take it he said yes?"

"And just a moment ago, you didn't think animals could speak. You're a quick learner."

Caden snorted and shook his head. "I'd rather be up there when they come out. Maybe we can hide among the rocks."

"Good idea."

They climbed up onto the ledge, and Caden hid behind a cluster of rocks on the left. Eira sprinted across the rock shelf and climbed up the face of the mountain to the right of the cave, taking a position above the entrance. She unslung her bow and nocked an arrow. Caden unsheathed his sword and tilted his neck to either side until it popped, then loosened his shoulders. He gave Eira a nod, and Rem ran into the cave.

Caden held his breath and waited. A commotion echoed out of the cave, and Rem sprinted into view, leaping over the ledge and disappearing. Caden adjusted his grip on the hilt of his sword as a tall brute of a man stepped out, carrying a large ax. Before Caden could engage him, Eira fired her arrow, striking the man in the back. His chest thrust forward from the momentum, and he staggered a few steps before tripping. He fell over the ledge, crashing to the plateau below. All went still, and for a moment, Caden thought the other soldiers weren't coming.

"Jon! Where'd ye go?"

A second soldier, this one shorter than the first, strode out of the cave, looking left and right. Caden looked at Eira, who nodded at him, signaling this one was his. He stepped out from behind the boulders and rushed the man, his sword flashing in the sunlight.

The man barely had time to draw his sword, but he brought it up in time to block Caden's strike. The clang of their steel echoed off the mountainside, and the alarmed shouts of the other soldiers joined the cacophony.

Caden feinted left and struck right, but the soldier parried the blow. He followed up with a kick to the knee, and the soldier stumbled. Seizing the opportunity, Caden aimed for the thin line between the man's armor and plunged his sword into the soldier's chest. The remaining soldiers emerged from the cave, temporarily startled by the scene.

An arrow struck one of them in the head, splattering the others with blood. Before Caden could engage another foe, Eira dispatched the rest of them with deadly accuracy, her arrows *whizzing* as they sailed through the air. With the thrill of battle ended, Caden wiped his sword on one of the bodies and sheathed it, then looked at the faces of the men. They wore Lord D'Lance's emblem, but they weren't Runesmen.

"That was easy enough," Eira said, joining him. "Look at their eyes, though. They look …"

"Sick?" Caden offered. "I thought so, too. At first, I thought it was the look of madness, but this is something else."

Caden looked at the cave entrance with renewed concern.

9

SINCE SHE WAS LEAVING SOON, Areg gave Mina the day off from training. He helped her pack supplies for the journey, and afterward, gifted her with a thick traveling cloak. She tried to refuse, but the elf wouldn't budge on the matter.

With nothing else to take up her time, she wandered to the chamber that held Lireth. The dragon wasn't pacing this time. Instead, she was curled up on the floor. Mina peered through the glass wall and the two locked eyes.

The smell of rose and orchid filled the air, and Mina knew beyond any doubt that Lireth was well aware of what was happening beyond her prison.

"You know they are coming for you, don't you?" she whispered to herself.

This place will burn, Lireth said, invading Mina's mind. She gasped in surprise and pushed the dragon away, forcing a mental wall up. Lireth rumbled heartily, then glowered as Gedrith sped through the hall to Mina's side.

Your draman will never make it through the desert, Gedrith replied, allowing Mina to hear his response. *And if they do, we will crush them like ants.*

We shall see, Lireth growled.

Indeed, we shall.

The two dragons glared at each other for a moment before Lireth turned her back to the cave wall.

Come with me, Gedrith told Mina.

He led her through the tunnels until they came to an area Mina had not seen before. Unlike the rest of the place, this chamber wasn't illuminated brightly. Gedrith paused at the threshold to swivel his head in her direction.

I can see well enough, she said.

He stepped into the cavern and Mina followed, her eyes slowly adjusting to the gloom. Once they did, she stiffened in astonishment. A literal hill of coins rose from the ground. Gold, silver, bronze … Mina guessed the value of it all was enough to rival even the High Price's wealth.

Take what you need for our journey.

Where did all this come from?

All across the dominions.

Mina had seen the spoils of Lord Klodian's hunts before, but this was hard to wrap her mind around.

There's something I've always been curious about. Why do dragons hoard money?

It has no value to us, Gedrith said. *Not in the ways it does to humans. We have it for more practical reasons.*

What do you mean?

When we are still in our eggs, our scales have no color. We are translucent by nature. These coins are mined from minerals within the earth, and those minerals give us our color. The larger the hoard, the more powerful a dragon is when it hatches.

Mina frowned. *I don't understand. There are all different coins here. How would a dragon's scales only be one color?*

Gedrith chuckled. *We are naturally drawn to one specific mineral. Though there may be different metals present, only the one we are attuned to affects our color. It is a mystery we ourselves have yet to unravel.*

What about the other dragons? The chromatic ones like Lireth?

They are drawn to gemstones instead of metals. Lireth was probably partial to onyx or obsidian.

Do only females hoard treasure?

No. Males will also do so when they are ready for a mate.

What metal gave you your color?

Copper, Gedrith replied. It was the same name he had given her when they first met. She found that funny.

Mina walked to the pile of coins and grabbed a handful. She held them up for inspection. Various inscriptions were on all of them. She recognized a few from the Thophate Dominion, and one from the Dracan, but the others were foreign to her. The coins clinked as she put them into her coin purse.

Is that enough?

More than enough, she replied, casting a look around the cavern. *Are there eggs in here?*

There are.

Gedrith drew near and used a claw to gently move some coins aside, uncovering an enormous egg. It was very different from the one she had taken from Lord Klodian.

Can I touch it?

Gedrith was silent for a moment, and she thought he would refuse. Finally, he lowered his head and nudged it out of the coins. Mina reached out and laid a hand on the egg. A steady pulse beat against the shell, and her eyes widened. She was amazed and humbled all at once, and tears stung her eyes.

This is amazing, she said. She ran her hand along the shell, feeling the many grooves and their hard texture. *How long before a dragon hatches?*

That depends on the dragon. Every hatchling is different.

Mina couldn't help but feel a sense of awe as she gazed upon the egg. She wondered what kind of dragon would emerge and what its fate would be. Would it be like Lireth, evil and imprisoned for eternity? Or would it be noble like Gedrith, free to roam the skies?

We should leave now, Gedrith said. *The eggs should remain undisturbed.*

Mina nodded and reluctantly removed her hand from the egg. She watched as Gedrith nestled it back into place, then scooped up a claw full of coins and reburied it.

Are dragons born already knowing their purpose in life, or do they have to discover it like humans? And is their purpose a matter of choice, or are they bound by fate?

Gedrith laughed softly, the sound echoing off the cave walls. *We are born with an innate knowledge of some things, but our fates are our own to decide.*

What about being bound to me? That wasn't a choice on your end. It was more a coincidence than anything. It's possible that could be the workings of fate, couldn't it?

Gedrith remained silent for a moment. *Perhaps. You have given me something to consider. Come.*

She followed him out of the cave and parted ways with him, returning to her chamber. Everything she planned on taking was packed aside from the cloak Areg had given her, and she rolled it up and set it next to her pack. A faint rustling sound caught her attention, and she turned to see the elf standing near the entryway.

"It nice. Know you."

"The honor is mine," Mina replied. "You've taught me so much. I'm indcbtcd to you."

"No debt. Do good. That repay."

"I will do my best."

Mina approached him and knelt, becoming eye level with the elf. "You are a great warrior," she said. "I hope I do not offend you, but may I give you a hug?"

A grin spread across Areg's lips and he wrapped his arms around her, squeezing her tightly. He was stronger than he looked, and she returned the embrace.

"Thank you for everything."

"No leave. Eat first."

"Eat?"

"Feast. Enclave give honor."

"To who?

"You."

10

"CAN DRAGONS CONTROL PEOPLE? THAT doesn't seem possible. They're just wild animals."

Caden considered sparing her the harsh reality, but he decided it wouldn't do her any good to believe that. They would eventually part ways, and after Lireth destroyed the Enclave, all of humanity might be her next target. It was better to give her a chance at survival. At least, that's what his conscience told him.

"Dragons are far more than wild animals. Unlike your fox friend here, they can do much more than speak."

Eira's face scrunched in confusion. "What do you mean?"

"It's too much to explain, but they are sentient creatures, more powerful than we know."

"So they *can* control people?"

Caden thought about his bond with Lireth. Had she taken over his will and controlled him? He didn't think so, but …

"That may be possible," he said. "I don't know for certain."

"Then we must kill them."

"No."

"Why not?"

"It would take a Dominion Lord with the power of many Runesmen to kill a single dragon. I'm certain there is more than one in there, and even if we could kill them, I don't want to. I need their help."

Eira stared at him curiously, waiting for an explanation.

"It's a complicated story, and one I do not care to tell. We can part ways now if you'd like. I understand if you don't want to involve yourself." Caden looked at the dead soldiers. "I appreciate your help with this lot either way."

"I have many questions, but I know when it is best not to pry." She paused. "I will see this task through with you, if for nothing else than to satisfy my curiosity."

Caden chuckled. "Very well. If things don't go as planned, flee. I don't need a hero trying to save my skin."

Eira bowed her head, but she said nothing. Caden didn't force the matter. If she wanted to face certain death, it was her choice. Sheathing his sword, Caden wiped the sweat that had collected on his forehead with the back of his hand and stepped into the cave.

The air was cool and damp, a welcome reprieve from the growing heat outside. He stepped lightly, careful not to kick any loose rocks. Eira was as stealthy as Rem, and he had to glance over his shoulder to make sure she was following him.

The darkness became all-consuming, and Caden had to feel along the wall to know where he was going. Eira tapped him on the shoulder, halting his steps.

"Rem can guide us," she whispered.

"Please," he replied, glad for the help. Walking blind was likely to get them killed, especially if they unknowingly stumbled into the dragons. He felt the fox brush against his leg as it took the lead, but he realized they still had the same problem. Rem could see in the dark, but they couldn't.

As if answering his unspoken concern, a faint green light illuminated the tunnel. Rem looked back, and Caden saw the light shining from the fox's eyes. His heart thumped in his chest at the eerie spectacle, but Rem turned his gaze ahead and trotted onward silently.

There was no denying the fox was a magical creature now. He was glad to have them as allies. The tunnel stretched for a few hundred feet before sloping downward and opening into a massive chamber. Rem's eyes abruptly stopped glowing, and before Caden could question why, he heard a hissing noise that echoed off the cavern walls.

Instinctively, his hand went to the hilt of his sword, but he knew it was foolish. The blade was useless against such creatures. He took a single step, and the sound stopped. He clenched his jaw, preparing for the worst.

I can smell you, a voice penetrated his mind. It overwhelmed his senses, nowhere near as controlled as Lireth's voice.

Then you must recognize my scent.

There was only silence, so he continued.

I am here on behalf of Lireth. The Enclave took her captive, and I seek your help in freeing her.

He heard multiple forms moving around in the darkness, and he fought the urge to turn and run.

If Lireth was weak enough to be captured, then she deserves her fate with the Enclave. Be gone, human, before I make you nothing more than a pile of ash.

Caden was afraid they might refuse. He needed to instill the level of fear that Lireth did, but how was he to do that when he wasn't a threat to them? Something tickled the edge of his senses. It was faint, so he knew it wasn't the dragon. Closing his eyes, he reached out with his mind. Like a bolt of lightning, he felt Lireth's presence invade his being.

"Fools!" she hissed through his mouth. "You will come to The Long Sands with my army, or you shall know my wrath!"

Just as quickly as she had come, she was gone. Caden dropped to his knees, overcome with weakness. The runes on his neck burned, and he reached back, rubbing at them feebly with his right hand. He tried to connect to her through the bond, but just as before, there was nothing but an empty abyss at the other end. Although he couldn't sense her, she knew what was happening around him.

Eira tucked her hand under his armpit and helped him back to his feet. The weakness faded, and the trembling left his knees. Taking a deep breath, he spoke aloud.

"You have heard the command of our master. Decide for yourself what you will do. You can find us in the same place we were before the battle at Velbridge, but it would not be wise to be seen. The High Prince has his men patrolling the area, and we don't need more problems than we already have. Meet us at the edge of the Dracan Dominion and be prepared to fight. The Enclave will not give Lireth up willingly."

Caden waited a moment to see if the dragons would respond, but they said nothing.

"Take us out of here," he said to Rem, hoping the fox would do as he asked. The green glow from the creature's eyes flooded the cavern, and Caden saw three black dragons staring at him. Rem scurried down the tunnel, and the darkness returned. Satisfied he had done all he could, Caden turned and followed Rem and Eira back out to the ledge.

They emerged from the cave, and Caden blinked against the sunlight. Eira stood at his side, but he found it impossible to read her expression. Rem watched him curiously, his head cocked to one side.

"I guess this is where we part ways," he said, looking out across the landscape. It was a long walk to the camp, and despite his exhaustion, he was eager to head back.

"I'm not sure what transpired back there, but I'm too invested to leave now. I'm coming with you. If you'll have me, that is."

Rem yipped, and Eira smiled. "If you'll have *us*."

"It will be dangerous," he warned.

"I've never been one to back down from a challenge."

"You will see things that have no explanation … odd things."

"Good. We should get going if we want to make good progress before making camp."

Caden watched Eira climb down the ledge. She remained a mystery for now, but all things would be revealed in time. He started down the mountain, determination guiding his steps.

Lireth was still with him, even if he couldn't feel her presence.

11

THE NEXT DAY, MINA WAS slow to rise. She'd eaten too much and was tired from having stayed up so late. Though dragons didn't consume alcohol, they could certainly host a grand affair. She groaned as she slipped on her boots. Wiping the sleep from her eyes, she noticed Areg was waiting near the entryway of her chamber.

"Sleep long," he said, a grin pulling at his lips.

"How are you so happy in the morning?"

The elf shrugged. "Natural."

Mina wished she had as much energy as he did. She stifled a yawn and belted on her sword, then grabbed her pack from beside her bed. Casting a glance around the room, she decided she was ready. While she was excited to be back among humans, she was nervous. What if the world didn't accept dragons as they once did?

You're awake, Gedrith's voice interrupted her thoughts. *Good. Come up here. We need to go.*

Mina sensed something pressing behind his words. *Sand wyrm?*

I'll explain on the way.

"What's going on out there?" she asked Areg.

"Draman march."

Mina hurried past the elf and rushed through the tunnels. Gedrith was waiting for her at the top of the sloped entrance. The sun was already high in the sky, and she blinked against the brightness. She strapped her pack across her shoulder and climbed onto his back. Before she could say anything, Gedrith leaped into the air. He flapped his mighty wings, rising higher and higher, then turned west.

Areg said the draman are marching. Are they coming this way? Mina asked.

We are not sure, but it would be foolish not to assume as much.

How close are they?

A few days away. Their progress is slow, but they are traveling east. We must stop them before they enter the desert.

Are more dragons coming to help?

No.

How will we stop them on our own?

We must remove the one that guides them. With him gone, the draman should lose the desire to free Lireth.

Caden. The image of him chained to the wall in Lord Culver's dungeon was seared into her mind's eye. She hadn't expected him to escape, but she also hadn't counted on the draman to regroup. Imprisoning him again wasn't the answer. She knew that, though she didn't want to admit it. He would have to die. That was the only way to sever his bond with Lireth. She steeled her heart, knowing if Gedrith didn't kill him with fire, she would have to do it with her blade. Mina's stomach churned with unease. She didn't want to kill him, but she knew it was necessary.

As they flew, she looked down at the landscape. They passed over blue rivers and green forests, but her mind was elsewhere. She was thinking of Caden, of the friendship he had offered her when they first met. He'd willingly put himself in harm's way to defend her from Thais. Mina smiled at the memory, temporarily forgetting what was to come.

As the distance passed, Mina's exhaustion grew. She laid against Gedrith's neck and closed her eyes, thinking only to rest them a moment. Darkness overtook her, but she jolted awake when she experienced the sensation of falling. She was relieved to find she was still safely on Gedrith's back, though the scenery below had changed.

Where are we? she asked.

We are approaching the Dracan Dominion.

Already?

You've been asleep for a while now.

Mina sat up and stretched her neck, feeling a kink in it. The wind whipped her hair about, and she pushed the strands aside and stared down at the ground. They were flying over farmland, and the tracts of various colors stood out among the surrounding landscape. She didn't see any signs of the draman, however.

Do you know where they are?

They should be in the woods outside Velbridge.

Gedrith sped up, and the wind buffeted Mina. She held on tightly to Gedrith's neck scales and kept her head down to protect her eyes. She remained in that position until he slowed his pace, then lifted her head to see where they were.

The ruined city of Velbridge stretched out below them. It was a sight both awe-inspiring and heart-wrenching. The once great city was now a shadow of its former glory. The buildings were empty shells, crumbled and charred, while the streets were littered with debris and ash. There was no sign of movement, and Mina knew the living had abandoned the place.

The fires must have burned the entire city down, she said. *Where did all the people go? This was the home of thousands.*

They are scattered to the wind, I am sure. There is no sense in staying in a place like this.

Gedrith landed near the center of the city, and Mina climbed down his shoulder to stand amid the rubble. Nothing was recognizable. She couldn't even pinpoint where she had killed Lord D'Lance.

I smell them, Gedrith rumbled.

Mina scanned the rubble, but there was no movement nor any sign of life.

Let's search them out, Mina said.

The two crossed over mounds of rubble, traveling east toward the forest. Ash covered everything, and by the time they reached the scorched wall, Mina's boots were stained black with soot. She stepped through a ruined entryway, the gate completely missing. Even the hinges were gone. Gedrith leaped over the wall, his trail smacking the upper stones. A few of them fell, clattering to the ground.

They trudged across a short, barren field and entered the forest. The outer edge of trees was dead, their leaves gone and their trunks blackened. Mina couldn't believe how far the devastation stretched, but as they moved deeper into the forest, signs of life returned.

The smell of burning wood reached Mina's nostrils, and she drew her sword. She turned to Gedrith and motioned for him to stay where he was. The trees ahead were thicker, and he would have trouble getting through without making too much noise.

I'll scout ahead, she told him.

Gedrith remained silent, and she stalked onward as quietly as she could manage. Voices drifted in the air, and she peered through the brush and saw a clearing. A group of draman was gathered around a campfire. A short distance away from them was another group, and another. Mina's eyes darted from one to the next, quickly realizing there were dozens of the creatures, if not hundreds.

There are many draman here.

Do not concern yourself with them. Look for the human that leads them.

Mina scanned the encampment, but she didn't see Caden anywhere. She crept closer, squinting at the groups further away. Perhaps the only good thing about there being so many draman was there would be no mistaking Caden among them. The draman near the campfire were talking, but she couldn't make out what they were saying. She inched toward the clearing, her heart pounding wildly.

The splintering sound of a twig breaking under her boot made her halt in place. She swallowed hard and waited. The draman didn't seem to notice the noise. She exhaled in relief and took one step before something heavy slammed into her from behind, sending her sprawling to the ground. Leaves and grit smothered her face, and Mina quickly scrambled to her feet, searching for her sword.

A draman towered over her, his scales glistening as if polished. The creature bared its fangs at her, and she snatched up her blade and took a step back. She brought the sword up and took a defensive stance, but she knew she was in trouble. The scores of draman behind her were quickly approaching, but she dared not risk a glance over her shoulder.

The ground trembled, sending vibrations up her calves. The draman who'd knocked her over looked around, his reptilian face wrinkling in what she assumed was confusion. Gedrith burst through the trees, his massive claw crushing the draman with hardly any effort.

Sorry, she said, whirling around to face the oncoming hoard. *I didn't see that one.*

Gedrith issued a deafening roar and stormed ahead. Tightening her grip on the hilt of her blade, Mina ran after him.

12

THE JOURNEY BACK TO THE camp took less time than Caden's foray into the wilderness, mainly because Eira took the lead. She knew the landscape better than he did, and Caden realized he'd originally taken a much longer route. They'd arrived late in the night, and to his surprise, she didn't seem taken aback by the presence of the draman. Bast gave her a tent, which she shared with Rem, and Caden tiredly collapsed in his own pavilion.

He slept without dreaming, and when he opened his eyes, he realized something had awakened him. The clash of steel, cries of pain, and the roar of a dragon. Caden sprang up from his bedroll and hurriedly put his boots and armor on, then scrambled out of his tent, looking to the sky.

It was difficult to see anything beyond the canopy of the forest, but there didn't seem to be any dragons overhead. Several draman rushed past him, heading toward the ruins of Velbridge.

"What's going on?" he shouted.

"We're under attack!"

Caden cursed and followed them, drawing his sword. As he drew nearer to the battle, he spotted an enormous red dragon. Why was a dragon attacking them? Was it rebelling against Lireth's command to aid her army?

And then he saw a human, a woman, clashing swords with a draman. Her blonde hair whipped about as she spun and twisted. His heart skipped a beat.

It was Mina.

A surge of conflicting emotions overtook him. Part of him was relieved to see she was alive and well, and the other part… well, he wanted to make her pay for leaving him to rot in a dungeon. He watched her fight, impressed with her sword skill. She'd clearly been training.

Mina parried the draman's strike, forcing his blade out wide, then stepped forward and rammed the hilt of her blade into the draman's snout. The creature stumbled back from the blow but didn't cry out in pain. Draman were made of tougher stuff than humans, a fact Caden continued to admire.

He continued to watch her for a moment longer, then shouted her name. All eyes turned to him, including hers. She briefly stiffened, but it was long enough that he noticed the reaction. Was it surprise … or fear?

Caden didn't have time to dwell on it, as Mina's dragon met his gaze. Raising his sword, he issued a battle cry and rushed forward. The dragon flapped his wings, and a powerful gust of wind sent the nearby draman tumbling backward. Too far away to be affected, Caden slowed his pace and changed direction, heading for Mina instead.

He was only a few feet away when her dragon let out a deafening roar that shook the ground beneath his feet. Mina didn't flinch. She swung her sword in a fluid motion and came at him. Caden dodged the attack and retaliated with a swift strike of his own. The clang of metal echoed off the trees as their blades met.

"What are you doing here?" he demanded.

"I should ask you the same thing," Mina replied. "You're supposed to be in Lord Culver's dungeon."

He could see it in her eyes. The fear. And it only fueled his anger. How dare she leave him in that cell? She'd betrayed him, and he couldn't forgive her for that. Her words came back to him.

Our destinies may be entwined, but they are not united.

She was right. Although he cared for her, he knew his feelings were deceiving. Their paths were too different, their goals at odds with one another.

"I'm sorry," he said.

Her expression morphed from anger to confusion, and she backed away a few steps. That was all he needed. With her guard down, he lunged forward, the tip of his sword aimed at her throat. Mina deftly sidestepped the strike, and he realized her confusion was merely an act. She came at him again, and Caden parried the attack.

"Why are you doing this?" she asked. "Why do you still follow Lireth after all she's done?"

"You betrayed me," Caden said.

"*I* betrayed *you?* You're the one who's gone down a dark path. Your dragon is evil, Caden! How do you not see that?"

They circled each other, both wary. Caden thought he had more experience with a blade than she did, but whoever had trained her did their job well. They matched each other evenly, and he knew the only way to win would be to disarm her. From his periphery, he could see her dragon was fighting a swarm of draman. He needed to end this quickly, before the beast slaughtered his men and killed him next.

Caden feinted a thrust, then swung his sword to the right, hoping to catch her off guard. Mina twirled aside, seeing through his trick. They exchanged blows, neither one gaining the advantage.

"Surrender," Mina huffed. Droplets of sweat rolled down her face.

"No."

"You'll never win, Caden. You're fighting for the wrong side."

"You're wrong about that. Stop trying to sway me. We have chosen our paths, and I intend to see mine through to the end."

Caden's muscles burned from the strain of his efforts. Fatigue was overtaking him, and he wasn't sure how much longer he could continue the fight. His forces easily outnumbered Mina and her dragon, but there was nothing that could defeat a dragon. At least, nothing at Caden's disposal.

Mina lunged at him, breaking his reverie. He blocked her strike, but there was an unnatural power behind her blow, and her sword shattered his to pieces. Caden stared dumbfounded at the broken blade in his hands. Mina wasn't a Runesman, so where had her strength come from? She leveled her sword at his throat. He looked up at her and could see the triumph in her eyes.

"It's over," she said. "You've lost."

A multitude of roars filled the air, and Caden saw Mina's eyes flick upward. The confidence in her expression faded. He slapped the flat of her blade, pushing it away from his neck, and tried to wrestle the sword from her grasp. Mina fought back, and for an intense moment, they were locked in an unwinnable struggle. With that same unnatural strength, Mina twisted the blade out of his grip and kicked him in the chest, sending him sprawling backward.

She turned and fled to her dragon, quickly climbing up his side. Caden scrambled onto his feet and turned to look toward the roars. Several black dragons, the ones from the mountain cave, were approaching the forest. Bast and a group of draman encircled him, forming a protective ring.

"They decided to come," Bast said.

"Lireth's wrath knows no bounds," Caden replied. "They feared what would happen if they did not obey her."

He turned back to look at Mina and saw she and her dragon had already fled.

"Should we pursue them, my lord?"

Caden stared into the distance for a moment.

"No," he answered, deciding to let her get away for now.

Her death would be much sweeter with Lireth watching.

13

I HAD HIM! WE NEED to go back!

Gedrith didn't respond. He continued flying east, away from the enemy.

Turn around!

Do not be foolish, Gedrith chided. *We could not have won. Not after those dragons arrived. They are as vicious and cruel as Lireth, and I can only do so much.*

Caden lost. I had him.

And yet you did not kill him when you had the opportunity. You hesitated.

Mina's anger deflated. She knew he was right. She had indeed held back. A part of her still cared for him, despite everything that had happened. But she couldn't let that cloud her judgment. He had made his choice, and even affirmed it. It was now her duty to stop him.

Where are we going? she asked, trying to distract herself from her thoughts.

Gedrith descended, landing in an open field.

We wait.

Wait?

We will wait and watch their movements. If they march toward The Long Sands, we will strike when the time is right.

What if we do not get a chance to strike at them?

Gedrith rumbled and pulled his wings against his body. *Then we will fight them in the desert.*

Mina dismounted and sat down on the grass, leaning her back against Gedrith's side. She closed her eyes and inhaled a deep breath. The battle had taken a toll on her, both physically and emotionally. Caden had almost fallen to her blade, but her emotions had once again thwarted her. She couldn't let her feelings get in the way of her duty. Not again. The steady rise and fall of Gedrith's body eased her mind, and she pushed the tumultuous thoughts aside.

The hours dragged on, and eventually, the sun set beyond the horizon. Mina had caught a rabbit, and it was cooking over a small fire Gedrith had made for her. She'd flattened the grass around the fire and ringed it with stones to keep it from spreading and burning the entire field. The sky was cloudless, and the moon shone brightly, providing plenty of light.

It was just as she was dozing off beside the fire that she heard it. The marching of soldiers. Mina's eyes snapped open, and she rose to her feet, her right hand grabbing the hilt of her sword. She looked at Gedrith. The dragon was asleep. Mina roused him by prodding his shoulder with her blade. He opened his eyes, and they reflected the moonlight, reminding her of a stray cat she'd once seen. They both turned their gaze toward the noise.

In the distance, torches flickered, and the rhythmic sound of boots hitting the ground grew steadily louder.

That can't be the draman, can it?

Gedrith silently stared into the distance for a moment, then turned his head to regard her. *It is them.*

Mina knew they were not ordinary men, but the distance they had traveled seemed an impossible feat. She had clearly underestimated them.

If the main force is this close, the dragons aren't far off, Gedrith said. *We must be wary.*

An idea came to Mina then, though she didn't know the likelihood of success.

If we can get close enough to find Caden, I can try to hit him with an arrow.

I do not think it is worth the risk.

You said yourself that if we cut the head from the enemy, the others will lose their desire.

I'm aware of my words, but even dragons can be wrong. And how will you hit him with an arrow? You do not have a bow.

Not yet, she replied. *If the main force is here, then I'm certain there are scouts nearby. I can take one of theirs.*

Do not grow smug in your abilities. Conceit is the downfall of many.

I'm not smug. I had good mentors who taught me much.

Flattery will not change my mind.

It was worth a try, Mina said, smiling at the dragon.

While I do not like the risk, the draman will be devastated if we can kill Lireth's puppet. Go and find a bow. I will remain here until you are ready.

Without any hesitation, Mina sprinted off. She would rather have Gedrith at her side, especially since she couldn't see as well as him in the dark, but it was probably better he stayed where he was. It would be hard to miss a dragon stalking about, and if he took to the skies, the other dragons would see him.

She ran toward the army, her sword pointed behind her. As she drew nearer, she could hear the deep, guttural voices of the draman. They marched in a loose formation, seeming unconcerned about potential enemies. Mina kept a safe distance, moving among the shadows as much as possible to keep herself hidden. She searched for a lone scout, one isolated from the main group.

It took some time, but she finally spotted one. He was walking on the outskirts of the formation, oblivious to her approach. The silhouette of a bow stretched across his shoulders. She thought it an odd way to carry a bow, but she had her target. She stepped lightly, her heart racing. Once she was within striking distance, she held her breath and aimed, then jabbed her sword forward with all her strength. The tip of her blade struck the draman between the scales on the back of his neck before slicing through his flesh.

The creature stumbled and collapsed with a wet gurgle. Mina pulled her sword free and looked around, making sure there were no other scouts. The army had halted its advance, but nothing seemed to be amiss. She knelt and grabbed the bow, only to realize it was actually a crossbow. She groaned but took the weapon anyway. It was one she had not trained with before, but it would have to do.

Glancing in the direction of the army again, she noticed they were setting up tents. It seemed even draman needed a break. She sprinted back to where Gedrith was and paused to catch her breath.

I found a crossbow, but there's only one bolt for it. There's something on the tip, too.

Let me see it, Gedrith said.

Mina removed the quarrel and held it up. The dragon sniffed the air near the tip of the projectile.

It's poison.

That should do the job. I just need to get near enough to hit him without getting caught.

We will fly over the camp.

What about the dragons? What if they see us?

We will be quick. Whether your aim is true or not, we will make one pass and then we shall return to the Enclave. They need to know what's coming.

Mina put the bolt back in place and stared at the weapon for a moment in silence. She had one chance to strike Caden. If she missed, then she knew killing him would have to be more direct. Issuing a plea to Avera, she strapped the crossbow over her shoulder and climbed onto Gedrith's back.

I've not used one of these. How does it compare to a bow? she asked.

It is more accurate, but it doesn't require the strength a bow does. I will fly as low as I can, but you will need to adjust how you aim.

Gedrith sent an image of Lucius, his previous rider, through the bond. Mina thought it looked easier than using a bow. She grabbed the crossbow and set it in her lap, holding it in place with her left hand while gripping Gedrith with her right.

I'm ready.

Gedrith stretched his wings out and leaped into the sky. The cool night air whipped around Mina, and she shivered as a chill ran down her back. The glow of campfires came into view, and she squeezed her knees tightly against Gedrith's sides and lifted the crossbow with both hands. As they reached the camp, Gedrith glided on the currents, flying little more than a dozen feet above the tents. Mina scanned the area, looking for Caden.

There, Gedrith said, sending the image to her. He was standing next to a draman, one she had seen before. The dragon changed direction, taking her straight toward him. She positioned the crossbow and aimed at him.

Time seemed to stand still. Her pulse pounded in her ears, overpowering the sound of the wind. Caden pointed at something, his lips moving with a command she couldn't hear. A wave of heat washed over her as she remembered their kiss. It had been so unexpected, but his lips had been soft and warm.

Focus.

Gedrith's voice broke her reverie. She closed one eye and centered her aim. Her finger tightened on the trigger, and her breath caught in her throat. It took everything she had to will herself to pull it.

Three, two, one…

Mina squeezed the trigger. The string twanged, and the bolt whizzed through the air.

14

"LET THEM REST UNTIL DAWN, then we continue to—" Caden's words were abruptly cut off as his world erupted in pain.

Bast turned and shouted orders, but the words were an incoherent jumble. Caden looked down and saw a crossbow bolt protruding from his chest. His eyes traced the length of it, then further away to see where it had come from. Sitting astride Gedrith was Mina, crossbow in hand.

"Mina," he whispered, his voice barely audible over the shouts of the draman. Caden faltered and dropped to his knees. A wave of dizziness swept over him, and he collapsed onto his right side. His vision swam, and pain spread throughout his entire body.

"Caden."

He was vaguely aware of someone calling his name. Mina knelt at his side and touched his face. She had just shot him. Why was she acting as though she was now concerned?

"Caden," the voice wasn't hers. He blinked several times and realized it wasn't Mina beside him. It was Eira. Was he delirious?

"Hold him down," she said.

Bast's face appeared above him, and the draman motioned with his hand. Another draman joined him, and the two of them pinned Caden to the ground. Eira grabbed hold of the quarrel and jerked it free.

Caden roared in pain. He felt as though his flesh had been ripped apart, and wetness seeped through his shirt. He tried to lift his head, but another wave of dizziness forced him to lie still. Fire blazed in his blood, burning through every inch of his being.

"He's been poisoned," Eira said, looking at Bast. "This bolt looks like one of yours. Is it?"

The draman nodded. "Yes, it is ours. That blasted woman must have stolen it from one of my men."

"What girl?"

"It's a long story, one that can wait. We need to get him to Lireth."

"He'll be lucky if he survives the night, judging by his current state," Eira said. "Is there a physician among you?"

"There is, but he cannot do anything about this."

"Why not?"

"The poison is made from Lireth's blood. It is the source and the cure."

"You don't have any of it here?"

"No."

"I see. We should make him as comfortable as we can. If he pulls through until morning, that's something."

Caden's vision faded, and silence followed.

He floated in a sea of darkness, barely aware of his body. There was no pain, and he could breathe without effort, but his face and neck were numb. He tried to move his head, but his body didn't respond. Wherever he was, it was cold and empty. He tried to speak, but his mouth was locked shut.

A sound like creaking leather caught his attention. It got closer, and a feeling of warmth and comfort washed over him. He felt completely at peace. The warmth intensified, and Caden could feel his body loosen. He flexed his fingers, and they obeyed. Able to move now, he turned his head to look at his surroundings and saw Lireth. The rustling sound he heard was her wings. She towered over him, impressive and powerful.

Where am I? he asked. The words echoed all around them.

You are safe, she answered. *What happened?*

I was struck by an arrow.

A mere flesh wound would not send you here.

I think it had a poisoned tip. Mina—

Lireth rumbled angrily at her name. *She tried to kill you? I will burn this world to ash!*

Caden shrank back, fearful of her wrath. The soothing feeling returned, and he looked up at her. She had never been kind, at least not since she first called him to her cave in the mountains.

You are on the doorstep of death, she said. *Come to me, and I will heal you.*

I don't know where you are.

When you reach The Long Sands, you will find guides. They are also allies. They will lead you to the Enclave. I will give you the strength to make the journey, but it will not be much. The distance between us is still too great. When you are closer, you will feel it.

Thank you, master.

My strength will only do so much. Your will to live must be great. Survive to avenge yourself.

Caden gasped and opened his eyes. He was lying in a tent. His head lolled weakly to the side, and he saw Rem was curled up nearby. The animal stared at him, deep intelligence behind its eyes. Hanging in the corner of the tent above the fox was a lantern. The flame burned steadily, providing plenty of light. Rem rose and stretched, then left the tent.

Caden could feel the dull pounding of a headache like a drum being played. He groaned, but the sound was weak and miserable. Why couldn't he move? Was it the effects of the poison?

Rem returned with Eira and Bast in tow. The draman stared down at him, his reptilian features creased into a smile, though it looked disturbing.

"You are strong, my lord. I am glad to see you are awake."

Caden licked his lips, but his mouth was dry and it felt like he was rubbing sand together.

"Swallow," Eira said, kneeling beside him with a waterskin. She poured a small amount of water into his mouth. It was cool and refreshing, and it washed the dryness from his throat.

"How do you feel?" she asked.

"Like … death," Caden managed to whisper.

"The poison has spread through your body," Bast said. "It is potent."

"The d—desert." Even breathing was a chore, and it took all of Caden's effort to speak the words.

"We will continue our march at dawn, my lord. Finding Lireth is the only way to cure you."

"No. March … now. Time … is … short."

Eira looked up at Bast, but the draman ignored her.

"My lord, you need rest. You cannot even sit up, let alone walk."

"Lireth … sustains me. March … now."

The draman hesitated but bowed his head. "As you command." He left the tent and began shouting orders.

Eira poured more water into Caden's mouth. He swallowed it and stared at her, wondering why she hadn't returned to wherever it was she called home. She didn't owe him her loyalty. If anything, he owed her for helping him find the dragons.

"Rem says something odd was happening to you while you were unconscious."

Caden nodded his head slightly, too exhausted to speak any more.

"Get some rest. You will need it. It will be a miracle if you are still alive in the morning. Rem will alert me if you need anything."

Eira stood and watched him for a moment, then backed out of the tent, leaving him with his thoughts and his pain. And Rem. The odd fox gazed at him knowingly.

15

MINA LAY ON HER COT, staring up at the cave ceiling. The image of Caden being struck by the quarrel was burned into her mind. It haunted her the entire way back to the Enclave, and it haunted her even now, keeping her from sleeping.

She had killed him.

Tears stung her eyes. She knew it was the right thing to do, but she hated herself for doing it. And she hated herself for being upset about doing what was just. It was her fault he'd found Lireth in the first place. She'd used her newfound position with Lord Klodian to send him away. Now he was dead, and at her own hands.

Mina wiped the tears that trickled down her cheeks and sat up. It hurt, but her sadness wasn't going to bring him back. She needed to take her mind off things and allow her emotions to settle. Rising from the cot, she left her chamber and wandered along the tunnels. She tried to clear her mind, but it was impossible to erase Caden's stunned look from her memory.

"What doin'?"

Her heart leaped in her chest, and she whirled around to see Areg. He was barefoot and looked as though he hadn't been awake long.

"Did I wake you?" she asked.

Areg rubbed the sleep from his eyes and yawned. "No. What doin'?" he repeated.

"Nothing. Just …" Just what? She didn't know what to say, and an overwhelming wave of emotions crashed over her. She sank to the floor and began sobbing.

Areg drew near and embraced her, his small arms strong and comforting. He said nothing as she cried, and eventually, the tears stopped. Mina pulled away from the elf and wiped her eyes.

"Thank you," she said lamely, avoiding his gaze.

"What wrong?"

"My friend is … gone."

"Caden?"

Mina nodded, sniffling.

"It not good reply. But time heal."

He was right. It wasn't a good response, but she knew he was trying to help. And his words were true. Time healed wounds, though she knew this one would affect her for a long while. It all felt like a dream.

"Need rest. Battle coming."

"I can rest later. The draman are still at least a day's march from The Long Sands. Two days from here."

"They in desert now."

Mina looked at him. "That's impossible. They stopped and set up—" Gedrith had been wrong. Removing their leader hadn't broken their ranks. "Does the Enclave know?"

Areg nodded. "Have time. You rest."

She was exhausted, but she doubted she'd be able to sleep. Despite that, she rose to her feet and walked with the elf to her chamber. Areg continued on his way, and Mina climbed onto her cot and tried to find solace in the darkness under her blanket.

Mina.

Someone was chasing her. It was a shadowy figure, the darkness of it constantly shifting about like dye poured into water.

Mina.

How did it know her name? She ran as fast as she could, but it was as though she moved through molasses. The darkness was closing in on her, wispy tendrils outstretched, reaching for her.

Mina.

She startled awake and kicked off the blanket. Sweat covered every inch of her body, and she realized there was nothing truly trying to get her. Gedrith was at the edge of her mind.

Are you all right? he asked. *The bond was filled with fear.*

I'm fine. It was a nightmare. I'm sorry.

Do not apologize. You cannot control your dreams. Prepare yourself and meet me above ground.

Mina dragged herself out of bed and donned her boots, followed by her armor. She buckled her sword around her waist and stepped out into the hall, pausing as her stomach rumbled. Breakfast could wait.

The tunnels were oddly silent as she made her way to the entrance of the underground fortress. When she climbed the steep slope and reached the top, she understood why. The dragons were all aboveground. Some were standing in the sand while others wheeled overhead.

What is it? Mina asked. She looked west, squinting.

The draman have arrived, Gedrith replied.

They traveled faster than I expected.

I'm sure Lireth had something to do with that.

She must have instructed them how to get here, too.

No, she does not know the way.

Then how did they know where to find us?

Come and see.

Mina climbed onto Gedrith's back and he took to the air. He didn't have to ascend far for her to see it. Numerous lines bulged in the sand, swaying back and forth.

Sand wyrms? But why—

They have aligned against a common enemy, Gedrith answered.

Mina stared in disbelief. At least a dozen of the creatures stirred up the sand, and behind them, the army of draman steadily marched closer. The dragons could easily defend against the smaller reptilians, but the sand wyrms posed a much bigger problem. This would not be an easy battle. She regretted not getting something to eat, but that was the least of her problems.

What's the plan?

We must keep them from reaching the tunnels. If they free Lireth, they will be emboldened.

You sound worried about that last part.

The scent of lavender reached her nostrils. Gedrith was afraid.

You don't think we can stop them? she asked.

I fear what we will lose with victory.

She didn't understand what he meant, and before she could ask, he said, *You will be on the ground. Focus your efforts on the draman. We will handle the sand wyrms.*

I would rather help you. I've killed a sand wyrm, and I can do it again.

The lavender smell turned to lemon and clove.

I do not doubt your abilities, Gedrith said. *But you must set your pride aside. In the time it takes you to kill one wyrm, we will have killed five. It is easier for me to fight with tooth, claw, and flame if I do not have to worry about you riding on my back.*

I understand, but what can I do against an army of draman?

Whatever you must to keep them from getting inside the tunnels. Areg will help you, and once the wyrms are dealt with, we will turn our attention to them.

The sand wyrms were only a few hundred feet away, and a few of the dragons were making dives, raking their claws through the sand.

It is time, Gedrith said. He landed on the ground, and Mina quickly leaped from his back. *Stay alive.*

I'll do my best, Mina replied.

That's all I require from you.

He returned to the sky, and Mina felt some relief as Areg joined her. He wore a polished chainmail shirt, and the sunlight glinted off the rings, making it seem as though he was glowing. A sleek silver helm adorned his head, and the design etched into the metal was as beautiful as any piece of art. Wings stretched back on the sides, and the nose guard resembled an eagle's beak. He held on to the haft of a long spear, and a sword was sheathed at his waist.

"Don't you look regal," she said, grinning at him.

"Ready to die," he replied. "Impress ancestors."

Mina drew her sword and turned her attention to the advancing army. The dragons continued to harass the wyrms, but it didn't seem to slow their progress.

They're getting close to the tunnels, Mina warned Gedrith.

Just a little further, he said.

She tightened her grip on the hilt of her blade. How much further did they need to get? A tremor shook the ground, followed by another, and another.

"Stone wall," Areg said cheerily.

"What?"

The elf pointed to the ground. "Stone under sand. Big stone."

Mina laughed. The dragons had placed a wall of stone under the sand. It was a brilliant defense. One of the wyrms broke the surface of the ground, its fleshy body undulating as it rose up, up, up into the air.

The dragons attacked without mercy, breathing fire and slashing with their claws. The beast shrieked in anger and pain, its open maw snapping this way and that, trying to retaliate, but the dragons were too quick, easily maneuvering out of the way. Mina watched the display with admiration until Areg pointed with his sword.

The underground stone wall had stopped the advance of the wyrms, but the draman continued ahead, coming directly toward them. Mina's heart pounded in her chest, but oddly she didn't feel scared. She felt determined. She glanced over at Areg.

"Ready to make your ancestors proud?"

"With honor."

The draman were so close now that Mina could see the details of their reptilian faces. Their eyes blazed with battle lust, and they roared in challenge. Areg drew the spear back and threw it. It sailed through the air, striking one of the draman and sending him into a backflip. Adrenaline coursed through Mina, making her vision blur momentarily. It filled her with an odd mix of excitement and fear, and she let out her own battle cry.

An intense wave of heat washed over her as a dragon flew overhead, bathing the draman in a torrent of flames. Many of them fell, burned beyond recognition. Those that weren't continued ahead, clashing blades with her and Areg.

The elf moved with fluid grace, his sword weaving a deadly dance, cutting down draman after draman. Mina fought with all her might, the clashing of steel a constant noise, like the cadence of a war drum. She dodged attacks, parried with her sword, and landed blows of her own.

The battle raged on, but she and Areg were outnumbered. Mina wanted to risk a glance to see how the dragons fared against the wyrms, but she dared not lose her focus.

"Me! To me!" Areg shouted.

Mina back peddled in the direction of his voice until she bumped into him. They stood back-to-back, barely fending off the draman that surrounded them. From her periphery, she saw several of the creatures rush down into the tunnel. There was nothing they could do to stop them.

They're in the tunnel! she screamed at Gedrith.

He didn't respond, but she could feel his rage through the bond. The flapping of wings nearby made her flick her gaze up long enough to see a few dragons swooping in. Her relief faded when she realized they weren't allies.

Ignoring her and Areg, they landed in the sand and scrambled ahead, entering the tunnel. The draman would have trouble breaking the walls that contained Lireth, but not the dragons. Hope was fading, and with it, Mina's strength. Her movements became sluggish, and a draman got his blade past her parry, slicing the flesh on her left forearm. Burning pain spread up the length of her arm.

This was it. This was the end for her. For all of them. She thrust her sword into the neck of the draman who cut her, then screamed. All her fear, pain, and loss were behind her cry, but there was more. Something deeper, hotter. It yearned for freedom, and she allowed it to come forth.

Gedrith's fire poured from her mouth, engulfing the draman nearest to her. The flames continued unabated, and she turned her head left and right, burning everything in her path. Shrieks of pain and surprise filled the air, and the inferno drove the draman back.

The fire faded, and Mina dropped to her knees, the last of her strength expended. Her fingers were too weak to hold on to her sword, and it fell to the sand beside her. She had done all she could, and it still wasn't enough. Mina searched the sky for Gedrith. A few of the wyrms had fallen, but there were more alive than dead. There were so few dragons the sky looked empty to her.

The ground trembled, grains of sand vibrating against one another. Mina glanced around, confused, and met Areg's gaze. He looked toward the tunnel. She guessed more sand wyrms were coming. The vibration increased, growing stronger. Mina gathered what little vigor she could muster and grabbed her sword, slowly rising to her feet.

The earth above the cave system erupted, sand and glass flying in every direction. Lireth's enormous bulk flew up into the sky, her black scales dark as night. The dragon opened her mouth and issued an ear-piercing roar.

<h1 style="text-align:center">16</h1>

CADEN LAY ON THE SLOPE of a dune and watched as the sand wyrms battled the dragons. As much as he would have preferred to be on the front lines with the draman, the poison running through his blood had wreaked havoc on him. When the sun rose, Eira and Bast were surprised to see he was still alive. If he were honest with himself, he was surprised as well. Despite Lireth's borrowed strength, it was all he could do to remain conscious.

"I've never seen anything like this," Eira said from beside him. "I didn't even know there was such a thing as a sand wyrm."

He didn't waste any words with her. His spirit was quickly fading. Although he'd made it through the night, he knew his time was running out.

Thank you for trusting me to lead your army, he told Lireth. *It has been an honor. They will free you soon, and you will get your vengeance upon the Enclave, but I fear I will not see it.*

You will not die. I will heal you.

Caden snorted a single laugh at the absurdity of her words. Surely, she could feel his connection to the bond slipping away. Or perhaps she was in denial, refusing to believe her servant was on the edge of dying. Either way, at least he'd had one final laugh before death took him. It felt good and temporarily drove the pain away, however brief.

"What is it?" Eira asked. "The dragon—Lireth?"

Caden nodded and felt his eyes lowering of their own will. He would have fought against it, but he didn't see the point. Rest was coming, and he welcomed it gladly. A flood of strength filled him, and he forced his eyes open. The battle was raging in every direction, and then Lireth burst out from the ground. His breath caught in his throat. She was majestic and beautiful.

I'm coming to you.

He wanted her to, but he knew it was a futile effort. Not even a dragon could defeat death. The dragons fighting the sand wyrms immediately broke away and flew straight for her.

A thunderous boom echoed off the dunes.

"The caves," Eira said. "They're collapsing."

Caden wondered if Mina was down there. He hoped so. She would die as he would, alone and forgotten. No family to mourn him, no friends to help him. Eira was a stranger, and Lireth … well, she was his master. There was no friendship between them. It was a bond of servitude. He saw that now, clearer than ever. Perhaps, in the end, Mina had been right.

He stared at the chaos unfolding and realized the truth. Lireth *was* evil. She had bound him to her without his knowledge or approval. Death, it seemed, brought clarity to many things. He deserved his fate, and he found it fitting the source of his death was poison made from the blood of the very creature who had saved him. Her call had been both a blessing and a curse.

And ultimately, he had failed. Not only Mina, but himself.

The thought of ceasing to exist, never to feel the touch of another, never again to be part of something more, never to atone for his wrongdoing filled him with grief and agony far more painful than the effects of the poison.

Lireth's strength began to fade again, and Caden felt something in the bond he never expected: anguish. And something else: guilt. Lireth felt guilty? That was the most surprising revelation of all.

He closed his eyes, and darkness enveloped him.

17

Gedrith and the other dragons who remained descended upon Lireth. The battle even consumed the attention of the draman. Mina kept her guard up, but the creatures were no longer concerned with her or Areg.

"What that?" the elf asked.

Mina turned to look in the direction Areg was pointing. Two figures were visible, away from the battlefield. The sunlight glared off the sand, and she squinted against the blinding light. Was that …

No. It couldn't be. He was dead. She's seen him fall with her own eyes. But she needed to be sure. She sprinted across the sand, and Areg followed after her. The draman ignored their departure, their focus still on their master.

As she drew closer, there was no mistaking it.

"Caden!"

Mina realized something was wrong. His flesh was pale, and he didn't seem to be conscious. A woman and a fox were with him, but she didn't recognize the person.

"Who are you?" the woman asked, stepping into her path.

"I'm a friend. Or, I was. Is he—"

"You're the one who struck him with the arrow, aren't you?"

Mina's cheeks burned with guilt. "Yes, but you don't understand. He's—"

"I don't need to understand. You should leave. He's in enough agony from the poison. Let him die in peace."

"I need to speak to him," Mina protested. "Please."

The woman rested her hand on the hilt of her sword. "No. Now leave, before I make you."

Mina looked at Areg, and the elf nodded knowingly.

"I don't know your connection to Caden, but I know him better than you. He would want to speak with me."

The woman drew her sword, and the fox at her feet bared its teeth and hissed threateningly.

"I don't want to fight," Mina said.

"That makes one of us."

The woman lunged forward, the tip of her blade aimed at Mina's neck. Mina parried the strike, the sound of metal ringing through the air. The woman came at her with fury, and they clashed blades. The fox darted around Mina's feet, trying to trip her up, but Areg snatched it by the scruff of its neck and held on to it.

"Do not hurt Rem," the woman growled.

Mina could tell the woman was skilled, but she was determined to get to Caden. She drew on Gedrith's strength, but she didn't pull much as she didn't want to disrupt his fight with Lireth. She siphoned just enough to invigorate her aching muscles and gain the advantage over the woman. Mina swung with all her might and shattered the woman's sword, just as she'd done to Caden in the forest.

The broken pieces of the blade fell onto the sand, and the woman hesitated. Mina sensed the woman had more fight in her, but she looked at her fox companion and backed down.

"I won't hurt him," Mina said. She stepped past her and knelt beside Caden. Areg had her back, so she wasn't concerned about the woman striking her when she wasn't looking.

"I'm sorry," she whispered. "I never meant for any of this to happen."

Tears slid down her cheeks, but she didn't bother to wipe them away. Caden didn't stir. She'd found him only to lose him again.

End him, Gedrith said to her. *It will weaken Lireth temporarily so we can defeat her.*

Mina froze and swallowed the lump in her throat. *Don't ask me to do this.*

I already did. Hurry!

She tightened her grip on the hilt of her blade, but she couldn't do it. It wasn't in her. Not this time. Not again. She dropped her sword and looked back at Areg.

"Must do."

"I can't," she whispered.

Areg started forward, but a noise like thunder cracked the sky. They both looked toward the battle. Lireth had unleashed some kind of magic, and it rippled across the sky. The surrounding dragons went limp and fell, crashing to the ground below. Her heart dropped into her stomach as she watched Gedrith spiral helplessly.

You must stop her!

Lireth bolted across the sky, faster than anything she'd seen before. The dragon opened her mouth, and flames poured out. Mina grabbed onto Areg and pushed him behind her, then summoned Gedrith's fire and breathed her own flames. The two streams collided in a blinding, searing display of power. Mina felt the heat on her skin, hotter than anything she'd encountered before. Sand and dust billowed into the air, and she gritted her teeth and pushed against Lireth's flames with all her might.

It wasn't enough.

Lireth's fire consumed hers, and the force threw Mina back, knocking the breath out of her. She gasped for air as she struggled to roll over. Her vision blurred and her head rang from the impact. Grit filled her mouth, but she didn't care about that. The dragon landed, and with a flap of her wings, she sent Areg and the woman tumbling along the dunes.

Mina's mind told her to get up, but her body wouldn't obey. She watched, powerless, as Lireth stood over Caden's prone form.

Gedrith!

His answer was a flood of pain through the bond. She pushed it back, blocking off their connection. For a long moment, Lireth did nothing. She merely stood there, looking down at Caden. Finally, she lifted her head and opened her jaws. An ethereal tendril slipped out, white as smoke, and it drifted on the wind before snaking down into Caden's nostrils.

"No!" Mina screamed.

She tried standing, but her legs wouldn't hold her weight and she fell back onto the sand. Pushing through the pain, she crawled instead, desperate to reach Caden.

The last of the ghostly tendril escaped Lireth's mouth and disappeared into him. Mina didn't know what it was, but it couldn't be good. Lireth's legs shook, and the dragon fell on her side, blocking Caden from her view. Mina continued scrambling on her hands and knees, forced to go around the massive beast.

She reached Caden's side and laid her head on his chest. His heartbeat was faint. She looked at Lireth, worried she was going to get up and attack at any moment. The dragon breathed raggedly, and her eyes slowly closed. A final breath escaped her nostrils, and she lay still.

18

WHEN CADEN OPENED HIS EYES, the first thing he saw was the white ceiling above him. The second thing he saw was Eira. She sat at his bedside, and Rem was curled up in her lap. Her eyes were closed, but Rem was watching him.

Surprisingly, he felt no pain. He tried to flex his fingers—and it worked. He didn't feel weak, either. Caden pushed himself up on his elbow and looked around. He was in an infirmary. It looked vaguely familiar, but he wasn't sure where he was.

"You're awake." Eira smiled at him. "The physicians weren't sure if you'd come to. I'm glad you proved them wrong."

"W—where am I?"

"Klodian Keep. I've never heard of the place, but I'm not from this area."

Caden laid back down and stared at the ceiling. Klodian Keep? Had he dreamed everything? No, of course not. Eira and Rem were here, which meant it had all really happened. But the last thing he remembered was hazy. He'd been poisoned and was …

"What happened?"

"What do you remember?"

"Not much. Bits and pieces of the march to The Long Sands. The wyrms were fighting the Enclave, and the rest is …" Caden shrugged. "Lost to memory."

"Lucky you. The draman freed Lireth from her prison. She battled with the Enclave before striking them all with a spell, then she stood over you and—" Eira looked off to the side, her eyes widening as if reliving the event, "—breathed something into you."

Caden repeated her words in his mind, trying to understand what it meant. Was it the cure for the poison? He reached through the bond, but there was nothing on the other end, just a vast abyss of emptiness.

"Where is she?"

472

"Mina?"

"What? No. Lireth. Where is Lireth?"

"She's … dead. Whatever she did saved your life and took hers."

At first, he felt the sting of agony. It slowly morphed into relief as fragments of his memory returned. He'd realized she was wicked, but given what he'd just learned, he questioned that. Would someone evil sacrifice themselves to save another? His first instinct was to say no, but perhaps he was wrong. Perhaps there was good in everyone, even if it was buried deep inside.

"You mentioned Mina. She survived?"

"Yes. She brought you here to heal. She brought us, too, but Rem didn't exactly like riding on the back of a dragon. He said it was too windy."

Caden smiled. Mina had tried to kill him, and yet she went out of her way to bring him home, his true home. Another mystery to ponder.

"How do you feel?"

"Good. Normal."

With Lireth's presence completely gone from his mind, he felt as though a great fog had lifted. His thoughts were clear, and his own. He looked down at his body. There were no cuts or bruises, and his skin was tan and healthy. It was as if he'd never been poisoned— in body or in mind.

Eira watched him with a curious expression. Rem stretched and yawned, then jumped off Eira's lap to investigate the room.

"You seem … different."

"What do you mean?"

"I don't know. You seem centered. More in control. Of yourself, I mean."

It was true. He felt a newfound sense of clarity. Lireth must have been more in control of him than he'd known. It was a frightening realization. He sat up and inhaled a deep breath. Everything felt … fresh. It was like Lireth had breathed new life into him. Perhaps that was exactly what she did.

Caden swung his legs over the side of the bed and stood. Things would be different this time. They had to be. He looked at Rem, who was now inspecting a vase of flowers on the windowsill, then at Eira who was still staring at him.

"Thank you for your help. What will you do now? Go back to wilderness?"

Eira shrugged. "I thought about sticking around with you. It's been quite an adventure so far, so why stop now?"

Caden chuckled. "I've got to make some things right, and I don't know how exciting that will be, but you're welcome to stay around as long as you'd like."

Rem yipped, and Caden looked at the fox. "The same goes for you."

A long road lay ahead, but with his new friends, it didn't seem so daunting.

19

Mina sat outside the mountain cave, watching the stars twinkle above. Areg sat next to her, a wistful expression on his face. They couldn't be more different, the two of them. The Enclave decided to leave The Long Sands behind and build a new home closer to civilization.

Lireth was dead, but that didn't mean more threats wouldn't arise. In time, they would reintroduce themselves to humans, and possibly even rebuild the riders. Gedrith told her the Enclave was happy with her actions, and she had done much to restore their faith in humanity. The draman had fled after Lireth fell, their ranks broken and scattered.

She had left Caden in Lord Klodian's care, though in truth, she knew he was in better hands with Eira. The woman had tried to protect him from her, after all. She'd failed, but it was the effort that mattered.

"There's something I've been meaning to ask you," Mina said, glancing over at Areg.

"What?"

"Where are the rest of your people? Before I met you, I didn't even know elves existed."

"Far. Past ocean."

"Do you think you'll ever see them again?"

Areg shrugged. "Know not. Banished."

"They banished you?"

He nodded.

"For what?"

"Bond to dragon. Against law."

Mina's face scrunched in surprise. "I thought elves also bonded to dragons before the world forgot the truth about them?"

"Only humans forget. Elves know still. Royalty only bond to dragon. Areg not royalty."

Many things made sense with that knowledge, and Mina nodded in understanding. "I'm sorry for asking. I'm sure it hurts to talk about it. I was a slave, but at least I wasn't banished from my own kind."

"Long time. No pain."

Mina didn't know if she believed that, but she wasn't going to press him about it.

"What do?" he asked.

Mina looked back up at the stars and admired their beauty for a moment, then turned her gaze back to Areg.

"A wise friend of mine once told me what I should do, and I'm going to follow his advice."

The elf looked at her questioningly.

"He told me, 'Do good.' So I plan to do good every day until I no longer walk this world."

Areg grinned. "Plan good."

"I thought so, too."

Mina sighed. For the first time in a long time, she was content. All was well, and she was going to 'do good.'

THE END

ABOUT THE AUTHOR

Richard Fierce is the author of over 30 books. He's been writing since childhood, but began publishing in 2007. Since then, he's written dozens of books, some of which have won awards.

In 2000, he won Poet of the Year for his poem The Darkness. He's the founder of the Acworth Book Festival, a literary event in Acworth, Georgia.

He lives in a small town with his wife, and has 3 daughters (pray for him), 3 grandchildren, 4 dogs (huskies!), and 2 ferrets. Basically, he has a zoo.

His love affair with fantasy began in high school when a friend's mom gave him a copy of *Dragons of Spring Dawning* by Margaret Weis and Tracy Hickman.

You can find more of his books at www.richardfierce.com and you can connect with him on social media.

YouTube - https://www.youtube.com/c/RichardFierceWrites

Facebook - https://www.facebook.com/dragonfirepress

www.ingramcontent.com/pod-product-compliance
Lightning Source LLC
Chambersburg PA
CBHW060723190726
48285CB00001B/41